S. S. BAZINET

Traces
of
HOME

book one
OPEN WIDE MY HEART

Renata Press
Albuquerque, New Mexico

This book is a work of fiction. Names, characters, places, businesses, organizations and events are either the product of the author's imagination or are used fictitiously. Any resemblance to actual persons, living or dead, events or locales is entirely coincidental.

Published by Renata Press
Albuquerque, New Mexico
www.renatapress.com

Visit the author's website:
www.ssbazinet.com

ISBN-13: 978-1-937279-22-6

For all those readers who enjoy an uplifting story about the bonds of friendship, family, and the healing power of the heart.

Acknowledgments

I have so many people in my life who have helped to make this book possible. My appreciation and gratitude goes out to all of my family for their continued, loving support. My son, Gabriel, deserves special thanks. He practically insisted that I publish this story. It had remained in some files on my computer for quite some time. Gabriel always encouraged me to publish it. Now, I think the time is right!

One

LEA STARED AT her watch. Why was it hard to read the second hand? She normally had perfect vision. Was she losing that too? What next? She didn't have time to worry about it. Matthew would be home soon. What if he found her packing? She balled up some jeans, threw them on top of her other clothes, and flipped down the lid of the suitcase.

"Dammit!" She couldn't get the zipper closed. Do something! Her hands trembled as she quickly refolded two pairs of jeans and a light jacket. She checked her watch again. Why was her heart pounding so loud? Breathe! You keep forgetting to breathe!

Slowly, her mind cleared just enough. Why was she worrying about Matthew seeing her pack? He knew she was taking a vacation to Florida. Her thoughts were getting more paranoid by the day. What was happening to her?

As soon as she asked herself the question, she knew she didn't want to know the answer. Nevertheless, something had to be done, and she had a plan. If she could pull it off, there was hope. Hope and her plan. Those were the things she had to cling to. Even if her trip to Florida was a lie. Even if she was running away, it wasn't a selfish act. It was for Matthew. She was doing it for the man who'd asked her to marry him. She slipped off her engagement ring and held it close to her heart. If Matthew knew what she was doing, he'd try to stop her. He was so naïve, so incapable of knowing what she was dealing with. And he'd never find out.

Reality was slipping away and taking any chance at happiness with it. She fought back, but the dark forces that wanted to control her were too strong, just like the monsters she'd faced as a child. Soon there'd be no Lea anymore, just a crazy, violent woman who hurt people. It was only when she was in Matthew's arms that she felt a little safer. But even that haven of comfort was drifting further and further away. The madness was winning.

Matthew was often its target. Her bouts of cruelty and foul words were becoming more and more frequent. Matthew made excuses for her behavior. He told her she was working too hard, that she was exhausted. He used his strong, unwavering love to ward off the hell she sent his way. Thinking about their last argument and how unreasonable she'd been, she heaved out a breath. "It's not right to hurt him like that. I can't stand what I've become."

The nightmares were getting worse. The voice in her head was getting louder. With each passing day, its accusations were more malicious. But was the voice wrong? No, it wasn't. That meant she had no choice. She had to go through with her plan. It was the only way Matthew would be safe.

Two

IT WAS EARLY morning, and the dreaded voice was already in Lea Ferguson's head. As the plane headed for Baltimore, she sat in her seat trying not to let anyone see how uptight she was.

"You're an evil, little witch! The devil's own! You should be locked up forever in the darkness, you wretched child! Now get in the closet where you belong!"

The shrill words were spewed out in a rage. They were part of Lea's past, part of a childhood she'd thought she'd left behind. She massaged her temples, trying to ease the pain of a throbbing headache. She had to remind herself of the facts. She wasn't a helpless child anymore. She was a strong, twenty-eight-year-old woman.

And as for that vile, old biddy who tortured me when I was a kid, she's probably dead. Her bones are probably long-buried and decaying in some grave.

The thought was meant to make her feel better, but her body wasn't buying it. Her muscles tightened even more. What if her old nanny's ghost was haunting her? What if the woman's decaying bones were reaching out again, trying to snatch away Lea's sanity?

It was a ridiculous idea, so ridiculous that she almost managed to smile. She'd always had a way of imagining things and scaring herself.

But some horrors aren't my imagination.

The voice that kept ridiculing her belonged to the woman who had taken care of her when she was too young to fend for herself. Now it was back, tormenting her again.

"You're black through and through! Do ya hear me? Wicked, that's what you are! And your precious daddy's gone and left you.

11

Nobody's goin' to save you now. You'll get the punishment you deserve."

Lea swallowed hard, trying to ignore the threats. But nothing could stop the visions that flashed through her mind. At times, she felt like that child she'd once been, a fragile little girl who was alone and helpless most of the time.

It was only when her father returned home that the darkness lifted and happiness filled her small heart. She was her daddy's little nightingale. He called her that when he came back from his frequent business trips.

"Come here, my little nightingale. Fly into daddy's arms!" When he stood in the nursery doorway, still dressed in his suit and tie, he was her hero.

She ran into his waiting arms, filled with the bliss of a child whose world was very small. "Daddy, Daddy! I missed you," she chirped when he lifted her up and held her close.

The memory of such moments could still make Lea's heart beat faster. For an instant, she was filled with the hope she'd felt. But she knew that in the end, her nanny had been right. Her father never saved her. He always went away and left her to face another day of cruelty and torment. Only her stuffed bear, Teddy, provided a little comfort. She held him tight as she rocked back and forth and tried to forget the last punishment she'd had to endure.

On one occasion, her nanny had tried to take Teddy away from her. "Give me that filthy thing," the woman demanded.

Lea had put up a fierce battle. Her bear was her only source of security when her father was gone. No matter how hard her nanny shook her, she wouldn't let go of him. The skirmish left bruises on Lea's small arm. When the nanny was asked about the telltale marks, she'd come up with a quick excuse. But she was careful after that. She had more devious ways of torturing her victim.

The hag covered her bases, that's for sure.

Lea sniffled and quickly grabbed some tissues. As she dabbed at her wet cheeks, she knew she needed sleep. She was so tired, so exhausted after weeks of battling the old woman who'd first reappeared in her dreams. Now, she was haunting Lea's waking hours. Every time Lea shut her eyes, the darkness closed in again. A shutter of despair grabbed hold when the screaming started. The darkness was filled with the cries of a terrified child, begging for help.

"Daddy, where are you? There's monsters in here! They goin' get me! Daddy!"

Those monsters had made their way back into Lea's adult life. Maybe it was because of all the stress she was under. Or maybe it was because she finally had a chance at happiness, and the nanny she thought she'd escaped wouldn't have it.

Whatever the reason, she often woke up in the middle of the night, barely able to breathe. She was in the suffocating closet again, fighting whatever was lurking in the darkness.

As each day passed, the monsters seemed to be gaining ground, just waiting for the time when they could drag her down into some hellish pit that her nanny had often described.

The thought made Lea retrieve a small, plastic bottle from her purse. As she struggled to get the top off, her hand trembled. In fact, her whole body felt like it was shaking apart.

She dumped out a couple of pills, swallowed them and waited. What could she tell herself that would allay her fears? How could she convince herself that she wasn't losing her mind?

Her eyes, half-closed, drifted to the window. The plane was flying through a thick bank of clouds. Thankfully, the powerful drugs she'd taken finally kicked in. As they did, the voices and the visions began to fade. Still, deep down, she knew she couldn't escape the inevitable. She was a pediatrician, a medical doctor, but she hadn't been trained to stop whatever it was that was slowly taking over her sense of self. As for her job, she explained that she needed to take an indefinite leave of absence.

As for Matthew? He thinks I'm going on vacation.

She thought about how often she lost her temper with Matthew. He was the man she loved, yet she said so many horrible things when they were together, things that were uncalled for and spiteful. But why would she do that? Was her nanny right? Was she a demon child who'd grown up and become an evil witch?

* * *

13

Lea exited the plane at the Baltimore/Washington International Airport with a degree of calm. However, her attempt at composure quickly gave way to doubt. As she made her way through the unfamiliar terminal, she knew she'd lied to herself about being a strong, capable woman. A strong, capable woman didn't walk around feeling that her medication was the only thing that kept her craziness in check.

And what about my plan to run off and hide myself away in a strange city?

Was she also fooling herself when she'd thought she could simply bow out of her life in Chicago? Maybe so, but it still seemed like her best option. If she could leave her old life behind, even for a month or two, she'd give herself time to deal with her emotional crisis.

Now, scared or not, she was rather proud of the way she was carrying out her plan. Hoping to cover her tracks, she didn't use the same airline as the one that was going to Florida, her original destination. Baltimore was picked at random. She also used a new credit card to pay for her ticket. Happily, the card wouldn't have an actual paper trail. She did everything online. Even so, she knew it would be better not to use it again. If Matthew or her father tried to find her, she had to do everything she could to foil their efforts.

Luckily she had cash. When she was in college, her father made sure she always carried the real thing when she traveled. A hefty sum was stowed away in a hidden part of her suitcase.

Still, after she retrieved her bag, doubt crept in again. She'd been rash in the past, but this time, maybe she needed to slow down and rethink what she was doing. It only took a moment to push the thought aside. She couldn't afford to think too much. She might weaken and run back to Chicago.

And then Matthew would be saddled with me again!

She couldn't do that to her fiancé. He was a good man, too good a man to be married to someone who was riddled with emotional problems. That singular thought gave her the strength to stop by a trash receptacle. After she ripped the tags off her bag and threw them away, she got out her wallet. She stared at her credit cards and driver's license one last time before she removed them from their plastic sleeves. After she dropped them into the container, she used some trash to cover the items. She was determined to leave all traces of the person named Lea Ferguson behind.

What about your phone? Don't you need to throw that away too?

She thought about the last time she'd used the device. After her plane landed in Baltimore, she'd sent Matthew a text message telling him not to worry about her. Now, she had to break her connection to Matthew completely. Her heart begged her to stop and reconsider, but she ignored its protest. She retrieved her phone with a trembling hand, turned it off and buried it too.

As she wheeled her suitcase towards the airport exit, she felt proud of herself. Throwing away everything that identified her as Lea Ferguson was the bravest thing she'd ever had to do. Of course, she wasn't really being brave, was she? If she had a problem, she could always call her father. He wasn't good for much in her life, but he'd definitely bail her out if she got into trouble.

* * *

The skies were heavy, crayon gray when Lea stood outside the airport. Wisps of a spring shower wet her face as she hailed a cab. The weather was dismal compared to the sunny skies she'd left in Chicago, but she felt better than she had earlier. The drugs were keeping the voices at bay, and she was almost excited about the prospect of taking control of her life.

She climbed into a taxi trying not to think about what she was doing. But it wasn't easy to ignore the heartache of never seeing her fiancé again.

He'll think I'm in Florida by now. He won't know anything about my deception. And when he eventually looks for me, hopefully he won't be able to trace my whereabouts.

She stared blankly out the cab window as a bleak, wet cityscape sped past. She had to ignore the rainy streets and focus on what was important. By leaving Matthew, she'd insured a better future for him. He'd be hurt initially, but he'd get over their relationship. The surgeon was strong and resilient. Unlike her, he didn't let his emotions rule his life.

The lofty thoughts didn't help her to breathe any easier. Her father hadn't been there for her, but Matthew was rock solid, someone she could depend on. Sometimes, when he held her very close, time stopped. She existed in a brief moment of lightness and joy. But the feeling never lasted. No matter how strong Matthew was, he couldn't stop what had hold of her mind. And she wouldn't put him through more of her abusive temper.

When the cab hit a pothole, she braced a hand on the worn seat next to her and recoiled at once in panic. She'd touched a dark, sticky stain on the upholstery.

Oh hell, I forgot to put hand wipes in my purse.

In the next moment, she reclaimed a bit of clarity and let out a mocking huff. Why should she care about germs when she'd already lost everything that mattered to her?

If only I could have been nicer to Matthew on our last night together.

The evening was a shining example of everything that she hated about herself. Of course, Matthew wasn't always the best at expressing his feelings either. As soon as the six-foot-three surgeon walked through the door of their apartment, the conversation turned confrontational. "You look like hell, Lea. Why aren't you taking better care of yourself?"

Matthew's voice had been brusque, but that was normal for Matthew. What wasn't normal was the worry that Lea saw on his face. His deep concern was obvious when his gaze flickered over her person.

Instead of being grateful, Lea was immediately angry. She didn't want his worry or concern. She wanted him to see her as someone who was pretty and most of all, normal. "I'm perfectly fine," she snapped back.

Matthew walked over to her carrying a bouquet of roses. As he presented them to her, his voice softened. "Lea, you have to get some rest."

She snatched the flowers out of his hand and took them over to a vase on the sofa table. Before she put them in the container, she hesitated. She bit her lip to keep from crying. Every one of the white roses was an example of beauty and perfection. But if someone examined her, what would they see? Would they find out how much of her mind was filled with black, wrathful thoughts?

Matthew came over to stand behind her. He put his hands on her shoulders and squeezed them ever so gently. "Maybe you should see someone. Maybe get some help—"

The thought sent a chill through Lea's body. She jerked around and thrust the flowers back at him. "Didn't you hear me? I told you I'm fine."

Matthew frowned mutely. Disappointment hung on his face as he touched one of the roses. His manicured fingers caressed the velvet, smooth petals before he set the bouquet aside. "Did something happen today?"

Lea tried to control her response, happy to change the subject. But the new topic made her angry too. "Our upcoming wedding happened. I lunched with mother, and of course she was self-indulgent and oblivious to my needs. I told her I wanted to keep things small and simple. She answered me with two words, 'How ridiculous.'"

Matthew shrugged. "Rita Ferguson is a pain in the neck. What else is new?"

"I am so sick of her elaborate meddling. She went on forever, talking about the guest list, the caterers, and everything else under the sun. I didn't think she would ever shut up."

"Why did you have to visit her today? You're leaving in the morning. I hoped that this evening we could enjoy each other. But I can see that isn't going to happen."

"You know this damn vacation I'm taking wasn't my idea, Matt."

Matthew's face contorted in anger, but he took a deep breath and remained silent.

Lea stared at him with hard questioning eyes. "What is it with you nowadays? Every time you get upset about something I say, you clam up. Spit it out! Tell me, was this stupid vacation my idea or not?"

Matthew came over and put his arms around her. His green eyes softened as he studied her. "I love you. Do you think I want you to go? But you don't sleep or eat, and you're as temperamental as hell. As for somebody clamming up, it's you. Why won't you tell me what's wrong?"

She pulled away. "I'll tell you what's wrong. You've changed. The Matthew Howell that I knew as a friend wasn't interested in crap like love and getting married."

Her statement seemed to shatter the patience the surgeon had been trying to exercise. He exploded. "You agreed to all that 'crap'! Besides, don't you think it scares the hell out of me too? Neither one of us went looking for a commitment. Lord knows you weren't what I thought I wanted. You're spoiled, head strong, and stubborn as a mule on your good days."

She crossed her arms. "Well, that makes me feel all better, Doctor Howell. You sure have a way of making a girl feel desirable." She stared down at the carpet. "But at least you sound like the Matthew I know."

Matthew paused. "Fair enough. Now can't we just call a truce?"

When she shrugged, he came over again. This time she let him hold her. As she buried her face in his chest, she inhaled deeply. Matthew always had a lingering scent of soap that mixed in perfectly with his expensive cologne. The combination was comforting, a blend of warmth and earthiness that also embodied a touch of something fresh and exotic. If she could only lose herself in Matthew's wonderful fragrance, maybe the rest of her problems would fade a little.

Matthew tilted up her chin and fingered her lips like the rose. "I never thought I could love someone like this." He bent down to kiss her and then explored her face with bright, passionate eyes.

"I want you, too," she whispered as she clung to him.

He kissed her again then stepped back and took her hand in his. "Let's go into the bedroom."

She remained steadfast, sucking in some air that had no scent of him. If she let herself feel Matthew too deeply, she'd never be strong enough to let go of him. The thought had been in the back of her mind ever since they got engaged. She needed to give Matthew a break, to dissolve their ties, not marry him. "Sorry, I can't," she stammered. "You're right, I'm tired, and I haven't packed yet. I don't have time to play around. Go somewhere and grab yourself a bite to eat while I get some things done."

"What do you mean? Don't you want to go to dinner? I made reservations at that new French place your father recommended last week."

At the mention of her father, Lea felt the sharp edge of her mind readying itself. "Forget my father. He's an idiot."

Matthew returned a look of confusion. "I know Rita's a pain, but Raymond seems to really care about you."

Her sharp edge was thrust forward, armed with feelings that Lea knew she should keep hidden. "My father's worthless!"

Matthew stared back cautiously. "What's going on here? A moment ago we were kissing each other."

What could she tell him? The truth? Not in a million years. "If you want to go to dinner, call my damn father and ask him out!"

"You're being totally unreasonable."

"Forget you, too!" After that she couldn't control her abusive tongue. Like her nanny predicted, caustic, hurtful language poured out of her before she could stop it.

Matthew remained the strong one, refusing to be part of her hostility. He did an about face and slammed the door on his way out.

After the scene replayed in her mind, Lea put her finger to the foggy, cab window and traced a heart on its cold surface. She looked at it longingly for a moment, and then smudged out the image.

She'd said things she later regretted. Now, her ugliness was proof that she was doing the right thing for Matthew's sake. A deep sadness took hold as she realized what that meant. "Everything I love, everything that makes life worth living is gone."

Three

LEA CHECKED INTO an aging, downtown hotel that the cab driver had recommended. With a number of large conventions in town, the nicer ones were fully booked. However, the situation turned out to be a fortunate one. Nicer hotels required a credit card, and she had impulsively trashed hers. The third-rate hotel accepted cash.

Lea felt like things were looking up until she saw her room. It was as dreary as the weather, with faded, lime green and gold furnishings. The only decorations were a chipped mirror on one wall and a large, yellowing picture of an old clipper ship opposite the bed. The ship was being tossed about in a storm, looking like it was ready to capsize.

Lea snorted out her cutting appraisal to the bellhop. "I didn't know the rooms were going to be so elegant."

He gave her a sideways squint. "Sorry, ma'am, but it's been very busy, and we've been booking rooms that are scheduled for remodeling."

Lea scowled. "Lucky me."

The thin, elderly man disregarded her comment and went about his duties. After he opened the curtains, he stepped back. "Nasty weather we're having, but the forecast should improve in a couple of days."

Lea stared at the grey skies and a steady drizzle splattering the window ledge. The scene added to the room's bleakness. She'd always stayed in five star hotels and felt a rising concern about her present accommodations. "Are you sure there's not something nicer? I don't think I've ever stayed anywhere like this before."

The bellhop shook his head, apologized again and left as soon as he got his gratuity.

Once Lea was alone, she gave the room another onceover. An involuntary shiver took hold. After being raised in an overly, opulent environment, she'd rebelled against excessive extravagance. However, her current quarters were definitely substandard. "If my mother saw me in this dump, she'd know I was going off the deep end."

She decided a shower would help to boost her mood. She quickly unzipped her bag and retrieved some toiletries. After she slipped off her clothes, she headed into the bathroom.

She had to tip-toe her way over the cracked tiles. As she moved about, she tried not to touch the dirty, gray grouting and the obvious neglect of some incompetent housekeeper. She refused to acknowledge the antique appearance of the toilet. Instead, she went straight to the shower. Ripping back the stiff curtain, she surveyed the chipped tub. Climbing in was another matter.

"Oh hell," she sneered with disgust. The shower was definitely lacking in cleanliness. It was the kind of place to get one of her phobias going. But backing away from what she'd started scared her even more. She had to forget everything but going forward.

As she stood in the shower and let the water soothe her body, she began to rally. Maybe she wasn't as bad a person as she thought. She'd put Matthew's welfare above her own. But then she thought about sleeping alone and cringed.

Normally, when she went to bed, she worried about the nightmares waiting for her. Sometimes, it was hard to even close her eyes. Matthew seemed to sense how she felt. He'd put his arms around her and pull her close. She knew he wanted to protect her. But from now on, she wouldn't have him to turn to. She was totally on her own.

* * *

After her shower, Lea pulled the old bedspread aside and laid down. She intended to simply rest for a few moments. Afterwards, she'd dress and go out for something to eat. Instead, she fell asleep. When she woke up, it was dark, and she couldn't get her bearings.

Where was she? Why did the air smell musty? It took a moment before she remembered she was in a hotel room. But there was something to be grateful for. She'd had a dreamless sleep, no nightmares.

She closed her eyes, still tired. Should she try to go back to sleep? No, it would be a mistake to stay in bed too long. She wouldn't be able to sleep that night.

She checked the clock on the side table. It was already late, and she was hungry. She hadn't eaten all day. With any luck, she'd find a restaurant or diner that was still open.

She forced herself out of bed and stretched. Her body was tight, even after her nap. She walked to the bathroom and flipped on the light. A bright, fluorescent glow filled the small space and made her squint. As her eyes slowly adjusted, she found herself staring at the mirror and immediately hated what she saw.

"How can Matthew think I'm marriage material?" she moaned.

Weighing in at ninety pounds, her small frame was gaunt and bony. All sign of womanly roundness was gone. Her skin appeared almost colorless. She ran a hand through her naturally wavy, dark hair. It contrasted sharply with her pale skin.

"I look like one of the walking dead."

As she continued to stare at herself, she thought about Matthew again, and how he'd professed his love. That was rare for the detached surgeon. He wasn't a man who naturally expressed his feelings. But he'd been insistent when he spoke. It didn't make sense. No matter how hard she tried to understand his attraction, she couldn't come up with a reason why he'd want her.

She thought about the painting in the other room. She was like the ship in the picture. It was facing a terrible fate. The treacherous waves were too much for it. It was going to sink. The voices in her head were treacherous too, repeatedly undermining her, swamping her ability to think rationally. She grabbed hold of the sink. How long would it be before they overwhelmed her completely?

* * *

Lea left the small, all-night diner feeling slightly nauseous. Her choices had been limited, and she ended up with a greasy burger and some overdone fries. As soon as she stepped out the door, she

22

paused under the canopy and took in a breath of the fresh air. After she felt a little better, she opened her umbrella. It was still raining, but she decided not to go back to her room. Instead, she started walking up the street. Puddles of rain splashed her slacks and blowing gusts wet her face. It didn't matter. Being a little wet was better than facing her depressing hotel room.

A short distance from the diner, she discovered a movie theatre. Fortunately, it was still open, a shelter in the storm. She'd not only get out of the weather, but she hoped to lose herself in some mystery or even an action film. She was so relieved to find a way to pass the time that she didn't bother to check on what was playing. After she bought a ticket at the box office, she walked briskly through the lobby. She barely noticed the posters of classic movies that lined the walls.

The lights in the auditorium were turned off, but the flickering illumination on the screen was bright enough to help her find her way down the center aisle. When she looked at the rows of seats, she realized that she had the entire space to herself. She groaned out her frustration. Normal people weren't at some late night movie. They were tucked away in their beds, dozing peacefully. "If only I could be like everyone else, I'd be snuggled up next to Matthew right now."

As soon as she thought about her fiancé, she felt a terrible twinge of regret. She hoped he was okay, that he wasn't worried about her. Even if he was tough, he did seem vulnerable when it came to her welfare. Had she been too hasty in running off without more of an explanation? Perhaps she needed to send him another text. She'd tell him that she needed some space and some time on her own to think things over. At least he'd know not to be too alarmed about her going missing.

She put a hand in her pocket and frowned. She'd tossed her phone away earlier. Probably a stupid thing to do. She'd have to buy a disposable replacement.

After she promised herself to contact Matthew early the next day, she found a seat halfway down the aisle. Taking off her jacket and settling in, she made a second promise. She'd forget everything for a few minutes and enjoy the movie. Maybe after some frivolous entertainment, she'd have the courage to return to her ghastly, hotel accommodations.

With that hopeful expectation in mind, she glanced up at the movie that was playing. It took a moment for her mind to fully engage, but as soon as she realized what she was looking at, she let out an involuntary shriek. A sea of brown insects, waving their long antennae, covered the screen.

Lea clasped a hand over her mouth. She couldn't tolerate any kind of horror film, but horror was definitely the focus of the movie she'd paid to watch. Cockroaches, large and small, swarmed everywhere. They were like a voracious, skittering army, and they were advancing on an old man.

Instant panic and dread electrified every nerve in Lea's body.

Get out of this place! Get out now!

She would have obeyed if she had any control over her movements. But whatever grabbed hold was too quick. Her heart raced, trying to pump blood into her muscles and brain, but her limbs were useless. A powerful force, a memory, held her in its vice-like grip.

Lea knew about roaches. As the insects on the scene multiplied into the thousands, she remembered her personal encounter with the ghastly bugs. Her calculating nanny used roaches very effectively when she was dealing with three-year-old Lea's innocent, receptive mind.

Sitting in the theater, shutting her eyes to avoid the dreadful creatures on the screen, Lea's own private movie began to play. She became a helpless, little girl again.

"I have something for you," her nanny said as she forced little Lea into the closet. "Something to keep you company."

Little Lea's eyes and mood brightened for a brief moment. "My Teddy? Can I have my bear?"

"No," the old woman giggled, "something better."

The woman thrust out her closed hand. It was only a few inches from little Lea's face when the big-boned fingers began to open.

"Play with this, you wicked child," hissed the nanny as she exposed a huge, flying roach. It perched on her hand for only a moment before it took flight into the darkness. After that, the old woman stepped back and slammed the door to the closet shut.

Lea fought the memory, trying to escape what was coming just as the little girl trapped in the closet fought her punishment. But no amount of pounding on the solid oak door helped the child. And nothing could stop Lea from reliving what happened next.

She was in the pitch-dark closet again. And the large, flying roach had landed on her face. She screamed for mercy as it crawled over her skin. But the insect paid no heed. Its sticky feet moved upwards slowly. When it reached her hair, it paused, nestling itself down in her fine baby curls.

Lea thought her heart would stop as she relived the terror she'd gone through. When it actually occurred, her little-girl self had almost passed out from fright. As an adult, she did a little better. After several minutes, she was able to bring herself back to the present and calm her shaking body.

She'd almost managed to begin breathing normally when she felt something on her leg. It was a familiar sensation, a terrifying feeling that made her breath catch so suddenly that she went mute. Another slight movement on her calf followed. The sticky feet she remembered were on her body again, under her slacks. A roach was making its way up her lower leg.

She couldn't manage any air. Her body was paralyzed as flashes of the alien monster in the closet buzzed her again and again. Now that alien thing was attacking her where she sat. There were probably countless more of the insects in the old, derelict theatre.

When the primal urge for survival finally kicked in, her body came alive with an explosive scream. In a frenzied state of near madness, she slapped her leg and stomped her feet. One thought kept repeating. She had to get away from the horrible menace that was back to torment her again.

She was soon in a full-blown panic attack. After racing up the center aisle, she picked up speed and tore through the theatre lobby. Everything became a blur, but she couldn't stop. She bolted out the glass door and into the rain. It was pouring down in driving sheets, but she didn't notice. Her mind was consumed by too much trauma as her past and the present merged. Her only choice was to try to outrun both. Without further thought, she darted out into the street. When she finally looked up, two spotlights blinded her.

"I hope you die, you wicked child!" The nanny shouted out the words just before a shocking force slammed into Lea, and everything went black.

Four

ERIC LLOYD EXITED Baltimore's Jones Falls Expressway. After barely braking at the stop sign, he continued on. A little earlier, he'd left his warm bed in the suburbs. He was on his way back to the Medical Center. There'd been an accident on the expressway that forced him to try an unaccustomed route. It was an annoying detour. He wanted to check on Bob Sims, a patient, as soon as possible. The thirty-three-year-old man had suffered a second heart attack.

Slunk down low in the leather, bucket seat of his white Porsche, he made his way through the sheets of spring rain that fell on the city's dark, deserted streets. Hospital personnel had told him that Sims was stable, but Eric was the man's cardiologist. He felt it was his responsibility to make sure his patient was getting the best care possible.

He brushed a lock of his white blond hair aside and kept his eyes focused on the road's mirrored surface. It had been a long day, and he was tired. But exhaustion was no excuse for shirking his duty. Years before, a fellow intern named Kevin Belford commented on Eric's attitude. "You got this 'save the lame and the sick' thing burned into you," the man insisted. When Eric protested, Belford brought Eric's father into the conversation. "I've heard the rumors. Your dad sounds like some kind of fanatic, general practitioner, a lone voice in the wilds of Appalachia, taking care of the hillbillies. And I bet you followed him around like he was a god."

Eric never admitted that Belford had been correct about his father being a zealot. He also failed to recognize his own zeal as he hammered the accelerator and brake alternately, speeding up between lights, then coming to abrupt stops when they flashed red.

The Porsche was an older model, but he loved its speed and responsiveness. He put it through its paces with smooth, quick movements. He turned on the fan when the windshield began fogging up. It made navigating even more difficult. Besides the fogging windshield, the shower suddenly turned into a heavy downpour. Gusting winds buffeted the car with drenching rain.

After a record breaking winter of ice storms, snow, and a spring assault of frequent rain, the roads were pock marked with holes. He did his best to avoid them, but when he hit one, he swore out in protest. His expletives were voiced in his soft, West Virginia drawl. He continued on his way, refusing to yield to the storm or decaying pavement. He had to stop at a red light and gunned the motor impatiently. His eyes, the palest shade of blue, were red with fatigue after a twenty hour day.

When the windshield cleared and the light turned green, he punched the gas petal and tore through the intersection. The Porsche's ghostly, white form was a fleeting image on the wet, shiny street. But his timing was off. There was another red light ahead at the next intersection. He geared down, slowing his speed, hoping the light would turn green before he reached it. He thought about his patient and gave voice to his concern. "Bob has four kids to raise. He's my age. He's too young to have two serious heart attacks."

His words were cut short by a movement in the street ahead. A figure, half shrouded by a curtain of rain, bolted out from between the parked cars. Someone ran blindly into the path of the Porsche.

The action was so unexpected that Eric froze for the briefest moment. Time knotted itself in his throat and stopped. In spite of the downpour, he connected with the eyes of the person in the road in front of him. They were fixated on the vehicle's headlights. Like the gaze of a suicidal animal crossing the highway on a moonless, black night, the person's stare was blameless and wild.

"No!" Eric's shout of disbelief started the clock ticking again. A sickening panic grabbed hold as he slammed hard on the brakes. The car responded, but not quite enough. Its momentum carried it forward.

Eric's hands were white knuckled on the wheel as he tried to steer away from the paralyzed figure that stood helpless in the street. The car half spun around on the glassy road surface. Then there was a thud just before the car came to a stop. It was the sound of the unforgiving machine hitting soft flesh and fragile bones. It was a sound that horrified him.

"No! Please, no!" The words slipped out in a whisper as he swung the car door open. An immediate blast of cold, driving rain greeted him as he tried to get out. His seat belt held him fast. "Don't let this be happening," he pleaded as he fumbled with the buckle and released the belt.

With his breath heaving, he finally managed to exit the car. For a moment he hung on to the door as the storm continued to pelt his face with its fury. It was an unholy baptism that he wished would absolve him of the revulsion he felt churning inside.

He rushed over to a small, still form and dropped to his knees. A person lay in a torrent of water that flooded the street. With the blinding rain, he wasn't sure if he was looking at a woman or a child.

"Lord, help me!" A clap of thunder drowned out his words as a rush of water cascaded past the face of his pale victim. It washed away the trickle of blood that ran steadily from a gash in their forehead. He fumbled for a pulse, his hands so shaky he could barely grasp the person's limp wrist.

* * *

She wasn't aware of anything but the beautiful dream she was in.
  She was floating . . . in golden light.
  Buoyed up by invisible hands.
  A perfect calm. Safe and warm.
  Free. Free to let go of everything.
  A sound. A voice calling.
  The sparkling light vibrating.
  A voice calling out again, "Wake up."
  Fighting the call. Holding back.
  Wanting to stay in the golden light.
  But coming to the surface instead.
  Breaking through.
  A sharp feeling. Slicing through everything.
  The voice still calling, "Wake up."
  Heaviness pushing out the light.
  The voice again, gentle and soothing, "Open your eyes."
  A touch, light as a hummingbird visiting a flower.

A touch, breaking the spell.

Leaden . . . weighted feelings.

Eyes, trying to open. So heavy.

The mellow voice again, reaching out.

"It's okay. You're going to be okay."

Eyes, like fluttering wings, wanting to open, opening.

A face. A celestial visitor. White blond, wispy-fine hair falling over the palest, blue gaze. The summer sky peering out of the portals of an angel.

As the dreamy images started to clear, everything became more solid. Objects came into focus. A man was looking down. A stranger. A question came out naturally. "Who are you?"

"My name is Eric Lloyd."

She blinked back. The name didn't mean anything. "Where am I?"

"Please lie still. You were in an accident. We're taking you to the hospital."

"Accident? I don't remember. I don't remember anything."

* * *

Eric abhorred violence, and yet he was standing in the ER, monitoring a person he'd run down. He could only be thankful that her injuries weren't worse. His quick responses and maneuvering, along with fast braking, had slowed the car enough to prevent the woman from sustaining any broken bones. Still, she had been unconscious for a short amount of time.

Currently, her condition was satisfactory, but she looked very fragile and frightened. When she stared up at him for reassurance, he kept his tone steady and calm. "It's okay. You're going to be okay."

She didn't respond, but her eyes did brighten a little.

When Eric's best friend, Jerry Norton, tapped his shoulder, he jerked around. Jerry was a neurologist. He was also a concussion specialist and a doctor who frequently helped out in the ER. Jerry signaled for Eric to follow him over to a quiet corner.

Eric tried to switch into a more professional mode, but he couldn't manage to keep his heart from pounding. "What's the verdict, Jerry?"

"I can't be sure, but I don't think she's suffered much physical damage. And there's no indication of a serious concussion."

"But I hit her with my car."

"Look, I can't explain it, but for whatever reason she's in remarkably good condition, especially for someone who wasn't in great shape to begin with."

"What do you mean?"

"Oh please, Eric, the woman clearly wasn't taking care of herself. She's probably one of those stressed out people who was living on the edge."

Eric rubbed his brow, trying to stave off a headache. "If only we knew who to contact, but she didn't have any identification."

Jerry returned a thoughtful smile. "Hopefully someone who knows her will come forward soon. In the meantime, go home and try to get some rest. When you come back in the morning, maybe there'll be more information on who she is."

Five

CHICAGO'S SPRING WEATHER was sunny and mild, almost perfect for a city that often felt the extremes of cold and heat. But for Doctor Matthew Howell, the pleasant weather went unappreciated. He was locked into a mindset that excluded anything positive. He couldn't get beyond his anger. Wherever he went, it was there. No one was spared, not even the people in the hospital where he worked.

At the end of another long and frustrating day, he slammed down a clipboard on the nurses' station. The intern who was waiting for him looked white-faced and nervous. Matthew returned a scathing scowl. "Get it right, Evans, or you're out. Is that clear? The next time I look at these records, they better be complete. If I see a dot missing over an 'i', you're finished."

"Yes, sir." The reply was shaky but loud, the way Martin Evans knew his superior wanted it.

"Well what are you waiting for?" Matthew shot back.

"Is that all, Doctor Howell?"

Matthew felt his exhaustion settling in deeper. It scared him. He was usually able to weather whatever life threw his way. Now, with Lea's disappearance, his nerves were getting worse by the day. "Get the hell out of here, Evans," he croaked in a weaker tone.

The intern was in motion at once, practically running in the opposite direction.

Matthew turned and headed down the hall. "Priscilla, I'm going home. I don't want to be disturbed," he called back to the nurse in charge. With an unaccustomed heaviness in his step, he headed for the elevator.

"What about your patient, Mr. Doyle?" the nurse called after him.

Matthew paused and closed his eyes. "Screw Mr. Doyle, I did my part already," he mumbled under his breath. He'd taken a case that no other surgeon would touch. Mr. Doyle pulled through the long and exhausting operation because of Matthew's expertise. Now he needed to go home and relax before his nerves went totally ballistic. On the other hand, he was always one for responsibility. He turned and glanced back at the nurse. "Tell Evans to keep a close eye on Doyle. If he needs to, he can call me."

"Evans is off in an hour."

"No, he's not! Tell him I said so."

"Yes, doctor," the nurse replied in a crisp tone.

When Matthew got to his car in the parking garage, he fumbled with his keys and dropped them. "Dammit!" he yelled as he bent over to pick them up. He was trying his best, but he couldn't ignore his fear. It had carried through after his lunch with his fiancé's father, Raymond Ferguson. The seventy-year-old executive had sounded worn and discouraged when they spoke.

"Listen, Matthew, my people started looking for Lea as soon as you found out she never arrived at her hotel. However, it's not easy because of the security measures that are involved. Thankfully, my man knows people, and we've been checking the airlines. From what we've learned, she never boarded her flight. We're also in the process of trying to check out other flights and airlines. But there are so many possibilities, and it takes time. And who knows with Lea, she's so unpredictable. She might still be in Chicago."

Matthew had sat back, trying to remain calm, trying to remember anything that he might add. "She sent me a text from the airport. She told me she was fine and not to worry. But I knew it was all bull. When I put her in a cab that morning, all I could think was that she should be checking into a hospital, not flying off somewhere. But you know Lea—"

"I do know her," Raymond said with a scowl. "She would have never forgiven you if you forced her to do something she didn't want. When she's like that, there's no reasoning with her. Believe me, I've tried."

"That's not the point," Matthew fumed.

"If it helps, there's no sign of foul play involved."

"Thank goodness for that."

Raymond raised his eyes in line with Matthew's. "I'm sorry to say this, but there is the possibility that she just ran off. That's what her mother thinks."

Matthew's response had been immediate. "I don't want to hear that, Raymond!"

"Matthew, I know how hard this is—"

"Hard? I love Lea!"

"And you think that I don't love her?" Raymond ran a shaky hand through his thinning hair. "I want her back too."

"So stop talking and keep looking for her."

Their discussion ended after that. But no matter how adamant Matthew had been with Lea's father, he had to face the truth. Maybe Lea's mother was right.

He unlocked his Mercedes and climbed in. He reached out to start the engine and hesitated. After his long day, thinking about Raymond's disturbing update added to his exhaustion.

"I'm so tired of incompetent people. Ferguson rules a business empire, and he can't find his only child!" After he blurted out the words, a rare jolt of panic hit. When he got home, he had nothing waiting for him but an empty apartment and more worry. How had his life spiraled out of control so quickly?

He looked over at the passenger seat. A few nights before Lea had disappeared, she'd been seated next to him in the car. "You were almost sweet, Lea. So what happened?"

They were driving home from dinner. At a stop light, he looked over and saw her playing with the engagement ring he'd given her. "A carat isn't big enough, right?"

Lea was dressed in a yellow sweater that offset her eyes. They looked tired and dull. But they instantly filled with fire when she glared back at him. "For the umpteenth time, it's a bigger diamond than I wanted. I hate when people have this 'show the world how much I've got' attitude."

"Yes, I know." He stared down at her purse and scowled. "You're constantly sticking that fact in everyone's face. I bought you a purse for your birthday. It set me back a grand, and you still carry around something that looks like it belongs in a thrift store."

"I like my purse."

"Okay, but when I bought the ring, I wanted you to know how important you are to me." He smiled. "Mrs. Matthew Howell. It has a nice ring."

Lea finally relaxed a little and giggled. "Do you realize that you're glowing when you talk like that?"

"I am not."

"Matthew, please, you're as bright as a 300 watt bulb."

"Somebody has to be happy about our wedding."

Lea snickered. "That's more like it. You always do the 'pout' look so well when you want your way."

"Obviously I can't 'glow' myself into your good graces."

Lea sat up straighter. "Pull the car over."

"What?"

"You heard me. Pull the car over."

Matthew protested under his breath, but he did what she asked.

As the car slowed to a stop, Lea smiled. "Can you hear yourself? You're an expert at whining. But I care about you anyway, Matt."

Matthew stared out the windshield with growing agitation. "I hope you do more than care about me. You care about every stray cat and dog that crosses your path."

"Okay, here it is. I'm going to make a statement that better shut you up. No more whining or complaining."

He saw her face go from womanly and preachy to innocent and open. "I live to whine and complain," he teased.

"Not tonight," she said with raised chin and insistent, dark eyes.

He reached out for her hand, studying its size. It was so small and delicate when compared to his own. Yet, she had an inner strength that could amaze him. It was one of the virtues that he admired. Lea could be a royal pain in the backside, but she did care, not just about animals, but she truly cared about him. She didn't only care, she accepted who he was, the good and the bad. She'd seen him at his worst, and she still wanted to be with him. He tried his best to be there for her too. "Fine, no more complaining tonight."

Lea smiled. "Good, because I have something very important to tell you, Matthew Howell."

He heard the conviction in her voice. If there was ever a person who'd give their all to help someone in need, it would be Lea Ferguson. Nobody had ever given a damn about him before, except for his grandpa. Lea was the exception. "So spit it out. What do you want to tell me?"

"I love you," she whispered.

His brows shot up in surprise. "Could you say it a little louder?"

"No."

"Why?"

"Never mind. I said it once. That's enough."

Matthew snorted out his breath. "Oh, I see. I'm sitting here trying to buy what you're telling me, but the truth is that your love only goes so far."

"And what about your love?"

He turned and stared out his side window. "All that I know is that I love you more than you love me. All this time I've successfully avoided the whole mess call romance, and now I'm trapped in a one-sided relationship."

Lea tugged on his arm. "First of all, you promised not to whine. And secondly, there's no way you love me more than I love you. Your little Grinch heart might be full to the brim, but I have more capacity to love."

"Really? Lea, please, you even hate your parents."

"Maybe, but it wasn't always like that, at least not with my father."

"So you loved him at one time?"

"With all my heart until—"

Matthew watched her bite her lip. "Oh hell, Lea, did your father do something to you?"

"No!" she blurted out. "Nothing. He did nothing."

Matthew relaxed back into his seat and sighed impatiently. "Never mind. Why should I care anyway? If you can't confide in me—"

"I am confiding. That's all that there is to it."

"Fine."

Lea smiled back. "No matter how I sound it times, Matt, I do care about us." She put her hand on his again and pulled it towards her, placing it over her chest. "You're a love-sick scoundrel, Matthew, and you've wormed your way into my heart. And no matter how hard I try to deny it, I'm infected with you."

"I sound like a disease."

Lea burst out laughing. "You know I didn't mean it that way. But I can see I have to be very clear about my feelings, so listen up, Doctor Howell. I love you! I love you! I love you!"

Matthew smiled as he remembered the conviction in Lea's voice that starry evening. So what happened after that? The night before Lea disappeared, she didn't shout out her love. All she could do was complain about their wedding.

"Dammit, that's it. She told me that she loved me, but she was lying to both of us. She wanted a friend, not a commitment. So guess what, Rita Ferguson was right. Lea ran out on me!"

As soon as he said the words, he felt like his world was crumbling. After being single and content as a bachelor, he realized how needy he felt. He had Lea on the brain. He wanted to go to sleep with her in his arms. He wanted to wake up in the morning and have her so close that he could feel her heart beating when he cradled her chest. He wanted her in his life, period.

He swallowed hard at the thoughts. "Lea was right about one thing. I am diseased. I've become some love-sick puppy."

He started the car and gunned the motor. Slamming the clutch into reverse, he shot out of the parking slot, then braked almost immediately. His anger was starting to escalate, and that wasn't good. Sure he yelled at interns and nurses, but it was a controlled anger. Emotional issues, those situations that really mattered, had to be handled with reason and logic. Nothing of benefit ever came from acting rashly.

He pushed back his shoulders and forced himself to take several deep breaths, slowing down that primal part that could override good judgement. "So what's it going to be? Am I going to let Lea ruin my life, or am I going to take the 'Matthew Howell' cure and move on?"

As the car idled, he continued to soothe his nerves. He'd let his guard down, yes, but that didn't mean he couldn't learn from his mistake. His entire childhood had been filled with disappointments and grief. But he didn't let any of it stop him. As a doctor, one of the best in his field, tough situations were the norm. But he never allowed circumstances to affect his performance. Now he had to be just as strong and unwavering with that elusive thing called love. He had to find a way to get past it and get on with his life.

Six

FORTY-FIVE-YEAR-OLD SARAH Kasner enjoyed being a psychiatrist. She liked helping people. She hoped she could help her patient. The woman sat in her hospital room, staring out her window. She'd been in an accident and had amnesia. Unfortunately, she didn't have any identification and had been given the name, Jane Doe.

Sarah looked at the clipboard in her lap. "Jane, since the accident, have you had any memories or feelings that you could tell me about?"

Her patient gave her a darting glance and returned her attention to the window.

Sarah frowned. She was usually able to remain very objective, but she'd noticed Jane's hollowed out cheeks and dark, forlorn eyes. They made her feel like she was working with a frightened, homeless child instead of an adult. Clearing her throat, she repeated her question and waited.

When Jane finally spoke, her voice was distant and wistful. "At first, I had vague, fleeting images. They seemed to be just beyond my reach." She paused and stared down at her tightly clasped fists. "I . . . I could almost see a face or hear a voice. But every time I tried to hold on—"

"Yes?"

Jane hesitated and slowly opened her fists. "No matter how hard I tried to remember, it was like a dream. Everything slipped away until there was nothing. Now, I can't remember anything."

"It's okay."

"No, it isn't!" Jane put her arms around herself, hunching her shoulders. "My mind is a blank, but my body feels like it's screaming . . . like it wants to run away."

Sarah got up, retrieved a blanket from the bed, and wrapped it around Jane's shoulders. "Is there anything else that you want to tell me?"

Jane's eyes went instantly bright with tears, but she quickly swiped them away with a tissue. "Tell everybody to leave me alone."

"Has someone been bothering you?"

"The nurses, the doctors, everybody keeps asking me the same questions. They want to know how I am, how I'm feeling."

Sarah smiled. "You were in an accident. It's important to know how you feel."

Jane looked down and began to twist the belt on her hospital robe. "But they look at me like I'm pitiful. And I guess they're right. When I see myself in the mirror, I hate what I see. I'm not just pitiful, I'm scary."

"Jane, I don't see someone who's scary. I see a young woman who might have lost her memory, but she's sensitive and very bright."

"I think you're the only one who sees me that way. Have you talked to Doctor Lloyd? He's nice, and he tries to be helpful, but—"

"Doctor Lloyd is very concerned—"

"I don't need his concern!"

Sarah looked down at her notes and took a deep breath. She knew what Jane meant about Eric Lloyd. He'd taken his part in Jane's accident very hard. "Jane, Doctor Lloyd genuinely wants to be there for you, to help you in any way that he can."

"But I don't want to be someone who needs his help. I want to remember who I am and get out of here." Jane looked up with hard, searching eyes. "Tell me why this is happening to me. Why do I feel so lost?"

Sarah went to the window, looking for a break in the weather. It was supposed to be getting sunnier, but so far the skies remained mostly gray. Ignoring the gloom, she turned back to Jane, determined to concentrate on her patient's needs.

She thought of herself as a woman of science, but she also believed in the human spirit and how strong it was. When she spoke, she made sure to engage Jane's disheartened gaze. "Jane, I promise that I'm going to do everything I can to help you find the answers to your questions. But you have to do something too. You have to hang in there even when you get discouraged. Can you do that?"

Jane looked up and blinked back warily. "I'll try."

Sarah sensed the turmoil and fear behind her patient's guardedness. The woman had amnesia, but Sarah suspected that it was covering up some much deeper trauma.

* * *

Jerry Norton paused in the hospital hallway watching Eric Lloyd walk towards him. Eric looked worn and drained after all the worrying he'd done. Jerry tried to lighten the mood. "It's the big day, right, old buddy?"

Eric paused and crossed his arms. "Yes, my mother and I are taking Jane home this afternoon."

"Fine, but you need to keep some facts in mind. We haven't been able to find any medical cause for her amnesia. Secondly, after assessing your Jane Doe, Doctor Sarah Kasner feels that the woman was probably a very troubled individual before the accident ever happened."

"That may be the case, but I'm dealing with the here and now. And Jane's not getting better. She's becoming more depressed and withdrawn every day."

"It's understandable. Amnesia can be difficult to deal with—"

"Difficult? Her world, everything that makes her a part of something, is gone. And Eric Lloyd, the guy who's supposed to help people, took it all away from her."

Jerry removed his horn-rimmed glasses and put them in his pocket. "Word of advice, Eric, you have to lighten up. You're not going to help this woman if you look at her like she's a goner."

Eric stepped back, frowning as he studied the floor. "You're right. I should know better."

"There is a bright side to it all. Except for some cuts and bruises, Jane Doe came out of a potentially, devastating accident unscathed physically. I'd say that's something to be thankful for."

"I am grateful, but what would you do if you were the one responsible?"

"Hopefully I'd listen to my friend, especially if that friend is also a very competent doctor."

"Jerry, I'm trying—"

"If you can, take it a day at a time. Putting pressure on yourself isn't going to help this woman you're taking home. And who knows, one of these days her memory could return."

* * *

Jane sat back in a chair in her hospital room, thinking about the name she'd been given. It sounded so uncomplicated, but she wished she could remember who she really was. It wasn't a realistic wish. As the days passed, her mind refused to come up with any new information.

At least she wasn't alone. Margaret Lloyd, Eric Lloyd's mother, was as nice and caring as her son. The tall, older woman was presently gathering up Jane's hospital belongings. "I guess there's not too much to pack." She paused and stared out the window. "It's funny. The nurses are happy for me. They told me I'm going home. But I don't know what that word means."

Margaret smiled back. "Then it will be up to Eric and me to try to help you learn what it means."

"I don't know. This might be a bad idea, Mrs. Lloyd—"

"Please, call me Margaret."

Jane frowned. "Margaret, neither of you should feel obligated to me."

"Dearest, our lives connected that awful night my son ran you over. Someday perhaps we'll understand why it happened. In the meantime, it would be impossible to feel you weren't meant to be a part of our lives. Besides, Eric has probably told you that I've only recently moved here from West Virginia. Living with him is nice, but he's gone so much, and I'm . . . well, I guess I'm lonely to tell you the truth. It would be wonderful to have you stay with us."

Jane stared back, amazed at how much Eric Lloyd and his sixty-five year old mother resembled each other. Both had white hair except that Margaret's was silver white and Eric's was blond. Their eyes were the same pale blue, and each had a face that radiated with warmth and caring. "You're much too kind. But we know from an eye witness that I ran out in front of Doctor Lloyd's car. And my amnesia doesn't seem to be physical. The psychiatrist seems to think it might be—" Jane hesitated, twisting and untwisting her tissue.

Margaret came over, staring at Jane with bright concern. "Jane?" She paused and took a breath. "Is it all right if I call you that?"

Jane nodded. "Sure, that's me, Jane Doe, the person with no past."

"I'm so sorry."

"I've been observing who I am, and I remind myself of a TV soap victim. I cry more and more every day. I pace the floor at night. I'm a wreck. You shouldn't get involved—" Jane couldn't stop the sob that came out as she spoke. "I'm sorry, it comes on so suddenly."

Margaret quickly pulled over a chair and sat down next to her. She put her arm around Jane's shoulders. "Oh, for heaven's sake, dear, I'd cry too if I lost all notion of who my family was. It's natural to grieve. Eric is the best son anyone could have, but that Porsche is his one downfall. I don't know why he couldn't settle for something sensible."

As Jane listened to Margaret's motherly concern, she felt her mood shift. Swiping at her face with her tissue, she smiled. "Margaret, a young, handsome guy like your son needs to have some fun. From what the nurses tell me, he can be an obsessively, caring doctor."

"I know that. So was his father. But he can be hard-headed too. Sometimes, it clouds his judgment. I just hope you can forgive him. I know how very sorry he is about that night."

"I have forgiven him, but he also seems a bit obsessive about guilt too."

Margaret's eyes sparkled brighter. "Then make him feel better. Come home with us like you told him you would. Maybe together we can straighten him out."

A male voice answered from the doorway. "Who is the 'he' that you two plan on straightening out?"

Jane looked up and saw Eric Lloyd. He was looking back at her with his usual serious expression, but after a moment, he let a little smile slip in. It changed his look so much that she laughed. "Nobody you know," she chided.

Eric's brows arched with surprise. "That's the first time I've seen you really smile since you've been here."

Jane observed his spotless, white shirt and tan slacks. His face was more relaxed. "And it's the first time that you seem like a normal human being."

Eric flushed with embarrassment. "I'm just happy that you've decided to join our family."

"I agree, Eric," Margaret chimed in. "Jane's exhausted from this whole ordeal. Now it's up to us to show her that things can change. For a start we can put some meat on her bones after this hospital food she's been forced to eat."

"She didn't eat much of it," Eric confided. He narrowed his eyes in Jane's direction. "Why do you think I've been so concerned?"

Jane crossed her arms. "The two of you both worry too much. I told your mother that none of this is your fault, Doctor Lloyd. You shouldn't feel guilty."

He looked down and swallowed. "I'm working on it. And please, it's just Eric."

Margaret cradled Jane's shoulder again and eyed Eric with impatience. "Is the paperwork done? Can we go home?"

Eric looked at Jane. His blue eyes flickered nervously. "Is that all right with you?"

Jane's throat tightened as she felt another wave of self-pity coming on. "I guess, but only for a little while."

Eric nodded with a smile. "Good."

* * *

Jane woke up breathless. It was her first night in her new home, and the moon was shining through her bedroom window. Its soft, shimmering light heightened her excitement. She'd just had the most wonderful dream.

Maybe my memory is coming back. Maybe somewhere in this world I have someone who loves me.

After feeling like her mind was useless, it was suddenly filled with vivid details from her dream. At first, she'd been walking on a beach. It was nighttime and the soft feel of darkness and the sound of the water lapping on the shore should have been comforting. Instead, everything reminded her of how alone she felt. She didn't know where she was or how to find her way back home. Even the word, home, had no meaning.

As her sense of hopelessness deepened, a man called out to her. "I've finally found you!"

The man's strong, confident voice parted the darkness with a resonant determination. It also stirred something hopeful in her. Could it be true? Had she heard the voice of the man she loved? She turned around slowly, searching. As she scanned the darkness, the moon drifted out from behind a cloud. Its light flickered across the man's face. She only had a brief glimpse, but it was enough.

She put her hand to her chest, feeling the beat of her heart. It was speeding up, preparing her, letting her know that she'd found the person she'd been yearning for. As the man walked towards her, his presence had a strength that didn't allow for sadness. His presence was as familiar as her breath. Yet she was afraid to breathe. She was afraid that the man would disappear, that the darkness would swallow him up again.

"Where have you been?" he asked as he reached out for her hand. "I looked everywhere for you?"

She hesitated. What could she say that wouldn't break the spell that had brought them together? She knew it was a fragile enchantment, a bit of magic that could be lost as easily as a wisp of smoke on the wind.

The man was bolder, less afraid of violating whatever had intervened in their behalf. He touched her face, running his fingers over her cheek, caressing it ever so lightly. "I didn't think I'd ever see you again."

He bent down and barely touched her lips with his own. When he kissed her, it was a teasing kiss, a kiss that waited for her response. When she offered an eager smile, he kissed her again. But this kiss was more passionate. As the moon danced across his face again, his eyes were ignited with both yearning and pain. "Don't ever go away again. Promise me!" he demanded.

When she nodded back, he scooped her up in his arms. He pressed her so tight against his broad chest that she felt the beating of his heart. It was a powerful vessel, and she knew it housed the love he'd always have for her.

"I didn't know where you were," she whispered as her own heart synced with his.

He swung her around in a wide circle. "It doesn't matter now. We'll always have each other, no matter what tries to come between us."

As the world swirled around her, she was lost in their shared happiness. The boundaries of time became a blur. There was only one thing that mattered. She finally knew where home was. It was in his arms. "Never let me go," she repeated over and over.

After that, the dream ended abruptly. Jane woke up squeezing her pillow. Her heart was pounding, trying to hold on to what she'd just experienced.

As she settled back into a wistful state, the questions started. Did someone really care for her? Was there someone she belonged to? Someone who belonged to her?

As she relived the dream again and again, she knew the answers. A man existed who would never stop searching for her. He'd always love her, and she'd always love him. They shared a bond that would last forever.

* * *

Matthew opened his eyes and blinked at the darkness. His body felt alive again. When he took a breath, his chest could finally expand fully. For a few brief moments, a rush of happiness replaced all the cares and fears he'd been entertaining recently.

As he came awake more fully, he stretched out his hand, hoping against hope to find Lea next to him. But the space was empty. The sheets were cold. He closed his eyes again. "Dammit, I was just dreaming."

In spite of his protest, he felt like the dream meant something. A deep-down sense of certainty told him that he'd been given a message. He hadn't always believed in such airy-fairy nonsense, but one of his teachers in med school had made an intriguing statement. She informed the class that the best doctors were intuitive.

Matthew dismissed the claim at the time. It was only later that he understood its validity. When he was in the OR, he felt like he could read his patients on a deeper level than any machine. It wasn't something that he had to work at. The information was simply there for him to access.

As he lay in the darkness, his intuition urged him to take his dream seriously. When he went over the details, he decided to heed the advice. What he'd just experienced was very unique and different than other dreams. The sights, sounds and smells were as real as anything he'd ever known in the waking state. Not only that, but Lea felt real. Her hair, her eyes, and her body pressed against his were solid and tangible. He could still feel her in his arms. He could still feel her lips on his as they kissed.

He sat up and looked at the clock. It was a quarter 'til five in the morning. "This can't wait," he said as he grabbed his phone and called Raymond Ferguson. The older man answered on the first ring. That's when Matthew remembered that Lea's father was a very early riser.

"Raymond, it's Matthew. I want to talk about Lea's whereabouts. I know you've had problems with your investigation, but you have to keep going. It's urgent."

Matthew held the phone out from his ear as he listened to Raymond's reply. The man always spoke in an annoyingly loud voice on a call.

When it was his turn to speak, Matthew's voice was louder too. "I don't give a damn about some airline software glitch. Don't ask me how, but I know Lea's out there somewhere, and something's happened to her. That's why she hasn't contacted us. She's in trouble, and you have to find her."

After Matthew finished his call, he threw his phone on the side table and laid back. More of the dream's message filled his mind. He'd been wrong about Lea. She still loved him. She hadn't deserted him, but she was lost. He could only pray that she wasn't badly hurt or worse. Just the thought of her being in harm's way made his heart race.

"If someone hurts a hair on her head, I swear, they'll live to regret the day they were born."

Seven

MARGARET SMILED AND took in a deep breath of the outdoor air. Eric had recently prepared a garden area in the backyard. She bent down and dug in the loosened soil with her bare fingers. She gave Jane a quick glance as she made a tiny hole. "Spring is my favorite time of the year. It's planting time. And now I can share that time with you."

Jane stood a few feet away. "I'm glad that you feel that way, but maybe I should go back in the house."

Margaret studied Jane's overall appearance. The young woman wasn't only frowning, her body looked rigid and stiff. "Please, stay out here for a bit," Margaret urged as she dropped a large, white bean in the hole she'd poked out.

"I don't understand. Don't you hate getting all dirty?"

Margaret laughed. "Planting vegetables and flowers and touching the earth makes me happy. Do you know I can almost feel the life force stirring in these seeds? I know each one of them is waiting for their moment to shoot out their tiny roots, to take hold of the soil and be nurtured by it, to grow strong and healthy."

Jane shrugged as she stared at the seeds in her hand. "They just look like dried out, little nothings to me."

"Come over by me, Jane, and we can plant those seeds together."

Jane stepped back. "I can't. I don't like getting dirty."

Margaret returned a look of concern. "It's alright. We're washable, and so are our clothes."

Jane's scowl deepened. "I better not."

"Please, indulge an old woman. I dreamed that someday I'd have a daughter to do things with. My husband, and now Eric, always tilled the garden for me. They got it ready, but I did the rest alone. And I enjoyed myself, but I always imagined what it would be like to have someone who enjoyed a garden too."

"First of all, Margaret, you're not an old woman. And I would like to help you, but I don't know anything about gardens. I'm sorry."

Margaret sat back on her heels. "It's easy. I'll show you what to do, but first, I have a favor to ask. When I look at you, I feel like you're family. Do you think you could just call me 'Mom' instead of Margaret?"

"Are you sure?"

"Of course, now please, grab those gloves over there on the ground. I can't stand to wear them, but they'll protect your young hands."

Jane cautiously slipped on the gloves and walked over to where Margaret was kneeling. "I hope this isn't a mistake."

"But how can you make a mistake enjoying this marvelous earth? Now, would you rather put in some tomato plants? Do you like tomatoes?"

"They're my favorite vegetable when they're not hot house grown." Jane hesitated. "Margaret . . . uh, I mean Mom, I'm confused."

Margaret stood up and dusted off her hands. "What is it?"

"How do I know these things about myself when I don't remember anything? I've been here for almost two weeks, and we both know that I have my likes and dislikes. I'm good at some tasks and terrible at others, especially taking care of a house. I don't understand any of it."

"I see. Let's go sit awhile and talk about it." Margaret gestured for Jane to follow her as she walked back towards the house. There was a patio area located there with a table and chairs.

After they were both seated, Jane studied the cotton gardening gloves she was wearing. "Sometimes I feel so angry and frustrated at myself."

Margaret sighed. "Oh, my sweet girl, if only I could give you all the answers. But the ways of our minds and most especially our hearts, are mysterious."

"What do you mean?"

"Sometimes all that we can see is what's on the outside of ourselves. We don't see the inner workings, how life is always trying to heal itself if we give it a chance. Like those little tomato plants. On the outside, it looks like they're too weak and small to ever produce big, juicy tomatoes."

Jane lifted her eyes and smiled briefly. "They do look tiny."

"Yes, but on the inside, something amazing is taking place. It's a process that's sure and unerring about what a tomato is all about. Come the middle of July, you won't recognize those plants. They'll all be five feet tall and two feet wide with dozens of fruit ready for the harvest."

"But I'm not a tomato. I might stay an empty bag of bones forever."

"Maybe, or maybe it isn't your season to know who you are. Did you know that a seed can remain dormant for years? But given the right circumstances, the life force wakes up. The seed shows everyone what it is. That seed might be a watermelon or a radish." Margaret leaned over and patted Jane's arm. "Or maybe a lovely carnation, which is, by the way, my favorite flower."

Jane let out a huff of doubt. "It sounds too good to be true."

"Let's just wait and see. In the meantime, do you think you could try putting in a couple of plants?"

"I guess I could try."

Margaret nodded. A few minutes later, she was able to encourage Jane to go back to the garden. But when Jane knelt down in the soil, she panicked and let out a cry of distress.

"What is it?" Margaret asked with concern.

When Jane stood up, she was trembling. "My jeans are getting muddy!"

Margaret hurried over and put her arm around Jane's shoulders. "It's okay. We'll take it slow."

Jane tried to pull away. "Touching the dirt makes me feel like something terrible might happen."

Margaret hugged her closer. "Maybe that's why we're together. I know things about the dirt."

"What do you mean? What things?"

"Dirt is Mother Nature's gift to us, did you know that? It grows food and beautiful flowers and trees. There's nothing more giving than dirt. It's something you can count on, no matter what else is going on in your life. See there, it even gathers up your tears."

Jane looked down as tiny droplets fell from her cheeks and disappeared into the soil.

Margaret bent down and gathered up the dirt where the tears had fallen. She held it tight in her hand. "Nothing is wasted here, not even our sorrow."

"Then I have a lot to give," Jane sniffled.

"Take a deep breath and tell me what you smell."

Jane did as she was asked and took in a ragged breath, then another. "It smells strange."

Margaret laughed. "Maybe you've never spent much time out-of-doors. But to me, newly dug soil has the smell of miracles." She winked at Jane. "And it's easy to be a part of those miracles."

"You make it sound so wonderful."

"It is, but first you have to bond with Mother Earth."

"How?"

"Since all this is new, we'll have a get acquainted party. So take off your gloves, stoop down and put your hand on this patch of dirt where I put in the beans."

Jane made a face, but she finally crouched down. "Okay, I'll do it, but it's only because I trust you." Timidly, she let one finger graze the surface of the dark soil. "It feels funny. It's cool and damp."

"As you get to know the earth better, you'll feel other things about it, beautiful things. When Eric, Sr. died, I was lost too. I often felt chilled just like you. I thought it was the hand of death reaching out to me that made me feel so cold."

Jane stood up. "I'm sorry. That had to be a terrible time for you."

Margaret raised her eyes and stared at the puffy white clouds above them. "So many times when I was alone, I'd just start crying. But they were angry tears. My husband left me so suddenly. Not knowing what else to do, I took long walks in the woods. I'd sit for hours by the lake, throwing rocks in the water. Sometimes, I fell asleep on the old quilt I brought along. I didn't want to go home to an empty house."

"What happened?"

"It took some time, but I felt a change. Neither my friends nor Eric knew how to reach me, but nature has its own way. When I was out in the woods, I began to feel a little better. The ground I slept on, the water, the sun and clouds over my head, all started to reach out to me, to tell me that I wasn't really alone. I guess only the earth could heal the emptiness that was eating away at me."

Jane stared at Margaret and smiled. "I want that too," she said as she reached down and carefully gathered up a very small clump of dirt. She held it for a long moment in her palm. Then she squeezed her hand shut. She shut her eyes too. "That's what I want more than anything. I want the emptiness inside of me to go away."

Eight

JANE STOOD BY the sink and stared out the kitchen window. As the summer months had gone by, she'd witnessed a miracle, just like Margaret said. The once barren, garden soil was now lush with healthy, vibrant plants. As she and Margaret weeded, hoed, and watered the garden, they were rewarded with the wonders the older woman had promised. Tiny seeds became giant bean stalks seven foot tall, and huge tomato plants grew heavy with fruit.

For Jane, the whole affair was a personal journey. Once she had the courage to "get her hands dirty" as Margaret said, she wanted to do what the older woman had done. Margaret had allowed Mother Nature to help her get past her grief. Jane hoped for another kind of healing. She wanted her memories restored. But she wasn't like the plants in the garden. While they grew and flourished, she remained in the dark about who she was.

With Eric and Margaret's encouragement, she tried to accept her plight. Still, it was hard. So was working in the kitchen. Even though tending the garden had become Jane's favorite chore, certain parts of kitchen duty were the exact opposite. With reluctance, she turned her attention to the potato peeler she was holding. She had it poised over a potato, determined to show the russet who was boss.

Margaret stepped behind her and peeked over Jane's shoulder. "Jane, dear, I told you that I'd peel those."

Jane turned around and tipped up her chin. "Absolutely not. I've got to learn. I can cook and bake with a fair amount of skill. Surely I can master the art of peeling a potato."

Margaret nodded. "Of course you can."

Jane hated when she raised her voice at Margaret. "Mom, I'm sorry."

Margaret went to the stove and turned down the burner under one of the pans. "Sorry? About what?"

"I don't know why I act like I do sometimes, but—"

"What is it?"

"It doesn't matter. Anyway, while I'm potato wrangling, let's talk about something else. Tell me how these Sunday dinners got started. They seem very important to you and Eric."

Margaret began to stir the gravy. "I suppose you're right. It's been that way for a long time. With Eric's father always on call, he missed a lot of dinners. He tried to make the one on Sunday an exception. No house calls were allowed unless it was an absolute emergency."

"Eric seems to have a similar rule," Jane said as she eyed her potato.

"Yes, he does if he knows what's good for him."

Jane held the potato firmly as she tried to guide the blade of the peeler along the skin of the potato. It was uneven, and the blade often slipped off before she did much damage. She wasn't deterred from her duty. In fact, she became more diligent and used quicker, more forceful strokes.

Margaret walked over to where Jane was working. "Are you sure you don't want to set the table instead? I know you're having a little trouble getting used to the peeler."

Jane's brows narrowed as she continued to nick and scrape her way around one of the spuds. "How hard can it be to master a potato peeler?" she mumbled aloud.

Margaret patted her arm. "I don't mean to upset you."

Jane paused and bit her lip. "It's not you. I think I'm just venting. You know I've been visiting Doctor Kasner these past months, but we aren't getting anywhere. I think I should stop going. It's a waste of Eric's hard-earned money."

"But you are happy with us, aren't you?"

Jane turned and smiled. "Of course I am. You and Eric are wonderful people."

"I wish you'd think of us as more than that. We both want you to think of us as family."

"That's very sweet, but let's face it, the truth is that I'm just some stranger off the street."

"Not to me, Jane," Margaret said in a stern voice. "And I'd love it if you could consider me as more than just some wonderful person."

Jane looked down at the potato in her hand. She held up the brown and white spud for Margaret's discerning eye. "What do you think?"

Margaret chuckled good-naturedly. "It has a case of freckles."

Jane turned back to the sink. "I'll get this right," she insisted.

"Honey, it's fine. I was making a joke."

Jane didn't reply. Instead, she brandished the peeler like a weapon, using it on the brown, spotted potatoes in her charge. For a long time she said nothing as she persistently went about her task. Finally, she looked up. "Okay, they're mostly white."

Margaret took the chicken out of the oven and set it on the counter. "That's good."

"Thanks, I'm ready to dice them. Are you finished with the cutting board?"

"I'll be happy to do that. Why don't you go upstairs and freshen up?"

Jane shook her head. "Not a chance! You always do everything for me because I'm a klutz. But if I'm going to stay here like you and Eric insist I should, I refuse to be catered to."

"Of course, but when you're cutting up the potatoes—"

"Please, Mom, you don't have to keep telling me to be careful."

Margaret clasped her hands. "Am I being too over-protective? If I am—"

"Yes, I think you are, but you also tell me how capable I am. So let me finish what I've started."

Margaret's brow was knitted when she handed Jane the cutting board. "I'll set the table."

Jane grabbed one of the larger knives out of its knife caddy. Cutting up a potato was no big deal. She'd watched Margaret perform the task on many occasions. The steps were simple. Put the knife over the potato and press down. She hadn't thought about the potato rolling when pressure was applied. It was a mistake. On her first try, the knife sliced her finger instead of the spud. "Ouch!"

Margaret came running back from the dining room. "Let me see," she said as she tried to examine Jane's finger.

Jane pulled it back. "It's just a scratch," she cried as she saw droplets of blood fall from her finger. "Oh no, now I've got blood on my new slacks."

"Jane, give me your finger," Margaret demanded.

Jane ignored her concern and grabbed a dish towel for her offended digit. "I can't do anything right!" she announced. A stream of tears was already wetting her cheeks as she ran from the room. She passed Eric on the stairs, giving him a hateful look. "This is all a mistake! I'm hopeless!"

* * *

When Eric asked his mother about Jane's unhappy state, Margaret suggested that Eric speak to the young woman. His mother explained that Jane had once again put too much pressure on herself. As a result, she'd ended up cutting her finger.

As Eric climbed the stairs to the upper bedrooms, he wanted to help Jane, but he wasn't sure his assistance would be welcome. The young woman was often sweet and anxious to please, but she could be easily upset over her lack of progress. He knocked softly on her bedroom door, trying to think about what he could tell her. He often felt lost himself when it came to advice.

When Jane didn't answer, he knocked harder. Finally, he let himself in. The bedroom was empty, but it was so neat that it reminded Eric of a hotel room. Not a slipper or bobby pin was out of place. He called out, "Jane, can I talk to you? Mom tells me that you cut your finger. Maybe I can help."

A shouted reply came from the bathroom. "Go away. I'll take care of this myself."

"Jane, please."

A moment later, Jane walked briskly into the bedroom, a dish towel wrapped around her hand. Her eyes were teary, but they were also bright with anger. "I don't feel like being sociable, Eric. So it's best that you leave before I start yelling at you."

"Go ahead, yell if you feel like it."

"Why are you always so nice? It's tiresome. It makes me feel like I'm always the problem." She fumbled with the double handled, dresser drawer. She tried to open it with one hand. "That's why I've got to get out of this place. I don't want to feel this way anymore."

She pulled on the handle but the drawer wouldn't budge. Finally, she threw the bloody cloth aside and grabbed for the dresser knob. Red droplets of blood fell from her exposed finger, spoiling the white carpet.

Jane looked up and grimaced. "I hate this! And I hate myself!" she exploded as she ran back into the bathroom.

Eric followed her, but he knew enough to be cautious. Wounded animals and wounded people had to be soothed before a person took action. He slowly reached out for Jane's hand and let their eyes meet. "Let me just put some pressure on it."

Jane shook with pain and a fury that seemed to need expression. "I'm trying everything to help myself, but nothing works. It's like there's a battle raging inside of me. Sometimes, I just want to end it all. It would be so much easier than living and not knowing who I am."

Eric held her finger and sighed. "I can understand the battle part, but you don't seem like the kind of person who'd give up."

Jane stared down and fingered her blood-stained slacks with her good hand. "I can't even peel a potato."

Eric smiled. "Neither can I. Mom thinks I'm too slow and ends up grabbing the peeler out of my hand."

Jane laughed and then frowned again. "It's not just my memory that frustrates me." She stared at the mirror. "It's the whole package. I'm so skinny. I look like a boy."

"I disagree, but what I think doesn't count."

"But it does!"

"What do you mean?"

"Your mom wants us all to be family, and I do sometimes think of you as a brother, but you're also a man. So tell me what you think. Do you think a man would ever want me?"

Eric tilted his head and studied her. "Do you have a man in mind?"

Jane blushed. "I had this dream. And yes, there was a man in it. And I think we loved each other, but as time goes by, the dream is fading like everything else."

"Did you tell Doctor Kasner about all this?"

"She wasn't able to help."

55

"I'm sorry."

Jane straightened and gave him her full attention. "Have you ever been in love, Eric?'

Eric didn't want to answer the question. Just thinking about it made him tired. But Jane's eyes were so imploring that he had to say something. "No, not really."

"Are you sure?"

A long-forgotten memory stirred, making him avoid Jane's eyes.

"Won't you tell me?"

"It's ancient history. She was an older woman. I was only a boy. One of those one sided affairs. I don't think it counts."

Jane's face softened. "I think that all love counts. When I lay in bed at night, I sometimes remember that feeling I had in the dream. Being with him was—"

"Was what?"

"It's like the world feels sweet and safe. For a few moments, nothing else matters but knowing that I'm wanted by someone whom I love."

Eric let out the breath he was holding. "Yes, you're right. Love does strange things to us. It can make the darkest night feel somehow full of promise. But that promise can turn empty with the light of day. In the end, we're forced to face facts."

Jane put her hand over his, the one holding her finger, but she remained quiet. Finally she spoke. "I'm sorry."

Eric swallowed back his feelings. It had been a long time since he'd thought about the terrible crush he'd once had. He'd thought he'd put it behind him. So why did it feel painful to think about it again. "Jane, you just told me you were sorry. Why would you say that?"

"Because I realize that I'm not the only one who feels the way I do."

Eric shrugged. "Whether we like it or not, life goes on."

Jane scowled and tried to pull away. "That's depressing."

Eric held on to her. He knew he was failing her. "Promise me something."

"What?"

"That you'll give life . . . that you'll give love a chance. Because you're right, it is important."

"And what about you? Can you promise the same thing?"

56

Eric tried to smile away her question. "I don't have time." He looked at her hand. "Anyway, I think your finger is better. The bleeding's stopped. Let's put a bandage on it."

Jane stiffened. "Eric, don't do this, please."

"Do what?"

"Shut out what's important and get all busy. It makes me feel so alone again."

Eric hesitated. He wished he could give her more, but sometimes he felt like his own life was almost as empty as Jane's. Or maybe it was his heart that felt empty. Still, he did have one pledge he could offer the woman in front of him. "Don't worry. You're not alone, I promise. No matter what you need, you can always count on me and Mom."

Jane didn't comment. After she went downstairs, Eric wandered back to his own room. There was a picture of his mother and father on his dresser. Everyone always thought they were the perfect couple. He wanted to believe it too, just like he wanted to believe his life was perfect. Then he ran a woman over with his car. The event didn't just impact Jane's life. When he hit her, he suffered a blow too. Now, he couldn't come to terms with what was stirring inside of him any more than Jane could get her memories back.

Nine

JANE SAT AT the Lloyd's backyard patio table. It was a warm day, but fall was fast approaching. She studied the freshly picked bouquet that lay on the table and ran her finger over the petals of a rose. A hint of sadness crept in, but she dismissed it. She picked up the rose and placed it into a milk-glass vase. She was becoming very adept at arranging flowers. When Margaret came out of the house, Jane gave her an expectant smile.

Margaret set two glasses of iced tea on the table and pulled out a chair across from Jane. "I know that look," she teased. "What would you like to know today?"

Jane didn't hesitate. It was a perfect time to learn more about the Lloyd family history. "Tell me about Eric's father. How did you meet him?"

"Oh my, that seems like such a long time ago. Give me a moment." Margaret picked up a carnation, inhaled its fragrance wistfully and finally continued. "We met in Baltimore. Eric, Sr. was an intern at Johns Hopkins Hospital, and I was an art student. We both lived in the same apartment building."

Jane continued arranging the flowers, adding red roses to the carnations and daisies. "I bet he was handsome."

"Yes, and he was also brilliant, serious and oh so shy. In fact, my first thought was that he was a snob. Later, I found out that he'd had a crush on me all along."

"Of course, you were gorgeous," Jane exclaimed. "Eric showed me the family album. You could have been a movie star with your natural, white hair and your willowy figure. Poor Doctor Lloyd didn't have a prayer when he saw you."

"Jane, please, you're embarrassing me. I didn't think I was pretty. I was too tall. I towered over some of the men at the art institute. And I felt very plain."

"You're kidding."

"Besides, I didn't think in terms of a relationship. All I dreamed about in those days was my art. I even had visions of going to Paris and setting up my easel on the left bank." Margaret took a sip of her iced tea. "Strange, I haven't thought about all that in so many years. Just talking about those days seems foolish now."

"It sounds exciting to me. Did you ever exhibit your work?"

"Only at the institute." Margaret giggled to herself. "I took first place in a school contest. I painted an abstract that was quite bold."

"What happened to it?"

"I sold it. I needed money for the rent. I was thrilled that someone wanted to buy it. A business man liked it."

Jane watched Margaret wipe the condensation from her glass and the table. "What made you stop painting?"

Margaret returned a polite smile, but her eyes were distant. "Once I got to know Ricky—"

"Ricky?" Jane asked.

"My husband's full name was Eric Richard Lloyd, but he liked when I called him Ricky. Anyway, he was strong and handsome. Everything a girl could want in a man. When he asked me to marry him, I was shocked. Of course, I said yes. After we were married and moved to Elkville, I didn't have the time or money to indulge in such a frivolous pursuit as painting anymore."

"But it's what you loved to do."

"I guess I agreed with Eric's father. He always said that there were more important things in life. He was a very determined person. He'd grown up in poor circumstances, but he put himself through medical school by working at all kinds of odd jobs. When we moved to Elkville, he said that we could raise a family in a place where there were no row houses or hoodlums."

"Did you feel the same way?"

Margaret shrugged. "I looked up to Ricky and admired what he wanted. And he didn't just think about himself or his family, he wanted to help others. And the people of Elkville certainly needed help. Many of them didn't even have indoor plumbing."

Jane put the last rose in the arrangement. "Do you have any regrets?"

Margaret sucked in a hasty breath. "Of course not. It could be a hard life, but Ricky pressed on no matter what. I was very proud of him and what he did."

* * *

Eric rolled up his sleeves, grabbed a pan off the stove, and took it to the sink. "Gosh almighty, Jane, I do believe that you and Mom must have preserved, canned, and frozen enough vegetables these past couple of months to feed the whole block."

Jane smiled happily. "It took all summer, but I have finally mastered my way around the kitchen."

Eric began to scrub the pan. "And the hospital too. How is your volunteer work going? You're not over doing it, are you?"

"I feel good when I help others. Your Mom told me about your dad, how he single-handedly took care of an area that went for many miles in any direction. You must have been so proud of him."

Eric paused and thought about the last conversation he'd had with his father. It hadn't gone well. But his father was dead. It made no sense to think about their argument now. "My father was an amazing man," he said quietly.

Jane took a dish out of the drainer and started to dry it. "I think you must be a lot like your dad."

"No, not really."

"But you became a doctor, too," Jane protested as she put the dish in a cupboard. "I know you really care about people."

"Maybe, but it's different. I wouldn't measure up in the conditions he was working under."

"Medicine has come a long way, I'm sure."

Eric rinsed the pan he'd washed and handed it to Jane. "I'm not just talking about medicine. I'm talking about the mountains, the people."

"Living in the country must have been wonderful."

Eric jerked around and stared at her. "The country? Appalachia isn't like the farmlands in Iowa. It's wild and harsh, even primitive in some places."

Jane gave him a curious look. "What do you mean by primitive?"

Eric stiffened. He didn't want to think about what the word meant. But he couldn't stop the memory that defined his version of its meaning. He was only eight when he saw and heard things no eight-year-old should experience. There was a boy, all bloodied and stone-cold, who was lying in the dirt. Words blistered the air. Eric's father was cussing out some farmer who lived high up in the hills. His words could still make Eric's breath catch. "What in the hell is wrong with you, John? You beat your own flesh and blood to death! You killed your son!"

Eric shuddered when he thought about the violent episode again. A tug on his arm made him come back to himself. He looked up. Jane was staring at him.

"Eric, are you okay? You look pale."

Eric turned back to the sink, thrusting his hands into the soapy dishwater. "I spaced out for a moment, but you were asking me about—"

"We were talking about Elkville. Did you like growing up there?"

Eric fished some canning tongs out of the soapy water and rinsed them. "It's a tough place, not a place for the faint at heart."

"Your mother lived there, and she did okay. When she talks about her friends, they sound nice."

Eric continued washing more utensils, forcing his unwanted memories back into the past where they belonged. "Yes, her friends are very nice."

Jane leaned against the counter. "Your mom must have had a lot of adventures living in a place like that. It must have been so different than living in the city."

Eric scowled. The concept of adventures didn't have anything to do with his mother's life. "My mother is a very strong woman."

"You're right there. I can barely keep up with her."

Eric needed to steer the conversation towards a more neutral topic. "How are things working out with you and Jerry? He asks about you whenever I see him."

61

"He's a great guy. We have fun when we go to dinner or the movies."

"Do you think you might like him?"

Jane blushed. "Eric Lloyd, that's none of your business. But if you must know, Jerry's a friend, that's all."

Eric gave her a teasing smile. "I'll be sure and tell him that."

"Don't you dare tell him anything," Jane protested. She folded her dish towel and draped it over the stove handle. "Do you mind finishing up? Your mom promised to show me how to knit a scarf."

"Good idea. When winter arrives, you'll be ready."

After Jane left the kitchen, Eric quickly drained the dishwater and tidied up a few more things on the counter. He was about to turn out the light when another flash from childhood came out of nowhere. He saw his father's face glaring back at him. Eric had disobeyed his father's instructions.

"Didn't I tell you to stay in the truck? Didn't you hear me, Eric? I told you to stay in the god-damn truck!"

The words were burned into Eric's memory. And no matter how old he was, when he thought about the day his father had yelled out those words, he regretted his disobedience. If only he'd stayed put like his father told him, he wouldn't have seen a boy who'd been horse-whipped to death. He wouldn't have seen how his father reacted to the man responsible for the boy's death.

Eric's fists closed on themselves as he tried to come back to the here and now. "Jane has the wrong idea about my family and the place where I grew up. It was such a relief to leave it all behind."

* * *

Margaret woke up with a start. Her jaw was so tight she could barely move it. She told herself that she'd simply had a nightmare, nothing more. But the terrible feelings and ghostly apparitions from the dream seemed to follow her back into her waking world. That fact was confirmed when a terrible chill took hold and wouldn't let go.

She quickly reached over and turned on the bedside lamp. Could her Ricky be back from the grave? She pulled up the cover, trying to get warm, trying not to think about the past. "Ricky, please, if you are here, let go of the misery. You always did your best," she pleaded.

She glanced around the room. It was bathed in soft shadows, but there was no sign of her dead husband. As she let out a sigh of relief, she felt another chill. Ricky's voice was close. He was whispering to her, sharing his secret again.

Margaret put her hands over her ears. "Ricky, don't! Stop torturing yourself!"

His response was immediate. "How can I forget what I did? How can I ever forgive myself? Help me, Margaret! You're the only one I could ever confide in."

"So long ago, it was so long ago."

"Help me, Margaret!"

Margaret wanted to reach out to him like she had on so many nights when he was alive and needed her. But the room suddenly felt empty. Ricky was gone.

She got up and grabbed her robe. Walking over to the window, she hoped to see some glimmer of light, but it was still dark outside. "Oh Ricky, I thought your pain died with you. Why am I remembering these things now?"

The answer came quickly. She saw Jane's bright inquiring face. Almost daily, the young woman asked about Margaret's life, pulling out the details, one by one. Margaret ended up sharing things that she had never spoken about with anyone else. Now, Margaret's secret thoughts and those of her dead husband were coming back to haunt her.

Ten

MATTHEW PUT A hand to his head and groaned. He definitely had a fever. And why wouldn't he be sick after all the stress he'd been under? "Dammit, Thanksgiving is supposed to be about gratitude. But how can I be grateful after what I've experienced these past months?"

He'd declined an invitation to spend the holiday with the Fergusons. It seemed that every year, Rita insisted on hosting a lavish dinner for friends. In spite of the fact that her daughter was missing, Rita carried on as usual.

On the other hand, Matthew's life had gone totally off course. His Thanksgiving meal was a frozen dinner. It was a poor substitute for a proper meal, but it didn't matter. He was ill, and his appetite was gone. His partner, Ralph, expressed concern. He reminded Matthew that he needed to take care of himself. His patients depended on him.

At one time, that would have been enough of a reason for Matthew to rally. He liked what he did, and he liked that people were eager for his services. It was a win-win proposition.

But circumstances had changed. The only person who truly mattered to Matthew was gone. Lea, the woman he was engaged to marry hadn't warmed his bed in months. People said that time healed everything, but he knew it wasn't true. As time went by, his anxiety was growing. He was certain that Lea was out in the world somewhere. Ever since his dream, he hoped desperately that she was safe. But at times, he'd almost given up on ever seeing her again. Raymond Ferguson was still searching out every lead, but he hadn't been able to trace his daughter's whereabouts.

Matthew shuddered and grabbed a fleece throw to wrap around himself. He held it close, hoping the medication he'd taken would help him feel a little better. But what about Lea's welfare? What if someone was using or even abusing her, taking advantage of some misfortune she'd had?

The horrible visions were becoming more frequent. Then there was the guilt. He should have done more than insist that Lea take a vacation. She was so frail, so fragile. It was easy to see that she wasn't well. He should have found out what was going on with her emotions. Why did she sometimes shake at night, even when he held her close? Why did she wake up crying?

If Raymond didn't find her, Matthew would never get any answers. Then his life would become a permanent hell. Not only would he have to live without the woman he loved, he'd have to live with the fact that he'd failed her completely.

As the thoughts ravaged his mind, his teeth chattered and his body ached. His throat was so sore he'd barely been able to swallow his food. He probably had the flu. Ralph would have to find someone to take over his duties for the next few days.

* * *

Eric watched Jane as she wiped her mouth and put her napkin back on the table. "You look very satisfied," he said with a smile. "Did you enjoy your meal?"

Jane patted her tummy. "That was the best dinner ever." She looked at Jerry Norton who sat next to her. "Don't you agree, Jerry?"

Jerry smiled. With a clean-shaven, boyish face, and happy, light brown eyes, he surveyed his plate. It was empty except for a stripped-to-the-bone turkey drumstick. "I love Thanksgiving. It's my favorite holiday, especially when I spend it here. It's almost as good as being at home with my folks and siblings in Illinois."

Jane pushed back her seat and stood up. "I feel like I'm about to explode." She looked at her fingers and began to count them off. "I had mashed potatoes, stuffing, candied yams, cranberries, peas, gravy, and turkey."

"No room for dessert, Jane?" Margaret asked as she came in from the kitchen. She had a pie in each hand. "Remember, we baked both pumpkin and mince."

Eric jumped up and helped her put the pies on the table. "You don't have to ask me twice. I still have room."

Margaret looked at Jerry. "Can I take your plate now, Jerry?"

Jerry gathered up his dishes. "I didn't want to hold things up, but I couldn't help myself. I had to have a third helping."

Eric stared back. "How can you eat more than anyone I know and stay so thin and fit?"

Margaret patted Eric's arm. "Jane and I are flattered. Jerry does justice to our cooking."

Eric frowned back. "Jerry's not the only one. If you noticed, I did my part, too."

"Don't show off in front of our guest, dear," Margaret replied in a motherly tone. "And please go get the whipped cream in the refrigerator."

Jerry stood up. "I'll be happy to help."

"Let me," Jane said. "I was going to the kitchen anyway. I wanted to help put things away."

"No, stay put both of you," Eric said. "I've got this."

"Come along then, Eric," Margaret said as she headed to the kitchen.

Once Eric and Margaret were alone, Eric pulled her over to a corner. "What do you think? Is Jane starting to warm up to Jerry?"

"Oh please, Eric, it's none of our business."

"But I was hoping they might—"

"Dearest, are you trying to play matchmaker?"

"I know Jerry. He's easy-going, steadfast and responsible. He'd make the perfect husband."

"Why are you worried about all that?"

"It's just that some months ago, we talked. And Jane said she wanted someone in her life."

Margaret put her hands on her hips. "I wonder why she never said anything to me."

"It was one of her low moments, and she was upset about cutting her finger."

"Oh yes, I remember. She was having a hard time in the kitchen. Thank goodness she's finally sure of herself." Margaret paused and glanced up at Eric. "But still, we have to let her find her own way."

Eric crossed his arms. "I guess."

"Do you want to know what I think? I think you're starting to act like her big brother."

"I wouldn't know. I was an only child."

"Do you wish you had brothers and sisters like Jerry? I gather he came from a large family. I hope you didn't get too lonely with just your dad and me."

"It doesn't matter now. What's done is done."

Margaret pursed her lips and frowned. "Do you believe that? Can we forget the past and simply move on?"

"Jane has."

Margaret's frown deepened. "I never thought of it that way."

Eric walked over to the refrigerator. After searching the shelves, he found the whipped cream. "I wonder about it all sometimes. Maybe Jane's condition is a blessing, not the curse she thinks it is."

Eleven

JANE SAT ON the living room floor. She was surrounded by boxes, Christmas paper, and colorful ribbon. She looked over at Margaret. The older woman was wrapping a present, making sure the paper was folded straight and at just the right angle. "I think you're crazy about Christmas, Mom."

Margaret smiled back. "I love every part of this time of year. I've always looked forward to it."

Jane grabbed a pen to address a name tag. "Christmas in Elkville must have been different. There were no malls to shop in."

"Heavens no, most people had to mail order everything or make it themselves. But presents were only a small part of the holidays back then. I remember how special it felt after we put up the decorations. And if it snowed, oh my, it changed the look of everything." She paused as she tried to put a bulky, man's sweater in a box that was too small. "Jane, pass me that large box please."

Jane did as she was told, but her face was bright and expectant. "Go on, you were saying—"

"Oh yes, when it snowed, there weren't many cars, so the road stayed white longer than around here. Indoors, the smell of pine boughs would mix with the aroma of clove-studded oranges drying by the fire."

"It sounds like a wonderful dream."

"When I think back, I remember sitting in the living room with Ricky and Eric. We'd drink homemade cider and string popcorn garlands for the tree."

Jane cut a big piece of green ribbon for a box wrapped in Santa Claus paper. "We could string popcorn again. What do you think?"

Margaret laughed. "Yes, I suppose we could. But I doubt if Eric will have time. He's been so busy lately."

Jane sniffed the air and got up to check the turkey breast roasting in the oven. "Maybe, but he's had time to keep an eye on what I'm doing."

Margaret called after her. "What is he up to now?"

"He's being a real bug about Jerry and me. I got in late from our date last night, and Eric was sitting up in the living room reading. As soon as I came through the door, he started asking me questions. I told him I didn't feel like talking right then, but he was a total pest."

"Really, he wouldn't leave you alone?"

Jane smirked. "He was nice."

"But he got his way?"

"Yes, I had to tell him where we went and what we did."

"Oh lord, I'm going to talk to him."

"No, that's okay. I guess it's natural for him to be curious. After all, I am dating his best and just about only, close friend."

Margaret stood up and walked Jane into the kitchen. "I wonder when Eric will start dating. I think it's time."

Jane opened the oven door and began basting the turkey breast. "I'm sure lots of women would love to go out with him. He's a real catch. He's handsome and as sweet as can be."

"Yes, but I better stay out of it. Eric is a grown man."

"You must be so proud of him."

"Of course I am, but enough about Eric. How is it going with Jerry?"

Jane closed the oven door and frowned. "I hoped we might, you know, feel more about each other as time went by."

Margaret sighed. "And?"

"He's still just a friend."

* * *

Margaret sat in her bed with a tissue in her hand. When she looked up at Eric, she couldn't hold back her disappointment. "I can't believe I'm sick. Christmas is only two days away."

Eric closed his medical bag and shrugged. "Sorry, but you have a fever and your throat is inflamed. I think you have the current virus that's been going around. You'll have to take it easy for a few days."

"But what about the Christmas Eve dinner? And on Christmas day—" Margaret's protest was interrupted by a fit of sneezing.

"We'll just have to cancel."

Margaret looked at him with woeful eyes. "What? I haven't missed a Christmas celebration since I can remember."

Eric sat down on the bed next to her. "I know, but you've been looking worn lately. You must be over doing it."

"Nonsense." Margaret barely got the word out before she sneezed again. With impatience, she grabbed another tissue. "Jane is really looking forward to the holidays. I wanted to make them special for her, and of course for you, Eric."

Eric smiled. "All my Christmases have been special, and this one will be too. Even if we have to open the gifts right here in your bedroom, we'll celebrate, I promise." He leaned over and kissed her cheek. "In the meantime, I want you to take care of yourself."

Margaret bit her lip and sniffled.

Eric gave her an anxious look and reached out for her hand. "What is it? What's the matter?"

She shook her head and sucked in her breath. "I don't know what's going on with me. I've been so emotional lately. I want to cry at the drop of a hat."

"Are you homesick for Elkville and your friends?"

She covered her face with her hand as her tears started in earnest.

Eric moved closer and put his arm around her. "I'm sorry if I took you away from everything you love. I guess I didn't know how much you'd miss it."

"It's not that. I keep thinking about your dad. I haven't been able to sleep very well lately. He's been on my mind."

Eric frowned. "You were so close."

"It was such a shock when he died. I guess I always thought he was so strong. Afterwards, I thought I'd worked through things." She sniffled and blew her nose. "I thought I was reconciled to his death. I was even starting to feel like I could take care of myself, but—"

Eric held her closer. "What is it? Tell me."

"Living here, I don't feel very independent anymore." Her announcement was accompanied by another crying spell. It was followed by more coughing. When she recovered her voice, she sighed. "I didn't realize it until your dad died, but I guess I needed him more than I thought. Now, I seem to need you and Jane like I needed your father. Instead of having my own life, my mind is always busy with what you two are doing. But some day, both of you will leave."

"I just wanted to take care of you."

"I know that, Eric," she sobbed. "But why do I feel like I'm becoming an old woman who can't take care of herself?"

Jane walked into the room carrying a tray with tea and toast. She quickly put it on a side table and went to Margaret's bedside. She sat down opposite Eric. "What's the matter, Mom?"

Margaret pulled herself out of Eric's embrace and sat up straighter in the bed. She blew her nose in an effort to quell her feelings. "I'm all right, Jane. I must be venting some unfinished business. That's all."

Jane looked at Margaret and Eric, then stood up quickly and backed away. "I interrupted. You and Eric were talking. I'm sorry. I'll go back downstairs."

Margaret reached out for her hand. "No, don't leave. You're part of the family. I was blessed with a wonderful son. Now I feel like I have the daughter I always wanted too. I may be confused about a lot of things right now, but I'm sure of one thing. I think of you as my own child." She stopped and stared at Jane through her tears. "If that's all right with you, Jane."

Jane's expression wavered between a look of surprise and joy. Within moments, her dark eyes became bright with her own tears. "That's the most precious gift anyone could give me."

Margaret felt her mood lift. Jane had changed drastically since that fateful, rainy night on a Baltimore street. It was a comfort to observe the young woman's beaming smile and the confident, poised way she held herself.

Eric seemed to be thinking the same thing. He stood up and smiled. "I think you're wonderful too, Jane. You're exactly the type of person I would want for a sister."

"Really?" Jane wavered for only a moment before she leaped forward and onto the bed. She grabbed Margaret and pulled her close. She looked at Eric with a happy grin on her face. "What a wonderful Christmas this is! It's like I've been given the best present of all, my own family!"

* * *

"Can you believe that it's New Year's Eve?" Jane's hair was pulled back into a short pony tail, but a delinquent curl dangled on her forehead as she finished the last of her chores. She tried to blow it out of her eyes as she climbed a stepladder in the family room. "I've had so much fun cooking and baking and decorating for the party we're having tonight."

"Well, I wish you had let me help you," Margaret replied as she handed Jane a streamer. "You've worked all day."

Jane stretched on tip toe to attach the decoration. "I'm happy that you listened to me and Eric and rested. You don't want a relapse."

"And now you need to be careful. That ladder looks a bit unsteady."

Jane laughed. "Listen to the two of us giving each other orders all the time. I'm telling you to take it easy, and you're making sure I'm careful. Soon you won't be able to tell us apart."

"I think Jerry will be able to tell us apart," Margaret laughed. "When he sees you in that new, green dress, he won't be able to take his eyes off of you. That color suits you perfectly."

Jane blushed. "Thank you, but Jerry probably won't notice. He doesn't say very much to me about how I look."

"Typical man, but I know he's taken with you. He's always telling Eric about how pretty you are. He's just too bashful to tell you directly."

"Speaking of Eric, has he seemed a little busier than usual to you? I've hardly seen him the past two weeks."

"I suppose there are a lot of sick people at this time of year. But you're right. He does seem preoccupied, even when he's home."

Jane got down off the ladder. Her brows were knit with a tinge of dismay. Sometimes when she talked about the cardiologist, she felt a little distracted, even wistful. But she ignored her feelings and surveyed her handiwork. There were balloons and streamers strung everywhere, and a Happy New Year sign brightened the fireplace wall. "It looks okay, doesn't it?"

Margaret glanced around the room and smiled. "It looks very nice."

"Good, then we're all set for our guests and some fun."

As Jane dressed for the party, she felt like the moment of truth about Jerry's feelings was at hand. She'd spent an extra hour making sure that her makeup, hair, and Kelly green, satin dress looked perfect. If Jerry saw her and still didn't care to comment on how she looked, then maybe Margaret was wrong. Perhaps she was just a plain Jane. It wasn't a comforting thought.

She didn't have time to indulge in self-pity. The doorbell rang as she took a last look in the mirror. "That's the best I can do, Jerry."

When she walked out into the hall, she saw Margaret coming out of her bedroom. The older woman was decked out in a champagne-colored, lace and chiffon dress. It emphasized her height and trim figure. Jane sighed with approval. "Oh Mom, you look gorgeous."

Margaret paused. "Are you sure I look alright? Eric insisted on taking me shopping and buying me this new dress."

"You should be ashamed of yourself for thinking you're getting old. You're beautiful."

"And you look like a fairy princess," Margaret said as she reached out for Jane's hand.

As they started down the stairs, the doorbell rang again. Jane laughed. "Probably Jerry. He's always the first to arrive when there's food around."

By the time they got to the foyer, the doorbell rang a third time. Margaret gave Jane a teasing glance. "Jerry must be anxious about more than the food the way he's ringing that bell."

Margaret hurried to the door and opened it. As soon as she identified her guest, her voice took on a scolding tone. "Eric Lloyd, why did you keep ringing the bell? Why didn't you let yourself in?"

Jane stared at Eric too, but her thoughts were anything but scolding. She was totally taken by the man who stood in front of her. She'd been living in the same house with him for the better part of a year, but she'd never allowed herself to acknowledge how handsome he was. And on this occasion, he was even more striking to behold. Dressed in a black tux, white shirt, and a Christmas plaid cummerbund, Eric made Jane's breath catch. And when she caught a glimpse of his bright, topaz-blue eyes, her heart fluttered like that of a bird gazing at the morning sun.

"You look incredible, Eric," Jane managed when she finally found her tongue.

Eric stood in the middle of the doorway and seemed oblivious to her comment. Instead, he gestured excitedly to her and his mother. "Mom, Jane, I want you to meet someone," he said as he stepped aside to reveal a woman who stood behind him. Putting his arm around her shoulder, he brought her forward into the light.

"Teresa, this is my mother, Margaret Lloyd, and this is our sweet Jane." He turned to his date. "Ladies, this is Teresa Willis, Doctor Teresa Willis, a fellow cardiologist."

Teresa put her hand out to Margaret and then to Jane. "I'm so happy to meet you. Eric has told me so much about you both."

Jane stood frozen in place as she blinked back at the tall, slender woman by Eric's side. Teresa had long, fiery, red hair and translucent, white skin. Her eyes were a beautiful, sparkling emerald green. But more than anything, Jane was transfixed by Teresa's radiant face. Teresa looked like a painting of a Madonna, a Madonna who had a gorgeous smile.

When Jane's mind began to function properly, her first thoughts were devastating. *Eric's found someone else! But how can that be? He belongs to me!*

Somehow she'd hidden her love for Eric from herself until that moment. While she tried to digest that revelation, Eric spoke and acted as if he'd struck gold.

"Mom, Jane, you both told me that I would feel different about a relationship if I met the right person. And you were right. Teresa and I have worked together off and on for quite a while, and I never suspected. Then one night a couple of weeks ago, we talked, and well, I think she's everything I could ever hope for, don't you?"

Jane could only stare back at the couple. As Eric hugged Teresa and glowed with the joy of new love, she could hear what he was saying. She could understand his every word because each one was so devastating. Each one hit her chest like an arrow. The pain that followed was summed up in a phrase. It repeated in her mind. *I've lost the man I love!*

Twelve

MATTHEW DIDN'T KNOW how he got through the Christmas holidays. The flu he'd had at Thanksgiving left him feeling constantly exhausted in spite of the medications he took and the healthy food that he forced himself to eat. He knew his emotional woes were probably a major cause of his lingering ills. He'd always been very healthy until he'd become obsessed with finding Lea.

His partner, Ralph, helped as much as he could. The older man tried to shoulder more of the patient load himself. But it began to take a toll on Ralph. He couldn't handle the long hours. That's when Matthew made a decision. He had to change his attitude. Or more precisely, he had to go back to his old one. He couldn't keep caring about Lea. He had to shut her out of his mind once and for all. He had obligations, patients to care for.

As he distanced himself from the idea of a relationship, he began to feel better. After Ralph's efforts on his behalf, Matthew also felt like he had a friend. It was something new for him. He'd always been a loner.

Still, there were days that were almost overwhelming. He'd start thinking about Lea again, and the pain would resurrect itself. On one of those days, a nurse named Nicky invited Matthew to coffee in the hospital cafeteria. Matthew had interacted with her on a number of occasions, but he'd never dealt with her personally. She wasn't young or even pretty, but she had a reputation for being kind and generous. Those were not traits that Matthew valued when he was at the top of his game, but after the emotional blows he'd had, he was more open. He cautiously accepted her invitation.

Nicky sat in the hospital cafeteria, sipping tea and glancing at Matthew Howell. He sat across from her, hunkered down over his coffee. His expression was sullen, almost hostile when his brows narrowed. But Nicky wasn't fooled. After being a nurse for so many years, she recognized pain. "Thanks for meeting me, Doctor Howell."

"What's the deal here, Nicky," the surgeon asked in a brusque tone.

Nicky laughed. "Let's just say that I've been around long enough to know when someone is at the end of their tether. I also know enough about you to keep my distance, but if you ever want to talk or just have a meal here in the cafeteria, I'm your gal."

The doctor sat back and tightened his jaw. "I have two words that sum up my life. It sucks."

Nicky's smile broadened. "Been there. In fact you're preaching to the choir. But unless our hearts stop, we have to go on, don't we?"

He glared back. "Got any more pearls of wisdom?"

Nicky ran a finger over the rim of her cup. "I'm sorry about your fiancé. I met her briefly a couple of times. She was—"

He shoved his chair back. "That's none of your business. Now, if you'll excuse me—"

Nicky held up a hand. "Please stay put for a few moments."

He crossed his arms, clearly suspicious, looking almost panicked by her request. "What now?" he growled.

Nicky stood up and walked around to the surgeon's side of the table. "I know it's asking a lot, but maybe you could relax just a little."

"Why?"

Nicky put her hands on her hips and stood back. After years of interacting with doctors, she'd come to a decision. When it was appropriate, she'd say what she felt needed to be said. "Let's get something straight. This hospital needs men like you, Doctor Howell. The patients need you. You're the best we have. So please, sit still for two minutes and let me work on those tight shoulders of yours."

He calmed down enough to start rubbing his temples. "My head's about ready to explode."

"I might be able to help. So while I massage your shoulders, breathe."

His eyes flared in her direction. "Fine, but don't apply too much pressure."

Nicky didn't respond, but she understood what he was telling her. Matthew Howell was probably one of those people who had a very tough exterior, but they could also be very sensitive in their own way. She knew to be careful when she put her hands on his broad shoulders. As soon as she began to knead them, she could feel his knotted muscles. Neither of them spoke as she worked on the knots. After a couple of minutes she paused and backed up. "I hope that helped a little."

He looked at her guardedly and finally nodded. "Thanks."

Nicky gathered up her things. "We work with people's bodies all day long, but we forget to take care of our own. You need to go home and take a long, hot shower."

He scowled again, but his eyes looked a little brighter. "Yes, ma'am."

As she started to walk away, he called out to her. "Take care of yourself too, Nicky."

She didn't look back at him. She didn't want him to see her face. She was sure she looked upset and even saddened by the man's situation. With her job, she tried to maintain a healthy emotional distance with her sick patients. However, when she interacted with Matthew Howell, she was surprised at how easily she slipped into a more personal mode.

As she reflected on what his body was telling her, a deep need to nurture was activated. Something was tearing Matthew Howell up inside, and he was clearly floundering. She wished she could do more to help. She'd told him that he was an excellent surgeon, but she sensed that he was also a good man at heart. She hated to think that he wouldn't find a way to get back his sense of self.

Thirteen

THE BALTIMORE SKY was a consistent gray throughout most of January. Dense clouds hung over the suburbs. It was too warm for snow, but the damp cold could be dismal and numbing. Jane's clothing never seemed to keep her warm enough.

When she and Jerry double-dated with Eric and Teresa, Jane was the only one who was always shivering. When they sat in a coffee shop, she seemed to bring the cold in with her. She needed to keep her coat on, or Jerry had to put his arm around her if she wanted to stay warm. Even the Lloyd's home felt perpetually chilly.

Margaret seemed determined to correct the situation, to keep Lea's chattering teeth and goose-bumps at bay. "Have some tea," she suggested as she brought over a cup and handed it to Jane. "A hot drink in front of the fire will make you feel better."

Jane pulled a colorful, peach and green afghan around her and reached out for the steamy mug. "Thank you. I'm sure it'll help." It was a polite lie. She knew the cold she harbored was too deep to be affected by a hot beverage.

What did affect her on all levels was Eric. Every time she heard his voice or he glanced at her across the dinner table, the chill got worse. She often chastised herself when that happened. Eric had the role of a brother in her life. He'd never acted in any way to encourage any other kind of relationship. Why had she let herself think of him as something more?

After Margaret sat down on the sofa, she eyed Jane with a motherly stare. "I think I know how you feel. Sometimes a body gets a chill that won't go away. My last winter in Elkville was the worst. I didn't dare stick my nose out the door without putting on my coat. I never fared well with the cold, but this was different. Just going to the mailbox by the road was a chore that year."

"What do you think made you feel that way?"

Margaret took up her yarn and needles and began knitting. "I don't know for sure. My friend, Florence Bowan, says that a widow is always cold. She told me that a man takes his wife's warmth with him when he dies. He uses it like a shield for his spirit when his body is lying cold in the ground."

"That doesn't make sense. A spirit has no need of another person's warmth."

"Tell that to Florence. She has a reason for everything that happens, whether it makes sense or not. I think she just likes to hear herself ramble on about things." Margaret paused and unrolled the soft, fuzzy ball of yarn that sat next to her. "But maybe there's a grain of truth in what she told me. When Ricky was alive, we liked to sit in the parlor every evening. He'd smoke his pipe and read while I knitted. Sometimes we'd talk. He'd remember the patients he saw that day and bring me up to date on things like how Mrs. Farley's baby was beginning to talk. Or I'd tell him how the plans for Jessie Novak's wedding were progressing, how she'd lost twenty pounds so she could fit into her mother's bridal gown. I know it sounds silly, but we enjoyed those times."

Jane watched Margaret's hands. They moved quickly and precisely as she worked on her newest project, a winter hat. "What you two had was beautiful."

Margaret looked up and stared straight ahead. "Yes, I suppose so. When Ricky was gone, the evenings seemed empty, like he took what made life special with him."

Jane held on to the afghan like a life jacket despite the fact that her body refused its warmth. "You loved him so much."

"I saw a lot through my husband's eyes. He never stopped appreciating the beauty of his rural paradise." She laughed. "That's what he called Elkville. We never went for a ride without him pointing something out. He always saw the prettiest wildflowers blooming by the side of the road or a chipmunk sitting on a fence post. To him, it was all so splendid, and he made me feel the same way when he shared his world with me. Maybe that's why I was cold all the time when he died. He gave me his passion, his fire. And when he was gone—"

Jane bit her lip. She appreciated Margaret's plight, but her own difficulty seemed just as painful. Why did she keep having flashes of Eric and Teresa in each other's arms? Why did she torture herself with the thought that she might always be alone? She looked down and sighed. "It's scary."

Margaret kept knitting. "What's scary?"

"Loving someone so much. In the end, all that's left is pain."

Margaret put her knitting aside. "Oh my dear, what have I done? Telling you all my troubles. I'm sorry."

Jane stared back. "I don't understand something. You were an artist before you met Doctor Lloyd. You had your own fire. Why did you let him take that from you?"

"Is that what you think?"

"But it's true. You relinquished everything when you married him. When he died, he even took your warmth."

"If that's what happened, I don't blame Ricky. You might think he took my painting from me, but it wasn't that way. I wanted to marry him more than anything."

Jane shrugged. "Then something must be wrong with love."

Margaret frowned and picked up her knitting again. "I can't believe that, but perhaps people don't know how to be in love. Nowadays, women and men are more independent. But in my generation, it wasn't that way. If I lost part of myself along the way, I blame myself. I must have been too needy."

Jane saw the anxious look in Margaret's eyes. "I'm sorry if I've made you feel bad. I'm sure you've always been a perfect example of what a loving person is all about. That's why I'm grateful when you tell me I'm part of the family."

Margaret hesitated. "Tell me about you and Jerry. I've been hoping that you two might—"

"I hate to say this," Jane interrupted, "but there's not even a little flicker between us. I guess not all of us can have fairy tale endings like Eric and Teresa."

Margaret smiled. "Give it time."

Jane tried to smile back. She was tired of thinking about love or suffering over the lack of it. She needed something to take her mind off her unhappiness. "Maybe I should put my focus on other things. I'm thinking of going back to school or at least taking some courses at the community college."

Margaret's eyes brightened. "I think that's wonderful."

"We could take some courses together. You could take some art classes."

Margaret shook her head. "No, I don't think so. I'm too stuck in my ways."

"Are you sure?"

"Yes, maybe at some later date, but I have enough to keep me busy for the time being."

Fourteen

MATTHEW STOOD AT Nicky's apartment door and gave it a number of hard raps. He'd had coffee with the older woman a number of times in the past couple of weeks. They were slowly getting to know each other. He found Nicky's no-nonsense manner and frank attitude refreshing. She was also very understanding when it came to his moods. She didn't let them affect her. Matthew had come to the conclusion that he now had two friends in his life, Ralph and Nicky.

When Nicky didn't show up for her shift, Matthew was concerned. He'd queried the nurse in charge and was told that Nicky went home sick. From what he knew, Nicky had no family or close friends. She was a people-person at her job, but a loner otherwise. He knocked on her door again. "Nicky, it's Matthew," he called out.

After his announcement, he heard the locks being turned back. The door slowly opened, and Nicky peeked out.

"Doctor Howell, what are you doing here?"

Matthew had instructed Nicky to call him by his first name, but she insisted on a level of formality when they talked. "Can I come in?"

Nicky clung to the door. "You better not. I think I have the flu."

Matthew had always thought of Nicky as a certain type of woman, the strong, durable type. She was the perfect nurse, someone who could lift patients and do all the tough jobs required around sick people. Now her face was flushed and drawn. Her eyes were barely open. "The flu? We can commiserate. Mine still comes and goes."

"Just don't get too close," Nicky said as she opened the door.

Matthew stepped inside and quickly noted the tidiness of the space. The living area was the exception. There was a pillow and blanket on the couch. Bottled water and a couple of over-the-counter medicine bottles littered the end table. He smiled as he followed Nicky into the living room. "Reminds me of my place."

Nicky sat down on the couch, clutching at her sweater. "Damn bug is a real pain. I feel like I fell off a building."

Matthew came over and felt her forehead. "You're burning up. What meds have you been taking?"

"Some crap from the drugstore, but it's not doing the job."

Matthew noticed a thermometer on the side table. "When did you take your temperature last?"

"I checked a few minutes ago, it was 103."

Matthew frowned. "That's getting up there."

Nicky fell back on the pillow. "Yeah, tell me something I don't know. But I'll be okay. I always am. This body just won't give up." She glanced at Matthew. "You look worn out. It must have been a long day for you. Go home, Doctor Howell."

"Don't worry about me."

She sighed as she closed her eyes. "But I do worry. You're my son's age. Call it motherly concern."

Matthew smiled. "You're not old enough to be my mother."

Nicky peeked up at him. "I had my baby when I was thirteen. I'm old enough. I had to give him up, but sometimes when I think about him, I picture you. It makes me feel better. I'd like to think my son turned out to be a good man too."

"Is that how you think of me?"

"Of course, under all your bark and bluster that is. Now go away so I can rest."

Matthew sighed. "You know, Nicky, if I was your son, I'd consider myself lucky."

Nicky's eyes welled up with tears. "That's the nicest thing anyone's ever told me. But don't say anything more, or I'll be bawlin' my eyes out. Then I'll be even more miserable."

* * *

Matthew stayed the night in Nicky's apartment. After he did what he could to get her fever down and make her more comfortable, he sat

83

in a chair and listened to her breathing. As he noted each rise and fall, he realized that he'd started to worry about her. The woman was becoming a friend he could talk to when life got too hard. To think that anything would happen to her was unacceptable.

He finally fell asleep in his chair around midnight. When he woke up, the first light of day was seeping into the apartment. He looked at the sofa and noticed that it was empty. He also noticed the smell of coffee. He sat up and rubbed the sleep from his eyes. "Nicky? Nicky, are you okay?"

The tall woman was smiling as she came out of the kitchen carrying two cups of coffee. She paused half way to the living room and took a deep breath. "I'm better, but I'm still not one hundred percent."

Matthew stood up and took the cups out of her hands. He gave her a stern look as she sat down on the sofa. "You should be resting, not traipsing around this place making coffee."

Nicky laughed and then started coughing so hard she couldn't catch her breath. When she could finally breathe again, she shook her head at Matthew. "What's wrong with you? You have surgery later this morning, right? You need to stop fussing."

Matthew stared back and knew he wasn't the only one who'd known very little kindness. The harsh realities of life were etched in Nicky's face. "How do you do it?" he asked as he handed her a cup.

Nicky took a sip of coffee and frowned. "Do what?"

"You're one of those nurses who guard the flock. You work long hours, yet you're always compassionate. From the little I know about you, your life has been very hard. A baby at thirteen? I can't imagine. What kept you from being bitter about it all?"

Nicky took another sip of coffee and paused. "I just never saw a reason to be as ignorant as the people who raised me, or the uncle who raped me. I wanted something better for myself. I can't say I've always been happy. I just try to hold on each day. I do what I can to help others hold on, too. There're a lot of people out there who are worse off than me."

Before Matthew had a chance to think about Nicky's thoughts about life, his phone sounded. It was Raymond Ferguson's ringtone. He excused himself and answered it. Raymond's voice was even louder than usual as the man blurted out some news.

Matthew mumbled back words he'd never dared hope to express. "You found Lea!" He began to smile. Unfortunately, his surprise and relief were quickly swept away. As Raymond continued to relate more of what he'd found out, Matthew's mouth went dry. His joy quickly turned to shock. After only a few more disclosures, his heart was pounding with fresh panic. He couldn't believe that his horrible visions concerning Lea seemed to have come true.

Fifteen

ERIC SAT IN his office chair, staring at his phone. After the conversation he'd just had, he knew he needed to take the rest of the day off. He told his receptionist to cancel his afternoon appointments. He was going home.

By the time he pulled into his driveway, his emotions were even more volatile. He paused for several minutes before he got out of the car. He had to put a lid on all of his feelings before he talked to his mother. He couldn't pass his burden on to her. Or at the very least, he had to be very careful about what he told her.

He walked into the kitchen and hesitated. Margaret stood at the counter. As usual, she was busy, cutting up apples for a pie. Her constant devotion to her family made his heart sink even further. After all that she'd done, after all her sacrifices for others, she didn't deserve the blow that was coming. And Eric had to deliver that blow. It couldn't be avoided. "Mom?"

Margaret glanced up and smiled. "Eric, I didn't expect you home so soon."

Eric tried to steady his voice. "Mom, you'll never guess what happened."

Margaret blinked back with a frown. "Eric Steven, are you alright? You don't look yourself."

He forced himself to say what had to be said. "After all this time, I got a call from Jane's family. They traced her here."

"Jane's family?"

"Yes, her real name is Lea Ferguson."

Margaret stepped back as if she needed a moment to understand what he was saying. After a long pause, she moved to the window. "Oh my! After all this time, I hoped, but I never thought this day would come."

Eric could hear both the wonder and the disbelief in Margaret's voice. She'd totally given in to the idea that she had a daughter. Now that daughter was being snatched away. "Yes, from what I can tell, they never stopped searching for her since she disappeared."

Margaret turned and stared back at him. "Of course they never stopped. Our precious Jane must mean everything to them."

Eric avoided her eyes and sat down at the kitchen table. "There's more. I spoke to Jane's fiancé, Doctor Matthew Howell."

Margaret walked over and sat down too. "Our Jane is engaged? Did he sound nice? Oh heavens, this is all so amazing." She looked around. "Let's get Jane! She's upstairs! She needs to be told about all this."

"I know, but I want to talk to you first." Eric reached out for his mother's hand. She'd suffered so much grief after losing his father. Was she going to lose Jane too?

When he hesitated, Margaret spoke up. "I know you're fond of Jane. She's like your sister. Are you afraid that will change?" She pulled her hand away and put it in her lap. "We both forgot that she's not really ours."

Eric shook his head. "That's not it. Of course, I'm surprised too, but I'd be happy for her, knowing that she was going to be reunited with her real folks again. But it's this guy, Matthew Howell. He was so incredibly rude when I spoke with him."

"Rude? How?"

Eric's feelings were still very raw. He had to be careful with what he divulged. "I just didn't get the best feeling about him. But maybe I read too much into the conversation."

"I don't understand. Wasn't he happy to find Jane after all of this time?"

Eric evaded looking at her. "He probably thought the worst after a while and is still feeling the aftereffects."

Margaret wasn't satisfied with his answer. "Don't fib to me, Eric. If there's something I should know, please, tell me."

Eric thought about some accusations that Howell had made. "He sounds like the angry type, that's all."

Margaret covered her mouth. "Oh Eric, I just had a thought. What if our Jane was running away from a bad situation? What if she was trying to get away from him. Do you think he—" Margaret's face crumpled in dismay. "Eric, what if he hurt her?"

Eric knew he needed to comfort his mother, but he didn't know what to tell her. He hated conflict, and after a short conversation with Howell, he felt like the man was definitely hostile. "Let's not jump to conclusions. I might be totally overreacting. But I swear, if he tries anything, I won't let any harm come to Jane or you."

"Is this Matthew Howell person coming here?"

"Yes, and Jane's parents are coming too."

Margaret's eyes brightened. "Her parents? Well, that's good. They wouldn't let anything happen to their daughter, would they?"

Eric sat up a little straighter and pulled his shoulders back. "No, I'm sure you're right. Anyway, the three of them are flying out of Chicago early tomorrow morning. They'll be here around noon."

"Tomorrow?" Margaret's voice dropped to a whisper. "Are they planning on giving our Jane some time to adjust? In her condition, they'll be strangers. Will they want to take her back to Chicago right away?"

"I don't have any answers. I wish I did, but there's nothing we can do about the situation. It's her family. If she chooses to go with them, we have to let her."

"Even if this Doctor Howell is abusive?"

Eric stood up. "Maybe we should stop talking about all that. We have to think of Jane. She's very sensitive. If we act worried around her, it's not going to help. We'll tell her the good parts, and we'll reassure her that she can stay with us no matter what."

Margaret stood up. "This whole thing scares me."

"That's my fault. I shouldn't have burdened you with—"

"Stop it, Eric. You've always tried to spare me and everyone else." She paused and wrapped her arms around herself. "But you can't bottle everything up in yourself. You'll have a heart attack like your father!" As soon as she made the statement, Margaret slumped back down in her chair. Tears flooded her cheeks. "I'm losing Jane. I don't want to lose you too. I couldn't bear it."

"It's okay, Mom, please—" Eric pulled her up and hugged her. "You're not going to lose anybody. I promise."

"Your father promised things too, but he couldn't keep those promises!"

Eric knew she was right. He'd been as devastated as she was when his father died. But he had to keep his deeper feelings hidden. He had to forget about everything but his mother's welfare. He would also do everything in his power to protect Jane.

* * *

Jane lay in her bed smiling. Margaret had put a thick featherbed over her mattress. And she was snuggled under layers of soft, fluffy covers. All in all, she felt like she was in a delightful nest of sorts. It was the one place where her chilliness was banished, and she felt totally warm.

"Lea Ferguson," she repeated to herself. "My name is Lea Ferguson." When she'd first heard Eric say her name, she waited and wondered. Maybe the name would spark something inside. Maybe she'd remember something of her previous life. She was disappointed when nothing happened, but she soon recovered. She told herself to be patient. Once she actually met her parents, her memories might come back.

She smiled as she thought about another facet of her life. She was a doctor, a pediatrician. If she could recall that part of herself, she wouldn't have to go back to school. She could help kids like the ones she'd met when she volunteered at the hospital.

She stared out at the barren branches of the tree that grew outside her window. Soon spring would arrive and the branches would be decked out in beautiful green leaves. "And I'll be warm again, knowing who my parents are and knowing someone loves me."

She paused and savored the idea that she was engaged to Doctor Matthew Howell. She was reminded of the dream she'd had when she'd first come to stay with the Lloyds. She was certain that the man in the dream was Matthew. Unfortunately, she couldn't remember his face anymore. With time, it had grown fuzzy like some of the other details. Only one fact remained as sure and true. "We were crazy about each other."

The thought helped her to push back her feelings for Eric. She couldn't just forget about how much she wanted him, but she told herself to appreciate what she did have, a man who loved her so much that he'd asked her to be his wife.

She sighed wistfully. She'd been wrong about how unfair life could be. Eric and Teresa weren't the only ones who could have a fairy tale ending. She could have one too. When the doorbell rang the next day, and she went to meet her family, everything would change. She'd be reunited with those she'd lost. She'd begin a new, amazing life.

Sixteen

MATTHEW STARED OUT the window of the Ferguson's private jet. He was clutching the report that Raymond had given him earlier. He'd read it over several times. He didn't want to miss any important facts.

Raymond approached Matthew's seat. "Mind if I sit down and talk for a few minutes?"

Matthew nodded. "I wanted to ask you some questions about this report."

Raymond settled back in his seat. "I thought you would."

"How accurate do you think it is?"

"My man in the field is excellent. I have no reason to doubt what he gave me."

Matthew handed Raymond the report with a scowl. "What the hell has Lea gotten herself into?"

"I don't know. I'm trying not to worry too much, but—"

Matthew stared out at the heavy layer of clouds. "This hillbilly doctor who took her home, you don't think he tried anything with her. Because if he took advantage—"

"No, let's not go there. You read what it says, he's dating someone else."

"Maybe he got tired of Lea, and—"

"Let's try not to think the worst. Lloyd might be from West Virginia, but he's well-educated."

"That doesn't mean a damn thing, Raymond. Education doesn't change a man. Eric Lloyd grew up in some godforsaken place that you can't even find on most maps. A town in the Appalachian Mountains. I don't know about you, but when I think about the locals in a place like that, I think about 'Deliverance,' that movie with Ned Beatty."

Raymond pulled a handkerchief out of his pocket and patted down his brow. "Let's keep our voices down. Rita is asleep. She doesn't know what's in the report. I didn't think she'd handle it well."

Matthew clenched his jaw and slammed the seat in front of him, cursing quietly. After venting a sudden burst of anger, he looked at Raymond. "I'm sorry, but I keep thinking about Lea living with some weirdo. How was she supposed to help herself with her memory wiped clean?"

Raymond patted Matthew's shoulder. "We can't go there. We have to think clearly. That's one thing I've learned in business."

"Think clearly about what?"

"Since Lea has amnesia, she won't recognize us. On the other hand, she's been living with Lloyd and his mother. She might think of them as her saviors."

Matthew glared back. "Saviors? The neighbor told your guy all about the Lloyds. The mother had the nerve to brag about how she taught Lea to take care of the house and grounds. The neighbor says Lea worked in the garden for hours on end. And here's the kicker. My fiancé, who refused to turn a hand in the kitchen, who never made me a single meal, spent hours on end canning a crap load of tomatoes! And you're sitting here, telling me not to worry. What kind of person in this day and age makes someone can tomatoes?"

Raymond shrugged. "My mother canned tomatoes."

"Yes, Raymond, because your mother was coming out of the depression. But that's not the point. The Lloyds obviously saw a good thing. They took a woman who Lloyd ran down with his car, and they brought her home. Once they isolated her, they turned her into a domestic."

Raymond shuttered and loosened his tie. After a few minutes, he nudged Matthew. "There is something else that's not in the report I showed you."

Matthew had his head against the window, nursing another headache. He'd taken something for it, but nothing could touch the pain slicing through his brow. Now his stomach was off too. He forced himself to sit up anyway. The tone in Raymond's voice had an ugly edge to it. "What now? Spit it out."

"Well, like I said, my man is very thorough. He's used to digging deep. So he looked into Eric Lloyd's background. The man's father was a doctor too, but he almost went to jail."

"What? Why?"

"Lloyd Sr. must have been a violent person. He almost killed a man in a fight."

It was the final straw for Matthew. Putting his hand over his mouth, he edged past Raymond and ran for the bathroom. All his fears about Lea's safety were correct. He'd let her go off by herself when she was in terrible shape, and now she was suffering because of his carelessness.

When he got to the toilet and started throwing up, his hands were shaking, and he'd never felt so weak. He'd always been strong and sure of himself, but after all that he'd been through, including the latest news, he wondered if he'd ever feel better.

When his stomach settled, he flushed the toilet. He told himself to hold it together for a little while longer. When he looked in the mirror, he issued orders to himself. "No matter what it takes, you are going to get Lea back. After that, you'll deal with the scum who took advantage of her. He'll pay for every minute he abused her."

* * *

With the mid-morning, winter light streaming in, Margaret sat in the living room recliner with her knitting draped across her lap. Positioned next to the large picture window, she was able to watch the street as she worked on a white, basket weave sweater.

She had promised Jane, who was now Lea, that she would announce the Fergusons' and Matthew Howell's arrival as soon as she saw them pull up. In the meantime, Lea had gone upstairs to change her clothes for the third time that morning.

Margaret glanced at Eric. He was sitting on the sofa reading. It was obvious that he was trying to keep his mind occupied. Yet, every couple of minutes he'd check the time.

Margaret decided some small talk might help them both. She smiled at Eric. "First, Lea put on a dress. Then she decided it was too formal, and she changed to slacks. Now she's gone back to her first choice. She thinks the dress would be more appropriate."

93

Eric didn't look up. "What difference does it make? They just want to see her. Forget what she's wearing."

"Changing clothes gives her something to do. She's nervous."

"Aren't we all?"

Margaret sighed. "Yes, I feel like I can barely sit still. I lost count with my knitting so many times that I think I'll call it quits. But at least I'm over my crying spell. That was so embarrassing last night. I went in to see Lea to make sure she was alright, and I got upset."

Eric put his book aside. "What did you get upset about?"

"I guess I was being selfish. I'm having a hard time thinking she'll be leaving, and I might not see her again."

"I'm sure Jane, I mean Lea, will make sure that won't happen."

"She told me the same thing," Margaret said with a smile. When she glanced at the window, a movement caught her eye. She stood up immediately, dropping her knitting and the white ball of yarn. "Oh, Eric, they're here."

Eric hurriedly picked up her sewing. "Please, come away from the window. They'll see you."

"But Eric, that man who's getting out must be that awful Doctor Howell you told me about. He looks like he's about your age, but my goodness, he's a big man. He must be at least six three or four. He's dressed nice, in a suit and tie, but you're right. He doesn't look friendly at all. Oh, that must be Lea's mother and father getting out."

Eric came over and stood behind her. "The mother looks fairly young, but severe. All that makeup and her hair pulled back so tight. And if that's her husband, he must be twenty years older than her."

Margaret stepped back and bumped into Eric. "Quick, they're coming up the walk. Go get Lea."

"No, you get her. I'll show them in."

Margaret stared down at herself. "Do I look alright?"

"You look great. Now stop fussing and get Jane."

Margaret held her chest and took another breath. "Her name is Lea, remember?" As soon as she corrected Eric, her tears started in again.

"What is it?"

"What if they're all terrible people?"

Eric took her hands in his. "We'll take it one step at a time. But for now, go upstairs, wash your face and announce our company."

Raymond helped his wife out of the car, straightened his suit and tried to adopt an optimistic attitude. He didn't get very far. There was too much family history involved. It was history that was filled with turmoil. And something told him that his reunion with his daughter was going to add another unhappy chapter to that history.

As they drove from the airport to the Lloyd residence, he'd felt a familiar anxiety in his chest. Besides Rita, Lea was everything to him. All he ever wanted was to make her happy. He'd succeeded when she was very young, but that changed. He never knew why it changed, only that their relationship had been an extremely rocky one for years.

Now, looking up at the Lloyd residence, he had to mop the sweat off his brow. The temperature was cold enough to freeze his breath, but his body was overheating. He took it as a sign. His physical vessel was letting him know that finding his daughter after her disappearance might not be all sweetness and light.

Then there was Matthew. He was another concern. When Raymond had first been introduced to the surgeon, he was impressed. Matthew had no time for chit-chat or getting chummy, but he did seem to have integrity. And he did love Raymond's only child. He'd even wanted to marry her.

Matthew was also a man who had an excellent reputation. It was backed up by his powerful presence. He exuded an energy that Raymond looked for when he dealt with others in the world of business. That presence told him a lot. People who had it could be depended on when times got rough.

However, when Raymond met Matthew at the airport that morning, he was deeply disheartened. The road Matthew had traveled since Raymond saw him last had been more than rough. The doctor's eyes had lost their clear focus, and he seemed to be physically ailing. Raymond could only assume that Lea's disappearance had affected him deeply.

Raymond could relate to Matthew's situation. Trying to find his daughter had put him through almost a year of frustration and heartache. As he watched Matthew walk to the porch and reach for the doorbell to the Lloyd house, Raymond sighed to himself.

You poor soul. I think my daughter has just about done you in too.

He turned to Rita, hoping his wife was doing alright. "You've been very quiet."

Rita's delicate features paled. "I'm preparing myself, Ray. But I don't know how much more I can take."

* * *

When Lea heard the door bell, she paused by her bedroom door. The first thing she did was remind herself that she wasn't Jane. From now on, she had to think of herself as Lea. The name felt foreign and added to her shakiness. What would her parents be like? Would they be anything like Margaret and Eric? Would she be what they expected? Of course her questions were useless. She'd never regained any of her memories, so what good did it do to probe for answers.

There was a knock on her door, and Margaret peeked in.

"Dearest, are you ready?"

"What shall I say to them, Mom? I want to make a good first impression."

"You're going to be reunited with your family. I'm sure they're just happy they've found you."

"I hope so."

Margaret took her hand. "Let's go downstairs."

She nodded and followed Margaret. When she reached the foyer and checked out the living room, she saw a gray-haired man getting up from the sofa. She assumed it was her father. "Dad?"

The moment she said his name, the man came forward. "Lea! My little girl!"

Lea expected him to hug her. Eric and Margaret had shown her that a hug was the proper greeting for a family member. But her father just stood in front of her and looked at her instead. She decided to be bold and hug him anyway. When she did, he gasped.

"I never thought I'd feel your arms around me again," he whispered.

A dark-haired, pretty woman came over to join them. "Baby?"

Lea let go of her father and turned to the woman. "Rita? Mother?"

The woman nodded as she nervously reached out a hand. Instead of taking it, Lea embraced her mother too. She was surprised by Rita's reaction. Her mother felt tense and stiff as if she was almost panicked by Lea's touch. When Lea let her go, her mother's face was filled with surprise and maybe even panic.

Lea's father put his arm around Rita and tried to soothe away the awkward moment. "You look very well, Lea."

"Thank you," Lea said as she stepped back. Even though she was confused by the way her parents were behaving, she hadn't forgotten that someone was missing. Where was the man who was supposed to be her fiancé?

Lea's father seemed to understand her questioning gaze. "Matthew will be right back. He forgot something in the car."

A moment later, the front door opened. Lea jerked around and saw a tall, sandy-haired man letting himself into the house. He wasn't as amazing as Eric, but he was handsome enough. He was carrying a bouquet of roses. "Matthew?"

Hearing his name, the man stopped in his tracks. When he stared back at her, he didn't appear happy. In fact, his eyes were filled with worry and concern. For a long moment he seemed incapable of moving or uttering a sound. When he finally regained his composure, he dropped the flowers and rushed over to her. Without further hesitation, he scooped her up in his arms. He pressed her tight against his body. "Finally, I've found you," he whispered.

Lea trembled with excitement. In the dream she'd had, her lover had said something very similar. Now, she was back in his arms. Everything was wonderful as he embraced her with strength and conviction. The reunion was everything Lea had imagined until Matthew put her down. As soon as he did, her feeling of euphoria vanished completely. When she glanced up, she was staring at a stranger.

The stranger's brows were narrowed when he questioned her. "Are you alright?"

His demanding tone made Lea a little uneasy. "Yes, I'm fine."

He held on to her hands and stepped back. After he scanned her over from head to toe, he let out his breath. "Look at you! You're beautiful!"

She blushed. Whether she remembered the man who loved her or not, it was nice to know that he found her pretty. She smiled. "Am I?"

Lea's parents had retreated to the sofa, but Lea's mother, Rita, let out a little sniffle. She tugged on her husband's arm as she dabbed the tears from her cheeks. "Raymond, it's so strange," she cried out. "I've never seen Lea smile like that before."

Her teary statement seemed to affect Matthew. He pulled back, and took a deep breath. "Rita's right. What's with the big smile? And you never wear dresses. What's going on with you?"

Lea shrugged and peeked at Margaret for support. "I like to smile, don't I? And I like dresses."

Margaret was sitting quietly nearby, but she immediately straightened her shoulders. "Yes, of course you do!"

Lea gave Matthew a puzzled frown. He was asking her some very strange questions. And why was he waring such a stern expression? It was making her uncomfortable. She carefully pulled her hands out of his. "Shall we sit down and chat?"

Matthew crossed his arms, but he didn't move.

She squinted back. "Is there something wrong?"

Her father quickly answered her question. "Matthew's just surprised, Lea. You're so different than any of us remember."

Her father's statement made Lea clasp her hands anxiously, not knowing how to respond.

After a moment of silence, Eric came to the rescue. He stood up and cleared his voice. "Can I get anyone something to drink or eat?" he asked. "Lea was very busy yesterday. When she heard that her family was coming, she baked a pie and a cake. Or you could try her zucchini bread. It's very good, very moist."

Rita's mother covered her mouth and stifled a gasp. "My baby has never lifted a finger in our house. Why would she do that?"

Lea relaxed a little. She was proud of her newly acquired skills. "I made those desserts because I like baking," she said with another smile. "Mom has been kind enough to teach me all kinds of things."

Rita blinked back. "I have done no such thing. I never asked anything of you."

Raymond pulled her closer. "My darling, I think Lea is referring to Mrs. Lloyd."

Rita looked like she'd been slapped. "What do you mean?" Her lip trembled as she stared at Margaret and then Lea. "Is it true? Do you think of this woman as your mother?"

Lea shrugged. "Well, I suppose I do in a way. She's been like a mother to me. When I didn't know who I was, Margaret and Eric took me in. So I'd think you'd be grateful for their concern. I know I am."

Matthew stumbled over to a recliner and sat down. "This is worse than I thought." He frowned at Raymond. "There's no trace of her left. They have her completely brainwashed."

Raymond swallowed hard. "Take it easy, Matthew. Let's not jump to conclusions."

Matthew rubbed at his forehead. "I'm not jumping to anything. All I know is what I see and hear. The woman I was going to marry is gone."

Lea didn't understand what Matthew and her father were talking about, but she was determined to find out. She approached Matthew and reached out to touch his shoulder. He'd been staring at the floor and startled so badly that he scared her. She jumped back too. "What is wrong with you? Why are you acting like this?"

Matthew's eyes flared in her direction. "Please do not touch my person," he ordered.

Lea bit her lip. "That's a strange thing to say."

Eric came over to where Lea was standing and put his arm around her shoulders. "Lea, don't upset yourself."

"But Eric, what's going on? I don't understand the problem. I'm behaving properly, aren't I?"

Margaret got up and hurried over too. "Of course you're behaving properly. I couldn't be prouder of you."

Margaret's fervent praise seemed to bring Matthew out of his daze. He stood up and shot Rita and Raymond a determined scowl. "I'd had all I can stand of this insanity. Let's go, both of you. If we take Lea out of this little slice of Appalachia immediately, maybe we can get her back to Chicago before nightfall."

Lea stiffened. "I'm not going anywhere with you. Not when you act so rudely around the two people I care about most in the world."

Eric stepped in front of Lea. "Doctor Howell, you're upsetting her. Maybe you should all leave and come back tomorrow. We can resume our talk in the morning."

Matthew glared back. "You'd like that, wouldn't you? And when we came back, she'd be gone. You'd have her canning tomatoes in some isolated shack in the wilderness! We'd never find her again."

Lea pushed Eric aside and stared up at Matthew. "Do you hear yourself? You're ill-mannered and totally insane to make a statement like that."

Matthew didn't answer. Instead he reached out and grabbed her wrist. When she resisted, he started dragging her towards the foyer.

Eric immediately tried to come to her aid. "Take your hands off of her!" he shouted.

His words triggered an instant response from Matthew. He swung around and hit Eric square in the jaw. The blow was enough to send Eric reeling back and crashing into a bookcase.

The violent act set off a chain reaction. Margaret cried out and rushed to Eric. Lea started yelling at Matthew. "How dare you hurt the man I love, you monster!"

Matthew turned and stared back. "The man you love?"

Lea dropped her eyes and sucked in a breath. "I mean the man I love like a brother."

Matthew let go of her wrist. "No, that's not what you mean." He glowered at Eric who was struggling to get to his feet. "You said what you meant. You're crazy about this jerk. I saw it in your eyes."

Raymond and Rita had hurried over to where Matthew was standing. Raymond reached out for Matthew's arm. "I'm so sorry, son. But I warned you about Lea when you asked for her hand. I told you she'd break your heart. I know she's broken her mother's heart and mine."

"Yes, that's what you told me, but I was too stupid to believe you."

Rita reached out too. "You tried, Matthew, just like us, but Lea's always had a mean streak in her. Maybe she can't help herself."

Matthew pulled away from both Rita and Raymond. Giving them a final look of revulsion, he turned and started for the door. "I'll be out in the car when you're ready to go, with or without her. But this is the end for me. I can't care about her anymore."

After he was gone, Raymond turned to Lea. "He was the best thing that ever happened to you, Lea. No other man could put up with your temper and ugly moods. Now, you've driven him away too." He pulled out a card and handed it to her. "If you ever need anything or want to visit, call me. But otherwise, Matthew's right, it's just too hard to keep trying to love you. None of us can do it anymore."

Seventeen

MATTHEW FLEW BACK to Chicago with an ongoing headache and muddled thoughts. Only one thing was clear. The "new" Lea was in love with someone else. At first, it was a blow, a terrible betrayal that made him want to vomit again. Slowly, as he watched the clouds from the plane window, he began to understand what had happened to him. He realized how he'd allowed himself to become Lea's latest victim.

A month before Lea's disappearance, he hadn't heeded Raymond's warning. It was voiced when Matthew paid Raymond Ferguson a visit. He'd wanted to ask for Lea's hand in marriage. Lea wasn't on friendly terms with her father, but Matthew liked the idea of being respectful and following certain protocols when approaching such a big, life-changing event. After all, he didn't operate on people's bodies without an extensive education, why would he rush into marriage without covering all of his bases.

His meeting with Raymond hadn't gone as planned. Matthew expected a quick answer, a yes or a no. Raymond knew him well enough, and Matthew was certain that the straight-forward man would quickly voice his opinion. Instead, Raymond had retreated to his office chair. He sat down very deliberately. He avoided Matthew's eyes and arranged some papers on his desk.

As Matthew waited, he observed Raymond's furrowed brow, the way his hands trembled slightly as he fiddled with his papers. As the moments dragged on, Matthew prepared himself for rejection. Instead, he got a warning. Yes, Raymond would hand over his daughter into Matthew's care, but he wanted Matthew to know what he was taking on. He explained what Matthew already knew about Lea. She was difficult and headstrong, but Raymond also talked about his only child's capacity to wreak havoc in a person's life.

"She could end up breaking your heart, my boy."

Raymond's voice was weary and strained when he said the words. His eyes expressed a deep sadness as if he were looking at a person headed for the gallows instead of marriage.

After the meeting, Matthew was unnerved, but he ignored the advice. He knew that parents often saw the worst in children who were independent and determined. In Matthew's case, his father made it clear that Matthew was a disappointment. When Matthew chose medicine over the law and joining his father's law firm, his father essentially disowned him. They didn't speak or have anything to do with each other since.

Now, coming back from Baltimore, Matthew realized he hadn't understood Raymond's advice. He hadn't understood that Raymond was trying to protect him from Lea's need to punish those who cared for her.

Matthew should have paid more attention to the way Lea treated her father. She often had angry outbursts and temper tantrums. Matthew had suffered from her behavior too, but he thought he was tough enough to withstand what she threw at him. He thought they were a good match, that they understood each other. He believed that there was more to Lea, that she was capable of loving him.

"Maybe she did love me, but Raymond was right. She wouldn't let go of her hateful attitude." It was the only conclusion he could come up with. It would explain why Lea ran away. "Maybe she's afraid of love."

Rubbing his sleep-deprived eyes, Matthew felt like Raymond looked. The man was very capable when it came to business, but affairs of the heart were a different matter. The situation was taking a toll on Raymond. His hair had lost all color. It was a solid gray. His skin was losing color too. And he rubbed at his chest in an uneasy way. Matthew had advised Raymond to see his doctor. He was surprised when Raymond patted his arm and smiled.

"Me? Have you looked in the mirror lately, Matthew?"

Matthew didn't want to look in the mirror. He didn't want to think he could be as bad off as Raymond. That's when he decided to put the "Lea" matter to rest. He had to forget everything they'd had, at least for the time being.

He turned his thoughts to a new and brighter part of his life, Nicky. The woman was totally dependable in spite of the fact that she must have had a terrible childhood. She was little more than a kid when she had a baby of her own.

Matthew tried to imagine what that was like. How did a child of thirteen deal with something like that? How did she deal with the fact that the baby's father was someone who had raped her?

Yet, Nicky didn't reject her baby. She'd been forced to give him up, but Matthew could tell she'd never stopped loving him. Nicky's eyes glowed when she talked about her son. It was as if she'd never let their bond be truly severed.

Then she'd turned those glowing eyes on him and made an announcement. She hoped her son was good and true like Matthew. Her sincerity was so tangible that he almost felt like he was that lost child. For that brief moment, he saw life so differently. If Nicky were his mother, he would have grown up being the object of her love. When pain and hurt came his way, he would have had someone there to comfort him. Nicky wasn't the touchy-feely type, but she'd have made him feel like he was wanted.

But Nicky wasn't his mother. Caroline Howell was his mother. There was no bond to be severed. When Caroline looked at him, he seemed to be simply an inconvenience. She made sure he was fed and clothed and sent to the proper schools, but she didn't make him a part of her life. She was too busy with her career and entertaining her friends on weekends. Even now, his mother simply put him on her Christmas list and sent him a card from wherever she was at in her travels. That was the extent of their mother/son connection.

As an adult, he existed in a world of separation, and he got used to being his own person. He learned not to need anyone else.

No wonder I'm screwed up when it comes to relationships. I've never expected much from my mother or the women I dated.

When he met Lea, he thought he'd found a kindred soul.

Talk about isolated. Lea lived in a far-away universe of her own.

But slowly, they began to matter to each other. After living in his own closed-off world, Matthew was willing to reach out to someone. He'd even let himself dream. He saw himself at the altar, taking Lea's hand in his and never letting that hand go. He'd be there for her. No matter how scared she was, he'd hold on to her. He'd convince her that she wasn't by herself anymore. But the dream became a nightmare. And he was just waking up from that nightmare.

* * *

Raymond's reunion with his daughter had not gone well. By the time he said goodbye to Matthew at the airport, he felt like he needed a long vacation. When he mentioned the idea to Rita, she didn't react like he'd supposed. Instead of being the excited woman who never turned down a chance to have fun, she shrugged. When they got home, she excused herself and said she needed to rest.

Raymond was understanding, but inside, his world was shaking. For all her childish behavior, Rita had always been someone he could depend on to keep things on the lighter side. Her ability to enjoy life was like his safety net. It helped him to get through all the troubles he'd had with Lea.

To see Rita depressed was an unwanted development. It obviously stemmed from Rita's recent interaction with Lea. But it still surprised Raymond. His wife wasn't the kind of person who let life affect her too deeply. Of course, Raymond knew why Rita was what she was. He knew her background, but he never expected her to change the way she dealt with life's blows.

Later, he crept into Rita's bedroom, wanting to check on her. He needed to touch her lovely face again. He smiled when he looked down at his petite wife. She was under the covers, asleep. His smile disappeared when he saw the prescription bottle on the side table. Rita didn't take any medications. She was very careful with her body, always eating properly and exercising. So what was she doing with his sleeping pills?

Grabbing the pills from the side table, he snapped off the cap and felt a wave of relief. The bottle was still full. "Oh, thank goodness," he gasped.

Rita's eyes opened, and she looked up at him. "I only took one. I hope you don't mind."

Her voice sounded too quiet. And her eyes, what happened to them? Why were they dull and vacant instead of sparkling with life?

That's when his world went from shaking to falling apart. Life wasn't getting better. His daughter was far away, living and loving strangers instead of him. Now Rita looked like she might be slipping away too. He scooped her up in his arms and started to weep.

Rita stirred enough to smile at him. "I'm here," she said quietly, as if she knew what he needed.

For the better part of the past year, he'd held his emotions at bay. When he thought about Lea's disappearance, he'd tell himself to stay calm. He thought about Lea's strength, and how she could take care of herself. He'd promised himself that he'd find her.

Behind the promise, he lived in fear and constant dread. Questions were always in the background. What if Lea threw herself in some river or took a plane somewhere only to later crash her car and kill herself?

There was something seriously wrong with his daughter. He'd known the truth for years. He'd tried to help. When she was a teenager, he'd hired the best therapists, but she was so stubborn. She claimed she hated them all, that they were incompetent. In the end, he did what he always did. He let her have her way.

Now, the search was over. Lea hadn't done herself in, quite the contrary. She looked like she was happy. How strange. He and Rita and Matthew couldn't believe it when she smiled at them.

New questions pinged Raymond's gut. Was the Lea they all knew still hidden beneath the smiles? Was she playing some new game with a new identity?

Raymond was too exhausted to search for the answers. He could only hope that his daughter would stay safe in her new home.

* * *

Matthew should have gone straight to his apartment from the airport. His exhaustion was so overwhelming he barely made it to the cab. But in spite of his physical woes, his thoughts kept returning to Nicky. How was she doing? She looked better when he left her apartment, but that fact wouldn't quiet a nagging feeling in his gut. It was the kind of feeling he sometimes had in the operating room. It let him know when all hell was going to break loose.

He tried to call Nicky, but the phone rang repeatedly and went to voice mail. Next, he called the hospital and talked to her supervisor. Nicky was a resilient woman. Maybe she'd recovered and had gone back to work. Wrong. Her supervisor told him that Nicky had called in early that morning and quit her job. No explanation, just a quick statement of fact.

After that, Matthew didn't go home. He gave the cabbie Nicky's address. Once he was at her apartment, he used what energy he had left to pound on her door. He called to her, but there was no answer. When a neighbor came out into the hall and asked who he was, Matthew explained the situation. Once he showed the woman his ID, she retrieved a key that Nicky had left with her.

As soon as Matthew walked into the apartment and saw Nicky, he couldn't breathe. His new friend lay very still on the sofa, looking somehow smaller than before. Obviously, she wasn't as strong as he'd thought.

Turning to the neighbor, he ordered her to call 911. Then he rushed over to Nicky. "Nicky, can you hear me?"

Nicky's pulse was rapid, and her breathing was labored. Finally, she opened her eyes and blinked back with heavy lids. "Oh good, you've come in time," she whispered.

"Hold on, the ambulance will be here soon."

Nicky's eyes turned hard, and she frowned. "No, I'm going home."

"You're going to the hospital. You're going to be alright," Matthew insisted. His resolute tone was as much for him as for Nicky. He had to be sure about something in his life, and keeping people alive was something he was good at.

Nicky's frown deepened. She tried to raise her hand as her finger pointed upwards. "No, I'm going home. This body is finally letting go of me."

Matthew pulled back. He understood what she was trying to tell him. "Absolutely not!"

Nicky lifted her hand again. This time she tried to touch his face. "Don't forget what I said," she mumbled as she tried to get a few snatches of air. "You're a good man. You're needed."

Matthew grabbed her hand, but Nicky didn't squeeze it back. "And you're needed too."

Nicky tried to smile and started coughing. Matthew lifted her up and tried to help, but a moment later her eyes closed and she went limp in his arms. Another unacceptable situation.

"Not again. I refuse to lose another person I care about!"

* * *

Ralph and Matthew had been partners for a number of years, and Ralph considered himself a lucky man. He was headed for retirement, and he needed someone to do more of the heavy lifting. Matthew seemed like the ideal candidate. His bedside manner was totally nonexistent, but he did what was needed and he did it beautifully. Ralph could settle for that.

When he heard that Matthew was in the hospital with a patient, at their bedside, Ralph knew he had to investigate. He walked into the room with a curious frown and stared at the sleeping patient. She seemed familiar. He finally remembered a nurse named Nicky. She'd been around for years. Still, he'd never paid her much attention. She was a plain woman, and she didn't make any attempt to be seen.

Ralph also noticed Matthew. His partner was sitting in a chair by the bed. He was leaned over on the bed with his head resting on his arms. His eyes were closed. He was sleeping too.

Ralph understood the situation. Matthew was running on empty. The man had had a tough year. First, he got engaged to a highly-strung, fellow doctor who ran off and disappeared. Unfortunately, the usually cool-headed Matthew reacted by going into a panic and driving himself crazy. Then he got the flu and never completely recovered.

Ralph walked over and shook Matthew's shoulder. "Time to go home, Matt." When Matthew moved slightly, but didn't wake up, Ralph shook him again. After a pause, he stepped back. "I knew it was more than the flu."

Ralph checked Matthew's pulse and felt his forehead. "It's a good thing I'm so understanding, and that I've got an excellent bedside manner. I'm sure you're going to be a terrible patient during your stay here, Doctor Howell."

Eighteen

"I'M NOT CALLED Jane anymore, Mrs. Miller. My name is Lea, remember?" Lea asked as she backed away from the neighbor's fence. "Anyway, I hope you enjoy the cookies."

In the weeks that followed the visit by her parents, Lea had been busy reminding everyone that they needed to call her by her legal name. Most folks made the adjustment quickly. Others, like absent-minded Mrs. Miller, had a harder time.

As Lea walked back home to the Lloyd residence, she wondered why it was so important for people to get her name right. Maybe she was trying to convince herself that she liked it. When she thought about its meaning, she wasn't sure. It was derived from a word that meant "weary." She hoped her appearance or her personality didn't fit the description.

She took a deep breath of the fresh, crisp air. The weather was still wintry, but the temperature that day was in the fifties. The sky was sunny and pleasant. But the best part was that Lea didn't feel cold all the time.

After her announcement that she loved Eric, there had been conversations. Margaret, Eric and Lea sat around in the family room sipping hot cocoa and talking about Lea's feelings. It helped. She realized that it was natural to be attracted to someone handsome and kind. Once her secret was out in the open, her crush started to fade away on its own.

But her feelings for Matthew Howell were growing. He was in her thoughts throughout her day. Reminiscing on their time together, she felt like she was beginning to understand his behavior a little better.

From the conversation everyone had during Matthew's brief visit, it was apparent that Lea was very different than the person she'd once been. Lea's parents and Matthew were practically in a state of shock when they interacted. Still, Matthew's eyes were filled with passion. Lea was sure he still loved her.

When the situation turned ugly and Matthew hit Eric, there seemed to be more than anger in Matthew's expression. He seemed almost frightened by the Lloyds. He seemed to be further traumatized by Lea's declaration of love for Eric.

All in all, the visit had been a dismal failure. The only moments that stood out as special and happy were those moments when Lea was cradled in Matthew's embrace. When she let herself feel those moments again, her heart sped up with excitement and desire. After a lot of soul searching, she decided that she wanted to see Matthew again. She even called him. But when she tried to reconnect, he'd politely let her know that he'd moved on.

She had to honor his decision, especially after she'd labeled him a monster. With uneasiness and regret, she'd deleted his number from her phone. But she hadn't expected Jerry Norton to bail out. Just when she'd decided to give the relationship more attention, he'd broken up with her. He'd been very nice about it. He'd apologized a number of times as he told her about a girl he'd met at his cousin's wedding. He explained how they hit it off right away.

So Lea's love life was as barren as the trees in the Lloyd's front yard. But instead of fighting it, she decided she had to accept it and make peace with her life. Her father had said she'd been a very hurtful person before her amnesia. She was determined not to be that person any more. Happily, she'd made a lot of progress since her accident the year before.

The Lloyds had helped her to be more patient instead of always getting upset. She'd also learned a lot about self-confidence. When she took stock of herself, she knew it might take time, but sooner or later, she'd master whatever she put her mind to.

Dr. Kasner helped Lea to deal with her amnesia more effectively. The psychiatrist pointed out that Lea wasn't alone when it came to difficult challenges. Some people lost their sight. Others lost a loved one. Some people were going through a very tough divorce.

The point was to find a way to make peace with a situation and embrace life again.

Lea felt like she was finally doing just that. As her attitude improved, she was even somewhat pleased when she looked in the mirror. And when it came to interacting with other people, she liked being friendly. It made her feel warm inside when she smiled at someone, and they smiled back.

She was smiling when she opened the door to the Lloyd residence. She was counting her blessings. What a lucky person she was to have someone like Margaret waiting for her to return.

"Mom, Mrs. Miller says thanks for the cookies," she announced.

"I'm in the kitchen," Margaret replied.

Lea followed her nose. There was the delicious smell of chocolate cake in the air. There was going to be a special dinner that night. Eric and Teresa were celebrating their engagement. Margaret had wondered about it being a little too soon, but Lea felt differently. One look at their faces told the story. They belonged together.

* * *

Matthew hated to admit it, but he looked forward to his dinners with Nicky and Ralph. Most of the time, they ate at Nicky's apartment. She was an excellent cook.

It had been a month since Matthew's hospital stay, and he was finally feeling well again. Nicky had recovered very nicely too. She never verbally thanked him for saving her life, but she usually gave him a motherly smile when they got together. His partner, Ralph, kept an eye on him too.

However, when Matthew checked out the large salad that Nicky put in front of him, he balked. "Not more rabbit food, please! I need a substantial meal, Nicky."

Ralph smiled as he forked at some baby greens and stared back. "Eat up, Matthew, and afterwards you'll get lasagna."

Matthew turned towards the kitchen. "I thought I smelled Italian. But really, I had a salad at lunch."

"Ralph and I spent quite a while working on this salad. Please appreciate our efforts," Nicky pleaded.

Matthew stared at his plate. "Appreciate your efforts? Don't you think you went overboard? Every vegetable in the produce department is represented on my plate. Did you at least douse this garden delight with my favorite dressing?"

Nicky patted Ralph's arm and frowned. "What are we going to do with this guy? He's a constant complainer."

Matthew took a bite, chewed and swallowed. "This complainer saved your butt. Please don't forget to mention that."

Ralph sat back and nodded. "Matthew is right. I'm very grateful that he got here in time."

"What do you mean?" Nicky protested. "I waited for him. I wasn't going to go to the great beyond without reminding him that he needs to take care of himself."

Ralph studied Matthew and looked at Nicky. "I think you were wasting your last breaths, Nicky. I lectured him for weeks about taking care of himself, and he paid no attention. Then I had to pick up the pieces when he fell apart."

"Can we change the subject?" Matthew asked. "By the way, the salad dressing is different, but it's okay."

Nicky got up and went to the kitchen. "Thanks, and yes you can change the subject as long as you don't talk about me."

Matthew took another bite. "I was simply going to ask how you liked your new job."

Nicky returned carrying a water pitcher. "I'm getting the hang of it."

Ralph beamed out a smile. "She's doing terrific. Our files were a mess after that last temp. Nicky, on the other hand, seems to know everything about everything. She's also a genius on the computer."

Nicky refilled their glasses. "I like technology. If used properly, it's a great time saver."

Matthew looked back at the kitchen counter. "Didn't I bring over a bottle of wine?"

Ralph sat up straighter. "It's important to stay hydrated, remember? However, I think the wine is being served with the lasagna."

Matthew scowled. "My lord, I feel like I'm having dinner with two irritating parents."

111

Ralph wiped his mouth with a paper napkin, smiled at Nicky and then back at Matthew. "Thank you, son, I'll take that as a compliment."

Nicky glanced at Matthew and then looked down at her salad. "I don't want to sound like a nosy parent, but I just want to make sure you're doing okay after—" She hesitated. "After everything that happened with—"

Matthew quickly broke in. "With my former fiancé?"

Nicky gave him the briefest glance. "Yes."

Matthew speared a tomato and grimaced. "I'm fine, Nicky. That's all behind me now. So let's forget the whole thing ever happened."

* * *

Raymond held the phone close to his ear, trying to avoid Rita's efforts. She was following him around, trying to get his attention by tugging at his sleeve. When he finally glanced her way, she gestured to him. He understood what she was trying to say. Raymond was talking to Lea, and Rita didn't want their conversation to include anything about her.

When Raymond hung up the phone, he looked at his wife as she took a seat by the window. She was wearing a full-length, white silk robe over her matching pajamas. "Sweetheart, what are you doing out of bed? I thought the doctor said you needed to rest."

Rita returned a pouty look. "I just can't bear the thought of Lea finding out that I'm sick."

"Don't you think she has a right to know if you're not well?"

"I spent a few minutes with her and went into a hell dive for days. What if she feels obliged to come here? I'll never get better."

"Rita, I don't think we can blame Lea for all our problems."

"Maybe you're right, but she certainly has a knack for making things worse."

He walked over to where she sat and took her hand. "You know, this might be an opportunity for the two of you to get to know each other."

"What? Now?"

"She's changed. I've been having these weekly chats with her, and I'm beginning to think the amnesia might have saved our little girl's sanity. She's not so nervous and upset all the time."

"I don't know. She scares me."

"She's our child, Rita. I think you'd both benefit if you could at least talk to one another."

"She doesn't want to talk to me."

"You know that's not true. She always asks about you, but I make excuses because you tell me to. So what if I invite her here for a weekend? You could have a pajama party together. What do you say?"

"I guess I could give her one more chance." Rita looked up at him with flashing eyes. "But if it doesn't go well, that's it."

Raymond kissed her cheek. "I promise. If she doesn't behave herself, I'll never ask you to see her again."

Nineteen

MARGARET STOOD IN her bedroom packing. She was going to accompany Lea to Chicago. It was a depressing thought. Ever since Lea's family found her, Margaret did her best to adjust. But it was one of the most difficult things she'd ever had to do. The person she'd thought of as a daughter wasn't a daughter at all. Lea belonged to the Fergusons.

When Margaret first met Rita and Raymond, she resented them when they barged into her house. She knew she should be happy for Lea, but she couldn't help herself. The event signaled the end of a time that Margaret had come to treasure.

She and Lea had done everything together for a good part of a year. If Margaret was honest with herself, she'd have to admit that she'd never spent that kind of quality time with Eric. When he was growing up, she'd been too busy. With no modern conveniences, her days consisted of taking care of one chore after another. Washing, at first on a scrub board, could gobble up most of a day. When she finally got a machine and an iron that plugged into electricity, she felt like she had a new lease on life.

"We were so poor for so long," she sighed as she put her nightgown in the suitcase. But how could she complain when she was so much better off than the people living in shacks in the hills.

Still, she often wondered why Ricky had wanted to move to such a remote area. That's when he'd take her in his arms and explain his reasoning. He told her that the mountains were wild and open, a place where they could experience the true beauty of nature. "God's resplendent earth," he'd say. She hadn't known the real reason until a number of years later.

114

"Mom, do you need any help?"

Margaret turned and looked at Lea. The young woman was standing in the doorway, looking very stylish in her new, pale-gray slacks and a white sweater. Raymond Ferguson was always sending Lea money, telling her to buy herself whatever she liked. "You look very nice. Are you finished packing already?"

Lea smiled. "Yes, my suitcase is downstairs."

"I'm almost finished too," Margaret said as she folded a couple more garments.

Lea came over and began to help. "Thank you for coming with me. I'm starting to feel comfortable talking to my dad, but still—"

"I'm sure you're first trip home is going to be fine."

"I don't know. My mother has hardly spoken to me. Dad says she's just nervous. Plus, she hasn't been feeling well."

"What's wrong?"

"They don't know. She's had tests, but so far it's a mystery." Lea paused and twisted a button on her sweater. "I've been thinking about what my father said the day they were here. He said I broke my mother's heart. He said I broke his too."

Margaret dropped the shirt she was folding. "Oh dearest, don't think about any of that. You're sweet. I couldn't ask for a sweeter person in my life."

"I know, but I don't think the old me was like that. Matthew found my diary a while back and sent it to me. It was awful. The things I wrote were so dark and spiteful."

Margaret stood up and crossed her arms. "You're not that person now."

"You're right. I wouldn't write those things anymore, but—"

Margaret put an arm around Lea. "What's bothering you? Please tell me."

Lea let out a ragged breath. "When Matthew hit Eric, I felt something take over. I felt so much anger inside. I wanted to hit Matthew, to really hurt him. I called Matthew a monster, but I think the real monster is inside of me."

Margaret's mind flashed to the time that Eric's father had shared his secret. Ricky knew all about the monster that Lea was talking about. "I'm going to tell you something important, my darling girl. You're right. There is a monster inside of each of us. It's the part where all the hurt and pain is stored. And that hurt and pain makes us think we have to fight everything to survive. But that monster can't hurt anyone unless we give up on the real us. So we have to hold on to our goodness and believe in it, do you understand?"

"But what if I can't? What if I become that other Lea again?"

"That's what family is for. It's there to let you know you're not alone with the monster. If you hold on to those who truly love you, they'll do their best to be there for you."

"Mom?"

"Yes?"

"What do you think about Matthew Howell?"

Margaret had to pause, to put aside the fact that the man in question had assaulted her son. As soon as she did, she remembered Matthew's eyes. When he stood in the foyer, staring at Lea, they were so full of pain. They were also overflowing with something else. "I think when he came here, he wanted to protect you. He wanted to keep you safe."

"I wish he still wanted that. He won't even talk to me now."

Margaret reached out for Lea's hand. "Just like you can't give up on yourself, you can't give up on love. If the two of you are meant to be together, you'll find a way. But no matter what, remember what we discussed."

"What was that?"

"You told me that I gave up part of myself to be with Ricky. I think I understand what you were getting at. So if you want to have someone in your life, take every bit of your true self into that partnership. Let go of the hurt parts and be strong, and help your partner be strong too. It's the only way to have true happiness."

* * *

When they arrived at the Ferguson mansion, Lea held on to Margaret's hand. They both agreed that the place was enormous. When they were greeted by a maid and asked to step into the foyer, Lea noticed Margaret's nervousness. The older woman glanced around the expansive space with an overwhelmed look in her eyes.

Lea was quick to give her a reassuring smile. "I like our house. It's homey and inviting. These high ceilings and marble floors are too much."

Margaret blushed. "Thank you, dear, but how about you? Does anything here feel familiar?"

Lea looked around again. "It's strange, but all I feel is bored."

"Bored? We can't have that," Raymond said as he came out of a side room.

Lea took a hasty breath. "Hi . . . Dad."

Raymond came over and hesitantly leaned in to kiss her cheek. "Hi, kitten, uh . . . I mean Lea. Forgive me if I say the wrong thing. I think I'm just excited to have you here after—" He stopped himself and stepped back. "Am I crowding you?"

Her father's voice had an anxious tremor when he spoke. Lea stepped forward and gave him a hug. She remembered that he'd seemed to like her embrace the first time they met in Baltimore. "It's nice to be here."

He smiled. "Thank you for coming."

Lea stepped aside. "You remember Margaret Lloyd, don't you?"

Raymond sobered as soon as he was introduced. "Mrs. Lloyd, I hope you know we didn't intend for things to get so out of hand that day we met. Again, accept my deepest apologies."

Margaret nodded. "Thank you."

Lea glanced around the foyer. "Is Rita, I mean Mother, going to join us?"

Raymond tried to paste on a smile, but his brows were pinched. "She asked to be excused this evening. She hopes it's alright if you two get together in the morning."

Lea shrugged. "Of course."

"Ladies, would you like to come in and sit down before dinner? Or would you like to see your rooms?"

Margaret touched Lea's arm. "Dear, why don't you go with your father while I get my things unpacked?"

Lea knew that Margaret wanted to give them privacy. "Come down when you're ready, Mom." As soon as she said the word, Mom, Lea saw Raymond's eyes flicker painfully, but he quickly called for a maid to escort Margaret to her accommodations. Afterwards, he invited Lea in to a large room that looked like it served as a library. At the far end, there was an oversized fireplace.

"My goodness, look at all the shelves of beautiful books," Lea exclaimed.

Raymond nodded. "I collect them. Electronic books might be the rage in some circles, but there's nothing like holding the print version in one's hand."

After that they chatted. As they exchanged ideas, Lea knew she liked Raymond. He was a gracious person whose eyes were filled with a guarded kindness every time he looked at her. So why did she write about how she hated him in her diary?

Twenty

THE MORNING AFTER Lea arrived at her parents' home, she felt tired. She hadn't slept very well in the bedroom she'd been given. It was so big, and the dark furnishings were depressing after living in the more upbeat Lloyd house. But she told herself not to get sidetracked. She was there to get to know her parents.

After dining on a generous breakfast with Margaret and Raymond, Lea sat on the edge of Rita's lavishly outfitted, king-size bed. Rita was seated against a number of silky, white pillows. Her nearly black hair was pulled back at the temples, exposing her pretty face. This was the first conversation Lea had had with her mother, and she didn't want to start off on the wrong foot. Inspiration took hold when she took a closer notice of her surroundings. "I don't know much about decorating, but this is a very impressive room. The furniture, the huge crystal chandelier, and the lavish curtains make me feel like I'm visiting a movie set in Paris. I think it's the prettiest room I've ever been in."

Rita leaned forward, her dark, perfectly plucked brows poised attentively. "Why that's the nicest thing that you've ever said to me!"

Lea couldn't hide her surprise. "Really?"

Rita dabbed her eyes with a hand embroidered handkerchief. "Did you have a nice breakfast? I made sure that our chef did his best."

Lea patted her tummy. "The peach crepes were delicious."

Rita nodded. "Good."

Lea noted how throaty the one word reply sounded. Then she saw the tears in Rita's eyes. She stood up and slowly approached the head of the bed. "Did I say the wrong thing, Mom, I mean Mother."

Rita sniffled a couple of times and dabbed at her eyes again. "You've never called me 'mom' before. It sounded nice."

Lea rested her hand on the bed, a few inches away from Rita's hand. "I'd like it if I could call you that whenever I see you," she said with an imploring smile. "I'm hoping that we can be—"

Rita's voice was barely a whisper. "Be what?"

"I'd like us to be able to start over again. Do you know what I mean?"

The simple question seemed to overwhelm Rita, and she burst into tears.

Lea quickly sat down next to Rita and reached out for her free hand. It was so delicate, smaller than her own, and it shook. Lea had barely said anything, and her mother was very upset. But why? Had she done something wrong again? She squeezed her mother's hand. "Please don't cry."

"I'm a terrible person!" Rita sobbed. "And I pray that I don't die too soon because I know I'll be damned. The devil is just waiting to throw me into the fire pit."

"No, please, it's not true," Lea pleaded back. She used her softest voice, a calming voice she'd learned from Margaret. But Rita only became more upset. Soon she was crying hysterically, shrieking wildly about punishment and hell's fires.

Lea's heart went out to her mother so completely that she thought she'd soon burst into tears too. But that wasn't going to help anything. Her only choice was to find her father. Maybe he could help the poor woman.

When she found Raymond outside, he was showing Margaret around the manicured gardens. "Dad!" she called out. "I think I upset Rita! We were talking, and she started crying. Now I don't know how to help her. You better go to her right away!"

Raymond let out a gasp and grabbed for his chest. "Oh no, it's starting again. I can't do this," he cried out. After a moment, he seemed to gather himself up enough to hurry towards the house.

Lea started to cry. "Dad?" she called after him. "Dad, I'm so sorry!"

Raymond didn't seem to hear her or maybe he didn't want to hear her. The only thing Lea knew is that she'd upset both her parents in the space of a few minutes.

Margaret rushed over and put her arms around Lea. "What happened?"

"I don't know. I was just trying to talk to Rita, and she started sobbing. She kept looking at me and saying things about hell and fire. She sounded so scared!"

"It's going to be okay—"

"No! It's not! You think I'm sweet, but I think I've fooled you too!" Lea reached in her slacks pocket and pulled out her phone.

"What are you going to do?" Margaret asked.

"I have to talk to Matthew. I have to find out why I'm upsetting everyone."

"But you said you deleted his number."

"Yes, but I memorized his office address. I'll call a cab and go to see him."

"But he might be at the hospital or—"

"I don't care! I'll camp out on the sidewalk in front of his building if I have to! Whatever it takes, I have to get to the bottom of this." She paused and stared at Margaret's blue eyes. "Don't you understand? No matter what you say, I must be a horrible person, and I don't want to hurt anyone else!"

When Margaret tried to reach out for her, Lea backed away. Margaret only saw her good side. But after reading the awful things in her diary, Lea knew there must be more, and she had to know the truth. What was it about her that frightened her father and sent Rita into hysterics?

She started running for the house. She didn't stop running until she got to the front entrance. She was about to call a cab when she saw a chauffeur standing by a fancy, black car. The grey-haired man was polishing a fender. She hailed him. "Hey, I'm Raymond Ferguson's daughter, and—"

The man smiled and tipped his cap. "I know who you are, Miss Lea. Welcome back."

"You know me? What's your name?"

"Joseph, Miss Lea."

Lea held up her phone and ran over to where Joseph stood. "Listen, Joseph, I need to get to this address. Can you drive me there? It's an emergency!"

Joseph peered closely at the phone and scratched his head. "I guess so. Did your papa say it was okay?"

"Yes, yes he did!"

Joseph nodded patiently. "Right this way, Miss Lea," he said as he turned and opened the rear door of the car. After Lea jumped in, he smiled at her and slammed it shut. Once Joseph was seated in the front seat, he pressed the push-button ignition, put the car in gear and slowly pulled away from the concrete curb.

"Joseph, please! Please drive faster!"

Joseph glanced at the rear view mirror. "Miss Lea, that's the first time you ever said please. It sounded real nice."

Lea's heart started beating harder. She was trapped in a crazy world. It was filled with ugly facts from her past. What kind of maniac was she? Even the chauffeur seemed surprised when she treated him with common decency.

* * *

Margaret was thankful that she'd learned to use a cell phone. She pressed it to her ear waiting impatiently. When Eric finally answered, she was almost too upset to speak.

Eric voiced his concern. "Mom, I can hear you gasping. What's wrong? Are you sick?"

"No!" Margaret finally managed to find her tongue. She'd been a doctor's wife for forty years. She knew how to stay calm in a crisis. But her fear was stronger than her training.

"Mom, is it Lea?"

She nodded. "I've never seen her like this. Her eyes were so frightened. And she ran off!"

"Where? Where did she go?"

"Doctor Howell's. She says she has to find out what's wrong with her!"

"There's nothing wrong with her. She was doing great when I saw her last. She looked so happy."

"Eric, she has some crazy idea that she's a monster, and that she's going to hurt someone."

122

"That's ridiculous! I've watched her with people at the hospital. She's the last person who would hurt anyone."

"All I know is that she's in trouble. You have to come here and help her before it's too late?"

"What do you mean too late?"

"You didn't see her. It's like she's in an all-out panic and running for her life!"

* * *

Matthew leaned back in his office chair and stretched. There'd been no surgery that morning. After seeing a couple of patients and catching up on his records, he was taking the rest of the day off. Ralph had made the suggestion, and Matthew was learning to take his partner's advice.

He'd go home and have lunch for starters. Nicky had brought in some leftover roasted chicken for him. After lunch, he'd finish reading a thriller he'd started earlier in the week. It was the perfect beginning of a long weekend away from work.

With a contented sigh he stood up and grabbed his jacket, thankful that his life was on track again. He was walking to the door when he heard voices in the waiting room. They were quickly escalating in volume. He opened the door to find out who was causing a problem. "Nicky, what's going on out here?"

"Matthew!"

Matthew recognized the voice yelling out his name and looked up. His jaw went rigid when he saw who was standing a few feet away. "Oh no, not you!"

Nicky was quick with an explanation. "I'm sorry, Doctor Howell, this woman came in here practically hysterical. I tried to get her to calm down, but—"

Nicky didn't get to finish her sentence. She was rudely pushed aside as Lea rushed forward and slipped into Matthew's office.

Matthew hesitated for a long moment, trying to rein in his emotions. "It's okay, Nicky, I'll handle this."

"She's very upset," Nicky said with a frown.

"What else is new?" Matthew asked as he turned and went back into his office. He found Lea sitting in one of the chairs with her hands wrapped around herself. He closed the door with impatience. "What do you want, Lea? I thought I made it clear that—"

"My parents!" Lea yelled out.

"What about them?"

"I was only visiting for a little while. Now I'm worried about them. Matthew, please, you have to help me."

"Why are you worried about your parents? You never gave a damn about them."

"You didn't see Rita! She wouldn't stop crying. And my dad looked like he was going to have a heart attack."

Matthew scowled and took out his phone. "Fine, I'll call them."

"No, not yet. First you have to help me."

"Help you do what?"

"You knew me. Why was I so terrible to everyone? I have to know."

Matthew rubbed his brow. "You just were."

"Didn't you try to find out why?"

"And get my jugular ripped out. I don't think so."

Lea slowly let go of herself and stood up. She took a step closer to Matthew. "Was I really that bad? Did I hurt you too?"

Matthew thought about all the times she'd cursed him out. He scowled back at her. "I survived, barely."

Lea swallowed hard. "So it's true. I go around hurting people."

Matthew had been over Lea's behavior so many times after she'd ran off. What he'd come to realize was that there were so many more bad times than good. He must have been out of his mind to think he wanted to marry her. "Lea, let me call your dad."

"No, please Matthew! I'm scared!"

He crossed his arms. Lea being scared was nothing new either. He'd held her night after night and tried to let her know that she was safe. What good did it do? Did she tell him why she felt like she did? No. In the end, she ran off without a word of explanation.

Lea came over to where he stood and touched his hand. "Matthew, did you hear what I said?"

Matthew pulled back. "Yes, I heard you. You said you were scared."

"Yes, of who I am. Margaret said I'm fine. She even thinks I'm sweet and—"

"Don't get me started on Margaret Lloyd!"

124

"What do you mean? She's wonderful."

Matthew thought about the private investigator's report he'd studied. "Your wonderful Ms. Lloyd was stuck in Appalachia for most of her life. She was married to some mad doctor who was holed up in some isolated hamlet."

Lea's brows lifted in surprise. "What are you talking about? Eric's father was a saint. He dedicated his life to—"

"Get real, Lea! Eric's father lost his Maryland medical license after he almost beat a man to death. He practiced in West Virginia because they were desperate for doctors and weren't too picky about who they licensed."

Lea backed up. "How would you know anything about the Lloyds?"

"Your father, Lea! After you ran off, he had to hire a slew of private investigators to find you. When they learned you were living with the Lloyds—"

"Stop!" Lea put her hands over her ears. "Those are lies! They have to be."

Matthew went over to his desk, unlocked a file drawer and withdrew a folder. "Here, read the report for yourself. Raymond gave me a copy."

Lea stared at the folder and bit her lip as her eyes filled with tears and overflowed. She didn't argue anymore, but her cheeks were wet and flushed when she looked up at Matthew. "Then you have to help me, Matthew, please. I don't have any place else to turn."

Matthew averted his eyes, letting his recent history with Lea unfold. He'd hoped and prayed for almost a year that Raymond would locate her. The stress took a toll on his health, but he overlooked that fact. The important thing was getting Lea back. So he flew to Baltimore. And what did that get him? Lea screamed at him, accused him of being a monster, and told him she was in love with someone else. Afterwards, his hands shook and his nerves were shot. It took almost a month to recuperate. For a while, he wondered if his career was over.

Lea stepped closer again. "Please Matthew, will you help me?"

"I'm sorry, Lea, I truly am, but I can't do this, not again."

Lea turned, went back to her chair and sat down again. After a moment, her face contorted into a sad grimace. "You said 'I can't do this,' just like my father this morning."

125

Matthew approached her. "Listen, your father is probably worried about you. I'll call him."

She stared down at her lap and shook her head. "He won't want me either. Nobody wants me now."

Matthew ignored her mood. Lea was always one for drama. He took out his phone and made a call. "Raymond, your daughter's at my office. I think you need to come and take her home."

* * *

Eric had been lucky to get a flight out of Baltimore a few hours after his mother's call. But it was dark by the time he arrived in Chicago. He took a cab directly to the Ferguson mansion. His mother was waiting for him when his cab pulled up. He got out quickly and went over to her. "What are you doing outside? It's cold."

His mother reached out to him. "When you called a few minutes ago and let me know you were almost here, I had to come out. I had to see you!"

Eric noted how icy her hands were and how they were trembling. "It's okay—"

"No! I think we've lost her, Eric."

Eric braced himself. His mother was wearing the same hopeless face that she'd had when his father died. "Don't say that, please. Our Lea's a fighter. We'll find a way to get her back."

Margaret shook her head. "How? After her father picked her up at Matthew Howell's office, she must have had some kind of breakdown. Mr. Ferguson tried to find out what was going on, but she wouldn't speak to him. Since he's brought her home, she's become completely withdrawn. It's like she's trying to shut out the world and everyone in it. Her father said he's never seen her like this. He's extremely upset too."

"Do you know what happened at Howell's office?"

"According to Lea's father, Doctor Howell told Lea that he couldn't be there for her anymore. I guess the whole ordeal of Lea running off left Doctor Howell so devastated that he won't take another chance on her."

Eric clenched his fists. "I can't believe he could be that cruel. Doesn't he know how hard we've worked to make Lea feel safe and secure?"

"Oh Eric, I don't think she even knows me. It's like she's in a different world." She took in a troubled breath. "Thank goodness her father contacted a specialist. He'll be here tomorrow."

"I want to see her."

Margaret nodded. "She's upstairs. Her father and I have been taking turns staying with her. But nothing I do or say seems to reach her. She just sits there rocking and looking terrified as she holds herself."

Eric followed Margaret into the foyer and up the oversized staircase. He hardly took notice of the interior of the house. What he did notice was the quiet. It reminded him of a mausoleum. The only sound he heard was the soles of his shoes tapping out on the marble steps.

A wide hallway led to Lea's room. Its walls were a gallery of paintings. Most were conservative, classical canvases with a sprinkling of modern pieces adding vivid color. But the splashes of color and creativity couldn't compete with the feeling of the house. Eric shivered. The space had a cold, empty feeling, as if something sinister had consumed all the warmth and happiness.

When they reached Lea's bedroom, Margaret stepped aside and let Eric go in first. "Maybe she'll recognize you," she whispered.

Eric glanced around and saw Raymond Ferguson sitting on a couch on the side of the room. He nodded in the older man's direction, but he didn't speak to him. He didn't want to startle Lea.

He let out a gasp of grief when he first saw her. Her eyes were open and staring blankly as she slowly rocked back and forth. She didn't look like the woman he'd seen a couple of days before. There was too much child in her. It reminded him of the first time he'd seen her on that rainy night a year ago, laying in the street. Now she looked even more wounded, more broken.

Ever so slowly, he walked towards her. When he was a couple of feet away, he stopped. He didn't say anything. He just stood very still and let her feel his presence.

After a moment, she stopped rocking. She slowly raised her eyes and stared back. They were bright with fear and panic. Moments passed as she continued to search his face. Finally she whispered out a few words. "My angel! It's really you. You're back."

Eric nodded and opened his arms in a welcoming gesture. "Yes, I am."

127

Lea hesitated again, but after another long pause she let go of herself and offered her hand. "I want to go far, far away. Will you take me there?"

Eric smiled and helped her up. "Yes, that's what angels do."

Lea fell against him, clinging tightly as he held her. She began to shake uncontrollably. Eric understood enough to know that the shaking was probably due to some trauma, and the body's need to release it.

When the shaking stopped, Lea shuddered out a few words. "I don't want to ever be in the dark again."

Eric gently cradled Lea close and kissed the top of her head. "Don't worry. I know all about the dark." As a child, he'd been so afraid. The darkness was where his nightmares lived. "I promise that we'll keep all the lights on," he whispered.

Twenty-One

DOCTOR PAUL GLASS had responded as quickly as possible to Raymond Ferguson's pleas on behalf of his daughter, Lea. Still, Paul wasn't able to get to the Ferguson mansion until the next day. During his travel time, he'd learned as much as possible about Lea's background and condition. Ferguson had emailed him copious amounts of information, including data collected by private investigators.

Once Paul arrived at the Ferguson home, he'd continued to search out any clues that might help him understand his patient. That meant that he'd even spoken to house staff who'd known Lea and who could shed some light on the situation. Paul knew his aggressive methods were sometimes unconventional, but that's why Raymond Ferguson had contacted him. As a psychiatrist, Paul often got results much more quickly than others in his field.

When he walked into his patient's bedroom, he saw that Raymond's daughter, Lea, was still asleep. Fortunately, when he took a closer look, she seemed quite peaceful too. He decided it was best to let her rest.

Instead, he continued on into the spacious sitting room that was located at the far end of the bedroom. An attractive, older woman was standing by the window. She matched the description given in one of the files that Paul had been studying. He smiled as he walked over to her. "You must be Margaret Lloyd," he said. "Let me introduce myself. My name is Paul Glass."

Margaret turned to greet him. "Yes, Mr. Ferguson said that you'd arrived. It's very nice to meet you."

"Raymond explained that you're Lea's friend."

His comment prompted an immediate reaction. Margaret stiffened and thrust out her chin. "I like to think that I'm more than that, Doctor Glass."

"Please call me, Paul. And if it's alright with you, I'd like to call you Margaret."

"Oh?"

"I want to surround Lea with a feeling of ease and friendliness as we all work together to help her."

Margaret's frown eased a little. "Good, I like that approach."

Paul offered Margaret his arm. "Could we sit down for a few moments. I'd like you to tell me more about Lea. Since you've helped her so much in the past, I think you could help her again."

Margaret paused, but she finally took Paul's arm and sighed. "I'd like that more than anything."

* * *

Eric woke up, glanced around at the unfamiliar room and quickly reminded himself of where he was. He was staying at the Ferguson mansion. His next thought was about the person who'd grown up there, Lea Ferguson. When he put the two together, they didn't compute.

After knowing Lea for the past year, he'd come to think of her as a sensitive, caring person. She was bright and inquisitive, and she'd become a beautiful, loving member of his family. When he thought about her cheerful, open smile and expectant eyes, he couldn't imagine any connection to the Ferguson mansion.

His first impression of its cold, empty nature hadn't changed. In fact, after spending a night in the large, foreboding structure, he felt a terrible heaviness settling into his bones. If he had a choice, he'd pack his bag and leave immediately. Unfortunately, that wasn't possible. He'd never abandon Lea, no matter what he felt.

He'd stayed up most of the night with her. And even though she never said anything after her initial acknowledgement, she did seem comforted by his presence. When she finally fell asleep in the early morning hours, she was still holding on to him. He'd gone to bed after that, too tired to do anything else.

* * *

130

It was already noon by the time Eric showered, dressed, and checked on Lea. She was still sleeping soundly. Next, he'd stopped in the dining room for a quick bite to eat. That's when he met a person named Paul Glass. Eric learned that Paul was the psychiatrist who'd been summoned by Raymond Ferguson. They had a brief chat during which Paul Glass was quick to inform Eric of the basics. The sooner they helped Lea to return to reality, the better.

After a hasty lunch, Eric went back to Lea's bedroom. He was pleased to see her still dozing. However, he heard muffled voices that were coming from a sitting room he'd noticed the night before. It was located at the far end of the bedroom. He was as quiet as possible when he approached it and opened the door. Like all of the rooms in the mansion, it was oversized and furnished in antiques. Paul Glass and Eric's mother were sitting on a fancy, tufted-back, gold sofa.

Eric's first thought revolved around his mother's and Paul's similarities. They both had white hair and blue eyes, and they appeared to be close in age. His second thought was more of a feeling. Something didn't seem right about the way the two people were interacting. His mother was reaching out to the psychiatrist, putting her hand on his arm, and Paul Glass was staring back in a way that was anything but professional.

Before Eric had a chance to process his feelings, Paul Glass looked up and noticed Eric's presence. He waved Eric over with a friendly smile.

"Eric, come join us," Paul said. "We want to work on a plan for today."

Eric took a deep breath and pushed back his weariness and personal concerns. A few hours of fitful sleep weren't enough to restore his energy, but he had to press on for Lea's sake. He strode over to the seating area and smiled at his mother. "How are you doing, Mom?" he asked as he leaned over and kissed her cheek.

Margaret shrugged. "I feel a little more optimistic. It seems that Paul has been very busy. For one thing, he called Lea's doctor, Doctor Kasner, this morning, right Paul?"

Paul's eyes sparkled brightly. "I sure did. I also spoke to Raymond extensively. I wanted to know everything he could tell me about Lea's childhood, especially about the time when he first noticed a change in his daughter's behavior. That prompted a conversation with Lea's mother, Rita. Raymond found out quite a bit from her and passed the information on to me."

Eric listened attentively. "What did you learn?"

"I believe Lea was fine until the age of about—"

A knock at the door interrupted Paul's answer and made everyone glance over at the tall man who was waiting in the doorway. Paul stood up and walked over to greet their visitor.

Eric crossed his arms when he realized who that visitor was. "What the hell is Howell doing here?" he asked in a sullen voice.

Margaret reached up for his arm. "Eric Steven, if Paul invited him, let's not cause a problem. We have to think about Lea's—"

Eric felt his face flush with anger. "I am thinking of Lea! And she doesn't need Howell! With his track record, she'll be catatonic next."

"Shh! Keep your voice down, please," Margaret chastised. "You don't want to wake her."

Eric held his tongue, but his feelings were a different matter. He could barely contain his resentment as Paul and Matthew Howell walked over to join them.

Paul Glass seemed to recognize the problem as soon as he saw Eric's face. "Is there something wrong, Eric?"

Eric let out a snort of half-contained rage. "Yes, there is. The man you're standing next to is a selfish, unfeeling jerk!"

The statement sparked an immediate reaction on Matthew Howell's part. He came forward and glared back at Eric. "And you're an ignorant fool, Lloyd!"

Paul stepped between the two men and gave each of them a stern look. "Let me explain how this works. I invited Matthew here after some extensive research on Lea's condition. For twelve hours I've studied every scrap of information I could get my hands on. My conclusion is that Lea needs all of you here. If you want her to come out of this thing sooner than later, you need to cooperate."

Eric let his shoulders drop. "You mentioned that earlier. What do you mean by sooner than later?"

"I've had very good results with Lea's type of withdrawal. But the more quickly we address the problem, the better. We don't want Lea to drift any further away from her family than she already has."

Matthew raised a hand, glanced back towards the bedroom where Lea was sleeping and scowled. "I'm not family."

Paul grabbed a thick folder off the settee table. "According to what I read, you were engaged to be married to Lea. That means you qualify."

Eric narrowed his eyes at Matthew Howell. "How can you stand there after being so heartless, Howell? Supposedly you loved Lea, but you wouldn't even help her when she came to you. She was desperate, and you shut her out."

Before Matthew could answer, Paul gestured for quiet and gave Eric an imploring look. "Eric, I know you feel that Matthew has let Lea down, but he did everything in his power to find her and help her when she went missing. In fact, his own health and wellbeing suffered as a result of all the stress he was under. So please, try not to be too hasty with your judgments."

"How do you know all that?" Matthew asked.

Paul smiled. "I'm very good at what I do, just like you're a topnotch surgeon, Matthew, and Eric is a first-class cardiologist."

Eric sat down heavily. "I'm just so damn frustrated. Lea was happy before she came here. Now, after all the hours with Kasner and all the time we've spent trying to help her, it's all come to nothing."

Paul sat down next to Eric. "That's not true. The time she spent with you and Margaret were a kind of a reset. She has more of herself to deal with the original problem."

Margaret put her hand on Paul's arm. "What is the original problem?"

Paul's easy going expression turned more serious. "From what I know, Rita hired a nanny, but the nanny wasn't qualified. Raymond is trying to trace her present whereabouts. But it's pretty easy to diagnose the trauma that Lea experienced when she was a three-year-old."

Matthew grimaced. "Three years? Some damned sadist hurt Lea when she was three?"

Paul nodded. "Some children survive better than others. In Lea's case, with an essentially non-existent mother and a father who was always away from home, she didn't have much of a chance of holding on to any sense of safety. Not only that, but children often think that they're to blame for what they experience."

Matthew stepped back, looking very pale. "Excuse me, I need some air."

133

Paul spoke up at once. "Matthew, please, don't blame yourself for Lea's current condition. I'm sure that you did your best."

Matthew huffed out his response. "Like you said, I'm a surgeon. There's no room for mistakes, but I made one in this case, and Lea's paying for it."

Paul nodded indulgently. "Please stay close in case—"

Matthew returned a hateful look as if he was being asked to remain for his execution. "I'll be down the hall. Is that close enough?"

After Matthew left, Paul turned to Margaret. "Margaret, do you think you could talk to Matthew?"

Margaret shrugged. "Me? But I wouldn't know what to say."

Eric stared back at Paul. "Why do you want my mother to talk to Howell?"

Paul smiled. "Because she's a mother. She's raised a son who's a very understanding and giving human being. From what I've learned about Matthew, he could use a little of that kind of nurturing."

Margaret stood up and started out of the room. "Maybe you're right, Paul. At least I'd feel like I was doing something besides sitting here."

Eric stood up too, looking first at his mother and then at Paul. "Are you sure Howell's safe? I don't want my mother—"

Paul sat back and rubbed his eyes. "Believe me, Eric, I would never put your mother in danger. But Matthew can use some help, and he needs to feel good about himself. He's got a big job ahead of him."

"What do you mean?"

"From what I read in Lea's diary—"

"You read her diary?"

"Certainly, she had it in with her socks."

Eric sat down again. "How did you have time to find out all this stuff?"

Paul chuckled. "Like I told you, I'm the best in the business of helping when people lose their way. At least I'm the best person that I know. I understand how to look and where to look."

Eric rubbed at his jaw. "If you help Lea, I might have to start seeing you myself."

"Are you talking about your night fears?"

"How could you possibly know about my night fears?"

134

Paul leaned in and retrieved a recording device from his briefcase. "After Raymond called me, I had him record everything that was said in this room last night. That includes your comments about the dark."

"Isn't that invasive?"

"We're trying to save Lea from drifting away permanently. You tell me if I did the right thing or not."

Eric looked through the doorway that opened into Lea's bedroom. Lea looked very small lying in the king size bed. Eric wasn't surprised that she was still asleep. He'd held her most of the night, but she'd fought closing her eyes. When she finally dozed off in his arms, he prayed for help, for a miracle that would restore her sanity.

Glancing at Paul, Eric hoped the psychiatrist might be an answer to those prayers. But if nothing else, Paul Glass seemed very capable when it came to dissecting the situation. Eric almost smiled when he asked Paul a light-hearted question. "Would you like to know my shoe size too?"

Paul shrugged. "Ten and a half, right?" He smiled. "Just guessing, but I'm pretty good at observation and deduction. I'd say I'm almost in a class with Sherlock Holmes."

Eric squinted back. "You're one of a kind, Paul, I'll give you that. I'm just grateful that you're modest too."

* * *

Margaret glanced to the right and left as she walked down the broad corridor. She was checking rooms as she went, looking for Matthew Howell. Not finding him at first, she paused in front of a large painting that included red roses.

With her background in art, she could appreciate the use of colors and the composition of the piece. But it was the subject matter that drew her in. The wilting roses had been scattered over a grave. The artist had done a very good job of depicting the finality of death, too good a job. Margaret's mind shifted, throwing her backwards into that miserable time when she was standing over Ricky's grave.

She knew she couldn't give in to the memories. It served no purpose. Instead, she continued down the hall, picking up her pace. It seemed she was constantly trying to outrun her grief. But how could she distance herself from something that was always so close? Once her sorrow was activated, it could blot out everything that made life worth living. She was left in some black void where she couldn't see any way out.

She put a hand to her mouth, trying to stop herself from going into that void again. Only the thought of being there for Lea could stop her tears. She'd been doing so much crying recently, and it wasn't helping anyone. With determination, she swallowed back her misery and pressed on. Besides, something told her that if she started crying now, with Lea in such a bad way, she might never stop wailing. Life kept piling on the blows, and she had to keep going.

As she searched out more rooms, she turned her attention to Matthew Howell. She had to figure out what she could say to the imposing surgeon. Paul seemed to think she needed to help him. She'd only just met the psychiatrist, but his presence was calming and inspired confidence. When their eyes connected for a brief moment, she even felt stronger.

But that didn't mean she'd know what to say to Matthew Howell. At first, like her son, she'd been angry at Matthew. But as she thought about her husband, her feelings softened. Men took heartbreak very hard, maybe harder than women. She'd witnessed that fact, day in and day out, for almost forty years. During all that time, she tried to help her husband forgive himself, but she knew it wasn't that simple. That monster that Lea had mentioned lived inside Ricky too. And her husband was scared to death that he wouldn't be able to control it.

"So you drove yourself to your death, my poor dear, trying to prove to yourself that you were more than that."

She let out a heavy sigh of regret. Ricky was a wonderful healer, but he never let himself be healed. He walked the path of guilt instead. So what about Matthew? Yes, he'd been hurtful with Lea, but Margaret knew there had to be a reason behind his actions.

With that attitude in place, she'd put her judgment aside long enough to observe the surgeon earlier. It helped her to form a new opinion. When Matthew heard the news about Lea's childhood, his face went white, and he almost stopped breathing. It was clear that he still cared deeply. So why was he so afraid to get involved?

When she finally located Matthew in the last room on the right, she collected her thoughts, smoothed out her blouse and knocked on the doorjamb. "Doctor Howell? Matthew?"

Matthew stood at one of the large windows, staring out, but her greeting made him swing around. His face was hard and questioning as he stared back at her. "Please, Mrs. Lloyd, I'd like to be alone."

Margaret smiled to herself. She recognized his stern tone. Matthew was using his doctor voice, the one that ordered people around in an emergency. Only this time, she knew the emergency centered around what was happening to him.

Margaret could also sense a deep fear. After being with Ricky, she was an expert at identifying it. She saw it hiding behind Matthew Howell's tough exterior. He'd already mentioned that he'd made a mistake, and it was clear that failure was eating away at him. If he didn't come to grips with it, he'd turn out like Ricky. He'd always be trying to prove himself, to outrun the monster.

Margaret walked over to an adjacent window. The sun was out and shining brightly. Its light sparkled on the water of a pond that lay beyond the formal gardens. The trees were budding out, adding a sprinkling of spring green to the scene. "So much beauty," she sighed.

Matthew grunted out a response. "Yes, but Lea won't see any of it, will she?"

Margaret ran her finger over the window sill. Its surface was slightly uneven and rough. Margaret was surprised to see tiny cracks in the paint. At first glance, the Ferguson mansion looked immaculate, but it was a very large structure. It was probably hard for Raymond Ferguson to keep up with the care and wellbeing of his home. It made her wonder about the man. Now that Lea's father knew he hadn't kept up with his daughter's care and wellbeing, what would happen to him?

Margaret sighed as she walked over to Matthew and touched his arm. He jumped back and stared at her with glaring eyes, but she held her ground. "Paul is right," she announced quietly. "You're not the cause of what Lea is going through."

Matthew's eyes hardened even more, and he let out a bitter laugh. "That's like saying I'm not responsible for an accident victim in the emergency room. Lea came to me for help, and I ignored her. It's as simple as that."

"I don't think you were purposefully trying to hurt her."

Matthew hesitated, but he remained adamant. "Oh, but I was, maybe not consciously, but I told her things I shouldn't have. I told her about you."

"Me? What did you say about me?"

Matthew turned and stared out the window again.

Margaret grabbed his arm. "Matthew, Doctor Howell, please tell me what you said?"

When Margaret asked the question again, she saw the surgeon's struggle. The man's eyes reverted to those of a boy, a boy who'd done something he shouldn't. They were eyes that also wanted forgiveness, but the person behind those eyes knew it would never be given.

"Please," Margaret pleaded.

Matthew finally drew himself up and confessed what he was holding back. "I inferred that you had lied to her. That you hadn't told her the real truth about yourself and your family."

It was Margaret's turn to pull away. She knew she shouldn't question Matthew further, but again, she had to be strong. "What truth are you talking about?"

Matthew's gaze grew more intense. "I told her about your husband, and how he'd lost his license. That he was hiding out in those mountains because of what he'd done."

Margaret stared at the surgeon, but as she processed his words, something inside of her stalled. Her life, her love for Ricky, all the days she'd tried so hard to raise a son and care for a husband, all of the time she'd prayed that the son wouldn't be privy to the sins of his father, all of it seemed to be pressing down on her now. The burdens she'd carried were suddenly crushing the air out of her.

She thought about Eric's face, his beautiful, caring face. It was still so innocent. And she had tried so hard to protect that innocence. Now, after what Doctor Howell told her, she didn't know how to do it anymore. The secrets she'd carried were exposed. They were going to destroy everything she'd tried so hard to safeguard.

As a feeling of dread began to seep in, all she could think about was how she wished she was in the grave too. And how she hated Ricky for leaving her behind. After all the pain she suffered with him, after all the nights she lay beside him in their bed and tried to be there for him, he'd abandoned her.

She couldn't breathe. She couldn't face life anymore. But most importantly, she couldn't face her son. "Oh my goodness, poor Eric! He'll find out about his father! Oh no!"

She tried to reach for the wall to steady herself and couldn't find anything to support her. She felt herself falling. But in that moment, it's what she wanted. She wanted to fall into a hole in the ground, one that was eight foot deep. When she landed with a thud, she'd know her personal hell was finally coming to an end. She'd be covered up with dirt. It would be the merciful answer she'd needed. It would be the blanket that would finally shut out the world, once and for all.

* * *

Matthew knew when he told Margaret what he'd done, that it would be painful for her. He never suspected that she'd react like she did. He barely managed to catch her as she fell over. He'd seen her face as she was collapsing, and it reminded him of Lea's face. The woman he'd loved had come to him, begging for understanding, and he'd done more than pushed her away. He'd destroyed her faith in a woman she depended on, a woman she seemed to think of as her mother.

Now, he was helping that woman to a sofa, hoping that she didn't follow Lea into the unknown. In the span of his career, he'd seen a lot of people who were terrified, and Margaret Lloyd was definitely vying for a spot at the top of the list.

Once he got her to a couch, he recognized another look he didn't want to see. Margaret had had enough of life's blows, and she wanted the same thing that Nicky had wanted. He was surprised that Margaret wasn't pointing to the heavens like Nicky had.

He had to do something. He tried to think about what she'd said before she passed out. She mentioned her son, Eric.

Oh hell, her son doesn't know about his father. Oh hell.

After he steadied Margaret on the couch, he grabbed a large, white knitted throw off a chair. With care, he draped it around Margaret's trembling shoulders. He had to get her attention as quickly as possible.

"Margaret, listen to me, Margaret!" He snapped his fingers, trying to get her to focus. "Margaret, I won't tell him! I won't tell your son anything, okay?"

The words were no sooner out of Matthew's mouth when a voice called out from the doorway. "What do you mean? What won't you tell me?"

Matthew turned and saw Eric Lloyd standing eight feet away. Before he could say anything more, Eric was rushing over to where Margaret was sitting.

Eric pushed Matthew aside and knelt down in front of his mother. "Mom, what's the matter? Mom?"

Eric's panicked voice seemed to rouse Margaret from her stupor. Matthew understood why. Mothers looked out for their children. At least they were supposed to look out for their children. Margaret was an example of that primal directive. She seemed driven to help her son. She looked at him and began to tremble even more violently. She grabbed his hand in a fierce protective gesture as if she was trying to save him from drowning. The next moment, she was looking up at Matthew. Her eyes were wild and imploring. "Please!" she cried out. "Please don't tell him anything!"

Matthew didn't know if he had his own primal directive, but he instinctively reached out. Margaret couldn't stand another shock. He understood that much, directive or not. He had to do what she wanted. "I promise," he said in a firm, assertive tone.

Twenty-Two

AS PAUL'S FIRST day at the mansion gave way to late afternoon and evening, he felt like he was a one man taskforce trying to put out a half dozen fires.

The Fergusons, Rita and Raymond, were both wounded and hurting. They were holed up in separate bedrooms. When Raymond Ferguson learned about the uncertified nanny from his wife, he didn't react at first. He knew he had to keep it together until he informed Paul about his discovery. Later that afternoon, when Raymond confronted Rita again, his anger came to the surface. His daughter had suffered at the hands of a ruthless woman whom Rita had hired. Rita's reaction was normal for Rita. She did what she usually did and cried like a child herself. But her tears fell on deaf ears. Raymond turned his back on his wife. He cloistered himself in a dark room and refused to see anyone. His reaction sent Rita into a further tailspin. Neither party left their room for the rest of the day.

Then there was Margaret. Paul knew he shouldn't let himself get personally involved, but his heart fluttered as soon as he first saw her. That was an unexpected and totally new reaction for him. He was pushing seventy, and he'd loved every minute that he'd been a confirmed bachelor. But his bachelor heart thawed every time he looked at Margaret. Still, he didn't have a chance to admire her once the fires started. She was another victim of circumstances. After her talk with Matthew, she too had shut herself away in her room. She didn't want to talk to Paul or anyone else. She even took her meals in her room.

Eric Lloyd remained true when it came to caring about Lea's wellbeing. However, after he made sure that Paul was keeping a close eye on her, he turned his attention to a personal matter. He was very upset over his mother's condition. When she refused to tell him what was wrong, he went from bright and compassionate to sullen and angry. He begged, even threatened Matthew Howell to disclose some secret between Eric's mother and Matthew. But Matthew wouldn't utter a word. When Paul tried to discuss the situation with Eric, Eric walked off.

Matthew's mood was similar to Eric's. He made sure that Lea was alright, but that was the extent of his involvement. Paul knew that Matthew was having a very difficult time with all that he'd learned about the origin of Lea's problems. The man insisted on keeping his own company for most of the day.

Lea, the patient whom Paul had flown in to help, was actually the bright spot in the whole affair. She'd been very receptive to Eric Lloyd's intervention. Afterwards, she was obviously worn out and slept peacefully until late afternoon. When she woke, she seemed somewhat confused but stable. However, the conditions around her, the people she needed for her security, were definitely in a state of chaos. Paul didn't want Lea to get upset again, and he opted for sedation. It was best that she sleep through the turmoil. Blazing, emotional wildfires were ravishing the Ferguson home, leaving no one in their path unscathed. Luckily, Paul was used to emotional wildfires. They were part of the job.

At the end of the day, he found himself in the kitchen. The servants had gone to bed, but Matthew sat at a table across from Paul. They were drinking coffee.

After a long silence, Paul tapped the handle of his mug. "Well, Matthew, it looks like it's up to us."

Matthew narrowed his eyes. "To do what, Paul? I think enough has been done already."

Paul sat back and rubbed his hands together. "Oh no, we're just at the beginning of this ride. So hold on tight. It's going to be a little bumpy at times, but we'll straighten things out."

"Bumpy? Are you nuts? This ride was devised by the Marquis de Sade himself."

Paul smiled. "Faith, my boy, you have to have faith."

"No," Matthew replied in a resolute tone. "I don't have the energy to have faith. I am sick and tired. And I mean that literally. I do not want to go on thinking life can straighten out as you say. Because it doesn't. It just keeps going downhill."

"But can't you see what's happening? All the pain is rising to the surface where we can deal with it. And I'm telling you, Matthew, we are going to do just that."

Matthew sat back and sneered. "Damn, you are the most confident and arrogant shrink I've ever met."

Paul grabbed his mug and sat back too. "I like that description. It fits. I think I'll add it to my resume."

Eric came walking into the kitchen and immediately targeted Paul with a contemptuous look. "Put what on your resume, Paul? That you're a quack?"

Paul shook his head. "No, that might turn some people off."

Eric ignored his remark and stared at Matthew. "And you! You could help my mother by simply telling me what's going on. But no, you sit there refusing to utter a word."

Paul cleared his throat. "Eric, your father almost beat a man to death. There, the truth is out."

Matthew jumped up and scowled at Paul. "Paul! I promised his mother—"

Eric looked back at each of them and let out a bitter laugh. "Is that what my mom is so upset about?" Without waiting for an answer, he went to the coffee maker and poured himself a cup of coffee. "I know about all that. I was eight years old. I saw it happen."

Matthew blinked back. "Damn! And I thought I had a crappy childhood!"

Eric came over with his cup, put it on the table, and pulled out a chair. "Relax, Howell, let me tell you about something you don't know. While you were growing up in a city with policemen and laws, I grew up in a place where a man could horsewhip his son to death, bury him in a field and start in on the next kid."

Matthew sat down cautiously and clamped his hands together. "And you saw your father—"

Eric tried to bring his mug to his lips, but he had to set it back on the table. His hands were shaking as he continued. "Yes, and I saw a dead boy. He wasn't very old, maybe five." He stopped, took an unsteady breath, and swallowed hard. After a moment, he continued. "My father was so angry. He grabbed the whip and—" He paused again.

143

"Keep going, Eric," Paul urged.

Eric looked down at his trembling hands and nodded. "I cried! When my dad heard me, he dropped the whip. We never talked about that day. But I guess my dad told my mom what happened. They shared everything."

Paul reached out and put his hand on Eric's. "Your father was a very passionate man. He cared deeply. But that wasn't the first time he acted out in violence."

Eric stared back, but he didn't interrupt.

Paul continued. "There was a child in a Baltimore hospital emergency room. The little girl was pretty broken up. Your dad couldn't control himself when he met the father. I think that's the secret that your mother has been keeping from you. Afterwards, he lost his license to practice medicine in that state."

Eric shoved back his chair and stood up. His face was pale, but his eyes flared with anger. "So you're telling me that my father retreated to some backwoods place where people would put up with someone like him, right? Is that what you're saying?" After heaving out some breaths, he turned and stormed out of the room.

Matthew sat back and glowered at Paul. "Are you satisfied? Do you like going around bringing everybody's pain to the surface?"

Paul leaned in. "I know my methods might seem harsh—"

"Harsh? Why don't I start operating without anesthesia?"

Paul sighed. "I don't always blurt things out like that. In this case, Eric was going crazy worrying about what his mother and you were keeping from him. I suspect that he's been feeling shut out most of his life. Like he said, his parents shared everything, but not with him. And a child's imagination, coupled with the violence Eric was exposed to, add up to nightmares that he's had for most of his life."

"Yes, but you saw his face. He's beyond devastated. He's the son of a nut case, a person who took justice into his own hands. Who goes around whipping people like that? That's not a comforting thought."

Paul sucked in a breath. "No, it's not. I'm afraid there're going to be more bumpy roads ahead."

Matthew slammed his fist on the table and stood up again. "Why are you telling me that? I'm not like you. I can't sit by and watch people falling apart like you do. Keep your damn bumpy roads to yourself! I'm going to bed!"

After Matthew left, Paul took out his notebook. He began to record the interactions he'd just witnessed, but his hand stalled. He looked up and stared at the empty chair where Matthew had been sitting. "No matter what you think, Matthew, I don't like seeing people in pain. That's why I'm doing this job. If possible, I'd like to make their lives a little easier."

He closed his notebook, stood up, and looked at the clock. It was past midnight. Dare he try to get in a nap? He didn't think so. It was going to be a long night.

With a heavy sigh, he went to the refrigerator and grabbed some sandwich items. He'd make himself eat so that he had the strength to travel those bumpy roads that Matthew hated. He'd been hoping that Matthew would be there beside him, to help him do what had to be done, but he might have to go it alone.

* * *

Matthew looked at the miniature, Spanish table clock on his nightstand. He hated it. He hated the way it kept ticking and ticking and reminding him that he couldn't sleep. He hated his depressing bedroom with its heavy, antique furniture, heavy lined drapes, and a four-poster bed with columns the size of small tree trunks. He longed for his own place and the simplicity of modern furniture. "Two o'clock in the damn morning, and I'm not even close to going to sleep."

He threw back his covers and got out of bed. Maybe he'd go back down to the kitchen and pray he wouldn't meet up with Paul again.

After he stretched some of the soreness out of his muscles, he glanced down at himself and realized he hated his pajamas too. Black silk with gold trim. He hadn't expected to stay the night and hadn't brought sleepwear. One of the servants found some of Raymond's pajamas that he could borrow. There was also a robe. Neither fit properly. Matthew was much taller than Raymond. He put on the robe and cinched the belt with a fast jerk. "I look like a damn clown."

He paused and hated the way he was cursing all the time. It reminded him of his days with Lea. She was a great one for cursing. He hadn't been much on swearing himself, but he soon picked up the habit. Now, he was determined to break it. Maybe he'd feel more like himself if he could at least express himself without profanity.

He was able to get to the kitchen without running into Paul, but the kitchen was occupied. Eric was slumped over the table. The cardiologist was sound asleep. Matthew quietly mumbled out his discontent. "Glad somebody in this house can get a few winks."

He didn't want to wake Eric, but then he saw the coffee maker. It was turned off, but there was coffee in the carafe. After he walked over as quietly as possible, he gave the carafe a careful touch and pulled his finger away. The pot was still hot. He glanced at Eric and figured the man had probably turned off the coffee maker before he went to sleep. The coffee would probably taste like mud, but Matthew was desperate. He reached out for the carafe. If he couldn't sleep, he needed his old friend, coffee, to help him get through the night.

"Stop right there!" a voice yelled out.

Matthew was just pouring himself a much needed cup of joe, but the unexpected shout startled him so badly that he slammed the carafe down on the marble countertop. Hot coffee and glass went flying. So did all hope of breaking his swearing habit. "Damn!" he bellowed when his skin was doused with the coffee. "Damn it to hell!"

Matthew's outburst woke up Eric. He was at Matthew's side almost immediately. "What happened?" Eric asked as he swiped at his sleepy eyes.

Matthew waved his hands in the air, trying to calm himself. "You yelled out like some maniac, and I burned myself! That's what happened!"

After Eric surveyed the damage, he looked repentant. "I must have been having a nightmare and shouted in my sleep! I'm sorry!"

Matthew hated being out of control with more passion than he hated anything else. It was important to remain unemotional in his line of work. He tried to do some deep breathing, but his hands hurt. Then the fear kicked in. How severe were the burns? Would he be able to operate again and when?

While Matthew was figuring out if his future was at risk, he was being guided over to the sink.

Eric turned on the taps and gave Matthew instructions. "Keep your hands under the cold water."

Matthew obeyed, knowing it was sound medical advice. He also tried to be a little more optimistic, but he didn't get very far. His painful hands and his fears ganged up on him. Some crazy thoughts slipped out. "I think this house is cursed," he mumbled. "There's a chance none of us will make it out alive."

Eric didn't respond, but his face was a picture of concern.

Matthew cleared his throat. From all that he'd observed, Eric didn't fit the description of the bad guy that Matthew had once imagined. He was a person who had tried to be there for Lea. Matthew let out a heavy breath. "Anyway, Eric, I want to say that I'm sorry. I'm sorry for everything. I wish I knew a way to prove it, but hell, at the rate this bumpy ride is going, I probably won't survive 'til morning."

Eric glanced at him, paused and burst out laughing. "Matthew, I've known a few pouters in my time, but you're really convincing."

Matthew stared at his hands. Still red, they were sticking out of his ill-fitting robe, looking like he'd crawled out of the lobster pot. He sighed. "Lea used to call me a pouter and laugh at me too."

Eric stepped back. "I'm sure it was very difficult when she—"

"When she ran off and ruined my life? Yes, it was a little rough. But that didn't give me an excuse to turn her away."

"Why did you?"

Matthew continued to stare at his hands. "Do you know how many times I took her back? She'd throw a fit about anything. It was like something just set her off. And I'd swear that was it. No more. Relationship over. Finally, I thought that maybe she needed a commitment, something that proved she could trust what we had. So I asked her to marry me. Next thing I know, she was gone without a trace."

Eric examined Matthew's hands more closely. "Thankfully, I don't think your burns are too bad."

"Good, the way things are going, if I end up in a wheelchair, I'll be able to push myself along."

147

Eric saw Matthew's half-smile and smiled back. "I think that if we had met under different circumstances, we could have been friends."

"I'd agree and shake on that, but my hands still hurt."

"Matthew, what happened?" a voice called from the doorway.

"Dammit," Matthew groaned. For the time being, he'd thought he'd escaped Paul Glass. "Go away, Paul. Nothing to see here."

Paul seemed to be encouraged rather than deterred. He closed the distance between the doorway and the sink so quickly that Matthew startled again.

Eric saw Matthew's distress and intervened. "Don't crowd him, Paul!" he ordered. "He's had enough of your bedside manner for the night."

Paul stepped back, but he was still trying to look at Matthew's hands. "I have some salve in my bag. I got it on a trip to South America. I think it might help."

Matthew opened his mouth to protest, but Paul was already headed out of the kitchen. Matthew looked at Eric. "Listen, I'll pay you a thousand bucks if you can keep that guy and his special salve away from me."

Eric shrugged. "I could use a thousand bucks. Goodness knows Mom is going to need a lot of therapy."

Matthew's brows narrowed with concern. "Again, I apologize."

"Look, Matthew, I thought a lot about my dad and everything before I fell asleep. And I was angry at you and Paul . . . at first. But it was also a relief to know what happened. Mom's been acting weird for years. Whenever I'd ask anything about my dad and his days in Baltimore, she'd clam up. Now, maybe we'll have a chance to get past all that."

Matthew nodded. "Good."

"I'm just worried about my mom. She looked so frightened."

Matthew stiffened. "And I don't want Lea to slip away again."

"If she recovers, do you think there could be hope for the two of you?"

"I don't know. My thinking capacity has hit a new low."

"I'm back," Paul called out as he rushed into the kitchen.

Eric quickly blocked his path. "No way! Just turn around and go to bed. You have people to torture in the morning, remember?"

Paul gave him a surprised look, lingered for a moment and then turned around and left again.

Matthew smiled as he patted his hands on a clean towel. He held them up for Eric to examine. "They look pretty good."

Eric shrugged. "Yeah, but I do have some stuff in my medical bag."

"Really? That might help." Matthew started to go over burn medications in his head. "What do you have?"

Eric rubbed his chin and gave Matthew a mischievous look. "Well, this old gal in the hills, we called her Wild Nelly, and she brewed some powerful herbs—"

Matthew held up a wounded hand. "Do you want that thousand bucks or not?"

Eric grinned back. "Yes, I do. As soon as you can hold a pen properly, I'll be expecting a check."

Twenty-Three

PAUL WOKE UP and realized that Eric was shaking his shoulder. "What time is it?"

"It's time for you to do your job. Raymond wants to see you."

Paul forced himself to sit up and do a couple of shoulder rolls. He'd been in observation mode during the night. He'd hardly slept, but he had to be ready for whatever came next. He suspected that fires from the previous day were not only still blazing, they could be growing in intensity. He looked at Eric and felt somewhat encouraged. "Did you and Matthew get a chance to talk last night?"

"Matthew is a decent enough guy once you get to know him a little better. I think he cares about Lea after all."

"Good, and your Mom? How is she doing?"

"She's still in her room."

"And Lea?"

"She was very quiet this morning, and I thought it best not to engage in any conversation yet. The good news is that she doesn't seem to be terrified anymore. In fact, I was able to get her to eat some toast."

"And Matthew?"

"He's staying with her and catching up on his reading. He tried to talk to Lea, but she ignored him."

Paul went to the dresser. "Would you see if your Mom would join us at noon?"

"She won't talk to me."

"How are you doing with her attitude?"

"I guess I'm coping." Eric paused and targeted Paul with a stern grimace. "As for you, I hope you're planning on helping my mother as soon as possible."

"Believe me, I'm working on it. In the meantime, I hope that Matthew didn't fall asleep."

Eric frowned. "Matthew looked very tired this morning. What time did you have him take over?"

"Around three."

"Around three in the morning? He didn't get any sleep at all."

"I know."

Eric started for the door. "I better relieve him."

"You'll do no such thing."

"Why?"

"Because you need to check on Rita."

"Raymond's wife? The person who's responsible for—"

"You're a doctor, Eric. Act like one and check on the woman while I talk to Raymond. It's important."

"Fine, but like I said, you have to help my mother. She's punishing herself, and I can't get through to her."

"I will, but some things have to fall into place first."

"What things?"

"You'll find out soon enough. Now go, please."

* * *

Matthew knew all about all-nighters from his days as an intern. Presently, he'd been keeping an eye on Lea for most of the night. When she woke up in the morning, he tried to talk to her, but she ignored him. After a couple of attempts to communicate, he gave up. However, he couldn't help but wonder what was going through her mind.

"Minds, they're so intangible," he mumbled to himself.

Maybe that's why he worked on bodies. At least he could help a broken body, but how did he mend a broken mind? How did he remove a hellish ordeal that someone experienced as a child? The more he contemplated the issues involved, the more confused he got.

He was also agitated by his hands. They hurt every time he moved them or tried to turn the pages of his book. All in all, he felt like he was surrounded by pain in one form or another. And he was exhausted. Again.

The good news was that he expected Paul or Eric to relieve him soon. He was having trouble keeping his eyes open. He tried to read, to keep focused on a story in a book, but he started to nod off. After a brief moment, he blinked himself awake. It happened a second time. And a third.

"Matt, come to bed."

Matthew heard Lea's voice and knew it was a dream. "Be there in a minute."

"Matthew, now! Come to bed."

It was a pleasant dream. It reminded him of when they had been living together. Almost every night, they'd gone through the same routine. Lea always went to bed first. He stayed up and tried to catch up on the latest and greatest in his field.

"Matthew Howell, honey? Please come here."

He put his book aside and stood up. His eyes were half-open as he made his way to the bed. It would feel so good to let go of everything and rest. He held on to the satisfying thought as he was about to climb into bed.

"Not with your clothes on, honey. Take off your shirt and slacks."

"Yes, dear," he mumbled back. It was so strange to be sleepy in a dream, but he didn't care. He was too tired to question what was happening. After he got out of his clothes, he practically fell into the bed. Once he was settled, he felt himself being covered. Then he was wrapping his arms around Lea. It was a wonderful dream. It was so wonderful that he smiled as he drifted away from all his worries.

* * *

Raymond got up and pulled open the window curtains. After sitting all night in his chair, his body felt stiff and old, but his mind was still chugging along. It was like a mule at a grain mill. It kept going round and round hoping to reach that carrot, that place where things felt good again.

His daughter had suffered a terrible setback, and his wife had fallen so far out of his favor that he doubted he could ever forgive her. Still, it was wrong to blame Rita. He might want to shift the yoke of responsibility to her pretty shoulders, but it was his stupidity and arrogance that had turned his life into a horror show.

He'd paved the way to unhappiness thirty years earlier. After achieving the status he wanted in the business world, he decided to get married. His criteria were simple. He wanted a woman who was young and beautiful. He wanted someone he could show off. Someone who made him feel young too. And along came Rita, the perfect fit.

At first, all was wonderful. He took her to the finest Paris salons and dressed her up like a beautiful plaything. But it wasn't a one-sided affair. Rita had no problem with being fussed over. She even doted on him and made sure he could be proud of her.

Instead of being content with what he had, he wanted more, a family. Rita didn't. She liked being the only one in his life. And she made it clear that she wasn't the motherly type.

But Raymond was used to getting his way in the world, and he didn't hold back at home. Finally, Rita gave in and got pregnant. It was a very difficult birth, and she never let him forget it. In Rita's eyes, Lea was considered a source of pain from the start.

Raymond tried to work around the situation. He told Rita to hire a wet nurse for the baby. When their daughter was a little older, the wet nurse was replaced. A couple of nannies came and went, but Raymond was too busy to pay them much attention. His business was expanding, and he loved spending his time helping it grow.

When he managed to spend some time at home, he adored his baby girl, but his spare time was limited. He had a wife who was used to his full attention, and she wasn't going to give up that position in his life without a fight.

So it was easy to forget about a little girl in a nursery at the far end of the corridor. Raymond told himself that they'd do things together when Lea got older.

His attitude almost shocked him now. How could he have allowed his only child to be shepherded by people he didn't check out himself. He certainly didn't handle his business that way. He was known as a take-charge guy.

He'd sat up all night praying that Paul Glass could do something for Lea and for his conscience. Still, when he heard Paul knock and announce himself, Raymond froze. Paul had a reputation. He got results. He ferried out the chaff from the wheat better than anybody in the mind-fixing business. Raymond already knew he'd been worthless as a father. Would he have any self-respect left after Paul got through with him as a person? He had initiated their visit, but now he was afraid of what it might entail.

* * *

Paul stepped into Raymond's room, happy to see that the drapes were open. He enjoyed the morning light, and the cheeriness that it brought to the room. When he glanced at Raymond, he knew they'd need every bit of cheeriness they could get. "Morning, Raymond, you asked to see me."

Raymond hung back. "Yes, I did."

Paul waited for more of an explanation, but Raymond was clearly stuck in some powerful, emotional turmoil. They were close in age, but while Paul still felt like he was full of "piss and vinegar" as his mother used to say, Raymond looked like he was quickly giving in to time and circumstance.

Paul walked over to a glass front cabinet and looked at the collectibles it housed. "You have some interesting figurines." He paused. "The unhappy clown is thought-provoking."

"Rita wanted it for her collection. But Lea never liked clowns."

"And what about you?"

"I'm in agreement with Lea, but I'd never let Rita know that. She'd have a—" Raymond paused. "But I don't want to talk about Rita."

"Really? Why's that?"

"Dammit, Paul, you know why."

"And how are you doing with what she told you? Were you surprised?"

"Of course I was surprised!" Raymond paused again. "But what did I expect? I'm married to a child!"

"And do you want to stay married to Rita?"

"She's been my wife all these years! What am I supposed to do? Disown her now for something that happened so long ago?"

"That's up to you."

"Why did I have to insist on Rita having a baby?"

"That's a good question."

Raymond's face turned angry, and he came up with an answer himself. "It's what people do! They get married and have a family."

"Not always. Some people prefer not to have children."

"I was entitled to children. I was hoping for a boy—" Raymond stared down. "But I loved my daughter. I'm sure of it."

"Good, then you'll do everything you can to help her now."

Raymond lifted his eyes. They were stuck under hooded lids and a heavily, lined brow. "Yes! I just want to put things right."

Paul knew what Raymond was really saying. The man needed a way out of his pain. And being a man of action, he'd do just about anything to lessen that pain. "You can start by visiting your wife. I think she needs you."

"How's that going to help Lea?"

"How's it 'not' going to help her? She needs functioning parents, not guilt-ridden, frightened ones."

"I've been guilt-ridden for years. I guess I always knew I'd failed Lea, but I just didn't want to admit it. It was easier to see her as the problem." He looked up at Paul. "You must pity me, right? Self-delusional. Always in denial. Neglecting his child."

"I don't approach situations that way. I look for solutions."

Raymond blinked a few times. "Actually, that's a sound business tactic. When something goes wrong, you have to adapt, find a new way to handle things." He glanced up at Paul. "Thank you for remaining positive. Anyway, I think I'll take a shower and get dressed."

"And put on something that you'd wear to a nice business luncheon."

"A business luncheon?"

"Yes, later, when you're around Lea, it'll make you feel more like your capable, business self. And that's something Lea needs. She needs to feel like you regard her in the same way that you regard that business empire you love so much."

Raymond stood up and came forward. "I think I see what you're getting at. I've always worn two hats. The business hat and the family hat. Maybe it's time to combine the two."

Paul smiled. "Maybe it is."

* * *

Eric walked into Rita's bedroom carrying his medical bag. Taking care of Lea's negligent mother was the last thing he wanted to do. But he'd put his feelings aside. After finding out more about his father's past, he certainly didn't want to allow his emotions to overrule his medical duties. Doctors were there to protect lives and to do whatever they could to encourage healing.

He glanced at the woman who was sitting in the bed. When she looked up and saw him, he offered a brisk greeting. "Good morning, Mrs. Ferguson."

Rita didn't say anything. She started crying. Her eyes were already red and swollen, but she still seemed to have an abundance of tears. Finally, she sobbed out a few words. "You hate me, don't you!"

The way Rita Ferguson screamed out the question took Eric by surprise. He had to quickly remind himself that the person in his care wasn't rational. He turned to face her, ignoring her question. "How are you feeling today?"

"Don't give me that!" Rita sobbed again. "I know what's going on! Everyone thinks I'm a witch! Maybe I am! So go ahead, hate me all you want!"

Eric paused. As much as he wanted to agree with Rita, he couldn't ignore a person who was suffering. "I'm sorry if—"

"Sorry, for what? I saw you when we flew to Baltimore. You're some golden boy with a sweet momma. And Lea adores you! As much as she hates me, she thinks you're so wonderful!"

"And I feel the same way about her, Mrs. Ferguson. I'd think you'd understand that since you're her mother."

"I never wanted to be her mother! I pleaded with Raymond to leave me alone! But he wouldn't stop." She took a gasping breath. "So I gave in. I had that wretched child after forty six hours of labor! Afterwards, I was so torn up inside that I didn't think the pain would ever go away." She looked up at Eric again. "That doctor should have let me bleed to death. Isn't that what you're thinking? Well, maybe he should have. Then I wouldn't be sitting here waiting for the devil to collect his dues."

Eric paused. He had to take a few breaths. As Rita was waiting for the devil to collect his dues, he had to collect his thoughts. They were scattered from a Chicago suburbs all the way back to the hills where he'd grown up.

When he went on calls with his father, he'd witnessed so many births. Women in pain, always in pain. Now he realized that Rita might have suffered even more than those women. Most of those women in the hills felt better after a child was born. They loved that child as much as poverty and lack of resources would allow. But Rita wasn't like that.

Eric walked over and sat down in the chair by the side of Rita's bed. "Why did you hate the idea of children?"

Rita pulled her cover up to her chin. "I've always hated them, from the time I was just a kid myself. They're wretched little creatures. Always screaming. You can't get away from them no matter how much you want to. Then it starts." Her eyes drifted as her body shuddered. She took breaths, sucking in air in little gasps.

"It starts? What do you mean by that?"

Rita's head slowly turned in Eric's direction. Her eyes grew darker and wary, as if she needed to warn him about some danger she'd seen. Her voice dropped to a whisper. "Every day, their cries get weaker. The sounds they make are so horrible. I hate those sounds. I still hear them in my dreams. Why can't they just shut up?" She put her hands over her ears and began to rock herself. "Then one day you look in that crate where they're kept and—"

Eric leaned forward, feeling like he wasn't just a doctor. He was Rita's confessor. "Please, tell me what you see in that crate?"

Rita twisted her body, rubbing her head on her shoulder. "Nothing. It's empty. It's empty 'til the next one comes along."

* * *

Eric left Rita's room hoping the sedative he gave her would help her to sleep. Perhaps, for a few hours, she could forget about the devil that was after her. When he thought about her future, he shuddered himself. Rita was going to need more counseling than his mother. And even with counseling, something in his gut told him that the woman might never recover from what she'd witnessed as a child.

He rubbed the sweat from his brow. "Matthew was right. This place is cursed!"

He had to steady his thoughts and find Paul Glass, the expert. He'd bring him up to date on what he'd just been privy to. He'd also find out what Paul had in mind as far as a plan. Hopefully, they could still save Lea from the demons that roamed the halls of the Ferguson mansion.

When Eric couldn't locate Paul, he sent the man a long text, explaining the gist of what he'd learned while talking to Rita. Paul wanted all the information he could get. And from what Eric had just learned from Rita, a more complete picture was falling into place.

Eric's next thought was about Matthew. He hoped Paul had relieved the surgeon. If not, he knew he better step in and take over. When he got to Lea's room, he opened the door without knocking. If Lea had gone back to sleep, he didn't want to disturb her.

"What in the hell!" Eric yelled out his shock before he could stop himself. He was in full-out brother mode as he continued to yell. "Howell, what are you doing sleeping with Lea when she's in the state she's in?"

Matthew came awake instantly, rubbed his eyes and stared into space. "What is it? Who's gone crazy this time?"

A moment later, Lea sat up. She'd obviously been in Matthew's arms. When she blinked around the room and saw Eric, she frowned. "Eric Lloyd, please stop yelling. Matthew and I were once engaged, remember?"

Eric knew his mouth was hanging open. Matthew looked just as confused. His eyes were completely dazed as if he'd been jettisoned into outer space.

Lea seemed to be the only one who was okay with the situation. Still frowning, she made a little shooing gesture in Eric's direction. "Eric, stop standing there gawking. Give us some privacy, thank you."

Eric backed up and quickly closed the door. He tried to process what he'd just seen and heard, but it didn't make sense. He definitely had to find Paul Glass now.

* * *

Matthew figured he was still dreaming. But it was the most lucid dream he'd ever had. It was only when Lea ran her hand over his chest that something clicked. He reached up, touched her hand and verbalized his surprise. "Oh hell, I'm not dreaming."

Lea seemed oblivious to his situation. "Matthew, what happened to your beautiful hands? They're all red."

Matthew didn't know what to do next. Lea was talking to him. That was the good part. But she was acting as if the past year of their separation had never happened. Questions started popping up so quickly that he decided not to do anything. Maybe it was best just to remain as still as possible and see what happened next.

Lea carefully pulled one of his hands towards her and examined it more closely. "Matthew, when did this happen to you? Does it hurt much?"

"Yes, it hurts," he mumbled. He tried to gather up his thoughts, but his mind felt useless. He'd always heard the expression a "deer in the headlights." Now he knew how the poor animal felt.

Lea was his opposite. She sighed contentedly. "I love your hands. They're strong and very well proportioned."

"I like them too," he gasped. He didn't know why, but he was starting to panic, saying crazy stuff and taking in more than a reasonable amount of oxygen. He couldn't keep up with the way reality kept changing, the way Lea kept changing.

Lea returned his hand and peeked at him, trying to get a better look at his face. "Matt, you seemed so tired earlier. Now, you look very stressed."

He blinked back and tried to smile. "I'm okay."

"Just try to relax. Maybe you can go back to sleep."

"Yes, that's probably a good idea." Matthew kept his tone even, but he was praying that Eric had gone to get Paul Glass. He didn't want to make a wrong move with Lea. What if he sent her spiraling into craziness again? Not only that, he needed someone to rescue him. The way his breath was heaving in and out, he might start hyperventilating at any moment.

"Matthew?"

"Yes?"

"We haven't made love in a long time. Do you ever miss being with me?"

Matthew knew his voice was failing when he tried to answer. He took in more breaths, more air. A knock on the door interrupted the moment. When the door opened, Paul looked in on them. "Hello, anybody home?"

Matthew exhaled deeply and gave thanks. He'd never been one to beseech a higher power too frequently, but he knew he was going to give the idea more consideration.

Twenty-Four

AS MARGARET WAS confronted by another day in the Ferguson mansion, she still couldn't bring herself to face Eric or anyone else for that matter. For most of her adult life, she'd been carrying around a secret. How could she let her son find out the truth about his father? That was the question she had asked herself every time her burden got too heavy. Now, she knew that carrying that burden was all for nothing.

Earlier in the morning, when she refused to talk to Eric or to discuss the current situation, he'd done what he thought was helpful. He told her about what he'd witnessed with his father when he was a boy. As she tried to process that horrendous piece of news, he went on to say that Doctor Glass was kind enough to fill him in on his father's entire past, even the part about his father losing his license in Maryland. His statements left Margaret dumbstruck.

"I've been such a fool," she hissed.

She continued to pace the length of the large bedroom she'd been given. The Ferguson mansion was the last place she wanted to be, but she couldn't even leave her room. She was too embarrassed. She felt trapped and didn't know what to do next. Some rapid knocks on her door made her sigh with weariness.

"Mom? It's Eric."

"Go away, Eric, please."

"Mom, something's happened with Lea."

Margaret quickly opened the door just a crack. "Lea? Is she okay?"

"Yes, I wanted to tell you that she's doing much better."

"Really?" Margaret took a deep breath. "Are you sure?"

"Yes, I think she's coming back to us."

Margaret stared back, barely able to process the good news with her own pain so close. "I'm so happy to hear that, but—"

Eric carefully pushed the door open a little more. "Please, we need to talk."

"I'm sorry, but I'm too ashamed—"

"Ashamed? Why?"

Margaret shrugged. How could she explain anything? When she thought about her life and the choices that she'd made, it was too much for her. She couldn't make sense out of any of it. And she didn't know how to go forward.

Eric tipped up her chin and brought her eyes in line with his own. "The only thing I know is that you've always tried to be the best mother any son could hope for."

"But that's not how I see myself, Eric!"

"Maybe not, but you and Teresa and Lea are the most important people in the world to me. I don't think I could draw breath if something happened to any of you. I love you. Don't you understand that?"

"I love you too, and no matter what you might think, your dad was—" She bit her lip, trying not to cry again. It was so painful to think that the man she'd loved and still loved was anything less than a good man.

Eric took her hand. "Come with me. Let's take a walk in the garden. I think we could both use some fresh air."

* * *

Eric's suggestion ended up being a good one for Margaret. After they spent time strolling through the gardens, she felt better, even hopeful. When Eric talked about Lea's turnaround, Margaret's own world felt brighter too. But once they were back in the house and walking towards Lea's bedroom, she hesitated.

"Eric, you've been so understanding about everything, but what about Lea? She knows the secret I've been keeping, too."

Eric hugged her shoulder. "No matter what, I'm sure that Lea loves you and wants to see you."

"That might not be a good idea. All this time I've been telling her things, all the good things. What if she thinks I've been trying to deceive her?"

"Stop torturing yourself," Eric said as he took her arm and tugged her forward. When they got to Lea's room, he stopped. "Try to relax a little."

"I don't know," Margaret protested. She pulled away, suddenly letting her shame overwhelm her again. "Maybe I should wait."

Eric knocked on the door. "Trust me. I know Lea."

Before Margaret could respond, the door opened and Lea stared out. She had her hair combed, and she looked her pretty self again. "Mom, I've been worried about you."

Margaret clasped her hands. "I've been worried about you, too."

Lea threw open the door and came forward. With a broad smile, she threw her arms around Margaret. "It's so good to see you."

"Really?"

"Of course. You might not be my birth mother, but you're still 'mom' to me. That will never change."

Eric smiled and backed up a few steps. "I'm sure the two of you have a lot to talk about, so I'll go check on Paul and Matthew."

Margaret could see that Eric was still tired after everything he'd been through recently. "Yes, why don't you relax for a while," she added.

* * *

Lea was grateful to have Margaret sitting across from her. They were having lunch in her room. Being together brought back memories of all the happy times they'd had in Baltimore. "Can I talk to you about something?"

Margaret looked up from her soup and smiled back. "You know you can. Whatever you want to discuss, I'm here for you."

Lea grabbed her napkin and quickly patted her mouth. "Maybe I should start with our trip to Chicago. As you know, things didn't work out with my parents. So I went to see Matthew. But that didn't go well either. It was horrible."

Margaret put her spoon aside and sat back. "I'm sorry I couldn't help."

Lea paused and twisted her napkin. "I wanted to run away from everything after that. I remember rocking, hoping to shut it all out. But then I looked up, and there was Eric."

"He cares about you, my dear. He came here as soon as he could."

"It was such a relief to see him. I was in a very dark place, but when I caught a glimpse of his eyes, they were full of light. All I wanted to do was reach out to him. He was so welcoming and kind. And he kept telling me that I didn't do anything wrong."

"It's true, you didn't. Whatever upset your mother and dad wasn't your fault."

Lea put her napkin aside and nodded. "Eric helped me to understand that. As I listened to him, my mind began to clear. No matter who I was before you took me in, I knew I wasn't that person anymore. When I recalled what happened with Rita, I knew that I desperately wanted to help her, not make her cry."

Margaret reached out for her hand and patted it. "You don't know how wonderful it is to hear that."

"But it's strange."

"What's strange?"

"My diary made some things very clear about how scared I once was. I think my mother and the old me shared some terrible fear. Rita called it the devil."

Margaret stared at her lap. "Fear goes by many names, but in the end, it robs people of their lives." When she looked up, she frowned. "I was so worried that it would take you away from us."

"I guess it almost did, but both you and Eric keep making sure that doesn't happen, don't you?"

"You're our precious Lea. Eric and I would do anything to keep you safe."

"Eric made me feel like that. As the hours passed, something happened, it's like all the pain started to fade away, and I fell asleep." She laughed. "Goodness, I feel like I was dozing forever after that."

"Oh, I think Doctor Glass gave you something to make you sleep yesterday. He thought it might help you recuperate after all that you went through."

"Maybe that was a good thing. This morning I woke up feeling different. The darkness was gone."

Margaret gasped. "My goodness!"

Lea's eyes flickered in a shy sort of way. "Seeing Matthew in my room was a surprise. I couldn't imagine why he'd be here after the words we'd had at his office. But I found myself glancing at him, thinking about our recent interaction. Then I had another flash of clarity. When I went to see him, I was the old me, so full of fear. Matthew didn't know how to handle the situation any more than I knew how to handle Rita's outburst."

"I suppose that makes sense."

"Yes, but he didn't run away like I did. He came here."

"I think he wants to help too."

"When I saw him in his chair, and how he kept glancing up to check on me, I realized how happy his presence made me."

Margaret leaned forward. "What happened after that?"

Lea giggled. "Matthew started looking so pathetic. He kept falling asleep and waking himself up. And it's almost like I remembered seeing him that way before."

"What do you mean?"

"I'm not sure, but I think some of my memories came back."

Margaret's eyes sparkled brightly. "Your memories? Really?"

"I had this warm feeling inside. I felt so happy that I did something without thinking."

"Yes?"

"I told Matthew to come to bed." Lea paused. "I didn't even think about it. The words just slipped out."

"The point is that you trusted what you felt, and you acted on it."

"I wanted Matthew to hold me and when he took me in his arms, I felt like we belonged together." She glanced up at Margaret bashfully. "It was totally different than Eric holding me."

Margaret laughed. "I understand."

"Later, when Eric came into my bedroom, everything was dreamy. I didn't want anything or anyone to spoil the feeling I had being with Matthew. Still, as I came back to myself, I realized that my feelings and reality were mixed up. And Matthew's face seconded the motion. He looked very uncomfortable being in bed with me."

Margaret hesitated. "Honey, what are you trying to say?"

"Was it wrong to want him next to me? When I think about it all now, and how Matthew didn't want a relationship anymore, maybe I acted inappropriately."

"I wish I had the answers, but what I do know is that Matthew still cares deeply about you."

"Do you think so?"

"Lea, you woke up and felt good. That's what's important."

Lea looked away. "If only my memories would really come back—"

"Dearest, let me tell you something. If I had a choice, to remember everything or to just enjoy the good parts, I'd happily choose the latter."

"Would you?"

Margaret let out a bitter laugh. "Yes, I'd consider myself blessed. Take it from one who knows, memories are overrated."

* * *

Paul Glass and Matthew Howell met in one of the Ferguson's many spare bedrooms. Paul understood the surgeon's pleading gaze. When Matthew woke up in Lea's bed, it scared him. Matthew had been at a total loss when it came to knowing what to do about the situation.

Paul patted Matthew's arm reassuringly. "Well, Matthew, things have already turned out better than expected."

Matthew's green eyes flared with fresh anger. "Better? How can you say that things are better?"

"Lea's made progress. She looked happy this morning. Isn't that a good thing?"

"She's still delusional, Paul. But what happens when her 'happy' bubble bursts?"

"Why should it burst?"

"She's living in the past. She's gone back to a time when we were engaged."

"Not true. When I spoke with her this morning, she was totally aware of the time she'd spent with the Lloyd family. And from what I've gathered, they helped her to find ways to enjoy being herself. When she was with you this morning, her behavior was in line with what she'd learned. I'd say things are looking up."

"But what am I supposed to do with her? She's even mentioned the idea of making love. How am I supposed to work around that if she gets more insistent?"

"You're smart. You can suggest other things you could do."

"Like what?"

"What did you do when you were living together?"

Matthew shrugged. "We had dinner, watched something on the tube or read, and then we went to bed." Matthew hesitated and ran a hand through his hair. "Talking about it, I guess our life was pretty boring."

"So now is the time to find new ways to be with each other. You could take her for a ride in the country or go for a walk in the park."

"What if we're strolling through that park you're talking about and Lea freaks out again?"

"Call me. You'll find my number in a text I sent you."

"How did you send me a text? You don't have my information."

Paul grinned. "I certainly do. I got it from Raymond when I arrived. I also know that you once liked to bowl and that you're crazy about certain kinds of French pastries."

"Was all of that in Raymond's report?"

"No, of course not. You're using an old bowling alley slip as a bookmark. And as for the French pastries, you passed up every dessert at the little buffet we had last night. Then you spied a Napoleon pastry and your eyes lit up in spite of your otherwise poor appetite."

Matthew backed up a few steps. "You don't miss anything."

"I can't afford to miss anything, not in my line of work. Helping people through their mental constraints and faulty belief systems requires diligence and staying power."

"About that staying power, why didn't you relieve me this morning? I ended up in Lea's bed because I couldn't keep my eyes open."

Paul winked back. "Yes, everything worked out perfectly. And let's admit it, Matthew, waking up with your arms around a beautiful woman is rather nice."

"Are you saying that you planned what happened and that you were watching us?"

"It would be negligent if I didn't keep an eye on things. Fortunately, there are hidden cameras in several places in the room. Raymond had them installed when he was spying on some business people."

"How did you know Lea would want me sleeping next to her?"

"I didn't, but after Eric left Lea, she seemed very peaceful. I hoped that having you close would be helpful too." Paul shrugged. "And when it came to your condition, I figured you would be too exhausted to think about anything but going to sleep. So you'd be completely unthreatening. Oh, and there was that other thing."

"What thing?"

"I observed what was happening with Lea on the closed-circuit display. This morning, Lea kept glancing over at you with that look in her eye."

"A look? What's a look got to do with anything?"

Paul smiled. "You'd be surprised how much a look can hold. But I've practiced for years to hone that skill."

Before Matthew could comment, Paul's phone chirped, and he answered it. "Yes, I see. Please meet Matthew and me in the library, and we'll take it from there."

"Who are we meeting?" Matthew asked.

"That was Eric. He says that Lea and Margaret are chatting over lunch." Paul paused, looked at his watch and frowned. "Oh my, I forgot."

"I don't like your tone, Paul."

"No, it's fine. I just have to meet Raymond in Rita's room."

"Rita's room?"

Paul nodded. "Yes, Eric only gave her a very light sedative. It should be wearing off about now. So I think it might be a perfect time for the couple to reevaluate their relationship."

"Doctor Glass, may I remind you that you're juggling a lot of lives right now. I hope you don't drop any."

"Don't worry. I was in the circus once. Juggling was my specialty."

Matthew winced. "You're right. I need to get out of here for a while. Unfortunately, Raymond sent his chauffeur to pick me up the other morning. I don't have my car here."

Paul reached into his pocket. "Here, take my keys and use mine. You and Eric both need some space, so take him with you. Go to your apartment and pick up your car, some clothes and proper sleepwear. Eric can drive my car back."

"You want me to spend another night here?"

Paul crossed his arms. "Oh yes, I know I've pointed out all the positives, but we have to keep the momentum going."

167

Matthew crossed his arms too. "And what is the goal of that momentum, Paul? I don't think you ever made that clear."

Paul laughed. "Heavens, I don't have a clue. That's why I love my job. There's mystery and magic in every case, but outcomes are never predictable. Anyway, I can't stay and chat. I have to see a man about his wife."

* * *

Raymond had been staring out the window of Rita's bedroom for at least ten minutes, waiting for Paul Glass. He'd always liked the view, but he barely focused on the gardens or the pond. He'd been informed that Lea was better, and that was wonderful news. Hopefully, his daughter would continue to improve, but what about Raymond's marriage. When he'd lost his connection to Lea years before, Rita was the person he depended on for emotional support.

He turned and stared at his wife. Rita was sleeping, but not peacefully. Her pretty face was spoiled by a deeply troubled brow and the turned-down set of her mouth. Many years before, she'd had a worse expression when she told Raymond she was pregnant. She'd agreed to a child, but when she knew she was actually going to have a baby, her outrage was so violent that the household staff ran for cover. The thought of that terrible time made Raymond rub his chest, hoping his angina didn't act up.

A wave of relief followed when Paul Glass knocked lightly and entered the room. That relief didn't last once Raymond gauged what he was dealing with. Paul Glass embodied a number of diverse elements. Take the Mona Lisa's smile, mix in the Laughing Buddha's wisdom and combine them with the tenacity of a Jack Russel terrier. The good doctor used all of those elements in his approach to his job.

Unfortunately, Raymond sensed that he was facing the Jack Russell. Paul Glass had gone easy on him earlier in the day, now Paul's face couldn't hide his need to flush out the rabbit in the hole. And Raymond knew he was that rabbit.

Of course, Jack Russell terriers are very smart dogs. They don't always come at a problem straight on. In this case, after Paul's friendly greeting, he began to question Raymond.

"Did you get my last text, Raymond? I asked you to bring your medication with you. Can you let me see what you're taking? Toss me the bottles."

Raymond dug in his pocket, produced a couple of vials and threw them, one at a time, over to where Paul was standing just inside the door. "You said to bring my heart meds, right?"

Paul examined the prescriptions. "Yes, that's right. By the way, I'm looking at these prescriptions and wondering."

Raymond didn't like the tone of Paul's voice. There was a tinge of concern. "Wondering what?"

"Any adverse side effects?"

"Nothing I haven't discussed with my doctor."

"Right," Paul sighed. "By the way, how are you feeling with everything that's happened recently?"

"How do you think I'm feeling? I'm stressed."

"Yes, of course you are."

Raymond tightened his jaw. "Is there anything else, Paul?"

Paul glanced up and smiled, but he didn't answer. He went back to studying a label on one of the medications.

As the moments passed, Raymond felt his resentment take hold. He didn't need more aggravation in his life, but Paul seemed intent on being deliberately annoying. It started after their morning conversation. Paul had texted Raymond, suggesting a time for him to visit with Lea. Raymond looked forward to the meeting. It would be a relief to see his daughter looking better. However, a few minutes before the scheduled time, Raymond got a text from Paul postponing the get-together. There was no explanation given. Now, Glass was being evasive about Raymond's medication.

Raymond broke the silence. He needed some answers. "What's going on, Paul? Is there something wrong with what I'm taking?"

Paul shrugged. "I didn't say that."

Raymond rubbed his chest. "Just what the hell are you saying?"

A loud moan came from the bed. Raymond's raised voice had woken up Rita.

In their last talk, Raymond's wife had issued numerous, teary apologies. Now, he prepared himself for more teary pleas for forgiveness. However, after Rita blinked a couple of times and her eyes came to rest on him, they were anything but apologetic. They were dark and filled with unbridled fury. Raymond took a step back.

Rita had come from the poorest of slums, but she'd once told Raymond about a relative who'd had a very different lifestyle. Her mother's brother, Rita's uncle, had never migrated to America. He remained in Spain. The uncle was a proud man. When his sister, Rita's mother, married a cook's assistant working on an American cargo vessel, he disowned her.

The uncle had a colorful career. He was a much admired matador who flaunted his good looks in the bullring. His level of elegance and his fearless approach earned him many awards. He had been gored a number of times, but after he recovered, he always went back for more. All in all, the bulls didn't fare well. The man finally retired with honors, enjoying the fact that he'd won out in the end.

Raymond stared at his wife, the matador's niece, and felt a tremor take hold. His bride had changed completely since their last meeting. Rita was letting him know that he wasn't facing a sniveling woman-child anymore. Her aggressive scowl told him that she'd inherited her uncle's blood. And that blood was stirring, growing hot in her veins as she glared back at him.

When Rita spoke, her voice wasn't overly loud. It was more like a low growl. "You good-for-nothing! You're the one responsible for this hell I'm in!"

Raymond remained silent and watchful as Rita's eyes became fiery orbs, and she began to slowly dig her nails into her sheets. He knew that he was in for a battle. He was entering the ring, an old bull facing a slender matador who wanted to drive a sword deep into his soul.

Before Raymond decided on how to respond, Paul spoke up from his place by the door.

"Raymond, I better let you and your wife talk things over. But before I go, here are your medications."

Raymond caught the first bottle that Paul tossed his way. He missed the second one and reached down to grab it before it rolled under the bed. By the time he got hold of the bottle, Paul was gone.

Raymond started to get up and saw Rita glowering down. As he was getting his feet under him, she used her foot to push him over.

"I should have tied you to the bed when you got drunk. I should have made you suffer like I've suffered."

Raymond recovered enough to scurry away from the bed. "What's got into you? I thought you loved me?"

"And I thought you'd always be there for me. But I was a fool. In the end, it's always about you."

Raymond stared. "I took care of you. I gave you everything. I treated you like royalty!"

"Yes, you gave me everything, but what I needed."

"And what was that?"

"The ability to say 'no' to you."

* * *

After Paul closed the door, he remained outside of Rita's room and listened in on the couple's argument. He'd be there to intervene if things took a turn towards physical violence. As it was, the couple was having a 'discussion' that bordered on someone being murdered. That someone was Raymond.

But Rita's loud expletives and threats of harming her husband were necessary. After Paul read Eric's text, he had enough information to know that Rita's childhood was very bleak. The idea of children petrified her. After she married Raymond, she'd been forced into something she abhorred. She'd had a child of her own. It was a role she couldn't face or embrace. As the years passed, she had bottled up her feelings. In the current situation, she'd even allowed Raymond to put all the blame for Lea's condition on her shoulders.

Fortunately, after Eric's visit, Rita's contained rage had surfaced. After practically sleepwalking through life, Rita was beginning to function again. Now, she needed to express her feelings verbally.

Paul left his station when Rita finally began to calm down. He knew that she'd worn herself out. After confining herself to bed for days, her body tired quickly.

From the sounds that Raymond made, he'd survived too. He probably had a very bruised ego and a mild attack of angina, but he'd come through in one piece. For the moment, it would have to be enough. Years of dysfunction couldn't be mended in one blowout. When Paul thought about the couple's future, he wouldn't make any predictions. Still, he hoped that Raymond was prudent, and that he'd keep his pills handy at all times.

Twenty-Five

MATTHEW SAT BEHIND the wheel of the sporty, black Audi coupe. He hadn't pictured Paul owning such a high-end, high-performance vehicle. Taking it out for a spin was an unexpected pleasure. But when he glanced over at his passenger, he could see that Eric wasn't thinking about the car. "So Eric, how did it go with Rita earlier?"

Eric returned a sideways glance. His blue eyes were narrowed slits as if the sunny rays bathing his face were painful. "If you want my opinion, I'd have to say that the woman is one of the cursed that you talked about."

"What do you mean?"

Eric waved him off and laid his head back. "Please, I don't want to talk about her. If you're interested, Paul can tell you more about the situation."

"What about your mother? You've worked things out with her, right?"

Eric rubbed his temples. "Mom's tricky. She can act like all is fine and dandy. Then when she's alone, she retreats and starts worrying."

"It's strange. When I first met your family, you all looked pretty content. I didn't buy it for a minute, but still, it would be nice to think somebody on this earth is happy."

"I'm very fortunate to have Teresa. She doesn't seem to have any big hang ups. Plus, she was great about taking care of any emergencies with my patients while I'm here.

"Sounds like you're very fortunate indeed."

172

Eric sighed. "I wish you felt that way about Lea. I know you never saw the side of her that I have, but she really is amazing."

Matthew kept his eyes on the road, but he could feel his face getting flush. "I might have been privy to that side of her this morning."

Eric frowned back. "She was doing very well while she was living with Mom and me. Then you called and gave me the news about who Lea really was." He rubbed at his temples again. "It scared the hell out of me when I thought I might be handing her over to a maniac."

"Yes, I remember that call. When I heard that Southern drawl you have, all I could think is that some down-home crazy had gotten hold of the woman I loved."

Eric sat up attentively. "Do I still have that much of an accent? I've really worked on it."

"I'm sure it's not as bad as Wild Nelly's, but you don't sound like you came from New York."

"Maybe you were right to worry about me. I do have my father's blood in my veins. I might lose it someday."

Matthew laughed. "Don't worry about it. I've seen you angry. It doesn't require much muscle to take you out."

"Dammit, you decked me pretty good."

Matthew flexed his hand. "I have to be more careful. I can't afford to damage myself."

"That's the trouble with surgeons, they have a superiority complex."

"You can criticize me all you want, but surgeons need a superiority complex." He glanced over at Eric. "Would you want to switch jobs?"

Eric's blue eyes sparked a little as his voice turned playful. "Tarnation, Doc Howell, their'n those who oprate and theys who don't. Thang is, I don't have y'alls skills."

Matthew's brows arched with surprise when Eric went country on him. But after recent events, it was nice to relax a little. He even found himself joining in with the banter. "Tarnation, Doc Lloyd, seeins how you speaks the words so dang good, no wonder y'all was scarier than hell."

Instead of laughing, Eric returned a serious glance. "This damnable headache is getting worse."

Matthew knew all about headaches. "You just shush now, boy, soon we be fetchin yorn an aspirin at my place."

Matthew's attempt to lighten the mood seemed to affect Eric in an unexpected way. He suddenly jerked upright in his seat. "Oh goodness!" he called out in alarm.

Matthew went on instant alert and gripped the wheel. "What is it?"

"I just had a flash."

"Like a migraine coming on?"

"No."

"Vision impairment? You're not having a stroke, are you?"

"No, it's the gift."

Matthew found Eric's reaction unsettling. The man went from barely moving to being very animated. "I hate to say this, Southern boy, but Santa isn't coming by for quite a while."

"I'm serious. I was told I have this special gift."

"By Wild Nelly?"

Eric gave Matthew a forlorn look. "Yes, as a matter of fact, it was Nelly. Anyway, I get these flashes of the future. And when you told me to 'shush,' I saw you holding a baby. It was so vivid."

"A sick baby? I don't operate on—"

"No!" Eric said insistently. "It was your baby, yours and Lea's. And I saw a toddler too. He was tall and his pouty face reminded me of you."

"The curse," Matthew groaned. "It's still with us." He pushed down on the accelerator. "I've got to get you that medication. At the rate you're going with your so-called flashes, you'll have me in a rocking chair with a ten-year-old grandchild on my lap."

"You might think I'm crazy, but a lot of what I've seen has come true."

"Great, just what I want to hear," Matthew protested. "Now I'm getting a headache, you hillbilly psychic. From now on, keep your gifts to yourself!"

Eric went back to rubbing his temples. "Sorry, I didn't mean to upset you."

"Well, you did!" Matthew yelled back. The thought of marriage had been a big step for him. He wasn't prepared to think about a family too, especially with his current situation with Lea. He was instantly overwhelmed.

174

Eric stood in Lea's bedroom staring at Lea with guilt and embarrassment. He was happy to see her looking better, but that didn't help to soften her tone or what she'd been telling him. "I'm sorry, Lea. I never meant any harm."

Lea frowned back. "You two were out for a short ride in the car, Eric. And in that time, you managed to break my Matthew."

"I didn't exactly break him. He's just in bed with a bad headache."

"Oh, he's broken alright. Have you seen his face? He looks like he's been attacked by Rita's entire clown collection. And she must have a minimum of five hundred, scary clowns."

"Please, I never thought this would happen."

Paul Glass walked into the room scowling. "I'm a little taken back. Most people are very responsive to my acupressure treatments. I'm very well-versed in the practice, but Matthew's headache just kept getting worse."

"Don't give him any more pills," Eric said. "I had to grab the bottle out of his hand when he started acting like they were popcorn. He still managed to swallow more than the recommended dose."

"Should I check on him?" Lea asked.

Paul shrugged. "I think he needs quiet. So maybe we should let him rest."

Eric reached out for Lea. "Could you find my mom and keep her company. I'm worried about her, and I'd prefer if she wasn't alone."

Lea started out of the room. "Of course, I will, but you have to stay away from Matthew."

"I understand," Eric called back.

Once Lea was gone, Eric grabbed Paul's arm. "Is Lea right? Did I break Matthew?"

"It's more like that proverbial straw. Matthew Howell is a strong man, and he would never admit it, but he's probably more sensitive than you think. Most doctors are. But to be a surgeon, a sensitive person usually has to put up some heavy-duty walls, otherwise he couldn't do his job. Now, after all that's happened, Matthew's walls are crumbling. When you mentioned family to a man who's probably got serious father issues, he panicked."

"That's just great. Lea was right," Eric sighed. "So how do we fix him?"

"I haven't figured that out yet. There are still too many variables. However, there is a bright spot in it all. Having someone to love and care for, namely Matthew, is helping Lea reinforce her own recovery."

Eric stumbled over to an armchair and slumped down. "Still, I can't stop thinking that Matthew's got a gift too."

Paul looked intrigued. "What kind of gift?"

"He seems to be some kind of fortune teller. That night he burned his hands, he was relieved that the burns weren't bad. He said he'd need them."

"Of course he needs them. He's a surgeon."

"No, that's not it. He talked about pushing himself around in a wheel chair."

Paul laughed. "He's not that broken."

"I guess the good news is that Lea is better, but I don't understand it. She looked so bad when I first got here."

"True, but think about her trauma as something akin to a stroke. Early treatment helps a lot. If you can find a way to ease the blocks of fear and uncertainty quickly, there's a chance of getting the mind functioning again. In Lea's case, she's doing well. She's reestablished a connection to herself, at least certain aspects of herself."

Eric frowned. "When Mom said we lost her, I wouldn't let myself believe it."

"Eric, be proud. You and your mother gave Lea the foundation she needed for a faster recovery. Anyway, I don't have time to talk about it now. I have to make my rounds."

"Your rounds?"

"Yes, Matthew isn't the only one whose walls are crumbling," Paul said as he started for the door. Halfway there, he hesitated. When he turned back to Eric, he smiled. "And Eric, please stay focused on the present and making your best use of it. It'll help if you start on that downward slide that Matthew mentioned."

* * *

Eric couldn't help himself. After he made sure that no one would see him, he let himself into Matthew's room. If Lea was right, and he broke Matthew, he was pretty sure he could fix him. He hadn't felt that way earlier, but when another of his gifts kicked in, he changed his mind.

Matthew's room lay in deep shadows and gloom. Eric glanced around and had to immediately calm his breath. The antique furniture surely originated in times when wars were fought with armor and swords and blood ran deep on the fields of battle. Now that past and its violent nature seemed to fill the space. The room would never be a place of rest or comfort.

Eric came forward, half-expecting to see a knight lying in the bed. But this warrior, named Matthew, was clearly wounded. His eyes were shut tight and he wore a grimace of pain.

"You look like hell," Eric gasped.

A groan came from the bed. "What do you want, Eric?"

Eric walked over to the massive, poster bed. "Give me a minute to adjust. This place gives me the creeps."

"Please, go, now. Just talking to you is making the pain worse. And I'm already way beyond my pain threshold."

Eric cleared his throat. "That's why I'm here. I'm going to help you."

"Mr. Know-It-All has already tried."

Eric didn't answer. Instead he put a hand on either side of Matthew's brow and said a silent prayer.

* * *

Matthew didn't want any visitors. He could barely tolerate the insistent Paul Glass and his healing techniques. Now, Eric, the man who thought himself capable of forecasting Matthew's future was back. The day wasn't getting any better.

However, Matthew hadn't expected Eric to be so forward in his attempt to practice the art of healing. Matthew's eyes were still closed when he felt Eric grab hold of his head. He wanted to protest, but he never got a chance. There was an immediate jolt of current that interrupted his thoughts. After that, everything turned dreamlike.

His mind, that steady component of reality, seemed to slip out of its tormented state. His awareness floated free. After suffering from blinding pain that wouldn't allow for the slightest movement, he felt better than he'd ever felt. All connection to his body's ailments had been severed. There was no anxiety either, just a sense of euphoria.

He was too relieved to question what had happened. In the state he was in, he simply let himself relax in a sea of tranquil bliss. He didn't know how long he remained in that state. With everything so calm and unmoving, time was a concept he couldn't fathom.

As he began to come back to his normal awareness, he smiled. He remembered something amazing during his flight of fancy. He'd seen Eric's face, but it wasn't the normal Eric. He'd never seen anyone who looked so otherworldly and yet so real at the same time. "He looked like some damn angel." Matthew used the profanity in a reverent, prayerful manner.

The sound of someone vomiting brought him back to the bedroom. He wasn't floating any longer. He was lying in his bed. The good news was that he still felt physically well. Even his hands seemed fine when he rubbed them against the covers. But he was bothered by the retching sounds that came from the bathroom.

"Eric? Is that you?" he asked as he got out of bed. Once he was standing, he had to stop for a moment. A question needed answering. How could he feel so great after going through such a horrible year of stress? And recently, with Lea's traumatic turn for the worse, he'd been riddled with worry and guilt. When he tried to recall the terrible state he'd been in, he couldn't think in those terms. His mind was as clear as a carefree child's. And physically, he felt like he was ready to run a marathon.

The sound of more vomiting didn't belong in Matthew's untroubled, new world. But he couldn't ignore it. When he got to the bathroom, Eric was draped over the toilet. He was reaching for the handle to flush it, but he was missing the mark.

Matthew went over to help. "What's wrong?" he asked as he flushed the toilet.

Eric sat back on his heels and returned a frown. "It's okay. I'll be fine."

"Are you sure?" Matthew hesitated, but he was still feeling so well that he couldn't do much more than accept Eric's reassurance.

Eric put a hand on the vanity and stood up. He held on to the wall as he exited the bathroom. "I should go lay down. These things can take a few minutes before I feel myself again."

Matthew helped Eric over to the bed. "You can stay here, but I want to know what just happened."

"It's my other 'gift,' so I'm sure you won't want to know about it."

"Are you kidding? I feel like I've been reborn."

Eric lay back on the bed. "Some people are very receptive. I'm glad that you're one of them."

"I never thought of myself in that way, but I'm grateful."

"Yes, it's quite amazing, isn't it?"

Matthew stepped back, checking once again, making sure that the effects were still there. When he noted that he was still in an elated state, his curiosity kicked in. "You have to tell me what you did."

Eric sighed, gave him a beatific smile and closed his eyes. "I don't know what to say. I don't have much experience. The gift comes and goes on its own."

"You mean you can't control it?"

"No, it's more like I just know when I can help someone."

"When did you first realize that you had this gift?"

Eric smiled. "I was a kid wandering round the hills. I found a bird with a broken wing. So I did what kids do. I picked it up and started towards home. Further down the mountain, I got this great feeling that the bird would be fine. When I checked on it and felt its wing, it was perfect and the bird flew off. I didn't know that Nelly was watching me. She came up to me and touched my face. She told me I had a gift. I didn't understand what she meant, but I never forgot that moment."

"Wild Nelly?"

"Just Nelly. She was a nice old gal with a couple of teeth left in her head. Mom says Nelly saved my life when I was a baby."

"Where was your father?"

"He'd gone off to take care of an emergency and was stuck in a snowstorm up in the hills. Mom said she knew I was a goner. I was only six months old and running a high fever. My lungs were congested, and I couldn't breathe." Eric smoothed out the bed cover. "I guess Mom was beside herself when there was a knock at the door. Mom answered it, and Nelly barged in out of the storm. Mom said Nelly's clothes were little more than layered rags. The old woman didn't say much, but I guess she was very animated. When

179

she approached my cradle, Mom got scared and tried to stop her. Then she saw Nelly's eyes. Mom said they almost glowed. They were also very kind, and they made Mom feel better instantly. Anyway, Nelly must have had the gift because I'm here, right?"

"Did you ever see this Nelly person after she said you had a gift?"

"My father wouldn't have it. He might have doctored the hill folk, but he was appalled by their customs and superstitions. To think that his son might be influenced by something so 'barbaric' was unthinkable."

Matthew dragged a heavy chair over to the bedside. "That's quite a story."

"I guess so," Eric said as he held out his hand.

"What is it?"

"Help me up . . . I'm going to be sick again. Sometimes, it's one of the side effects."

"Dammit, there's always a catch," Matthew swore as he helped Eric to the bathroom.

After Eric threw up a second time and returned to bed. Matthew had more questions. "Does Teresa know about all this? What about your mother?"

Eric targeted Matthew with pale-blue eyes that seemed untethered to the earth. "No, just you, Matthew. And I want to keep it that way. You joke, but I don't want people calling me 'that freaky, hillbilly' doctor," he insisted. "Promise me. It'll be your payment for my help."

"I promise."

Eric seemed pleased as he drifted off to sleep. But as Matthew continued to study the man's fine, genteel features, his white-blond hair and his boyish face, he felt a chill. For just the briefest instant, he thought he was looking at an angel again. Another thought followed. What if Eric had helped Lea too? That would explain why she was so much better, so much more secure and loving.

Matthew scowled. "After what I just experienced, I feel kind of 'loving' myself." It wasn't the way he usually defined himself, and he tried to forget he'd ever had the thought.

Twenty-Six

LEA FIDGETED WITH a lock of her hair as she stood outside of Matthew's bedroom. Doctor Glass said that Matthew needed quiet, but Lea wanted to check on him. When she thought about that morning and waking up in Matthew's arms, she smiled. Even in his sleep, he held her so close, so caringly. She felt a wonderful ripple of excitement recalling the moment.

When Matthew returned from his outing with Eric, she'd taken her frustration out on Eric. She hadn't intended to put any blame on his shoulders, but she'd been upset. Matthew was in pain, and she couldn't stand the fact that she didn't know how to help him.

But now, she could at least check on him. She'd be very quiet, so quiet that he wouldn't even know she was there. She reached out, but before she could touch the knob, the door swung open.

"Matthew!" The excitement was back in an instant. But there was more than just excitement coursing through her body. Matthew's close proximity was enough to ignite a longing that was anchored deep inside. But she couldn't think about that now. She was still concerned about Matthew's physical condition. "How is your headache?"

Matthew put a finger to his lips and pointed to the bed. "Eric's sleeping," he whispered.

Lea peeked in. "Is he alright?"

Matthew edged her out into the hall and closed the door behind him. "Yes, he's just exhausted. Sorry, Lea, but we're dropping like flies around here."

"But you're okay?" She noted the serene look on his face. "You look a lot better."

Matthew nodded. "I am better, much better."

Lea stepped back. "I want to apologize for this morning. I think I overwhelmed you."

Matthew blinked back. "It was a surprise, but it was great to see you happy."

"I told Margaret that it was almost like a dream. But I know some parts of what I felt were valid. When I was in your arms, it was where I wanted to be. For a few moments, I realized how lucky I was to be in the embrace of the man I love."

"How do you know you love me, Lea? I thought you'd forgotten all of that?"

She looked down. "Yes, well . . . I don't know if you read my diary—"

"No, I only found it a couple of weeks ago, and I sent it to you straight away."

She stared up at him. "Thank you for that. After you and my parents visited in Baltimore, I needed to know who I was before my amnesia. So I studied my diary for days on end. I wanted to know about Rita and Raymond, but most importantly, about us. And I found out a lot. Throughout the whole journal, on page after page, you were the person I really wanted in my life. You were the one bright spot, Matthew. And the more I read the happier I felt." She touched her heart. "I felt it here."

"I wish I could have helped you—"

"I wrote about that too, how you tried, but I was so afraid. I thought I was going crazy. I didn't want you to be saddled with a mental case."

"And now?"

"I guess I'll have to wait and see. I hope I'm not headed for the looney bin."

Matthew reached out and brushed a lock of hair out of her eyes. "You look okay to me."

"Matthew, my feelings for you are coming back. But maybe you don't want to hear that. If that's true, I'll return to Baltimore and let you get on with your life."

Matthew's eyes looked hopeful, but cautious. "Can we forget about everything for now? Would you like to go someplace? We could get a bite to eat if you're hungry."

Lea smiled again. "Yes, I'd love that."

Paul was headed down the corridor when he heard voices ahead and quickly let himself into a side room. He smiled. The voices belonged to Lea and Matthew. From their tone and the brief glance he'd had of them, they were getting along nicely.

"I needed that," he whispered to himself. Between the Rita versus Raymond fight and hardly getting any sleep, it had been a tough day. When Paul checked on the hallway again, he noticed that Lea and Matthew were headed towards the stairs. A moment later, he got a text from Matthew. He and Lea were going out to dinner. "Good man, Matthew. You're remembering to keep me informed."

He had faith in the surgeon. Even if Matthew's walls were crumbling, he had great staying power.

But how was Paul Glass coping? He needed to stop and take a look at his own overall state. He was sighing a lot, even talking to himself instead of keeping up with his notes, but overall, he was doing okay. Of course, he knew himself very well, and he knew he had great staying power too. How else would he do his job?

He stepped back into the corridor. He thought about his last duty of the afternoon. He had to check on Margaret Lloyd. He walked up to her door and tapped it lightly.

Margaret answered before he needed to knock a second time. "Paul, it's you. I thought it was Lea needing something."

Paul smiled his best smile. The day might be catching up with him, but his heart was performing beautifully. It was letting him know that he liked Margaret more than he should. "May I come in?"

Margaret hesitated.

"Just for a moment. I wanted to talk to you about Eric."

"Eric? Is he alright?"

"Yes, yes, Eric's fine, perfectly fine," Paul stammered. He stepped back and immediately chastised himself for blurting out Eric's name. He was letting his feelings for Margaret affect his professional relationship with her.

Margaret noticed his uneasiness. "Paul, what's wrong?"

"I'm so sorry. I think I'm tired. These past couple of days—"

Margaret reached out for his arm and guided him inside. "You've been trying to take care of everything, just like my Ricky."

Paul walked over to the sitting area and slumped down on the couch. "Don't trouble yourself, Margaret. I'm used to long days."

"Well, I don't pretend to know you, but I have eyes. And you're plum tuckered out." She hesitated. "Oh my goodness, I never say things like that. I sound like I grew up in the hills."

Paul sighed. "My mother used that term. It brings back fond memories."

"You got along with her?"

Paul remembered his mother's face, so strong and kind throughout his life. "She was a saint," he blurted out.

"That's wonderful."

"Sorry, I didn't mean to raise my voice. I'm more tired than I thought."

"Do you need to rest?"

Paul made himself sit up more attentively. "No, of course not."

Margaret smiled. "Then what about a cup of tea. This room comes with an electric kettle, coffee packets and an assortment of tea bags."

"Tea would be great, but if you don't mind, maybe I'll have some coffee."

Margaret eyed him intently. "You look like you've had enough coffee. What about some herbal tea?"

"Thank you, herbal tea it is."

Paul watched Margaret head over to a Louis XV lowboy that served as a refreshment station. As she went about her duties, he knew that she was like her son, Eric. They were both nurturers to the core.

He leaned back and shut his eyes. His mother was nurturing too. He'd meant it when he'd said she was a saint. Storms came her way, hardships that would have broken a weaker woman, but she never let it affect the way she treated him. It was just the opposite. She'd been incredibly loving and supportive. Paul had never met her equal. "Until now," he sighed as he drifted off.

When Paul woke up, he noticed that he had a soft cashmere throw covering him from his neck down. After fully coming awake, he saw Margaret sitting across from him, reading a book. He sat up and quickly tossed the blanket aside. "I can't believe I fell asleep like that."

Margaret put her book down. "When did you eat last?"

Paul didn't remember. Had he bothered with breakfast or lunch?

Margaret crossed her arms. "I take your silence to mean you're not taking care of yourself. But you have to stop that. You need your strength if you're going to help Lea. I know she's better, but still."

Paul scratched his head. He wasn't used to the people in his care correcting his behavior. He stood up. "Maybe you're right. I'll go down to the kitchen—"

Margaret held up her hand. "Maybe we could contact Eric, and we could eat together."

"I'd like that."

"The kitchen staff said they were serving another buffet dinner since things are so—"

"Crazy around here?"

Margaret laughed. "Paul Glass, you're a psychiatrist. You're not supposed to use the word, crazy."

Paul laughed too. "Thank you, Margaret, I'll try to remember that. I'll also avoid using 'nuts' and 'mad as a hatter' when I'm making notes about my patients."

Margaret sobered and approached him. She reached out for his arm. "You don't think of Lea in those terms, do you?"

"No, I don't. In fact, I have every hope in the world that she's going to come out of this with a renewed sense of identity and wellbeing."

Margaret let out a breath. "I'm so relieved to hear that. She seemed fine until she came here. It was a shock—"

"Margaret, don't think about what happened here. Keep remembering that Lea is very capable, like you."

"I'd like to believe that about myself, but I don't feel very capable. I've been living with lies for too long. How can I trust myself again?"

Paul extended his arm and when Margaret took it, he winked at her. "If you can't trust yourself, try to trust me. After all the wackos I've seen, I know a delusional fruitcake when I see one, and you could never be put in that category, my dear lady."

"Oh Paul, you are incorrigible, aren't you."

Paul held Margaret's arm a little tighter when he saw her smile and try to hide it. "Yes, I suppose I am, but let me text Eric about dinner. He can meet us in the dining room."

Margaret pulled away and turned to face him. "What did you want to tell me about Eric? You never said."

Paul hedged. He'd been thinking about how Eric had helped Lea. The more he thought about that night, the more curious he got. His gut told him there was more to Eric than could be seen in a report or even in an interview. Paul wanted to question Margaret about Eric's childhood days. He'd have a more complete picture of what made Eric tick.

Margaret shook his arm. "Paul Glass, answer me. Are you concerned about my son?"

"Not concerned so much as impressed. He's so compassionate and supportive with Lea. You must be very proud of him."

"Yes, he's everything a mother could want."

Paul didn't say anything more, but Margaret kept making him think about his mother, Mary Glass. She was a tiny slip of a woman who used to make the same comment about him. She had led a long incredible life, but she'd died a few years before. Paul still missed her.

As he walked down the hall corridor with Margaret on his arm, he could almost see his mother smiling. She'd been disappointed when he'd never married. But he'd been too busy. He glanced at Margaret, and she smiled back. Was it finally time to rethink his life?

Twenty-Seven

ERIC WOKE UP from a nightmare with his heart pounding. He'd been dreaming about the dead boy. He rubbed the sleep from his eyes and tried to concentrate. "That was a long time ago."

The room was pitch-black. He couldn't see anything, but he could feel it. Sometimes the darkness had substance. Now, it was thick . . . suffocating, and it was closing in on him. He took a breath, trying to get some air.

"Calm yourself and breathe." He knew from experience that he needed to stay ahead of his fear. It had haunted his childhood, but he'd learned how to handle it. "Just turn on the light, and everything will be fine."

The words, spoken with confidence, would have worked if he could find the lamp. He groped in vain, reaching out and coming up empty. A warning made him hesitate. Should he have his hands outstretched? Exposed? Unprotected? What if he touched something he didn't want to touch?

As soon as he had the thought, a face appeared. It was the face of the dead boy from Eric's nightmare. It faded in and out as the boy spoke. His voice was a whisper in the darkness. "Don't let it happen again!"

Eric stood up cautiously. Had the apparition trailed after him? Why was the boy back after all these years?

Eric stumbled forward and bumped into some furniture. "Find the light," he ordered. The darkness was getting thicker, pressing on him, pushing him back, making him remember things he didn't want to remember. He fought to get more air, hoping against hope that he didn't remember everything.

But he knew how the darkness worked. If he lost control, if he couldn't find the light, the past would come alive again. He wouldn't only see a dead boy's face, he'd hear what he'd prayed he'd forget. And there was so much to forget.

How many long, winter nights had he lain breathless in his bed? He'd clung to his covers, listening. Sound was like the darkness, it surrounded him. It made him its prisoner. His bedroom windows rattled as the wind prowled the exterior, howling out its fury. A room away, another sound seeped in through the thin walls, the sound of his mother crying.

"Oh, Ricky, when is it going to end? When are we going to be free?"

The sound of his father's voice followed, reprimanding her. "Hush, Margaret, you'll wake the boy. We don't want him asking questions. Hush!"

Their conversations were like waves of hurt and sorrow, crashing into Eric's young bones, throwing him against the rocks of helplessness. But what were the sorrowful secrets of his parents compared to those of the mountains?

When people settled in the Appalachians, they brought everything with them, everything they were running from. All their hates and unfulfilled desires were stamped into the soil. Their curses and their children's screams polluted the air as generation after generation kept trudging on, eking out a pale existence. The pristine landscape was scarred, and the mountains wailed in protest. The trees creaked, and groaned and broke under the burden of too much grief.

At least when the deep snows came, the mountain's voice was muffled. White drifts covered everything including the untold miseries and the unmarked graves. But snow didn't stop people from whispering at the general store. Nobody could keep the old, grizzled men from spitting out their stories. Some would cup their deaf ears and stare with watery eyes, needing to add their tales too. They spoke of the restless dead who roamed the hills in hushed voices.

The children were a different matter. Nobody liked to talk about the plight of the children, those small beings whom Eric's father tended along with the adults. The doctor became that lone voice in the wilderness as he fought for their lives. All the while he hated the tales, the superstitions that would never go away. He hated that his own son was affected by such nonsense.

Now the country doctor's son was a grown man. He was a doctor too, like his father wanted, and he was still lost in the darkness.

"No, I won't play that game anymore," Eric insisted as he lunged forward and slammed into another piece of furniture. He hit it so hard it shook. A crash followed.

The sound was enough to make him pause again. He'd broken something, probably an expensive lamp. He was sure that the antique object cost more than what his father earned in a year back in Elkville. Poverty was a way of life for the doctor's family too.

The coming of winter was accompanied by his mother's lament. Trying to stay warm in the drafty, old house was a chore. She'd stare out a frosty pane of glass and pray. As a blizzard buried the house, inch by inch, she clutched at her sweater with hands that were stiff with the cold. Her dismay was joined by the wailing of the wind, always blowing, always driving the cold deeper.

His father's orders were loud and stern before he left to attend to an emergency. "Keep the stove going, Eric! Do you hear me! Don't let the fire go out."

So many times the wood pile was frozen. And Eric's hands were frozen too. Why was his father always gone when they needed him? As the years passed, the poverty remained a constant until his father's face was so tired towards the end. Yet, nothing changed his father's mind. It was steely and unbending, tempered by stubbornness and pride.

His mother couldn't stop crying at his father's funeral. Her heart was broken, and Eric couldn't put it back together. Even with his medical degrees and training, he was helpless, just as he'd been as a child.

His parents had always been a unit of two. He lived on the outside of their world. A ghost of a child, like the dead boy, trailing after them. Wondering why they couldn't find their way. Why was there always so much darkness?

Eric didn't have the answers, but he knew he couldn't give into the darkness now. He turned around in a slow circle and saw a sliver of light. It was coming in under the door.

"Just move forward slowly. There's a switch on the wall."

189

But why couldn't his mother move forward? Even after he'd brought her to Baltimore, she remained fixed and unmovable. But there was a reason. She was still attached to her Ricky. She still cried at night when she thought Eric couldn't hear her. But how could he possibly shut her out? The walls in his mind were as thin as the walls in the old house in Elkville. He heard everything he shouldn't.

Now, they were in a strange house in Chicago, and Eric had to keep his wits about him. He had to move with care towards the light and the door. He didn't want to pay for more broken lamps. After a half-dozen steps and a bit of fumbling, he found the switch. Light flooded the space. He blinked, trying to adjust his vision. The shadows were gone. He was standing in a room of old furniture.

His phone dinged as he made his way back to the bedside table. When he checked the text Paul sent, his face remained passive, but his fists closed on their own. Paul had asked him to come to dinner in the dining room. His mother would be there too. The three of them could have a meal together.

Eric sat down on the bed, still holding the phone. Before he thought about dinner, he had to let his mind collect itself. What were the memories trying to tell him? He closed his eyes and forced himself to steady his breath. He needed to stay calm if he wanted clarity.

As the pieces of his past began to fuse into a pattern, another light of sorts switched on. He was sending himself a series of warnings, or maybe the dead boy was cautioning him. But one bit of information stood out from the rest. It was the one that worried him the most, and it had to do with relationships.

Paul Glass was attracted to his mother. Eric felt it the first time he saw the psychiatrist look at her. It was such a familiar look. He'd grown up seeing that look on his father's face. He saw the way his mother responded, how she touched Paul's arm. She was always reaching out, leaving herself behind. She'd left everything behind when she married his father. A life of stress and hardship followed.

Eric started to get up, felt his body tremble, and he had to sit down again. He wondered if he had the strength to do what needed to be done. He was supposed to be in his prime, but his spirit was worn and threadbare. And the house that Matthew thought of as cursed seemed to be adding to his exhaustion. The Ferguson structure was cold and dark. After only a couple of nights under its roof, Eric had never felt so weary.

He stood up again, this time with a fixed determination. It didn't matter how he felt. He had to help his mother before it was too late. He had to make her realize that she couldn't keep looking to a man to define her life. Whatever it took, he had to help her sever the tie she was making with Paul and take a chance on herself.

* * *

Margaret looked up and smiled when she saw Eric coming into the dining room to join them. Since it seemed there were only going to be the three of them, she and Paul were sitting on one end of the long, formal table. Paul sat at the head, Margaret sat to his right. After Eric greeted her and kissed her cheek, he sat down next to her. He nodded to Paul Glass. "Good evening, Paul. So what's the latest? Bring me up to date."

Margaret and Paul already had their food, but Margaret was concerned about Eric. "Before all that, you need to get some supper. You look tired. Very tired. Are you alright? You're not sick, are you?"

Eric smiled. "I am a little tired, but that's part of the job, isn't it? Father was always coming home exhausted."

"Yes, you're right. He always gave his best."

Eric sat back and took her hand. "But there wasn't much left for you."

Margaret returned a little frown. Eric's tone was quiet, and he had a pleasant expression, but she could always tell when there was something wrong. "When I became a doctor's wife, I knew he'd have to put his work first. After all, people's lives were at stake."

Eric kissed her hand and returned it to her. "Yes, I know that. But it's not what I want. So I'm calling it quits."

"Calling it quits?" Margaret instinctively grabbed Paul's arm for support, like she'd grabbed Ricky's. She didn't even think about it until she saw Eric's eyes. He wasn't looking at her. He was staring at the way she was holding on to Paul.

Paul patted her hand, but he looked at Eric. "Are you saying you're giving up your medical practice?"

Eric sucked in a breath and raised his eyes to meet Paul's. "Yes, Paul, that's what I'm saying."

191

Margaret recoiled at the thought. "Oh Eric, I can't believe what I'm hearing. How can you throw away your career, all the hard work—" Margaret couldn't find the words to express her dismay. Eric was so perfect when it came to caring for people. "I don't understand."

"I never wanted to be a doctor."

Margaret brought her hands together, trying to hold on to something that made sense, but as she searched her mind, it felt like a chalkboard that had been wiped clean. "What about Teresa?"

Eric put his hands on the table. "I love her and I love you and Lea, and when I think of having a family, I want something different for my children."

Margaret stared back. "Oh, I see. What you're saying is that your father and I failed you."

Eric lowered his voice. "Please, don't go there. It's what you and Dad always did when I had something to say that didn't agree with your ideas. You made everything about you two. But this time, I want it to be different. I want us to go home and start a new life, one that's happy. You can paint again or do whatever you want. I'll find a way to support you and Teresa and Lea too, I promise."

Paul leaned in and smiled. "Margaret, is that what you want?"

"No, it's not." She bit her lip and stared at Eric. "I feel like you're doing this because you're angry at what you found out about your father."

Eric pulled back. "Are you talking about the fact that my father lost his license and used you? Maybe I am."

"What do you mean he used me?"

"Was Elkville your dream, Mom? An isolated, backwater village? Is that the kind of place you wanted when you thought of raising a family? Or did you let my father decide all that, a man running from his fists and an inability to control himself?"

Margaret couldn't believe what she was hearing. "That's cruel, Eric, very cruel."

"No, it has nothing to do with cruelty. Those are just facts. But you never let yourself think about those facts. You sacrificed your own needs and wants in favor of Dad's wants and needs. Can't you see that?" Eric reached for her hand. "But I want something different for you. You deserve a better life."

Margaret looked away. "If what you're saying is true, then I'd be exchanging one prison for another, you're father's dreams for your dreams."

Eric's eyes softened even more. "Please, I promise you, I don't have an agenda."

Margaret squared her shoulders. "Of course you do. You've just passed judgement on the last forty years of my life. Now you want to take me back with you so I can be the happy mother you think I should be. I'd say you definitely have an agenda."

Eric pushed back his chair, gripped the table edge and pushed himself up. "Nothing I say is ever right. I'm doing my best to be there for you, but you twist everything. I love you, but I don't know what more to say." He turned his eyes on Paul. "Goodbye, Doctor Glass."

Paul stood up too. "You're leaving? Now?"

"Why not? You're the man who has all the answers. You're the shrink. Do your job and straighten this mess out."

Margaret jerked to her feet. "So you're leaving without a thought about Lea? Do you know how important you are to her, and you're just going to abandon her?"

"I've done what I can. Now she has you and Matthew Howell. She's in good hands."

Margaret felt her anger hit with a terrible force. "I didn't raise my son to run off, to leave behind people in need. That's shameful!"

Instead of commenting, Eric turned and quickly walked out of the room.

Paul put his arm around Margaret's shoulder. "I think your son is trying his best, Margaret."

Paul's statement was delivered in a gentle, compassionate way, but all that Margaret heard was that she'd failed again. According to Eric, she'd failed him from the day he was born.

The idea was another shock that shook her world. She had to sit down in her chair and try to get her body to calm down. Paul took a seat too, but he remained quiet.

When she'd recovered a little, she stood up and looked at the psychiatrist. "I'm going to my room, Doctor Glass, and I don't want to be disturbed."

"What about Lea?"

"I've already ruined a son. I won't make another mistake with Lea. Like Eric said, you have to handle it."

* * *

Eric didn't know if he'd make it back to his room. Basic foundations were shifting. After talking to his mother, he'd managed to exit the dining room and get as far as the foyer stairs, but his body was collapsing under the weight of his mother's demeaning remark. She was ashamed of him.

All he could ever remember was that he loved his mother. As a child, he couldn't distinguish her pain from his own. Slowly, he began to establish his own identity, but that didn't prevent him from feeling her unhappiness. It took an act of will on his part to shut it out.

Yet, when he'd been at the dinner table, he'd suddenly felt the need to be his own person in a more forthright way. He knew he still loved his mother, but his feelings had rushed to the surface. His mother accused him of being cruel. Was she right? Was it cruel to finally express how unhappy he'd been growing up?

He started to climb the stairs and had to grab on to the railing for support. His father's face came to mind. As a child, he'd also felt his father's pain. Maybe that was why he'd become a doctor too. The practice of medicine was his father's way of dealing with pain. And since Eric was so able to feel his father's need to stop the suffering in the world, he joined forces with his parent. But his father never found a way to stop his self-inflicted torment. Now, Eric was caught in the same trap, and he didn't see a way out.

As he dragged himself upwards, each step became an obstacle that required more energy than he had to give. His body was telling him that it was exhausted by life, but he made himself climb the many stairs anyway. He had to pack his bag, call a taxi and flee the Ferguson mansion. It was the place where his life had started to unravel. Maybe it was because he could feel the pain of the structure itself.

So much misery, including Lea's tortured childhood, was stored in its walls. Since he'd been there, he'd heard her screams, screams that went on and on, a baby crying out and no one there to help.

They haunted the place. They filled the airways with their helplessness and despair.

They became the screams of the poor, little waifs Eric had heard as a child. Children who were beaten and slapped as consistently as they were given food and hand-me-down clothing. By the time he was an adult, Eric had had a lifetime of the innocent suffering. Cruel or not, he couldn't keep quiet about it anymore. Yet, he hated himself for making his mother look at him the way she had.

She'd taken what he'd said as an indictment of her own failing. He'd never meant any harm, yet now, he was full of the shame she forced on him. The bottom line was that he'd hurt his mother in a most grievous way. It was the last straw. He couldn't shoulder any more misery. He had to get away from it all.

Eric finally succeeded in getting to the top of the stairs, and faced his next challenge. He had to make it to his room and pack. He hoped that he had the strength to carry out his plan. Still, Matthew's statement kept repeating in his mind. After burning his hands, the surgeon was being sarcastic, but he'd also sounded half serious with his declaration.

"There's a chance none of us will make it out alive."

Eric had a terrible foreboding. "Matthew's right."

Eric Lloyd, the capable cardiologist, wasn't going to have to worry about giving up medicine. Before that happened, the Ferguson mansion would claim him as its latest victim.

Twenty-Eight

MATTHEW WALKED LEA back to her room with a sense of triumph. They'd had a delightful dinner at a small café. But the word, delightful, had never been in Matthew's vocabulary. So why was he thinking in those terms now? He let an inner smile inform him. Feeling a sense of wellbeing and even delight was one of the side effects of Eric's miracle cure.

It was a strange and utterly baffling experience. Matthew thought it would wane quickly. But as he drove to Pete's Café, he didn't lose his buoyant feeling. It stuck with him through his salad. He didn't even feel like complaining as he chewed a generous bite of leafy greens. He felt content through his fish and chips. Dessert was, dare he think it, exquisite. The warm cherry cobbler, with ice cream, and mounds of whipped cream was the most satisfying and tasty treat he'd ever experienced. The entire meal, and his new feelings were very scary.

Lea was a delight too. She was so pretty. She wasn't rail thin anymore, but rather a perfect example of womanhood. He loved her dark, shiny hair and her sparkling eyes. Why hadn't he ever appreciated what beautiful eyes she had? But her smile was her best quality. He felt like it could light up the entire diner. And when she smiled at him, he found himself smiling back with his own sparkling eyes. Again, very scary.

Where was his guardedness, that necessary shield that deflected life's many assaults on his person? The rude woman at the grocery store, banging her cart into his and then giving him hell for being at

196

fault. Cranky patients with unending complaints. People cutting him off in traffic. Why didn't he care to protect himself from all of it?

He didn't know the answer. He didn't know why he didn't feel the need to think about it. He just accepted feeling happy, almost like he'd accepted a cough after a cold. It would pass, and life would go back to its customary, tedious norm.

What Matthew didn't expect was to be standing with Lea, saying goodnight, and seeing Eric Lloyd. The man was walking, or at least stumbling, his way down the corridor. He was pulling his suitcase behind him, head down, not paying attention to his steps. Matthew had seen weary soldiers in war films who looked better.

Lea spoke up before Matthew had a chance.

"Eric, where are you going?" she asked as she hurried over to him.

Eric paused, looked up with listless eyes, and half-smiled. "Oh, good, I hoped to say goodbye."

"Are you going back to Baltimore?"

Eric frowned, blinked a couple of times and finally answered. "Yes, I am."

"I'll miss you. You're my angel, you know."

Matthew had been observing their exchange, but when Lea mentioned the word, angel, he came to full attention. His spine went rigid, as if he was ready to salute a superior. He quickly joined Lea and Eric, smiled and nudged Lea. "Did you call him your angel?"

Lea went all dreamy. "Of course, because he is."

Eric managed a better smile as he leaned down and kissed Lea's cheek. "Remember to be good to yourself."

Lea reached out for his hand and hesitated. "You're so hot. You're not well."

Eric quickly pulled back. "Goodbye, both of you. Hope you have a wonderful life."

Matthew put a hand on Eric's chest as the man started to move on. "Wait a minute. What's the rush? Do you have a plane to catch?"

"Yes, I do, in the morning. In the meantime, there's a taxi waiting. I have to go."

Matthew used his hand to hold Eric in place. It was an easy matter to see that he was looking at a sick man. "Lea's right. Something is wrong."

197

Eric's face flushed with anger. "Of course, something is wrong. My mother hates me, and I'm giving up my medical practice."

Lea grabbed Eric's arm. "Mom hates you?"

"You're giving up your practice?" Matthew asked with concern. He was taken back by Eric's announcement. How could someone like Eric, who was very good at what they did, just quit? "Lea and I were gone for three hours, tops. Did hell break loose while we were gone?"

Eric returned a sad look, the kind an animal has after a beating. "It's strange how quickly life can turn on a person. But you know that Matthew." He looked at Lea. "My darling, almost sister. I don't know how you survived in this place. Be so proud of yourself that you're still standing here."

Matthew blinked back. When he'd first met Eric, it wasn't under the best of circumstances. His first impression of Eric was confusing. Matthew expected to meet the enemy, some red-neck rube who had taken advantage of Lea. But Eric surprised him. With his bright, youthful face, Eric didn't look like he'd had a role in "Deliverance." His manner was soft-spoken and dignified, without the slightest indication of any malice or ego.

At the time, Matthew questioned Eric's attitude. They had both gone through the rigors of med school, internship and residency. Most people came out with an edge or at least a bit of aloofness, but Eric still acted like a Boy Scout. Now, that Boy Scout looked crushed, like he'd tried to save the world and failed.

"Eric?"

"Yes, Matthew?"

"I don't know what happened, but you need to slow down. You can leave in the morning."

Eric's face flushed scarlet. "No! I have to get out of here while I'm still able to walk. I'll be ready for that wheelchair otherwise."

"What wheelchair?" Lea asked.

"Never mind," Eric said. "I have to go."

Matthew grabbed his arm. "You better hold on to the railing going down those stairs."

"Thanks, that's a good idea."

"Do you want me to help you with your luggage?"

Eric hesitated for a long moment, scratching his head as if he was trying to understand a new theory on quantum mechanics. Finally, he eyed Matthew guardedly. "Yes, that might be wise."

Once they were on their way down the long corridor, Matthew felt like he was accompanying a nursing home resident. Maybe Eric would need that wheelchair he'd mentioned.

The journey down the stairs was worse. Matthew tried not to look, but how could he turn away from an accident in the making. Eric was holding on to the handrail with both hands, moving cautiously as his foot slid forward and dropped heavily to the next step. Almost more unnerving was the fact that Eric would look up at Matthew every few steps. In a breathless voice, he'd announce his progress. "I'm going to beat this thing. I'm going to make it, Matthew."

Matthew was afraid to reply. If Eric lost his concentration, the next phase of hell would ensue and Matthew would be calling 911. When he glanced up at Lea on the landing above, she was covering her mouth. Her sparkly eyes were wide with alarm.

Perhaps Eric would have made it to the floor below if it wasn't for Margaret Lloyd running up to Lea, then glancing down at Eric. Instead of covering her mouth too, she let out a little scream. "Eric, please don't leave! I'm sorry! I'm so sorry!"

Her shrill cry bounced off the walls and hit Eric's unprotected ears. Like any son who hears his mother's scream, Eric jerked around, letting go of the railing. He maintained his balance for approximately a nanosecond. Then he was falling.

Matthew was stifling his own cry of distress, but he quickly traversed the stairs to the floor below. When he got to Eric, the man was lying face down, with one hand up and his legs slightly spread out. It was a classic pose, often seen in one of those murder mysteries on PBS.

Matthew stared at Lea. She was running down the stairs. Margaret Lloyd was close on her heels. "Lea, call 911," he ordered. He was about to check Eric for injuries when Eric started to move. He was also saying something.

Matthew knelt down, keeping his voice as calm as possible. "Lie still, you've probably broken something."

Eric raised his head, still mumbling. "I'm okay. I know how to take a fall. I've watched training films." As Eric was speaking, he was gathering his arms and legs under him.

Matthew tried to appeal to Eric's common sense. "Please, moving is dangerous."

Eric's comeback was immediate. "Not as dangerous as staying here."

By this time Lea and Margaret had joined the party.

Margaret was gasping as she stood over her son. "Oh Eric, please tell me that you're not going to die!"

Her plea seemed to give Eric the impetus he needed. He was able to push himself up to his hands and knees, still issuing his own orders. "Don't concern yourself. This isn't the first time I've taken a tumble."

"What happened?" This time Paul Glass was traversing the stairs. "Is that Eric on the floor?"

Raymond Ferguson was also coming down, more slowly than Paul. He was holding his chest. "What's going on?"

Standing up, Matthew knew he had to take charge. He turned to face the small group that was gathering round. "Please, everyone, stand back and let me help Eric."

Eric moaned out a response. "Nothing broken. Just a few bruises."

Matthew glanced back at the injured party, surprised to see Eric slowly getting to his feet. Everyone let out a silent gasp, wondering how long he'd stay upright. Margaret was standing very close, but she was clasping her hands as if in prayer.

Eric took his time as he slowly straightened up, weaved back and forth a bit, and gestured for attention. "Look, no harm done. So everyone, please go about your business."

Matthew tried again. "Eric, listen to me—"

Eric targeted Matthew with a stern eye. "Sir!"

Matthew looked around, then back at Eric. "Are you talking to me?"

Eric tried to straighten up a little more. "Indeed I am. Would you please fetch my bag? I have a taxi waiting."

Before Matthew could do as he was told, Margaret was rushing over and grabbing his arm. "I've seen him like this before. He fell out of a tree, developed a fever and was slightly delirious for two days. I thought I was going to lose him."

Eric laughed. "Don't listen to that nonsense. Once I'm out of this house, I'll be right as rain." He stumbled over to a wall and braced a hand against it. He almost smiled. "I'm going back to Baltimore, handing in my medical license and marrying Teresa. She'll support us until I get a job at the pet store."

Margaret tugged on Matthew's arm again. Her face was almost as stricken as Eric's. "He loves animals. He'd be so good around them."

Eric tried to snap his fingers at Matthew and failed. "Come along, sir. It's time to leave."

Matthew remained frozen in place. He gawked at Eric like the rest of the group. When Eric managed to open the front door and go outside, Matthew started after him, stopped, and ran back for Eric's luggage. Margaret Lloyd called to him as he followed Eric.

"Help him, Matthew! Help my precious boy!"

When Matthew got outside, he didn't see Eric at first. After a moment of panic, he saw the weaving man walking down the driveway. Matthew sighed. He was getting better at recognizing someone on the edge of a mental collapse. He had to be very careful in how he handled Eric. "Eric, where are you going?" he asked in a casual tone.

Eric turned. "Matthew, where's my taxi? It should be here by now."

"Yes, about your taxi—"

Eric did a good imitation of a drunk at a Christmas party as he made his way back to Matthew. "Do you think there's a problem?"

Matthew knew he wasn't a doctor in that moment. He was just another bit actor in Eric's play. It was a dramatic composition that seemed to demand compliance on Matthew's part. He felt compelled to assist Eric, who had the starring role. "Give me your phone. I'll check it out."

Eric steadied a hand on Matthew's shoulder and fished in a pocket. "Check the last call I made. I'm sure I gave them the right address."

Matthew looked at the list and paused before he delivered his information. "Eric, my friend, it might be awhile before they get here." What he didn't say to Eric was a concern. He and Eric were standing in a suburb of Chicago, and Eric had called the Baltimore Yellow Cab company. A definite mistake on Eric's part.

"That's alright. I can wait," Eric said as he wandered over to the curb by the flower beds. After he managed to sit down, he sighed. "While I'm waiting maybe I'll catch a few winks. I think I'm tired."

Matthew sat down next to him. "I'm sure you are," he sighed as he felt Eric's forehead. Margaret was right. Her son had a fever.

Eric stirred and stared at Matthew with eyes that were only slightly open. "Promise that you'll wake me when the taxi gets here."

Matthew nodded. "You bet. It might take a couple of days, and you'll be looking at a heck of a bill, but I'll inform you the minute they arrive."

Eric slumped against Matthew's shoulder. "You're a friend, Matthew. Thanks." A moment later, Eric was dozing from exhaustion.

With Paul's help, Matthew managed to get Eric back into the house. Eric hardly took notice. He seemed too tired to fight anymore. Happily, Matthew didn't think Eric had seriously injured himself, and Matthew canceled the 911 call. He did stay with Eric just in case he went crazy again.

* * *

After all the excitement with Eric, Lea sat in Margaret's room, trying to comfort the older woman. Paul Glass was also there. He sat quietly in a corner chair as Lea talked to Margaret. "Mom, please remember what you're always telling me. You have to be kind to yourself. And as for Eric, Matthew is taking good care of him."

Margaret sniffled and rubbed her nose with a tissue. "My poor boy, he's never spoken to me like that before. I should have known he wasn't well. Now he's so ill that your Matthew won't let me see him."

Lea liked the way Margaret said, "your Matthew." She put her arm around Margaret's shoulder. "Matthew doesn't think Eric's in any danger. Eric just seems to be in a very emotionally charged state of mind."

Margaret looked up at her. "Eric has always been so sensitive."

Paul shifted in his seat. "Exactly what do you mean when you say he's sensitive, Margaret?"

"I don't think Eric was like other boys. Once, when I had a terrible headache, he sat very close. He was still small, and he kept rubbing his forehead. His eyes were so sad when he asked me why our heads hurt so much. I noticed that he always got sick when I was ailing."

"Hyper-empathy," Paul said. "Most people are somewhat empathic, but some are so sensitive that they can't separate their feelings from those of others around them, especially when they're children."

The information seemed to startle Margaret. "Oh dear, what must it have been like for Eric? He was surrounded by pain. At home, he must have had to endure his father's constant guilt and anger, plus my frequent crying spells. Then there were the house calls with his father. There was so much abuse and suffering in those remote areas. How did he survive?"

Paul had been taking notes, but he stilled his pen. "He has a very strong spirit, like you, Margaret. I think you're quite empathic too."

Margaret glared back. "Don't talk to me about my empathy, Doctor Glass. If I'd have been a little more empathic at dinner, Eric wouldn't be lying there in bed half out of his mind."

"But Margaret, every person has to shield themselves in order to function. You felt wounded, and you were only trying to protect yourself. You never meant to be hurtful."

"Who protected Eric all those years? Tell me that. You're supposed to be such a high-flying expert, but my son was fine until you started taking charge of things."

"I'm sorry," Paul said.

Margaret stood up and gave Paul another hateful look. "Your apology doesn't help!"

Lea hadn't wanted to interrupt the conversation between Margaret and Paul. She'd sat quietly and listened. When Margaret stormed out of her room, slamming the door on her way out, she looked at Paul. "Margaret is so angry."

"Yes, and I didn't help her. Quite the opposite."

"Paul, I don't mean to tell you how to handle this situation, but I'm a little surprised."

"What do you mean?"

"I've been seeing a psychiatrist for a while. When you talked to Margaret, you didn't act anything like Doctor Kasner. She usually lets me find the answers, but that's not what you were doing."

Paul put his notes in his pocket. "You're right. I wasn't being a professional."

"I don't understand."

Paul stood up and tried to adjust his posture. "I'm sorry, Lea. At this point, I think you're much better at helping Margaret than I am. Now, if you'll excuse me I need to rethink this situation."

"What situation?"

"As Margaret said, I don't seem to be helping."

"I'm sorry, Paul"

"Yes, so am I."

Lea watched Paul leave and wondered if he was okay. The man's voice had changed. It was weaker and more unsure than it had been earlier. But she couldn't worry about Paul. Other people had more serious problems. She didn't know if she should try to comfort Margaret again or check on Eric. She decided the latter was a better idea.

After she let herself into Eric's bedroom, she smiled and waved at Matthew. He was sitting in a chair close to Eric's bedside, reading a book. She traipsed over as quietly as possible and noticed that Eric seemed to still be sleeping. "How is he?"

Matthew put his book aside and shrugged. "I checked him over, and he doesn't seem to have any serious injuries. He was right about only having a few bruises."

Lea smiled again. "I guess he knows how to take a fall after all. So what is wrong with him?"

"He's obviously exhausted, and he has a fever. Other than that, he's doing okay physically."

Lea leaned over the bed and studied Eric's face. His brows were still furrowed. "Paul learned that he's hyper-empathic."

Matthew rubbed his chin. "I've read some articles about it. But that doesn't explain how he went from being fine when he got here to where he's at now."

"Matthew, I've been thinking about what Eric said to me. He said that I 'survived' this place. What's that mean?"

"I'm not sure, but he seemed hell-bent on getting out of here. You should have seen his face when he was waiting for that cab to pick him up."

"Matthew, have you ever been empathic? Like when you were a kid, did it bother you if one child hit another?"

"I suppose, but I can tell you this much, I've changed. I've got a reputation for having a non-existent bedside manner."

"That makes sense. You probably can't stand being around other people's pain."

"Are you saying that I'm hyper- empathic too?"

Lea leaned over and gave him a kiss on the cheek. "Let's not get carried away," she teased.

He frowned. "I hated seeing you unhappy. Does that count?"

Lea moved in front of him, unfolded his arms, and put his hands around her waist. "Yes, that counts. Like I said, I realize now just how wonderful you are. However, I'm curious."

"About what?"

"Did Eric ever do anything to you?"

Matthew let his arms drop. "Like what?"

"Like make you feel all better when you wanted to die?"

Matthew looked away. "No comment."

Lea grabbed his hands and replaced them on her hips. "There was an old television show that you probably never watched. It was called, 'Touched by an Angel'."

Matthew tried to pull back again, but Lea held on to his arms.

"What's your point, Lea?"

"I think we've both been touched."

"Look, I like Eric, but the man in the bed is flesh and blood. He's not an angel."

"But he could be a channel for one."

"Now you're scaring me."

"I've been reading up on it. It's an ability that some people have."

"Where have you been reading something like that?"

"Just do some investigating, Matthew, please. I'm not saying I'm right. I'm not saying I'm wrong. But I want us to be open to that type of thing."

"Oh hell, I'm getting in deeper and deeper."

Lea frowned. "What's the problem?"

Matthew swallowed hard. "I'm not trying to upset you. I just can't go where you're going."

Lea could see that Matthew really was frightened by what she was asking. "I'm sorry. Forget what I said. We don't have to agree on this stuff."

Matthew blinked back a few times. "You would have never made a statement like that before. You always insisted on being right."

Lea kissed his cheek again and sighed. "I know, but I've been touched by an angel. Now, I can't be that cranky person that I was. Do you have a problem with that too?"

Matthew stood up and pulled her into his arms. As he held her close, he tipped up her chin. "I don't have a problem when I look at how beautiful you are."

"I like that."

"I think about you a lot."

Lea took a deep breath, inhaling his cologne. "I think about you too."

The moment was interrupted by a moan from the bed.

Matthew glanced at Eric. "Uh, oh, he's waking up. He's going to go nuts when he finds out his taxi never came."

Lea heard the concern in Matthew's voice. "Should I get Paul? He's supposed to be the expert, right?"

Matthew stiffened. "If you want my opinion, I'd rather take my chances on Wild Nelly."

"I don't know who that is, but from what you said, Eric needs to leave this house."

"He's in no shape to go down those stairs again."

"We'll take the elevator."

"There's an elevator? I wish we knew that before Eric practiced his falling technique. But where will we take him?"

"To this really nice guest house on the property. My dad showed it to me the night I arrived. It's in a wooded area, very private."

"I wish I'd known that too. I've been sleeping in a room that's creepier than a morgue. But it's getting late. Will it be hard to navigate in the dark?"

"The path is well lit. It won't be a problem." Lea pulled Matthew over to a corner and kept her voice very low. "Eric seems to trust you, and I don't think it would be good if he loses faith in you now.

206

So here's my plan. Give him a little sedative, just enough to keep him drowsy, and we'll get him to the guest house. Maybe he'll sleep through to morning once he's in a peaceful setting."

"Tell me there are no antiques in this guest house."

"No, in fact, it's ultra-modern."

"Good, it sounds ideal."

Lea giggled. "You and me will go on a little mission together."

Matthew pulled her into his arms again. "You're still as clever as ever."

Lea stood on her tip toes, put her hands on his shoulders and lifted herself up enough to plant a kiss on his lips. "I can be clever about a lot of things," she said in a mischievous tone.

Matthew looked like he wanted to reply, but he let her go instead. "Anyway, we better get Angel Boy to that guesthouse."

Lea nodded. "Yes, we better do that before I ravage you on the spot."

Matthew blinked back, but he seemed incapable of replying.

Lea blushed. "Oh my lord, that just slipped out."

Lea's statement didn't seem to help Matthew. He remained speechless, as if some unspoken edict prevented him from using his vocal cords.

After that they both went about their duties. Matthew got Eric ready for a short trip to a happier place, and Lea grabbed some of Eric's things to take with them.

Twenty-Nine

THE MORNING GOT off to an early start for Matthew. It was only six o'clock when he woke up, checked on Eric, and got dressed. Lea was already in the kitchenette drinking tea. Matthew took the opportunity to ask her if she'd like to chat out on the front porch. He wanted to talk in private.

Thankfully, the spring morning was mild enough, but Matthew insisted on Lea wearing her jacket. He wanted to make sure she was comfortable when he discussed some important issues with her. He had to set some things straight before their relationship went any further.

Once they were settled in two all-weather wicker chairs, there was a long pause. The view from the porch was postcard beautiful. A scattering of pine trees led down to a pond that was surrounded by flowers coming into bloom.

Lea took a deep breath of the fresh air and sighed. "I got at least seven hours. How about you? Did you sleep okay on that twin bed in Eric's room?"

"Yes, it was fine. Eric never woke up after he got settled in. When I checked on him this morning, he seemed okay."

Lea reached out for his hand. "You sound a little distant. What's going on?"

Matthew looked at Lea's outstretched hand, but he didn't take it. "I can't go on fooling you like this."

"How are you fooling me?"

Matthew forced himself to look Lea in the eye. "I'm not worthy of your ravishing. There, I've said it."

Lea gave him a confused smile. "My ravishing?"

"Yes, last night, you distinctly said you wanted to . . . to—"

"To ravish you? I'm sorry. I keep forgetting that we're not exactly a couple anymore, at least not in your mind."

Matthew reached out and grabbed her hand out of her lap. "Lea, I failed you when you needed me the most. I'm sorry, but I can't fix what happened. I'll always be ashamed of my conduct, but what's done is done." He let go of her hand. "So, it's probably better if you find someone like Angel Boy. Because you deserve someone like him."

"Matthew, you're being silly."

"No, I'm not. The problem is you don't remember how horrible I was. If you did, you'd never want to see me again."

Lea directed her gaze at the lake. "But I do remember. I remember being very upset and going to your office. I remember your poor receptionist, and how I bullied my way past her. I remember you, staring down at me with those weary eyes, like a storm was battering at your door again."

"I'm sorry I was so callous."

Lea got up and stood in front of him. "Do you want to know why I love you anyway?"

Matthew didn't know if he did or not. He was still trying to process the fact that Lea remembered the events leading up to a near mental breakdown. But he had to find out what Lea saw in him. "Go on."

Lea reached down and pushed back the hair falling across his brow. "When you and my family found me in Baltimore and things didn't work out—"

"I'm sorry about that too. Now that I've gotten to know Eric, I regret hitting him. He's a good guy."

"And you're a good guy too. That's what I found out when I started reading my diary. It had details about our life together and how I acted. Frankly, I don't know how you put up with me. I was so horrible so much of the time."

Matthew shrugged. "It was tough, but on occasion you could be so—"

"Adorable?" Lea asked in a playful voice.

Matthew remained serious. "You didn't say much, but I could tell that you'd had a very rough time growing up. I kept hoping you'd let go of that part of your life, and we would—"

Lea hugged herself. "I know. The diary was very clear about how forgiving you were. Now, after learning about what happened to me as a child—"

"Did you talk to your psychiatrist about what happened?"

"No, I didn't have time to get into all that before I came out here."

"Raymond seemed shocked when he found out what happened."

Lea shrugged. "I guess I didn't think about that. Besides, when I read my diary, I often skipped the parts about hearing voices or other nutty stuff. I concentrated on the good parts."

"That was probably a wise thing to do."

"Yes, but I'm sorry for how I treated you. I don't have any excuses except that the abused can become the abuser. Still, I hated myself for being that way. That's why I ran. You didn't deserve to marry the ugly person I was."

Matthew's hands closed in on themselves. "I was so scared that you were dead or god-knows-what else."

"I wanted to disappear, and I guess I got my wish, but at your expense. That wasn't fair. So don't worry about the way you were at your office. I understand why you did what you did."

Matthew looked over his shoulder. "Yes, well Eric would have never behaved like that. He got on a plane and flew here as soon as he knew you were in trouble."

"Eric was lucky. He never knew the horrible me."

Matthew looked up at her. "I still don't understand why you love me. You have no memory of our time together."

Lea laughed. "I did have that one meeting when you came to take me back to Chicago."

Matthew blinked back. "When you told me that you loved Eric?"

"Please, it's hard not to love him. But even when I had that crush on him, I didn't want to—"

"Ravish him?"

Lea laughed. "No, I didn't. It was an innocent, little crush."

"Right. Who doesn't love an angel?"

"Anyway, when you took me in your arms that day, I felt your strong, beautiful heart, and I knew you wanted to love and protect me. Then as I kept going over what I wrote in my diary, and the picture of our life together filled in, I fell in love with you all over again."

"So the old Lea had some nice stuff to say about me?"

Lea laughed. "Yes, I think I already admitted that."

Matthew was studying the porch flooring, but he looked up. "Maybe I need to hear it again."

"You weren't the problem." Lea hesitated. "Anyway, when I came here to visit my parents, I got scared. I didn't know what to think and I wanted answers. So I went to your office."

"What happened when your dad picked you up?"

"I wanted to run away again. And I guess I did. I wanted to shut out everything. But then Eric showed up. When I saw him, I felt like a kid. All I wanted was for him to hold me, to tell me I wasn't so bad. When I woke up the next day, I felt different. I think I felt truly alive."

"Yes, I understand that feeling."

"Poor Eric, he didn't fare well coming here, did he?"

"Thankfully, from what I can tell, he's recovering. Of course, he'll probably think he's staying in a nice motel. We better be prepared if he freaks out again."

"I think he'll be fine as long as he doesn't go back to the big house."

Matthew laughed. "The big house? It sounds like a prison."

Lea glanced over at Matthew with soulful eyes.

"What is it?" he quickly asked.

"Do you mind holding me now? I mean, have your feelings truly changed since my visit to your office?"

Matthew stood up and reached out for her hand. "Give me a break, woman. You know the answer to that. So don't play coy."

"I'm serious—"

Matthew pulled her close and kissed her before she could complete her sentence. "Does that answer your question?"

Lea smiled. "You make my heart do funny things, Doctor Howell."

Matthew smiled back. He wanted to believe that he and Lea were finally getting a break. A flutter in his stomach made him wonder. He didn't know if it was a good flutter or a bad flutter. "I feel good too, but what if we're both being fooled? What if Angel Boy's magic wears off."

Lea laid her head on his chest and hugged him. "Then we'll have to find a way to make our own magic."

"Make magic? I'm sorry, but I'm just a practical surgeon, please don't ask for the impossible."

Lea looked up and laughed. "Don't worry. I can be practical too. Look at how I came up with a plan last night."

"Yes, well I wish you'd come up with a way I didn't have to return to the 'big house,' but I better check in with Paul and bring him up to date. He's probably wondering what's become of us."

Lea held him tighter. "Please be extra careful. After everything that's happened, I don't want that place affecting you too."

Matthew let her go and pushed back his shoulders. He didn't know about magic, but Lea was right. The Ferguson mansion worried him. Eric seemed to think the place was downright dangerous. That was probably just Eric's out-of-whack emotions, but still. Matthew hoped there weren't any more surprises waiting for him.

* * *

Matthew found Paul Glass sitting in the dining room and braced himself. Paul's body language was shouting out a clear message. The psychiatrist wasn't happy. Matthew cleared his throat. "Morning, Paul."

Paul looked up with bloodshot eyes. His hands were gripping a large mug. "Matthew, I was going to check on Eric, but I thought I better have a cup of coffee first."

"Eric isn't here. He's down at the guest house. The guy is freaked out by this place, so Lea and I thought we better do something about it."

Paul's worn eyes lifted briefly. "Sounds like a good idea. How about Lea? Is she okay?"

"Thankfully, she seems well enough. She's keeping an eye on Eric," Matthew said as he approached a massive, Victorian sideboard. He was about to get some coffee and hesitated. He'd avoided actually examining the furniture in the Ferguson home, but after Eric's

212

hysteria, he was a little spooked himself. He found the marble-topped mahogany piece almost intimidating as well as depressing. Besides those unpleasant qualities, it seemed like it was there to make a statement. The owner of the house was announcing his status by way of the size of the piece and its elaborate carvings and embellishments.

Matthew quickly got his coffee and took a seat at the table. "Paul, I have a question. Do you know anything about houses being a problem for certain people?"

"Some individuals get very upset in so-called, haunted places. They claim they can feel the bad vibes."

"Do you believe in that sort of thing?"

Paul had been staring at his mug, but Matthew's question brought him to life. His weary eyes turned hard. "I believe in people and the choices they make," he replied in a stern tone.

Matthew sat down at the table, cup in hand. "Is something bothering you?"

"I was up all night, thinking about things. After we got Eric to bed, Raymond called me. It seems that when he returned to his room, Rita was waiting for him. She told him she wants a divorce. I think he nearly had a heart attack. It wasn't easy to calm him down."

"I'm a little surprised. Since I've known them, Rita and Raymond were always very supportive around each other."

Paul slumped over the table. "You were right, Matthew, I have been juggling lives. And I can't juggle worth a damn anymore."

"Why do you say that? I thought you believed in—" Matthew paused to think about his conversation with Paul the day before. "You said we had to keep the momentum going, and something about the mystery involved."

"The rantings of an old fool."

"Paul, this thing about Rita and Raymond isn't surprising. I said they supported each other, but of course, we both know they also had a lot of problems. The information about Lea's childhood must have triggered something for both of them."

Paul glared back. "I triggered them! I took a couple of wounded people and threw them into a pit and let them fight it out."

"Why? What did you think you'd accomplish?"

Paul loosened his grip on his cup. He fell back in his chair. "I made a bad choice. What more is there to say?"

213

"Okay, but I've done a little research. You have a reputation for being good at what you do. The words, unorthodox methods, were used to describe you, but it seems you got results."

Paul pushed his chair back and stood up. "I got results here too. The Fergusons, two emotional cripples, are barely surviving. Eric nearly killed himself after processing the news about his father. By the way, I'm the one who delivered that news with my usual care and wisdom. Now he's forfeiting his career as a doctor. The man's talking about working in a pet store, cleaning bird cages for the rest of his life. Meanwhile his sweet mother, the most nurturing of women, will be forever beating herself up. Oh, and there's one more thing, she'll always remember me as the person who ruined her life!"

Matthew blinked back. He didn't know how to respond. Paul was standing on the other side of the table, breathing heavily. His misdeeds had been delivered in the fervent style of a pulpit pounder. Now his fire was gone. He was staring absently into space. Matthew cleared his throat, not knowing how to help. Some words escaped before he thought about what he was saying. "So what do you plan to do next?" As soon as he asked the question, he was slightly shocked at himself. It didn't come out the way it was intended.

Paul straightened up and glowered back. "What's my next trick? Is that what you're asking? I think that's obvious. I'm retiring. Hopefully, with my meditation practice for support and getting down on my knees and praying, I'll find a moment of peace before I take my last breath in this world."

Matthew remained quiet as Paul started out of the dining room. The man's shoulders were hunched and his gait was only slightly better than Eric's the night before. Another casualty. "Oh hell, I'm the only guy left standing in this place."

But Matthew wasn't standing. He was sitting in a quiet dining room, drinking his coffee. Plus, he'd had a great talk with Lea earlier. No matter what, he had to stay focused on the positive, not people's problems. He had to remain the calm Doctor Howell, the go-to guy who knew how to handle a crisis. "There's no curse. This house is just a house," he sighed.

He was enjoying a moment of calm when a woman's cry was sounded. It was Margaret Lloyd's voice. She came running towards him.

"Matthew, I'm so relieved to see you here!" she called out as she rushed forward.

He stood immediately, just in time for impact. Margaret slammed into him, and threw her arms around his body.

"You were such a godsend last night. Thank you for taking such good care of my Eric. I hardly got a wink of sleep thinking about how awful he looked. So terrified! In his condition—" Her voice broke into sobs as she continued to hang on to him, her embrace getting fiercer with each sobbing breath.

Matthew's heart started to pound. Margaret's strength was impressive. She'd probably developed a powerful body during those years as a poor, country doctor's wife, scrubbing clothes on a washboard and splitting cords of wood for the stove. Now she had him in a bear hug. He didn't know if he'd be strong enough to extricate himself if he needed to. After being sick and not getting back to the gym in quite a while, he'd lost some ground.

Margaret looked up at him with pleading eyes. "Promise that you'll stick by my boy, that you'll make sure he doesn't feel alone again. Please!"

Matthew's heart sped up. He remembered Margaret's last emotional storm and how she'd fainted. "I promise," he said quickly as he got her to a chair. Unfortunately, she wasn't ready to sit down.

"Matthew, tell me what I should do. How can I make it right with Eric after my inexcusable behavior?"

Matthew's mind was a blank. That file in his brain, the one that was supposed to contain words of comfort, that one that a doctor used as part of his bedside manner, that file was empty. "My goodness, Margaret, maybe if my mother were half as concerned about her son as you are, I'd know how to help. Unfortunately, I'm not very good with people. I'm sorry."

Margaret reacted immediately by letting go of him, quickly drying her eyes with a tissue, and straightening up to stare at him with an intense focus. "Matthew Howell, your mother didn't recognize how fortunate she was to have you. I only wish Eric could have had a brother like you, someone strong who would have helped him through the trials of life. So please, be that brother now, if only for a little while. Can you do that, Matthew, and save me from a broken heart?"

Paul Glass's pulpit pounding couldn't hold a candle to the fervor in Margaret Lloyd's motherly repertoire. As she spoke in the soul-stirring voice of a momma grizzly intent on getting its point across, Matthew's head was bobbing up and down on its own accord. He was saying things, but he didn't know where the words were coming from. "Thank you. You're very kind to say that. And certainly, I'll try to help Eric. I'll do everything I can—" He almost added, "I swear that we'll win this battle," but he finally regained a bit of his composure.

Margaret followed up by embracing him again. She was letting him know that they were now bonded in a common mission, to help her boy. As an added bonus, Margaret Lloyd was cementing that bond by hugging the life out of him.

The day had barely begun, and Matthew had already been the sounding board for two individuals in crisis. Paul Glass should have been the one who was taking charge of the situation. But Paul was one of the stricken. Matthew hadn't seen that coming. He hadn't expected to take on sibling status either. But again, he caved when it came to refusing Margaret Lloyd. Now he had to tread as carefully as possible before another emotional landmine came his way.

As he contemplated his chances of survival, of weathering the curse of the "big house," he could only hope that the taxi cab from Baltimore showed up sooner than later. Eric and he could both make an escape.

* * *

Eric woke up and blinked a couple of times. The darkness wasn't there anymore. The light of day was coming in through the partially closed blinds. He glanced around, but he didn't recognize the place. The good part was that he liked what he saw. The cool-blue walls and white woodwork delivered a sense of calm. The modern furniture, with light woods and straight lines, was easy on his senses. It felt safe to stretch out his sore muscles.

As he let himself relax, he appreciated the purity and comfort of the white bed linens. The sheets were soft to the touch, and the fluffy, nearly weightless comforter reminded him of something manufactured in the clouds. It felt so good to lie in the bed and enjoy the quiet.

The only part of him that moved was his gaze. It wandered around the room and came to rest on some framed photos of ferns. The pictures transported him back to the woods in summer. As he pondered the peacefulness of nature, he could breathe again.

He was climbing out of bed when a brief memory surfaced. While Eric had been in that state that was in-between the worlds of sleep and wakefulness, he thought he saw Matthew standing over him. He tried to remember why the surgeon looked concerned, but his brain felt tired, too tired for questions and answers.

He walked into the bathroom, stretching again and noticing that parts of his body hurt. But he forgot everything when he glanced up and became aware of the room itself. So bright, so refreshing. Walls and flooring were a pleasing off white. The built-in shelving and cabinetry hid any sign of clutter. The only other color came from several deep green plants. All in all, the word, perfect, came to mind. The room was a place for quiet relaxation.

He wandered over to the large walk-in shower. It was enclosed in glass and equipped with both a rain shower head and a body spray system. After he undressed and got in, he enjoyed the body spray. It had just the right amount of pressure to help him relax even more.

All was well until he washed his arms and noticed multiple bruises. As he studied the discolored areas, he remembered parts of some outlandish dream he'd had. He'd been running off somewhere. "And I fell down the stairs at the Ferguson house."

Memory started to return as soon as the words were out. His bout of madness hadn't been a dream at all. But at some point, he must have lost the ability to fully comprehend what was going on around him. He only had privy to some disjointed images. Lea and Matthew appeared in a collage of more craziness.

He turned off the shower, paused and thought about his morning. He'd come awake in a place that felt comforting and safe. That meant someone had rescued him from his nightmarish journey. He was grateful for that kind act, very grateful. He smiled as he remembered a little more. "It was Lea and Matthew. They make a great team."

Thirty

LEA WALKED UP the path to her parent's house with an extra spring in her step. Eric was quickly returning to normal. In fact, when she'd talked to him, he seemed to have a good idea about how he'd slipped away from reality the night before. When he'd met with his mother, he wasn't in a very good place. He was already suffering from exhaustion and some old fears he'd had as a child. When things were said by both himself and his mother, he must have panicked. Afterwards, his emotions continued to spiral.

His explanation made sense, but Lea felt he should remain at the guest house until he had a chance to talk to Matthew or Paul. In the meantime, she wanted to check on Eric's mother. She promised him that she'd convey his apologies.

Instead of using the main back entrance, Lea used the service door. She wanted to tell the cook to send some breakfast down to Eric. When she walked into the kitchen, she noticed the servants were gathered together in a group. They were whispering in an animated way that made her frown. She prayed that nothing had happened to Matthew. She'd tried to call him to check on the house occupants, but he'd forgotten to take his phone when he'd left earlier.

Now, with the servants gossiping, it was possible that the cursed house had claimed another victim, her Matthew. When she saw the chauffeur, Joseph, she called him over. She'd get the tall man to tell her all. "Joseph, talk to me. Has something happened?"

Joseph backed up. "That's not for me to say, Miss Lea."

Lea straightened and raised her chin. "I think if the servants know something about what's going on in this house, I'm entitled to know too. So tell me what you were discussing."

Joseph looked down, clasping his hat with both hands. "It's your mama, Miss Lea, she's leaving."

"Rita? Where is she going?"

"No, you don't understand. She's packing her things and leaving your papa."

"Now? She's leaving now?"

"Yes, ma'am."

Lea didn't know how to process the news. She hardly knew her mother. When Rita was mentioned in Lea's diary, it was clear that they didn't get along. When they had met a couple of days earlier, the meeting didn't go well either. Their brief interaction provoked Lea's guilt, and it was straight downhill for her after that.

Lea didn't blame Rita for her upset. It was Lea's choice to give in to the bad feelings she had about herself. Now, Rita was leaving, and Lea didn't know when she'd have a chance to see her again.

Lea reached out and patted Joseph's arm. "Thank you, Joseph. I'll go up to her room and wish her well before she goes. Oh, and would you have the cook send breakfast down to the guest house. Doctor Lloyd is staying there."

"Yes, Miss Lea."

Lea started for the service elevator when she heard Joseph call out.

"Miss Lea, if your mama's in one of her moods, you better mind your Ps and Qs."

Lea turned to look back at him. Joseph's face was old and lined, and his eyes were filled with concern. "I'll remember that, Joseph."

A short while later, when she stood in front of Rita's bedroom door, Joseph's warning made Lea cautious. She'd already experienced one of her mother's emotional flare-ups. She didn't want a repeat performance.

"Peace," she told herself. "This house needs peace, not more turmoil."

She knocked very lightly and waited. When there was no answer, she knocked on the door a second time.

This time there was a loud response from Rita. "Who in the hell is bothering me now?" she yelled out.

Lea opened the door a crack and looked in. "Mother, it's me."

Rita was coming out of her closet with clothes in hand. "Oh great, are you coming to gloat, Baby?"

Lea held her tongue, waited for Rita to say more and finally walked over to a chair by the window.

Rita glanced up as she folded a white, silk shirt. "I know you hate me, so just say it. Don't sit there looking all pretty and dumb."

"How can I hate you, mother? I don't know you. I don't know father either."

Rita put her hands on her hips. "Well, let me enlighten you. Before your so-called amnesia, you always made sure to let me know how you felt. I don't think I saw you smile a half dozen times in twenty-eight years. So please leave so I can finally have a little peace."

Lea didn't move. "Where will you go when you leave here?"

"I'll stay at a hotel until I can get my own place. And I'll enjoy life for a change. I won't have to be your daddy's pretty, little wife anymore."

"But you two always got along from the little I know."

"House of cards, Baby, built on shit. If I'd been smart, I'd have done what you did and got the hell out before I had you."

Lea stared back, calming herself, telling herself that she couldn't take the statement personally. "Why didn't you leave?"

Rita let out a forceful laugh. "You haven't a clue about what it's like to have nothing, to be nothing. No matter what happened to you, you never had to go hungry or lay on some filthy bed knowing some man was going to do things to you, and you'd have no say in the matter. So a person looks for a way out, any way out. They hope, they dream that they'll wake and the squalor will disappear." Rita put a shaky hand to her head. "And that's what happened to me when I married Raymond. I even thought we could be happy, but it wasn't enough for him. He just had to have a child, someone to take over his precious empire. And nothing I said would convince him otherwise. Now look what it's come to. You're sitting there not even knowing who he is . . . who I am. And for that, you should be damn grateful. If I could only forget—"

Lea realized that Margaret had said the same thing to her. She stood up. "I always upset you. I better go."

Rita went on packing, pushing down sweaters and bulky knits with forceful thrusts. But when Lea reached out for the doorknob, and it made a small clicking sound, Rita jerked around. "Lea!"

Lea startled and looked at her. "Yes, what is it?"

"No matter what you think, I did give you life, Baby. Remember that. Remember I could have gotten rid of you when I first got pregnant, and your father would have never known."

Lea's grip tightened on the door knob. "Why didn't you?"

Rita laughed, but it was laced with bitterness. "I don't know why. Maybe I'd seen too much ugliness already. So I couldn't kill you, but you nearly killed me. The doctor said I wasn't built to have children."

Lea glanced down, studying the plush carpet. "I wish I understood why there's so much pain in the world."

"There just is."

When Lea looked up, Rita's back was turned. She was packing again. "Goodbye, I hope things work out for you."

Rita glanced back. Her eyes, two dark pools of swirling anger, softened just a little. "Take care of yourself, Baby. Make my suffering count for something."

* * *

Matthew was still sitting in the dining room with Margaret. After she'd calmed down, he'd convinced her to eat some breakfast. He used the old ploy that she needed to eat for Eric's sake if not her own. She'd be stronger if her son needed her. The ploy was tried and true. Few mothers could refuse such a plea.

Of course, she'd turned it around on him, claiming he had to eat for the same reason. Everyone in the house needed him. When Matthew argued back that he didn't have an appetite, Margaret's plea was followed by a reinforcing technique used by mothers worldwide. Margaret gave him the 'mother's look.'

The day before, Paul had mentioned how much a look could convey, and Matthew was now getting a demonstration. Margaret's facial expression delivered a couple of firm directives. First of all, a child, or the person being treated like a child, needed to understand that they had no choice in the matter. Secondly, there was that persuasive undertone, an unspoken request that said, "Please, eat, do it for Mommy."

Margaret had honed the skill to perfection. Matthew sat hunched over his plate, trying to get down a large helping of eggs, hash browns and sausage. When he slowed in his effort to get his fork to his mouth, Margaret gave him the look again. She also added some words that Matthew knew were meant to coax a child along. A little sugar to take away the sting of doing what someone else wanted.

"Matthew, I want to thank you for being so understanding with me. And I want you to know that if you ever need an old lady's ear, you can call me. I probably won't have much of value to offer, but I'll always be there for you, just like you were there for Eric."

What could Matthew do after that sweet offer? He shoved the bite of food in his mouth and chewed. As he was being directed to take that last bite of sausage, he heard Lea's hail. When he glanced around she was coming into the dining room.

"Matthew, Mom, I was looking for you two," she called out.

Matthew started to stand, but Margaret was faster on her feet than he was. She sprung up out of her chair and practically ran to Lea. She soon had Lea in an embrace, but this embrace was more carefully applied. A gentle hug instead of a bone-crusher. Matthew felt his ribs. He was lucky they were still intact. For an 'old lady,' Margaret Lloyd was built for the wear and tear of battle conditions. If she ever got a hold of his hands, she'd probably put an end to his surgical career.

He stood back as he heard Lea filling Margaret in on Eric's condition. It sounded like the cardiologist wouldn't need a big brother after all. He breathed a little easier. Perhaps, the day had taken a dip, but now things were on an upswing.

He approached Lea after Margaret retreated a little. "I didn't mean to listen in, but I'm glad to hear that all is well."

Lea's eyes dimmed. "Yes, Eric is doing great, but Rita isn't in good shape."

Matthew's throat tightened when he heard Lea's distress. They'd had such an encouraging talk earlier. Was Lea's mood shifting again? "Yes, Paul just told me that she's divorcing Raymond. But Lea, I didn't know that you'd be affected—"

Lea sniffled. "I just talked to her."

Margaret reached out for Lea's hand. "I'm sorry if you're upset."

222

Lea shrugged. "I guess I shouldn't be. I don't have any memories about my mother, but the way she looked at me was hard."

Matthew quickly moved to Lea's side as soon as he heard the tone of her voice. It was an iffy tone. Lea could rally or quickly collapse into some unhappy emotion. He had to make sure she went the right way. Besides, he wanted to redeem himself after the incident at his office. "Lea, tell me what you need. I'm here for you."

Lea looked up at him. "Thank you," she said quietly.

Margaret let go of Lea's hand and grabbed Matthew's. "Look at you, Doctor Howell, being there for all of us. I told you that you needed that breakfast, didn't I?"

Matthew nodded as he felt her grip tightening. How many bushels of corn had Margaret shucked? Maybe she milked some cows too. He only knew his fears might come true if she didn't let up on his fingers. As he said a silent prayer, she finally released him. She reached up for his face instead, putting a powerful, warm hand on his cheek.

"You have a good man here, Lea. Hold on to him."

Lea's mood seemed to lift. She looked up at Matthew and smiled. "I know, Margaret. I'm very fortunate to have him, especially now, when I think about my parents. Their worlds are falling apart."

Margaret sighed. "Yes, that's the way life is sometimes. I can only hold on to that old saying, 'It's always darkest before the dawn.'"

Matthew sighed and began a new prayer. Like it or not, it was becoming almost routine to ask for help. As he faced the darkness that Margaret spoke about, any pride or thought that he could handle more people falling apart was gone. On the other hand, he was a recent recipient of Angel Boy's healing, and he was becoming a believer. He even managed to smile back at Lea and Margaret. "I don't know what to say. This is all so new for me—"

Margaret grabbed his hand again. "Stop worrying, Matthew, you're a natural healer like my Eric."

A shout came from the foyer. It interrupted any more thoughts that Matthew might manage. But he did recognize Paul Glass's voice.

Soon Paul was hurrying into the dining room. His eyes targeted Margaret than moved to Matthew. "Matthew, what kind of shape is Eric in?"

"He's doing pretty well. Why?"

Paul took a quick breath and continued. "Raymond asked me to come with him to Rita's room. He was about to knock on her door when it flew open. Rita was standing there with her luggage. When she yelled some obscenities at Raymond and pushed him out of her way, he grabbed for his chest and keeled over. I think he's having a heart attack. I called 911, but he's in a very bad way."

Matthew grabbed for his phone, but it wasn't in his pocket. Lea came to the rescue. She connected with Eric and handed her phone to Matthew. "Come up to the big house, Eric. Ferguson's had a heart attack."

Thirty-One

AS THE SOUNDS of the ambulance faded away, Paul Glass sat at the dining room table. "In all the years I've been at this job, I've never experienced anything like this."

"Who are you talking to?" Eric asked as he walked into the room.

Paul looked up and tried to smile, but he couldn't force his body to go beyond a feeling that it was lost and floundering. It was a state that matched his thoughts. But he had to put aside his selfish concerns. "How's Raymond?"

Eric sat down across from him and clasped his hands. "From what I can tell, he didn't have a heart attack. Maybe the shock of seeing his wife leaving brought on his symptoms."

Paul looked around, almost like he was waking up. He realized that he'd abandoned his post. When Raymond fell over, Paul had enough of his wits to summon help. Afterwards, he'd faltered. Instead of keeping an eye on those he was supposed to be helping, he'd been a little like Raymond. He'd collapsed into a terrible sense of failure. "What about Rita?"

"I think she was shocked too. She insisted on staying with Raymond when the medics were taking him away."

Paul nodded, trying to think, trying to put his thoughts in some kind of order. Finally, he was able to come back to the moment. He had to use his strength and determination just to stand. It was a strange feeling. Where was his normal mindset, that resourceful mechanism that propelled him through life? Where was the buoyant feeling that he could trust the circumstances around him, even when they were chaotic? He glanced at Eric. "Thank you, Eric. I'm so grateful that you were able to help. Now, if you'll excuse me, I need to pack."

Eric's brows went up. "What are you talking about, Paul? You called us all together. Now, are you saying that we should all go home?"

Paul shrugged. "You're so much more capable of assessing the situation. Do whatever you think is best?"

Eric frowned. "What's going on with you? Where's that cocky attitude you had when I first arrived?"

Paul blinked back, searching for an answer. Matthew was correct when he said that Paul had had a very successful career. Now, it was like that part of his life was over. The man who didn't believe in aging had left the building. A failing individual now filled his shoes. He walked over to Eric and managed a smile. "Appreciate yourself, Eric. You're very gifted, whether you acknowledge that fact or not." Paul stuck out his hand. "It's been a privilege to meet you."

Eric stood up and returned a handshape. "Okay . . . thank you."

Paul had been born with a psychic ability that few possessed. He usually had access to a much greater knowledge base than most. When he used his gift to tap into that knowledge base, his overview of a situation and his intuition were then used in conjunction with the facts involved. The process guided his actions and had always worked for him until he got involved with his current case.

"Take care of your mom, dear boy, but try not to be too overly protective. She'll find her way, I'm sure of it."

As soon as he made the statement, Paul quickly released Eric and hurried from the room. He had to put distance between himself and the Lloyd family. He suspected that they were the reason for his downfall.

* * *

Eric was still standing in place, wondering about Paul Glass, when his mother, Lea and Matthew walked into the dining room. They seemed to be in a better mood now that the ambulance was on its way. But when his mother looked at him, her face turned sad. Eric quickly walked over to her. "Mom, can you forgive me for what I said last night?"

Margaret didn't answer verbally. She hugged him. But after a moment, she pulled away with anxious eyes. "There's nothing to forgive you for, but can you forgive me?"

Eric smiled. Whatever craziness he'd felt was quickly falling back into the shadows. "It's this house. I think it brings out our worst."

Lea and Matthew walked over to join them.

"I don't believe in houses being cursed," Matthew said with a frown. "But I might have to make an exception with this place. I think we all need to leave."

Eric took his mother's hand. "Paul Glass seems to agree. He's gone upstairs to pack."

Lea hesitated. "So what are we doing now?" She looked at Margaret then Eric.

Eric reached out to her. "Are you ready to come back home with Mom and me?" He gave Matthew a quick glance. "Or do you have other plans?"

Lea smiled up at Matthew. "I want to stay in Chicago. I'm going to rent a place for a little while. I need to bridge the gap between my old and new life."

Matthew's face paled. "You could stay with me, couldn't you?"

Lea hugged his arm. "I want that more than anything, but after talking to Rita, I know I have to have some time. I want to think about my life and how to balance it out a little better."

Margaret nodded. "I know how Lea feels, I need some time too." She turned to Eric. "Honey, I can't go back with you, not yet."

It was time for Eric's face to lose color. "Really? Did I drive you away with my—"

"No, just the opposite, Eric. You helped me to see what I've been running away from. But now it's time for me to face my fears."

Lea's eyes sparked as she smiled at Margaret. "We could share an apartment if you'd like, Mom."

Margaret beamed back a look of happiness. "I'd like that very much."

Thirty-Two

CHICAGO'S SPRING WAS rainy and cool, but Margaret ignored the weather. She couldn't stop thinking about her decision to strike out on her own. It was a much bigger challenge than she'd anticipated. While living with Eric in the Baltimore suburbs, her life was simple and straight forward. She cleaned and cooked and did a little shopping at the grocery store. Except for living in a more populated environment, her life was similar to the one she'd had in Elkville. She'd done what she'd always done, she'd maintained her role as a mother. Now, there wasn't much to clean, and Lea didn't seem to need any mothering. The young woman was very self-sufficient.

With a sigh, Margaret picked up her cup of tea and walked it into the living room. Lea was curled up in a chair, scribbling in her diary. Seeing Margaret, Lea looked up and smiled. Margaret smiled back as she sat down on the couch. "Anything happy to report?"

Lea's eyes softened into a contented sparkle. "We've only been on our own for a short time, but I think we're both getting the hang of it, don't you?"

Margaret let her eyes drift to the window. The upper limbs of a maple tree were turning a bright green. The color contrasted sharply with the dreary drizzle that pelted the tree's new leaves. "Perhaps."

"Is anything bothering you? You're wearing your sad face."

"When I lived in Elkville, I spent a lot of time by myself. Ricky was always out taking care of people. After he died, I thought I'd learned to adjust to life without him." She smiled at Lea again. "Then I met you, and I really enjoyed our time together."

Lea put her diary aside. "But now? Are you glad that you stayed here instead of going back to Baltimore?"

"I don't think it matters where I'm at now."

"Maybe you're bored. We should get out and do some exploring. We've been busy gathering the basics for this apartment, but that's not the same as enjoying ourselves."

Margaret looked around. The apartment had two bedrooms, but its living area was small and sparsely furnished. "I'm glad we didn't spend too much. We aren't planning to stay here, are we?"

Lea shrugged. "I thought we said we wanted to take our time, you know, to think about everything before we make any big decisions."

Margaret glanced at Lea's diary. "Dearest, I think we both know that there is a certain doctor in your future."

Lea blushed. "I do love Matthew, but I've been thinking about what you said when you talked about being a doctor's wife."

Margaret put her cup on the end table and sat up straighter. "What did I say? I hope it wasn't something that would interfere with how you feel about Matthew. I've only spent a little time with him, but I think he's very nice."

Lea sat up too. "Being a doctor's wife is fine, but there has to be more, doesn't there? What about your own life?"

Margaret frowned and pulled her sweater closer. "Oh, I see. Eric pointed out the same thing, that I never learned to be my own person." She shrugged. "You're both right. I feel like I'm adrift, and I haven't a clue about what to do with myself now."

"Then we're in the same boat. I volunteered at a hospital in Baltimore, but I think I want to try something new. Even if I was a doctor before, I don't feel drawn to that profession."

"I don't feel drawn to anything either."

Lea stood up and stretched. She was still wearing her PJs and a fluffy pink robe. "We need to get out of here. Chicago is a big place. We could go to some art galleries. You loved painting."

Margaret glanced out the window again. "I don't know. The weather is dismal. It's not the kind of day that—"

"Please, listen to me, you would never let me talk like that when I was down. You helped me to keep moving and find things to do that made me happy."

Margaret let out a big sigh. "You're right. I sound like Florence Bowan. She could be very depressing with all her complaints. Now, I'm starting to know why she sounded like that."

Lea came over and sat down next to her. "We'll check out our options together."

"But we're different Lea. You're so young. You have your whole life ahead of you."

Lea gave her a puzzled look. "You're full of life too."

Margaret knew she couldn't burden Lea with her problems. It was better to give in to the young woman's suggestion than upset her. "You're right. Let's go out and see what happens."

Lea gave her a hug. "Good."

Margaret stood up and tried to smile. "I'll go get dressed."

Even as she said the words, she knew she was repeating an old pattern. How many times had she forced herself to climb out of bed in the morning, dress, and do whatever needed to be done for her family?

Year in and year out, there was never time to think about life outside of certain set parameters and duties. She loved being a wife and mother, but somewhere along the way, she lost touch with who she was. Would she settle for that kind of life again? Maybe she would. It certainly felt better than the alternative, sitting in her chair, feeling sorry for herself.

* * *

Matthew stood in the filing area of the office and pocketed his phone. He frowned at his partner, Ralph. "I wonder why Glass won't answer. I had some questions and wanted his advice."

Ralph put a folder in one of the cabinets and turned around. "He's that shrink, right? Maybe he's away or just avoiding calls. It sounds like he wasn't happy when you saw him last."

"But I've been trying to contact him for over a week. He should be bouncing back."

Ralph shrugged and glanced at the wall clock. "I'm ready to call it a day. What about you? Are you having dinner with Lea?"

"She didn't want to leave Margaret alone tonight."

"The woman who helped her after the amnesia?"

"Yes, now Lea's on the other end of the stick. She said that Margaret is getting more depressed by the day."

Ralph smiled. "Maybe Margaret should give Paul Glass a call. From what you told me, he's normally very good at what he does."

"Yes, he's respected, but he's got his own weird way of handling things. Still, when I think about Lea, I'm grateful. She's doing well. And as for Lea's father and mother, they're not in the best shape, but they're talking again and finally facing their problems. All in all, things worked out better than I thought possible."

"Except for Margaret."

Matthew sucked in a breath. "Yes, except for Margaret, and I suspect, Paul Glass."

Ralph clasped Matthew's shoulder. "I'm grateful, too. Recently, you've been looking a lot better. How about coming over to Nicky's tonight? She's making enchiladas."

Matthew returned a barely perceptible smile. "I think you like her."

Ralph let go of Matthew and headed for the door. "Maybe I do. So are you coming to dinner?"

"Thanks, but I have other plans."

After Ralph left, Matthew took out his phone and redialed. This time he left a message for Paul Glass. "Margaret Lloyd is very depressed. Just thought you'd like to know."

Before Matthew could pocket his phone, it rang.

As soon as Matthew answered the call, his face turned smug. He'd played his ace in a hole, and it worked. "Hi Paul."

Paul didn't offer a return greeting. He asked Matthew a question instead.

"Can you come over, Matthew?"

Matthew nodded. "Sure."

As Matthew was locking up the office, he paused. That unwanted feeling in his gut was suddenly making itself known. As it took hold, he hoped it didn't have anything to do with Lea. But he didn't think so. He thought about Paul and their short conversation. Paul didn't sound right. His tone was too edgy and unsure for a strong-willed guy who liked driving a sporty car with five hundred plus horses under the hood. "Great, if he's still in a slump, I'm the one who just had to call him."

Matthew was impressed with Paul's building. As he rode the elevator to the psychiatrist's high-rise condo, he was figuring out what one of the units would cost. By the time he got to Paul's floor, he knew the amount was definitely more than he was prepared to shell out.

In fact, after being subjected to the Ferguson mansion, he'd decided that he didn't need anything too extravagant when it came to a house. When he and Lea married, which looked like a promising prospect, he was thinking of a home in the suburbs. It wouldn't be too big, but something more like Eric Lloyd's modest residence.

He and Eric had talked a couple of times since Eric had returned to Baltimore. Their conversations had been pleasant, and Matthew was beginning to think of Eric as a friend, a friend with a gift that was still with Matthew. He kept waiting to wake up to his old, grumpy self, but so far so good.

Paul Glass was a different matter. Like Matthew had told Ralph, he was grateful to the man, but Paul had an edge that rubbed Matthew the wrong way. Recently, Paul had reined in his ego after a series of mishaps, but Matthew figured Paul had had enough time to get back to his former, over-confident self.

Matthew knocked on Paul's door and stood back. He was there to get some help for Margaret so that Lea could stop worrying. He was about to knock a second time when the door opened. He didn't see Paul at first. The room beyond was in shadows, and the man he'd come to talk to was mostly hidden behind his door.

"Come in, Matthew," Paul said as he opened the door a little wider.

Matthew stepped forward hesitantly. "Is there a problem with the electricity, Paul?"

Paul let out a faint sigh. "Oh, sorry, I've been meditating a lot. My eyes are used to candlelight. I'll turn on a lamp."

Matthew waited in the foyer as Paul wandered over to a side table by the sofa. After he switched on the light, Paul turned to Matthew.

"Come in and sit down."

Matthew stared at Paul's lamp as he walked over to the sofa. It was better than a candle but not by much. "Paul, that lamp of yours

232

must be putting out a good twenty-five watts of illumination. I can almost see my hand in front of me."

"Please excuse the inconvenience. I prefer the darkness right now."

As Matthew's eyes adjusted to the low-wattage, he got a better look at Paul. The man's thick, white mane of hair was no longer carefully groomed. It was hanging in Paul's eyes and generally unruly. Instead of a clean shaven face, Paul was sporting the stubble look.

Paul smiled knowingly. "I've had a lot of restless nights. I should have combed my hair or at least shaved when I knew you'd be stopping by. But you didn't come here to talk about my grooming habits. Tell me about Mrs. Lloyd."

"I thought we were supposed to call each other by our first names."

Paul shrugged. "Do whatever. I'm not involved anymore."

Matthew sat back on the sofa. "I don't agree. Our little group came together with you at the helm. We trusted you—"

"Well, I'm not at the helm now. That's why I asked you here. Whatever is going on with Margaret needs to be addressed. And as I see it, you're the man for the job. I saw how she clung to you when her son fell down the stairs that night. She trusts you now."

Matthew jerked up. "Me? I'm not a therapist. That's your department."

"Not anymore. I was thinking about retirement before the Ferguson case. It just pushed me in the right direction."

"Oh, how convenient for you. Screw up people's lives and run away."

"Think what you want, but I know what's best in this situation."

"You're concerned about Margaret, aren't you?"

Paul looked away, avoiding Matthew's eyes. When he spoke, his voice was low and soulful. "I don't know how to undo the harm I've caused. When I tapped into her feelings that last day, I knew she'd never have anything to do with me."

"What do you mean you tapped into her feelings? Are you saying you could read her mind?"

"No, but I do have a gift like Eric. I can sense the feelings of others as easily as I can feel my own. I've learned how to control my ability, how to shut out other people's turmoil, but in Margaret's case, I had to know."

233

"Paul, it's evident that you have a little crush on the woman, but—"

Paul burst out laughing. "I wish. I wish with all my heart that it was only a crush. I've had my share of them, but this is different. I've gone almost seventy years without this kind of thing happening."

"What? What's happened? Are you saying you've fallen for Margaret?"

Paul got up and started to pace. "I don't want to talk about it."

"Why?"

"Because you'll do what people like you do."

Matthew stood up too. "What do you mean by that?"

Paul turned and glared back. "You minimize other people's feelings because they make you uncomfortable."

"If that's so, why am I here, asking you to help Margaret?"

Paul's scowl deepened. "You want your life back, Matthew. And I understand that. You want Lea happy so you can get on with your lives. And all of that is fine. I don't go around judging other people's choices. I'm the guy they call when those choices go haywire and everybody's screaming. But I'm tired of it all. And most of all, I'm disappointed in the fact that I've become one of the screamers." He held out a shaky hand. "Look at me. I used to be rock solid. Now I don't dare peel an apple with a sharp knife. I haven't just fallen for Margaret, I'm falling apart."

Matthew sat back down on the sofa. "Maybe it's not you. Maybe the Ferguson curse is still at work."

Paul came over and stared down at him. "What are you talking about?"

Matthew leaned forward, clasping his hands. "Don't you think it's strange that first Eric, now you, have both gone haywire?"

Paul laughed again, but this time it was a good-natured laugh. "It has nothing to do with a curse."

Matthew glanced up, studying the twinkle in Paul's eyes. It had been absent until that moment. "So what's going on?"

Paul sat down and took a couple of deep breaths. "I've been asking myself that since I came home. I think I might have a partial answer, but you're not going to like it."

"Just say what you have to say."

"I don't believe the house is cursed in the way you think, but the place might retain a lot of negative energy. There are locations on the earth that amplify energy fields, negative or positive."

"That doesn't sound very scientific, but it's better than thinking the house is cursed."

"Plus there's the human factor. I believe that everyone in our group, Lea, you, Eric, Margaret and I, and even Raymond and Rita to some extent, are very empathic. When we came together and allowed ourselves to give in to our negative emotions, the pain factor that we all shared, increased."

Matthew tried to relate. "Like when families come together at Christmas and push each other's buttons."

"Yes, but if a hyper-empathic person like Eric is low on energy and gets his buttons pushed, he can overreact."

"Luckily, I came out just fine."

Paul gave him a sly smile. "You had a very bad headache, remember? But you recovered very quickly."

Matthew didn't say anything. He'd promised to keep Eric's part in the healing a secret. But what if Paul's abilities made a secret an impossible thing to keep? "Let me ask you something. Do you usually respect a person's privacy?"

"Of course I do. It's better for me. I can maintain an unbiased perspective of the group's dynamics."

"So what do you suggest we do with Margaret?"

"I told you, I'm out. However, you could let yourself come up with some ideas."

"I don't know why we can't simply get together for a nice dinner."

Paul pulled back. "What do you mean by 'we'?"

Matthew took out his phone. "I'll invite Lea and Margaret to my place. In the meantime, you take a shower. You look like one of the drifters hanging around the rail yards."

Paul held up a hand in protest. "I can't see Margaret Lloyd! I'll upset her."

Matthew gave him a stern look. "Since I'm in charge, you don't have a say in the matter. So go take a shower."

"What will you serve for dinner?"

"I can order some pizza."

235

Paul frowned. "If I'm going to see Margaret again, I'd like the dinner to be special. It will probably be my last chance to prove myself."

"Fine, what about Chinese takeout?"

"No, we'll stop at a market and pick up some things. I'll make dinner."

"I thought you couldn't safely wield a butter knife."

"You can help."

"I don't know anything about cooking, and I don't care to learn."

"Fine, I'll pull myself together in the shower. In the meantime, go in the kitchen and get my wok, some sauce pans, and my favorite knife. It's the largest one on the knife strip."

"Paul, is this really necessary?"

Paul was already hurrying out of the room, but he called back. "Yes, I'm going to make at least one nice meal for Margaret before we part company forever."

"Oh hell, he's got it bad," Matthew mumbled as he headed for the kitchen and switched on the light. "Finally, some decent lighting."

He took a moment to study the space. It was very different than his own. His kitchen inventory contained the bare essentials needed to prepare frozen dinners and an occasional foray into the exotic world of an egg scramble. Paul's kitchen was more like a chef's dream. It was spotlessly clean and well organized. Overhead, a large rectangular pot rack was filled with assorted pots and pans, including the wok that Paul mentioned. A food processer, slow cooker, bread machine and other appliances lined the pristine, white counters. Various kitchen utensils that Matthew couldn't identify were stored in a couple of stainless steel holders.

Matthew was particularly impressed by Paul's knives. A mounted wall strip hosted a number of extraordinary blades. Matthew wasn't an expert when it came to the culinary arts, but he knew quality when he saw it. He was drawn to the large chef's knife that Paul had wanted to take along. It was a beauty. The hammered, high carbon, stainless steel blade was polished and potentially treacherous if the user wasn't careful. Matthew tested the edge and let out a low whistle. In Paul's shaky condition, the man would definitely damage himself if his fingers slipped.

Matthew replaced the knife. "No way, Paul. You can use one of mine."

As he gathered up the kitchen items that Paul needed, Matthew realized how little he knew about the man. He could only hope that he wasn't making a mistake hosting a dinner that brought the psychiatrist and Margaret Lloyd together again. Still, he felt that both of them would benefit from closure.

"Closure?" he asked with a scowl. When had he thought in terms of a word like that? He almost smiled. Maybe he had more skills than he gave himself credit for. Or maybe he was getting in way over his head again.

No matter what the answer was, he knew that he wanted Margaret to be happy, and not just for Lea's sake. Eric's mother, like Eric, had done something to him on that day when she'd asked him for his help. Her eyes had branded him with a need to comply. As a result, he'd given Margaret his word. Now, he felt bound to carry out his promise.

After Paul finished his shower, they left the condo with supplies in hand. Paul seemed to know exactly where to get the ingredients for the dinner he had planned. After making a couple of stops, they finally arrived back at Matthew's apartment. As he carried in the last of the groceries, pans and numerous other items that Paul had insisted on bringing, he was tired. It had been a long day, and he wanted to relax. However, he soon realized that old saying, "no rest for the weary" applied to him. With Lea and Margaret scheduled to arrive in less than thirty minutes, Paul pressed Matthew into service in the kitchen.

It took most of the thirty minutes to wash a mountain of vegetables and to prepare a special sauce that Paul needed. When it came to chopping the mountain of vegetables, Paul faltered. He had not pulled himself together in the shower like he said he would. He was still shaky. When he picked up a large knife, Matthew held his breath. If he thought watching Eric navigate a flight of stairs was bad, watching Paul wield a sharp blade was worse. Paul insisted he'd be fine, but his hand slipped halfway through the first carrot. Luckily, he only nicked himself.

Matthew was forced to take over. His patience was long gone, but he kept reminding himself that Margaret's happiness hung in the balance. And if Margaret was happy, Lea would be happy.

Unfortunately, he'd never been a kitchen assistant and didn't have a clue about what to do. Paul, on the other hand, had exacting standards about the art of chopping and dicing.

While Paul was explaining that Matthew was doing everything wrong, the doorbell rang. Paul immediately went into a panic, but Matthew welcomed the interruption. He needed to rid himself of Paul Glass if only for a few minutes. "Go answer the door, Paul," he ordered through clenched teeth.

* * *

Lea stood next to Margaret in the elevator. As they waited for it to reach Matthew's floor, Lea checked on Margaret. "I know you didn't want to come this evening, but Matthew felt it was the right thing to do. He mentioned something about Paul needing closure."

Margaret adjusted her suit jacket and returned an unhappy look. "You don't have to explain it again, my dear. The fact is that Matthew is much too caring when it comes to other people's feelings."

Lea smiled just as the elevator reached their floor and dinged. "Matthew insists on just the opposite. He warned me that he has a terrible bedside manner."

Margaret exited the elevator and started down the hallway. "Lea, could I tell you what I think?"

Lea hurried to keep up with Margaret. The tall woman had a fast gait, especially when she was determined about something. "Please, I'd love to know your thoughts."

Margaret slowed a little and gave Lea a quick smile. "In a very tender moment, your Matthew confided in me. It seems he had a very critical mother. She probably convinced him that he was lacking in many ways."

"That might explain why he sometimes has a hard time expressing his feelings."

Margaret sighed. "Matthew is very sensitive, just like Eric. But in this case, he shouldn't be worried about Doctor Glass. The man is supposed to be someone people can trust. Yet, he totally mishandled things at your parents' house. So if he wants to call it quits and move away, maybe it's for the best."

Lea didn't know what to say. Margaret seemed to have her mind made up about the matter. When they got to Matthew's apartment, she quickly rang the bell.

Paul Glass opened the door. His face looked thinner than Lea remembered, but he offered them a warm smile. "Margaret, Lea, how nice to see you both again. Please come in," he said in a cordial voice.

"Thank you, Doctor Glass," Margaret said as she brushed past him.

Lea paused in the foyer. "How are you, Paul?"

Paul's face sagged a little. "I'm fine. And you?"

"I'm doing well. Margaret and I are excited about our new apartment."

Paul looked back with kind eyes, but he was gripping his hands anxiously. "You must tell me all about it later, but for now, I'm needed in the kitchen." He held up a bandaged finger. "After my clumsiness, Matthew insisted on taking over."

Lea smiled. "I don't think Matthew knows very much about cooking."

Paul grimaced. "Exactly, so please sit down in the living room for a few minutes while I check on things."

Lea walked over to where Margaret had already seated herself. She leaned in and lowered her voice to a whisper. "Paul looks a little nervous."

Margaret took a tissue out of her purse and put it in a jacket pocket. "I didn't notice, but it's very kind of Matthew to help out."

"Maybe Paul is trying to teach him to cook, like you did with me."

Margaret sat back. "Yes, I suppose."

A raised voice, coming from the kitchen, interrupted their conversation. It was Paul Glass's voice.

"Look at your carrot slices, Matthew!"

Matthew's reply was immediate. "What's wrong with them?"

"They're supposed to be the same thickness so that they cook evenly. But some of yours are twice as thick as others."

"I'm doing my best, Paul, okay?"

Paul let out a loud huff. "Well, try harder! I want this dinner to be memorable."

Lea glanced over at Margaret. "I guess Matthew is at the beginner stage. I remember when I had the same problem. You were very understanding."

Margaret frowned back. "Every teacher knows that a beginner needs a gentle hand. But if Doctor Glass doesn't stop criticizing poor Matthew—"

"Not everyone has your patience, Mom."

Before Margaret could reply, another shout came from the kitchen.

"Matthew, quick!" Paul yelled. "My sauce is boiling over. Stir it!"

"Ow!" Matthew yelped. "Damn it, Paul! Now I've cut my finger. Ow!"

Before Lea could respond, Margaret was already in action, jumping up and sprinting towards the kitchen. A moment later, she was issuing orders. "Paul Glass, leave this kitchen immediately! Matthew, let me see your hand? How badly are you hurt?"

* * *

Matthew couldn't believe how quickly Margaret ushered Paul out of the kitchen and then hurried over to where he stood. "I don't think it's too bad," he stammered.

"Put some pressure on it, just in case," Margaret instructed as she hurried to the sink, washed her hands thoroughly, and dried them on a paper towel. Then she was back by Matthew's side, taking his hand in hers. After she examined his wound, she let out a sigh of relief. "You're right. The cut is superficial, thank goodness. But still, do you have any bandages?"

Matthew nodded. "In the bathroom medicine cabinet."

Margaret looked at Lea who stood close by, observing. "Lea, would you go get the bandages while I rinse Matthew's hand?"

Lea nodded and hurried out of the room.

"Please don't worry about me, Margaret," Matthew said. "I'm sure I'll be fine."

Margaret looked up at him with pleading eyes. "Matthew, you have to take care of yourself. I know you want to minimize your injury, but even a small cut deserves the proper care."

Matthew shrugged. "I guess I'm not used to anyone being as concerned as you, Margaret."

240

Margaret's eyes softened into pools of motherly kindness. "Well, as long as I'm around, you don't have to worry about being neglected. Is that clear?"

Matthew nodded. "Yes, ma'am."

Margaret let out a heavy sigh, grabbed a tissue from her pocket and patted her eyes. "I'm sorry."

Matthew wondered what he could have said to make her look so distressed. "What is it? Did I say something wrong?"

Margaret bit her lip as tears started down her cheeks. "It's just that you remind me of Eric. I think I miss him more than I'd like to admit."

Matthew hesitated before he responded. Margaret was like a drill sergeant one minute and fragile as a teacup the next. "Do you want to know something? Eric is very lucky to have you as his mother." He held out his injured finger. "But you're here now, and my finger needs that bandage you talked about."

Lea returned and handed Margaret a small box. "Here you go."

Margaret smiled as she opened the box. "Thank you, Lea, and thank you, Matthew. You're both so kind."

Paul stood just outside the kitchen. After a moment, he stepped a little closer. "I want to apologize to everyone, but most of all, I want to apologize to Matthew. I can't believe I acted so inappropriately."

Matthew returned a weak smile. "You missed your calling, Paul. You belong in an upscale eatery's kitchen. You'd love bossing around a big kitchen staff."

Paul started to retreat. "Or maybe I belong at home where no one has to suffer from my bad manners. I'll call a cab."

Margaret turned around before Paul got very far. "Doctor Glass, I think it would be very rude of you to leave us all in the lurch. We were promised a dinner, and we expect a dinner."

Paul's face flushed a bright red. "Of course, but I'm out of kitchen help. Do you have any suggestions?"

Margaret shrugged. "Why don't you order pizza? Chicago is supposed to have some of the best around. I'd love to try one for myself."

Paul blinked back. "Really?"

241

Margaret walked over and eyed him from head to toe. "Yes, and make sure they're extra-large. You look like you could use a good meal."

Paul smiled. "It would be my pleasure."

Margaret returned to the kitchen and glanced around. "In the meantime, I'll straighten up in here." She looked at Matthew. "Dear, why don't you and Lea go into the living room and relax?"

Matthew gave her an indulgent smile. "But Margaret, you're supposed to be the guest—"

"Nonsense, I haven't done a thing all day. But you look exhausted. Go sit down."

Matthew knew the drill sergeant was back and dutifully started out of the kitchen.

Paul edged forward a little more. "Margaret, could I be of assistance? It would really make me happy if I could help out."

Margaret crossed her arms and hesitated. "Well, I suppose you could be useful as long as you don't start giving out orders again."

Paul held up three fingers. "Scout's honor. I won't say a word."

Margaret sighed. "But first order the pizza, please. I am getting a bit hungry."

Paul fumbled for his phone and turned to Matthew. "I've never ordered pizza," he confided in a whisper. "Can you suggest someone I can call?"

Matthew nodded. "I'll take care of it while you help Margaret."

Paul returned a grateful smile. "Didn't I tell you that you were the right man for the job? I should have listened to you from the start."

Before Matthew could protest that he was definitely not the person to take over the helm, Margaret called out from the kitchen. "Matthew, what are you going to do with all this produce? Will you use it, or will it end up in the garbage?"

Matthew sighed. "I'm sorry, but—"

"Just what I thought," Margaret said. "I really hate to waste food, but maybe I'll take it back with me. I can make dinner for everyone tomorrow night. How about that?"

Lea took hold of Matthew's arm. "And I could help." She smiled up at Matthew. "Margaret taught me how to cook and bake, right Mom?"

242

Margaret softened immediately and came over to put a hand on Lea's arm. "You're wonderful in the kitchen, Lea." She looked up at Matthew next. "Dear, can I borrow your wok and sauce pans too? We only have the bare essentials at our place."

Matthew glanced at Paul. "That's all Paul's stuff, but I'd like to make a suggestion. Why don't we meet at his house tomorrow? His kitchen is a chef's paradise from what I can tell."

"Oh?" Margaret straightened her shoulders and gave Paul another appraising look. "Do you like to cook, Doctor Glass?"

Paul nodded. "I hate to brag, but I have hosted some amazing dinners."

Margaret frowned. "That's all well and good, but I think you can leave the bragging part out. That sort of thing doesn't set well with me."

Paul's eyes widened at the censure, but he soon recovered and smiled. "Thank you for that reminder, Margaret."

Matthew noticed that Margaret raised her chin and gave Paul the slightest acknowledgment before she went back to the kitchen. That was the moment when he knew he didn't have to worry about manning the helm. Once Margaret Lloyd was on the scene, the position was definitely in her capable hands.

Thirty-Three

PAUL OPENED HIS eyes to the morning light, looked around his bedroom and moaned. "What's happening to me?"

He was sure that the question was the result of a nightmare he'd had. He'd been trapped in a world of chaos. He saw a wall with all his diplomas and awards on it, but the wall was sinking into a quagmire. He knew what the dream was telling him. His life's work was slipping away.

He got out of bed and went to the window. Pulling back the curtain, he gazed out at the beautiful cityscape in front of him. He loved Chicago. Why would he want to leave it? He also loved his job, so why was he retiring?

He leaned forward on the window sill and let himself appreciate the view and how lucky he was to be where he was. The longer he stared out, the better he felt. He enjoyed the peacefulness and the calm that settled over his mind.

He hadn't been so clear in quite a while. Like the dream had pointed out, he'd been operating in a kind of foggy, chaotic world. His decisions reflected that state. But that wasn't like him. His mind was usually razor sharp.

So what had caused the fog in the first place? Ever since he'd come back from the Ferguson house, he'd been trying desperately to understand how and why his life had changed so drastically, so fast. He'd thought the answer was simple. He'd fallen in love with Margaret Lloyd. With that came the classic symptoms of being in love.

That meant that Paul's emotional world became a roller coaster. He experienced highs of euphoria and increased energy and the lows of panic and despair. Sleeplessness, racing heart and panic set in when Margaret rejected him. He was so caught up in the cycle that he hadn't recognized the real truth. He hadn't questioned the idea of being in love in broader terms. Like many, he'd classified it as some mysterious, ethereal virtue. It was a heavenly state that swept him away from the daily affairs of life.

But now, in a moment of clarity, he had a different idea. He stepped away from the window and pondered his revelation. "My attention and focus were hijacked by Mother Nature," he whispered. "In short, I've abandoned my scientific training and put love on a pedestal."

His nightmare was there to get him back on track. It was letting him know that his life was in chaos, and the only way to bring order to that chaos was to face facts. Love wasn't an intangible virtue. Love was part of a primal need that was built into his physical mechanism. It was something manufactured. It was an experience that the body produced by way of hormones and chemicals.

Nature was always encouraging the male and the female to join together, to become a couple and ensure survival of the species. Paul had been lucky enough to escape that fate for nearly seventy years. In a moment of weakness, he allowed himself to be affected by a pretty, mature female named Margaret Lloyd.

After that, nature was in charge. Huge chemical changes took place in his body. It was flooded with dopamine, a neurotransmitter that some associated with the idea of "love at first sight." It also shifted his attention from normal reality to a euphoric feeling of walking on clouds. Other hormones were surely present too. They made up a nicely put-together cocktail of complex chemicals that were meant to encourage coupling.

Paul winced at the thought. He wasn't having a transcendent experience. He'd become an addict of sorts, and nature was his drug dealer. His body provided him with hormones and chemical compounds that interfered with his normal take on life. That's why he couldn't do his job properly.

The insight brought instant relief. He'd helped lots of patients beat their addictions. Now, with hard science as his counsel, he'd help himself beat his addiction to Margaret Lloyd.

His next thought scared him. "Oh no, the vixen is coming here to fix dinner tonight!"

He felt a shiver race down his spine. He was sure just the sight of Margaret Lloyd would activate all the unwanted chemicals again. It would be like waving heroin in front of a heroin addict. Would he be strong enough to refuse the temptation to indulge?

He squared his shoulders, determined to beat the chemicals and the powerful pull that would try to take over. He even made a silent vow not to give in to his body's crazy directives. No matter what, he'd reclaim his sovereign right to be happy and single.

* * *

Margaret had to take a cab to Paul Glass's high-rise condo. Matthew was going to pick her and Lea up, but he'd had an emergency to take care of at the hospital. Lea would have accompanied Margaret, but she'd gotten stuck talking to her father for two hours. She'd promised to join Margaret a little later. Margaret could have waited for Lea, but she had a lot of prep work in front of her, and she didn't want to be rushed.

When she arrived at Paul's door, Paul was very polite, but she sensed something different about him. It wasn't his clothes. As usual, he was dressed in a fancy sweater and slacks, and every hair on his head was in place. It was his attitude that had changed from the night before. When they cleaned up Matthew's kitchen together, Paul looked at her like a moony schoolboy. It was irritating, but she put up with him since he was trying so hard to be nice. She'd even started calling him by his first name.

Now, his eyes were much more distant and there was an aloofness in his attitude. It was a relief. She was there to fix dinner, not to engage with Paul socially. "So Paul, it seems that Matthew was impressed with your kitchen. It has me curious."

Paul's gaze went from distant to excited. "Yes, come this way."

Margaret heard the cockiness in his voice. It reminded her of when she'd first met him. She'd almost appreciated his self-assured attitude. It gave her hope that he could help Lea. Now, that same cockiness was grating.

Paul paused in front of a doorway, turned to face her, and then moved aside. "Tell me what you think of my little cooking space."

246

Margaret took a couple of steps forward and gazed at the room in front of her. She found herself trying to take in everything at once. "It's beautiful. It's the most beautiful kitchen I've ever seen."

All of the upper cabinets were a pleasing creamy white with glass fronts. The immaculate marble countertops were white with grey veining. The lower cabinets were adorned with modern, stainless steel pulls. A modest island sat in the middle of the space. A suspended pot rack with lamps hung down over it. The lamps lit up the island's pristine surface, making it the ideal place for food preparation.

Margaret walked over to the island and ran her hand over the cool marble. She turned and looked at Paul. "I'm afraid my old kitchen in Elkville looks like a museum piece in comparison."

Paul didn't respond. Instead, he went to the double door, stainless steel refrigerator and began removing bags of vegetables. "Shall we get started?"

Margaret nodded. "Yes, let me wash up first, then give me a knife. Old fashioned kitchen or not, I've chopped a few vegetables in my time."

Paul pointed to the mounted strip of knives. "Choose one that you think might suit you."

Margaret walked over and examined her choices. "This one might do the trick," she said as she removed the grandest chef's knife she'd ever seen.

Paul's face paled. "Oh dear, that one is very sharp, are you—"

"I'll be fine," Margaret interrupted as she held the large blade and evaluated its feel. A tingle of anticipation coursed through her body. She'd never imagined using such an exquisite example of craftsmanship and artistry.

Paul nodded and went back to the refrigerator. "Would you like a glass of wine or—"

"I'd like some coffee if you have it," she replied.

"Coming right up," Paul said with the kind of smile a waiter gave a patron.

Margaret put down the knife. "Paul, I realize that I might be bold in asking, but did something happen since I saw you last night."

Paul beamed back another generous smile. "Just coming to my senses, Margaret."

"Good. I'm happy to hear that."

After Paul gave Margaret a mug of coffee, he knew he should be pleased with himself. He was winning his battle with Mother Nature. Every time he felt a rush of emotion, he reminded himself of the truth. His body was producing hormones, nothing more was going on.

He felt almost relaxed as he sipped a martini served in a vintage, Waterford martini glass. When he took up a knife to chop celery, his hands weren't shaking anymore. He sighed, more to himself than to Margaret who stood across from him. "There's nothing like feeling at peace."

Margaret paused. Her eyes had picked up the light and were pale blue and wistful when she spoke. "That's all I ever wanted for my husband."

Paul looked back at the cutting board. "That's because you cared deeply about him."

"I loved him! I loved him with all my heart. And that love has never diminished even though he's no longer on this earth."

Paul swallowed hard. Margaret's voice was so passionate and adoring. Nature's "love cocktail" had obviously done a number on the woman. It made him wonder. Why was her body still producing chemicals meant for procreation? When he took a sip of his martini, he searched for answers and came up empty. He'd have to investigate the subject. "How are you coming with the broccoli?"

Margaret pushed a pile of broccoli florets off her chopping board and into a large bowl. "Almost finished."

Paul's phone sounded, and he quickly answered it. After talking to Matthew briefly, he looked at Margaret again. "Lea and Matthew are on their way."

"Good," Margaret said in a cheerful tone.

Paul admired her. The woman had opened her heart to Lea, a complete stranger, the year before. While still trying to get over the loss of her husband, Margaret had made sure to give Lea the love and care that a mother gives her own child. And it showed. Lea bounced back from her recent episode and withdrawal because Margaret and her son had given Lea a solid, safe foundation to work from.

He was about to tell Margaret what a good job she'd done when Margaret excused herself. She left the kitchen quickly, but Paul hadn't missed her teary eyes. He knew immediately that her brief but devoted profession of love for her husband, Ricky, had brought on a sudden bout of sadness.

Paul retrieved more celery, almost started chopping again and stole a glance at Margaret as she left the room. When she'd spoken about her dead husband, her eyes transformed. They became blue-fire stars soaring in another dimension. Chemicals or no, he wondered if anyone's eyes would ever light up that way for him. Sadly, he knew the answer was no.

He tried to push the thought away, but then he remembered Raymond Ferguson's eyes. The morning that Raymond went to see his wife, he was stunned to find out that she was leaving his house and his life. His eyes were full of grief. The successful, business man couldn't bear the thought of losing Rita.

Paul hadn't meant to let it happen, but he'd felt Raymond's misery just before the man collapsed. It had entered Paul's heart, filling his chest with an agonizing torment. Thankfully, the moment passed quickly. But the painful experience had left its mark. It had torn open a very old scar.

Paul had always cared deeply about others, but he'd never allowed himself to truly love another human being except for his mother. The roots went back to his early childhood. Paul was only four when his father had a fatal heart attack. Paul was there when it happened. He'd watched his father die. He was just a helpless, little boy who didn't know how to handle devastation, but it came anyway.

With his mother's help, Paul slowly recovered, but a part of him knew he couldn't face that kind of pain again. So his goal became a worthy one. He needed to find a way to alleviate suffering, but that need was externalized. He became a kind, considerate child who came to the aid of any sick animal. As he grew into adulthood, his efforts expanded. He'd studied traditional and alternative medicine. He'd traveled the world trying to learn some secret that would keep people safe from pain. But his focus was always on the outer world. He'd never let himself get personally involved.

But now, as he stood across from the empty place where Margaret had been, he knew he'd paid a price for walling himself off. And he didn't care if the feeling came from chemicals flooding his body or not. Damn the hormones and chemicals! He wanted more in that moment. He wanted to be a part of someone's life. He wanted to be a part of Margaret's life.

But it wasn't going to happen. He'd pushed away love for too long, now it was pushing him away. It was such a depressing thought that he grabbed his martini glass and took a large swallow of its contents. Without meaning to, he swallowed an olive and began choking. The olive had lodged in his windpipe, cutting off his air supply.

He needed to help himself, but instead, he became a four year old boy again, a child who wanted to scream when he saw his father dying. He wanted to rush over to the man who took him fishing and who sat by his bed when he was sick. But that child was so frozen with fear that he couldn't speak or move. Instead, he took on his father's pain. And the result was terrible. It crushed his small heart, punishing him for loving another. The horror and hurt was so acute and all-consuming that it took a year before that child could speak again.

Now, as Paul fought for air, that same pain was back, only it was much worse. It made his knees buckle. He started to fall and reached out for the counter, but his hand couldn't hold on.

* * *

Margaret stood in Paul's bathroom wiping her tears away, but a fresh batch kept replacing them. Her weepy spell had come on quickly. Maybe part of it was being in the kitchen with Paul. Unlike her times with Lea when they laughed and chatted as they made dinner, she and Paul didn't have much to say to each other. Then Paul got a call from Lea and Matthew saying they'd be arriving soon. That got Margaret thinking about the years ahead.

The couple had a bright future, just like Eric and Teresa. Margaret was happy for both couples. She knew how wonderful it was to have someone. But her own special someone was gone. She'd never see her Ricky again.

Instead, she was supposed to be making a new life for herself, but sometimes it felt like an impossible job. And as much as she hated to admit it, she often got lonely, especially when she thought about Lea.

They had been so close the past year, but Lea would soon be caught up in a life of her own. Just thinking about it left Margaret with that miserable "empty nest" feeling. When Eric went off to college, at least she'd had Ricky to soften the blow. But soon, she'd be completely on her own. And she refused to go back to Baltimore and be a burden to Eric. He and Teresa would be married soon, and they needed their space.

Even if Margaret became a grandmother someday, it wouldn't be the same. There was a lot more loneliness in her future, and it made her miserable when she saw the years span out in front of her. She'd refused to cry in front of Paul. He'd start asking questions. He'd want to help, but he couldn't do anything to change what she was feeling. So she'd asked to excuse herself.

As the last of her tears dried up, she did feel a little better. At least she knew she wouldn't burst into tears in front of Paul. And if she thought about it a little more, she knew she needed to enjoy what she did have. An evening with Lea and Matthew could be very pleasant. But as she walked back into the kitchen, she got a shock. Paul was lying on the floor with his hand at his throat.

"Paul! Paul?" She called out to him as she rushed over and dropped to his side. She kept calling to him, but he didn't seem able to respond. Her first instinct was to get help. She'd seen a landline in the living room and ran there to use it. After she called 911 and reported the situation, she hung up and ran back into the kitchen.

She had to catch her breath as she knelt next to Paul again. He lay on the tile floor, looking so still. Her fright escalated when she checked his breathing and found out he wasn't getting any oxygen. Then she saw glass fragments scattered over the floor. She'd noticed a couple of olives in his martini glass. He'd probably choked on one of them.

She'd seen numerous choking victims and knew what to do. She knelt over his prone body and began a series of abdominal thrusts, hoping to dislodge the obstruction in his airway. At least she prayed that was the problem.

As she worked to help Paul, her mind went over the countless occasions when she'd assisted with Ricky's mission of mercy. People were always looking to her husband to patch them up. They came with knife wounds, broken bones, and a variety of dire medical situations. Since there was no hospital close by, Ricky tried his best to do what he could. Sometimes he was away when people showed up, and she had to do what she could on her own.

Now, she was on her own again, at least until help arrived. But after a half dozen thrusts and no response from Paul, she started to panic and pray. "Please! Help me to help this man before it's too late."

Her plea was answered almost immediately. Margaret heard Ricky's voice. It was deep and caring, just like when he was alive. He seemed to be speaking to her, telling her to believe in herself, telling her how capable she was.

It was enough to restore her faith and keep going. "I can do this," she told herself. And she was right. Paul finally coughed. When she checked his mouth, she saw that the olive had been dislodged. Her relief almost made her cry again, but she knew she had to remain calm. She was about to start CPR when she heard a loud pounding on the door. The paramedics had arrived.

She got to her feet, letting herself take a quick breath. When she'd called 911, the dispatcher had been encouraging. She told Margaret that a unit was close by and would get there very quickly.

Margaret was more than grateful for that fact as she sprinted to the foyer to open the door. Once she handed over the burden of Paul's life to more capable hands, she stepped back and watched from the sidelines. She could already feel the aftereffects of staying calm in a crisis. Her body was doing what it always did afterwards. She was starting to tremble from head to toe.

* * *

After the elevator stopped at Paul's floor, Lea and Matthew stepped out and quickly headed down the hall. Lea held on to Matthew's hand. They'd seen an ambulance parked in front of the building and the doorman explained that the paramedics were there for Paul Glass. Lea tried not to think the worst, but she tightened her grip as they neared the door to Paul's unit. "Goodness knows what's happened to Paul. I'm also worried about Mom. I wish I could have been there for her."

Matthew looked down at her. "No matter what, we're here now. And let's remember that Margaret is a very strong woman."

"I know, but still. She's been very gloomy recently. Maybe it's because next week it'll be two years since she lost Eric's dad. She's tried really hard to adjust, but I think all the stuff that happened at my parent's house has affected her. She's having a hard time coping."

When they reached Paul's unit, Matthew glanced at Lea again. "Are you going to be okay with all this?"

Lea nodded. "I'm okay."

Matthew reached for the door knob, not bothering to knock. When he opened the door, the paramedics were in the foyer. He held the door open for them as they brought someone out on a stretcher.

Lea let out a little cry of alarm when she saw that the person on the stretcher was Paul Glass. He was being given oxygen, but his skin was grey, and he looked like he was barely conscious.

Once the paramedics were on their way, Matthew came over to Lea and put his hands on her shoulders. He made sure to connect with her eyes and gave her some instructions. "Stay here with Margaret while I find out more about Paul's condition."

She nodded again and watched him hurry off. She put a hand to her chest. Her heart was pounding, but then she thought about Margaret. She let herself into the condo. "Mom? It's Lea?"

She found Margaret sitting on the couch in the living room. Her shoulders were bent, and she was clasping her hands. Lea hurried over. "Mom, are you okay?"

Margaret jerked upright and stared back mutely.

"Mom, it's okay. I'm here."

Margaret frowned. "Oh lord, I think I spaced out for a moment. Where's Paul?"

"They took him to the hospital."

Margaret stood up, still clasping her hands. "Then we have to go to the hospital, too."

"Matthew is talking to the paramedics. He'll be back soon."

"Good, he can take us there."

"I know you're concerned about Paul, but how are you doing?"

Margaret backed away, letting her hands fall to her sides. "I'm fine, but Paul doesn't have anyone. From what he told me last night, he's all alone in the world. And I know how that can feel."

"Don't worry, we'll all be there for him, I promise."

Margaret looked away, but she didn't have anything more to say.

Thirty-Four

MARGARET SAT IN the hospital waiting room with Lea, staring at the clock and praying. Matthew wasn't there. His partner needed to talk to him about a patient who wasn't doing well. After what seemed like forever, Margaret was relieved to see Paul's doctor. He told them that Paul had suffered a mild heart attack, but he was stable. He recommended that Margaret and Lea go home and get some rest. Margaret resisted the suggestion, but Lea convinced her that she couldn't help Paul by sitting there. He was getting the care he needed.

After they took a cab back to their small apartment, Margaret felt numb. All her shakiness had given way to a dull feeling that nothing was real anymore. Lea tried to help, but Margaret explained that she was too tired to talk and retreated to her bedroom.

Instead of going to bed, she sat in the upholstered chair she'd picked out at a second hand shop. She'd liked the floral pattern and the yellow and pink colors in the fabric. It reminded her of a cheerful, spring day. But color had left her world. It had gone grey, like Paul's face.

As she clutched at her arms, her mind drifted in no set pattern. Current events and those from the past were jumbled together in a series of dismal images. Eric falling down the stairs, trying desperately to outrun some phantom ghosts. Raymond Ferguson being ferried off to the hospital. Ricky, her beloved Ricky, lying in a coffin. Trying to keep flowers at his grave, but knowing he'd never see them. And now, Paul Glass. He'd looked dead too, like her Ricky.

As she'd straddled his body, trying to help him, she'd thought he'd be lost too.

It was all too much. She didn't want to think anymore. She wanted to turn off her brain and forget everything. In fact, she wished she could shut her eyes and drift away forever. She didn't see the point of going on. Her Ricky was gone, and she wished she was gone too.

At some point in the evening, Lea came in to check on her. But not even the sight of Lea's pretty face could rouse Margaret's spirit. She simply got up and climbed into bed, clothes and all. She almost smiled when she thought of dreaming about her Ricky. She closed her eyes and yearned for sleep. But it didn't come. Her mind switched on again. The thoughts started up.

"Poor Paul, if only I could have been there when he first choked." While she was feeling sorry for herself, Paul was fighting for his life. Now, he was lying in a hospital bed, all alone. It wasn't right for her to turn her back on him. She had to pull herself together and be there for him if he needed her, at least until he was better.

* * *

Lea came out of Margaret's bedroom and closed the door as quietly as possible. Matthew sat waiting patiently on the sofa. "Matthew, you look so tired. You need some sleep."

Matthew patted the couch next to him. "I'm sorry I couldn't be here sooner. But come over and tell me how Margaret is doing."

Lea bit her lip, but she couldn't stop the tears. They ran freely down her cheeks. "I've never seen Mom like this. She wouldn't talk or even undress. She just climbed into bed and pulled up the covers."

Matthew stood up, came over and put his arms around her. "She's had a very rough day. The paramedics said she managed to get Paul breathing again, but I'm sure it was a very stressful situation."

"It's all so scary," Lea said as she leaned into Matthew's broad chest and sniffled back a sob.

Matthew held her close. "Paul's going to be alright, and so is Margaret."

Lea looked up at him and sniffled again. "Do you really think so?"

"Yes, I do," Matthew said as he reached in a pocket and retrieved a clean, monogramed handkerchief. He carefully patted down her cheeks.

Lea tried to rally. There was something so comforting about having Matthew's arms around her. But another thought made her pull back. "Matthew, do you think I'm one of those needy women?"

"What needy women?"

"The kind who have to have a man to feel secure?"

Matthew paused and frowned, as if he required a moment to think the question through. Slowly, a smirk slid into place. "No, I think you're someone who appreciates having a terrific guy like me around, but if I'm unavailable, you can take care of yourself."

Lea saw his teasing look. "Oh, that's reassuring. However, since you are such a catch, with your wonderful bedside manner and all, and sense you're so handsome—"

"So you think I'm handsome?"

It was Lea's turn to pause and evaluate. "Well, you have very nice, green eyes—"

"Like one of those jungle cats, right?"

"No, I'm thinking of the purring kind of cat."

Matthew was immediately offended. "I've never purred in my life! And if I did start purring, I'd find a vet and have myself put down."

Lea laughed. "What about pouting? You can't deny that you're an expert when it comes to pouting. I wrote all about it in my diary."

"That is your misinterpretation. I'm merely annoyed at times. And annoyance has nothing to do with pouting."

"Oh, how unfortunate."

"Why?"

"Because I love the way you look when you're pouting."

"And how is that?"

"Matthew Howell, look in the mirror sometimes. When something doesn't go your way, you cross your arms, adopt this unhappy power pose, and act like you're preparing for a tank to plow into you. Still, I find it endearing."

Matthew's frown deepened. "I find this conversation confusing."

Lea put her arms around Matthew and held on tight. "I'm sorry. I know you're exhausted."

Matthew let out a heavy sigh. "And so are you. I guess I should leave."

She pulled back enough to look up at him. "No, don't go. I don't want to sleep alone tonight."

"But I thought—"

"I know," she said softly. She stared at his face and appreciated the strength she saw there. The resolute set of his jaw and his intense, focused eyes told her that he was someone who would always do their best to protect those he loved. But his eyes could also be introspective and thoughtful when he didn't think anyone was looking at him. She suspected that his actions were guided by a wisdom that Matthew didn't know he had.

"Matthew, I said I needed time, but—"

"Yes?"

"Thank you for giving me the space I asked for. I know you don't want to ever push me into something too soon."

Matthew frowned. "What are you trying to say?"

She shrugged, not knowing what to tell him. Then the words slipped out. "Don't you know how much I love you, Matthew Howell?"

The statement made him pause, as if he didn't know how to process what she'd said.

After a moment, she looked away. She wanted to give Matthew the space he deserved, too. He'd expressed his feelings for her when she was recovering at her parents' home, but some time had passed since then. She wanted to make sure he still wanted her as much as she wanted him. "I know I'm not the person I was before. I'm not the person you fell in love with, so if you don't feel that way now—"

"But I do love you," he whispered. "I've never stopped loving you." He pulled her close again, tipping up her chin, gazing at her with eyes that were definitely untamed and wanting. "When I thought I'd lost you—"

"But you didn't lose me, Matthew. I'm here now, and from what I can tell, I'm a new and improved version."

Matthew's eyes became more fervent. "No, it has nothing to do with new and improved. You've just come back to yourself." He leaned down and brushed her lips with his own. "Behind all your anger, I knew you were fighting to find yourself. And I never gave up thinking that you would."

257

She blinked back fresh tears, but they were happy tears. She'd traveled so far away from herself and from Matthew. Now, that was all behind her. When she looked at Matthew and thought about a lifetime together, euphoria flooded her mind and heart. It was so powerful that she threw her arms around Matthew and squeezed him with all the strength she had. "I've never felt this happy before!"

Matthew embraced her too, but after long moments passed, he nuzzled her ear. "Lea, my darling Lea, can you ease up just a bit?" he said. "For a wisp of a woman, you're very strong."

She laughed and immediately relaxed the powerful hold she had on him. "But I can't help myself!"

Matthew's brows arched. "You have that look again."

She giggled, knowing exactly what he meant. "You mean the 'I want to ravish you' look?"

He nodded, kissing away the tears on her cheeks. "Yes, that's the one."

She pulled back. "I'm sorry, but you're mistaken."

Matthew jerked back. "Really?"

"Doctor Howell, you have it all wrong."

"I do?"

Lea ran a finger over his lips. "Yes, tonight I'm thinking that you should do the ravishing. Unless that's a problem."

He narrowed his eyes and gave her a curious look. "Well, give me a moment to think about it."

Lea stiffened. "What?"

Matthew held her at arm's length and studied her from head to toe. "Hmm, just as I thought."

Lea blinked back with confusion and surprise. "What? What is it?"

"After years of studying the human anatomy, I've come to a conclusion."

Lea crossed her arms. Matthew was a man of medicine. Like he just said, people's bodies were his stock and trade. She wondered for just a moment if hers measured up. "And what is that conclusion?"

Matthew swept her up in his arms. Holding her tight against him, he nuzzled her cheek again. "You, Lea Ferguson, are perfect. I can't think of anyone I'd rather ravish."

She noted the devilish glint in his eyes. It was something new and exciting, and she liked it. "Oh, you are a rascal, aren't you?"

"Point me towards your bedroom, ma'am, and you'll see just what a rascal I can be."

"Down the hall, first door at the end, Doctor Howell," she grinned.

Matthew almost got a chance to smile when his phone went off. "You have got to be kidding," he groaned as he set Lea down.

Lea sighed. "Duty calls."

Matthew answered the call halfway through the second ring. "Howell here," he grumbled as he stood listening and commenting. "He is? He what? He specifically gave you my name?"

Lea tugged at Matthew's arm as soon as he ended the call. "Is it the same patient as before?"

"No, Paul's been asking for me."

A door on the other end of the hall opened and Margaret stepped out. After a brief glance at Matthew, she hurried over and grabbed his other arm. "Matthew, I heard the phone. Is it Paul? Is he okay?"

Matthew sighed. "He's doing fine, but—"

"But what?" Margaret demanded. "I should go back to the hospital. Will you take me?"

Lea tugged on his arm again. "Why do you think he wants to see you?"

Margaret's eyes flared. "He wants to see you, Matthew? I'm not surprised. You're the one who cared about him when the rest of us ignored him. Poor man, I was so distant today."

"Margaret, don't upset yourself. After all, you did save his life," Matthew said. "But I better go and check—"

"I'm going too," Lea insisted.

"I'll get my jacket," Margaret added.

* * *

Matthew walked up to Paul Glass's bedside trying to put his best foot forward. However, that foot had been on its way to Lea's bedroom just a half hour earlier. A visit to the hospital was the last thing he had on his mind.

Matthew hadn't been allowed to complain about the trip. With Lea and Margaret both tugging on him at the same time, he'd felt like a turkey wishbone on Thanksgiving. He either submitted to their demands or else. Happily, he'd been able to leave the two women in the waiting room. Paul had specified that only Matthew be allowed to visit.

But Paul appeared to be Matthew's opposite. The man smiled, eager to engage Matthew in conversation.

"Matthew, I have so much to tell you."

Matthew decided that Paul was way too cheerful for a man who was hooked up to a heart monitor. "Maybe you should rest, Paul," he advised. "We can talk when you've had a chance to—"

"Nonsense!" Paul reached out a hand and put it on the bedside rail. "This is too important. I need to talk to you."

Matthew was trying his best to be pleasant, but it was difficult. He had no track record to fall back on when it came to sick people wanting something. As a surgeon, he did his part of the job to the best of his ability. After that, patients were supposed to be quiet and get better. If they had questions or complaints, his partner, Ralph, or a resident could offer a sympathetic ear.

But Paul fell into that terrible category called a friend or at least a colleague. They had shared a meal together at Matthew's apartment. Now Matthew had to dig deep and find a virtue called tolerance before he spoke. He almost managed. "What's so important that it couldn't wait until morning?"

Paul seemed to understand Matthew's plight. "I know this isn't convenient, but I had to confide in someone."

Matthew held up a hand. "Hold on, Paul, you have the wrong guy. Maybe you need a chaplain or a priest."

"No, no, no! They wouldn't do at all. I need someone who's broad-minded, who won't have me signed up for a psych evaluation."

Matthew started to back away. "Are you kidding. I'm totally narrow-minded about anything weird."

Paul squinted back. "Like Eric's healing abilities?"

Matthew clamped his jaws shut. Lea's statement came to mind. A tank named Paul Glass was getting ready to plow into him. Matthew needed to head him off. "Paul, I'm tired. It's been a very long day—"

Paul didn't seem to notice Matthew's discomfort. He began to smile again. "Matthew, I've played the game as you know. I've spouted off about the mysteries of life and all that stuff, but I guess deep down, I wasn't quite convinced. I tried to make my scientific mind go along with what I'd been told, but I never quite succeeded. Now, things have changed drastically."

Matthew stifled a yawn.

"Matthew, I wouldn't have asked you here if this wasn't important."

Matthew looked around and saw a chair sitting by the wall. He dragged it over and sat down. But he could tell by Paul's excited voice that he wasn't going to like whatever Paul had to tell him. "Oh here it comes, more of your grand ideas, just like the stuff you spouted off at the Ferguson house of horrors."

Paul's face suddenly went from happy to sullen. "Never mind, you're right, I should have never asked you to come."

Matthew slouched in his chair and closed his eyes. "But I am here. So spit it out."

Paul looked away. "No, forget it."

Matthew forced himself to sit up again. "Look Paul, Lea and Margaret are going to grill me as soon as I go back to the waiting room. I have to tell them something."

"They're here too?"

"Yes, they're both very worried about you."

Paul shrugged. "Tell them I'm fine. And thank Margaret. I've been told she saved my life."

Matthew sat up more attentively. "Oh hell, Paul, you know they're going to want more than that."

Paul closed his eyes. "Sorry, like you said, I need to rest."

* * *

Matthew had called it. After his visit with Paul and nothing to report, neither Lea nor Margaret was happy. But he'd been up since five that morning, and he was too tired to try to explain himself. Fortunately, his weariness seemed to work out nicely. The women blamed Paul for dragging Matthew out for nothing.

After Matthew took them back to their apartment and walked them to the door, he only planned to come in for a moment, but Margaret refused to let him leave.

"Matthew, please, you're worn to a frazzle. You're not going anywhere."

Lea joined in. "She's right. You could fall asleep at the wheel. You're staying here tonight."

Matthew perked up. Maybe his evening wasn't completely shot to hell. "Are you sure?"

Margaret smiled and came over to pat his arm. "Don't you worry, you poor thing. You won't have to sleep on the sofa. I have a queen size bed. Lea can sleep with me, and you can use her bed."

Matthew's shoulders slumped even lower. "Oh, wonderful. Can I use her PJs too?"

Margaret laughed and turned to Lea. "You never told me how funny he can be."

"I know. He surprises me too," Lea said as she grabbed Matthew's hand. "But I better tuck him in before he falls over on us."

"Make sure he has enough blankets. The weather has been a little chillier lately," Margaret said as she headed for the kitchen. "And I'm going to warm some milk for him. It always helped Ricky after a very strenuous day."

Matthew started to object. He didn't like milk, especially warm milk. Then he realized he didn't have the strength to go up against Margaret Lloyd. No matter how frail Lea claimed the woman could be, Margaret was always at her best when she had a duty to perform. And right now, she was intent on putting him to bed like a three-year-old child.

Lea came to his rescue. "Mom, when I was reading my diary, I learned that Matthew likes cocoa. I think we have some in the cupboard."

Ten minutes later, Matthew was propped up in Lea's bed, sipping his drink as Margaret wrapped a shawl around his shoulders. Shortly after that, his mind went mercifully blank, and he felt himself falling asleep.

* * *

Margaret sat in the living room with Lea after they got Matthew to bed. She felt better than she had earlier. "Your Matthew is a real trooper, isn't he?"

Lea swallowed some of her tea. "Yes, and I think he enjoys the way you pamper him."

"Really? I'm not overwhelming him, am I?"

"No, it's more like he's never had anyone care so much before. I don't think he knows what to do or say half the time."

Margaret sat back. Maybe she'd been too hasty to think her mothering days were over. "Well, I'll do my best to let him know that things have changed. However—"

"What is it?"

"I was thinking about Eric. I know he was fine with having a sister, but he might get a little jealous if he thinks I'm paying too much attention to Matthew."

Lea laughed. "Oh, I think you have enough love to go around. Nobody has a heart as big as you."

"Oh my, what a wonderful compliment."

Lea moved closer and put her arm around Margaret's shoulder. "We're all so lucky to have you. I hope you always remember that."

Margaret took a tissue out of her pocket and patted her eyes. "I guess I was wondering if I had any purpose now that you and Eric are in relationships."

"Are you serious? You asked me to call you Mom, and now I feel like you are my mom. You're also my friend, someone I can talk to when I don't feel anyone else would understand. You're wise and I'm always learning something new and important just being around you. So please, you asked me to believe in myself. Now, you have to believe in who you are."

Thirty-Five

ERIC PUT HIS PHONE on the counter just as Teresa came into the kitchen. "Mom says to say hi. She hopes you're not working too hard."

Teresa smiled and went to the stove and began to stir some soup. "How's she doing?"

Eric hesitated. "I don't know. I wish she'd come back to Baltimore."

Teresa walked over and reached out for Eric's hand. "Are you worried about her?"

"I guess I am. She just told me that Paul Glass had a heart attack."

"You're kidding. From your description, he sounded like he stayed in shape and had a very active life style."

"He almost choked to death. If Mom hadn't helped him, I guess he'd be dead."

"Oh, Eric, what is going on? First Lea had that unfortunate episode, then her father ended up in the hospital, now Paul Glass—"

"I know. And I feel like whatever it is that's happening, we haven't heard the end of it."

"What do you mean?"

"That's just it. I don't know what I mean. It's just a feeling I have."

Teresa stood back with alarm. "Honey, you look really upset. What's going on?"

Eric tried to smile. "Don't mind me. I'm sure I'm overreacting."

"Still, you're not usually like this."

"I'm not used to my mom sounding like she does. She's always been so resilient when it came to helping my dad and raising me. I don't know what's happening to her."

Teresa smiled. "Maybe that's just it. She always had your dad and when she moved here, she had you. Now she's on her own, and she's going through an adjustment period. I remember being very insecure when I first went off to college. I bet that you were too."

Eric came over and put his arms around Teresa. "I see your point."

"I'll tell you what. Why don't we fly to Chicago next weekend and surprise her. We both have that weekend off."

"Really? You don't mind?"

"Of course I don't mind. I enjoy your mom's company."

* * *

Paul insisted that he'd be fine when he came home from the hospital, but Margaret Lloyd had other ideas. She not only accompanied him home in a cab, but she wanted to stay and help out. He supposed that would be fine, but he found out that she could be quite bossy if she didn't get her way.

"Paul? What are you doing in the kitchen with that broom? I went to turn down your bed, and I come out to find you over-exerting yourself."

Paul frowned back. "I'm being careful, but there's still glass on the floor. I don't want someone getting hurt."

His excuse was useless. Without another word, Margaret marched over, took the broom from his hands, and pointed to the doorway. "I put your mail next to your living room recliner. If you have to do something, you can sort through the circulars."

"Oh yes, I have some bills I should take care of—"

"They're in your office. You can take care of anything stressful when your doctor gives you the okay. You shouldn't even be home yet, but I guess the poor man couldn't take any more of your complaining."

"It's my body, Margaret. I think I know best about what I can do and not do."

Margaret put the broom aside. "Really? If that's what you think then I guess I'm out of line. It's just that I was the one who found you on the floor, not able to breathe."

"I'm sorry. I'm sure it was very difficult to see me like that."

Margaret walked over to the sink, put her hands on the counter and leaned in. "Don't worry. It's not the first time that I've been faced with death. It's just that something like that makes me realize how easy it is for someone to leave this earth."

Paul came over and stood next to her. "Margaret, can I tell you about something strange that happened to me?"

Margaret looked up. "Of course, what is it?"

"I think I left this earth for a little while. I think I had what's referred to as a Near Death Experience."

Margaret smiled. "When I was eight, I nearly drowned. What I experienced while I was unconscious left me wondering about life. So I think I might know what you're talking about."

Paul's eyes brightened. "Can we compare notes?"

Margaret hesitated. "I don't think so. My mother forbade me to ever tell anyone what happened."

"I see. Forget I said anything."

Margaret put her hand on Paul's. "I'd like very much if you told me about what you experienced."

"No, maybe your mother was right. People seem more comfortable with the way things are. After all that's happened at the Ferguson house, I don't want to cause any more problems." He turned and started out of the kitchen. "I'll go check out those circulars."

* * *

Lea decided to drop in on Paul and Margaret. She hadn't had a chance to really talk to Paul since his accident. She also knew that she'd never let him know how much she appreciated what he'd done for her. When Margaret answered the door, Lea was happy to see her. "I thought I'd visit Paul."

Margaret gestured her into the hall and shut the door behind her. "I'm glad that you came. I think that Paul is a little down. And I think it's my fault. I might have been too over-protective."

Lea could see that Margaret was struggling. Her face was lined with concern. "Let me talk to him."

Margaret nodded. "While you're doing that, I'll make some lunch. Maybe you can join us."

Lea found Paul in his office. His smile was polite, but his eyes didn't have the focus she remembered. "It's good to see you again," she said as she sat down in one of the office chairs.

Paul nodded. "How is Matthew?"

"He's busy. But I came here to talk to you about what you did for me. I'm very grateful."

Paul gave her a dismissive smile. "You did it, Lea, not me."

"Paul, what's wrong? When you were at my parent's house, I remember how excited you seemed about life. Your attitude affected us all in a very positive way. Now, you seem so different. Does this have anything to do with my parents and the problems they're having?"

Paul let out a heavy sigh. "I hope they're figuring some things out."

"I've been talking to my father lately. He's struggling with the situation, but at least Rita has put off moving out of the house."

"I'm sorry about what happened."

"I think they were both living a lie. At least that lie is in the open now, and they can try to deal with it."

Paul shrugged. "I wish them the best."

"Are you still going to retire?"

"Yes, as soon as I can, I'll move—"

"Where? Where will you go?"

Paul's eyes drifted. "I haven't decided yet."

"From what I've learned, running away isn't the best way to handle a situation."

"I'm simply moving on."

"I heard that you think you failed everyone. I know that feeling too."

"That's understandable. As a child you were told things that destroyed your confidence in yourself."

Lea smiled. "Matthew said that I used my anger to hold on to what was left."

"Matthew was right."

"Where's your anger, Paul? You look like you've given up."

267

Paul looked around. "I used to be very invested in life, but now, whatever happens, it's okay. I've found a measure of peace."

"But are you happy?"

Paul stood up. "I'm sorry. I think I'm tired, that's all. If you'll excuse me, I think I better lie down."

Lea stood up too. "Margaret is fixing lunch, are you hungry?"

"Maybe I'll eat something later."

* * *

When Lea joined Margaret in the kitchen, she went over to where Margaret was standing at the stove. "Looks delicious."

Margaret smiled. "Is Paul ready to eat? He said that he liked fish, so I'm making salmon filets and a salad."

"He says he's not hungry. He went to lie down."

Margaret removed the fillets to a serving dish and turned off the burner. "Maybe I better check on him."

"Mom, I think something is wrong with Paul."

"What do you mean?"

"It was the way he looked at me, like he didn't care about anything anymore."

"I hope his heart isn't acting up."

"I think it's more than that. He's not the man who showed up to help me when I freaked out. It's like that person is gone."

Margaret wiped her hands on her apron and started out of the room. "I'll go see how he is."

Lea followed Margaret to Paul's bedroom. She waited as Margaret knocked lightly on his door. "Paul? Are you okay?"

Paul's voice sounded muffled when he answered. "Yes, I'm taking it easy like you suggested, Margaret."

Margaret opened the door and peeked in. "Are you sure? I made some lunch."

Paul was in an upholstered, lounge chair with a throw tucked around him. He was staring out his window. "Just eat without me. I need to rest."

Margaret shut the door and gestured for Lea to follow her back to the kitchen. "You're right. I don't know what's bothering him, but he sounds depressed. He tried to talk to me about something he'd experienced, but I think I shut him down." Margaret reached out for

Lea's hand. "Dearest, later, could you go back to the apartment and get a few things for me. I want to spend the night here in case Paul needs something."

"Of course, I'll pack some of my things too. I don't want you to do this alone."

"I'll be fine."

"I know, but Paul was really there for me. I found out that he flew back from Europe as soon as my dad contacted him. The least I can do is be here for him too."

"Well, he did seem to think that a group effort was a good idea when he was helping you."

"Strength in numbers?" Lea asked.

"Maybe."

* * *

Matthew was disappointed when Lea bailed on dinner together, but when he found out why, he wasn't hungry anymore. Lea and Margaret were very worried about Paul. They were staying at his condo to keep an eye on him.

Something told Matthew that the Ferguson fiasco wasn't done with them yet. Whatever had been triggered in the foreboding mansion was still active. And Paul, the person who had headed up an undertaking to help Lea, appeared to be the current victim who was quickly losing ground.

Matthew's problem was that he had no way of knowing how to tackle the situation. Then he thought of Eric. The man had strange abilities that Matthew didn't understand. However, he had been one of the recipients of Eric's extraordinary gifts. What if Eric could shed some light on what was happening to Paul? Matthew decided to give him a call.

As soon as Eric answered Matthew's call, Eric was the one who started asking questions. What was wrong? Were Lea and Margaret alright? Was Matthew well?

After Eric was satisfied that everyone was safe, Matthew got in a few inquiries of his own. "Eric, you said something about the Ferguson house and how it affected you. Do you think that it could have affected Paul Glass too?"

Eric didn't hesitate. "Yes, we both noticed how different he acted after being there for a short period of time. And I think it's because that place is a fortress of pain and guilt. Paul probably tapped into it and took it on. Unfortunately, unlike me, he probably doesn't know what even happened. If he's taken on a lot of guilt and feelings of failure, it would explain why he's giving up his practice."

Matthew ran a hand through his hair, trying to think of how to combat something that sounded very elusive. "So what the hell do we do? Exorcise the guy?"

Eric laughed. "Some of the hill folk I knew would probably try it."

"I'm serious, Eric. From what Lea said, Paul is going down for the count."

"Do you want me to fly out right away?"

"I don't think you should do anything that endangers your own stability. That trip of yours down the stairs scared the hell out of me. So stay put for the time being, and I'll check out the situation myself and get back to you."

"Matthew, be careful too. When I did that little trick that cured your headache, I found out that you and I are more alike than you'd think."

Matthew swallowed the lump in his throat and tried to lighten up the conversation. "Tarnation, Doc Lloyd, yall is scarier than hell right now."

"Matthew, I mean it. I know you have a different take on this 'gift' business, but a wrong decision could have serious consequences."

"What about Lea? Is she in danger?"

Eric paused. "I don't think so. She survived all those years growing up in that house."

"Yes, but she just about lost it recently."

"I know, but I think that was her final inoculation with the type of energy that we're dealing with. She's probably better off than the rest of us at this point."

Thirty-Six

MARGARET FELT A surge of relief when she answered Paul's entry door. Matthew was waiting in the hall. "Oh, it's so good to see you, Matthew."

Matthew blinked back anxiously. "Why? Did something else happen since I talked to Lea thirty minutes ago?"

"No, but I'm very concerned about Paul. He's been sitting in his bedroom for hours, and he won't talk or eat at this point."

Matthew stepped into the foyer. "Where's Lea?"

"She insisted on staying with Paul. We've been taking turns reading to him. We feel like it's something that might make him feel better. But come into the kitchen. I'm sure that you haven't eaten either, right?"

Matthew waved her off. "I had lunch."

"That's well and good, but Lea needs some supper. After I get her, the two of you can have the baked chicken I made. I'll stay with Paul."

Matthew looked at his watch and sighed. "Okay."

Matthew's distracted tone and his edgy look made Margaret take notice. Lea had said that the surgeon wasn't used to anyone really being attentive to his wellbeing. That fact tugged at Margaret's heart. She reached out and patted Matthew's arm. "Do you know that you're appreciated, Matthew?"

Matthew stalled, looking confused. "Appreciated? What do you mean?"

"I mean that I worry about you, too."

"That's not necessary. Look at me, I'm fine."

Margaret put her hands on her hips. "I am looking at you, and do you know what I see? I see a man who is always helping others. But once this whole thing with Paul is straightened out, I think you and Lea should get away for a while. You deserve some time to relax and enjoy your lives."

Matthew's brows arched with surprise. "Thank you, Margaret. You're very kind."

Margaret turned and headed for Paul's bedroom. "You're welcome. Now go get washed up, and I'll get Lea."

* * *

Matthew sat at the dining table with Lea. His plate was covered with heaping portions of chicken, potatoes, and green beans. Margaret seemed to think he needed extra fortification. Before dinner, she'd given him a thorough onceover and then shook her head like he was some orphan she'd found on the street.

He was about to take a bite of chicken and frowned. "This is ridiculous."

Lea swallowed her bite of potatoes and looked up. "What's ridiculous? Aren't you in the mood for chicken?"

Matthew threw his napkin on the table and stood up. "I'm not in the mood to let Paul Glass act like a child. I'm going to speak to him."

Lea put her fork down. "Do you want me to come with you?"

"No, please, stay here and eat. I'll be back very shortly."

Matthew's anger was coming to the surface. It was the first time he'd felt it flare up with such intensity since Eric took care of his headache. He didn't have the patience to deal with Paul's attitude. The man was creating a very stressful situation, and Margaret and Lea were letting him have his way.

When Matthew got to Paul's bedroom, he gave the door a couple of raps and let himself in. Margaret looked up, but she didn't say anything.

Matthew gave her the faintest smile. He didn't want to offend the woman, but it was everything he could do to keep his temper in check. "Margaret, could I talk to Paul alone?"

Margaret seemed to read his mood and nodded. After she left, Matthew approached Paul. The man hadn't moved since Matthew entered the room. When Matthew stood over him, Paul remained very still. His pale blue eyes were open, and he was staring at the closed window curtains. Other than that, there was no indication that the psychiatrist was aware of anything.

Matthew shook Paul's shoulder and stood back. "Paul, what's going on with you? Margaret and Lea are very upset by your behavior. Whatever you think you're doing, stop it. Pull yourself together and go out to that dining room and act like a normal human being."

Paul glanced up. "This is my home, and I didn't ask any of you to be here. So here's what's going to happen. You and Margaret and Lea are going to leave."

"Right, it's always your way. When we were at the Ferguson house, you ordered us all around too. But now that people care about you and are trying to help, you can behave like a spoiled child who only thinks about himself. Is that it?"

Paul looked up at him again. "I tried to talk to you, Matthew. I tried to talk to Margaret, but the bottom line is that people don't want to hear what I have to say. So I'm not going to converse with any of you from now on. I'm going to keep my own company which I do believe is still my right."

"So where does that leave the rest of us, the people who are supposed to care about the wellbeing of others?"

Paul let out a bitter laugh. "That's a problem I've tried to solve for as long as I can remember. And helping people is what made my life worthwhile. As a surgeon, you know what I mean, right?"

"Yes, I guess so."

Paul glared back. "What if something happened, and you couldn't do your job anymore? What if your career was stripped away? Because that's where I'm at, Matthew. It has nothing to do with acting like a child."

Paul's explanation hit Matthew where it counted. He'd been doused with the cold waters of truth. Like Paul said, Matthew's role as a doctor was a very, big part of his life. What if all of that was lost? "Maybe I didn't think your problem through, but—"

Paul shrugged. "It's not your problem to think about."

Matthew stepped back and heard voices in the other room. "Maybe not, but we both share another kind of problem."

273

Paul leaned his head back. "You're talking about Margaret and Lea?"

"Yes, Margaret's been cooking up enough for a small army. If you don't at least pretend to be hungry—""

Paul gave Matthew a worn look, but he forced himself out of his seat. "You're right. I better do as you say."

Matthew grabbed Paul's arm. "And please, try to get that grim look off your face, or Margaret's going to think you're dying again."

Paul blinked back intently. "Oh no, then she'll be hounding me constantly when the only thing I want is peace." He paused. "And I had that peace briefly when—"

Matthew waited for Paul to continue, but the psychiatrist's gaze grew wistful instead. "Paul, what's going on?"

"I'm just thinking that you're right, I need to make sure that Margaret and Lea don't worry."

Matthew nodded back. "And you'll feel better when you eat some dinner and join the living again, Paul."

"The living, that's what we doctors are always concerned about. But maybe someday there'll be more to study." Paul's eyes brightened. "Thank you for your help, Matthew. You've inspired me."

* * *

Matthew sat at the dinner table on one side with Lea and Margaret sitting across from him. Paul sat at the head of the table, looking his usual, put-together self. In the space of five minutes, the man had changed into a clean, white shirt, combed his hair and adopted a totally normal attitude.

At first, Matthew was pleased that Paul had taken his advice. Instead of being sullen and withdrawn, Paul brought an apologetic tone to the dinner conversation.

When Paul had first addressed Margaret and Lea, his voice conveyed deep feelings of regret. "I'm embarrassed by my earlier behavior. I know that both of you ladies were doing your best to cheer me up, and I was conducting myself very badly. However, thanks to Matthew, I've come to my senses."

As soon as Matthew heard his name mentioned, he felt uncomfortable. "If I was a little rough on you, Paul—"

"No, Matthew, you said what needed saying. If I was acting like a spoiled child, I needed to be aware of it. So thank you."

Matthew continued to plead his case. "Still, I don't want anyone to think I didn't appreciate your condition."

Paul looked at Margaret and then Lea. "I think all of us know that you had my best interests at heart."

Margaret smiled at Matthew. "Matthew, I want to thank you for getting Paul to take care of himself and eat. It's what his body needs if he's going to get well."

Paul chewed his bite of chicken and swallowed. "That's right, Margaret. And by the way, this meal is delicious. You're a wonderful cook. And did I smell cookies?"

Margaret blushed. "Yes, Paul, but I don't know if you should eat too many. I made them for Lea and Matthew."

Paul reached out for her hand and patted it. "I'll tell you what, from now on, I want your advice about such things. You seem to have a very good sense about what's best for me."

Margaret's blush deepened. "Well, perhaps it would be okay if you had some pudding. I made tapioca."

Paul's eyes sparked. "You're kidding. That's a favorite."

As Paul continued to go on and on about how everything was wonderful, Matthew started to feel more uncomfortable. He couldn't quite understand why his stomach was acting up. Maybe the food wasn't agreeing with him. Then he thought about another explanation. Maybe, he couldn't stomach Paul's upbeat, overly accommodating attitude. It didn't ring true.

Just a half hour earlier, Paul had stated that he felt like his life was essentially over. He didn't have a wife or family or even any close relatives. The only thing Paul lived for was his work. Since he was retiring, what would he do with himself? When Paul expressed his unhappiness to Matthew, he looked miserable. So why had he suddenly become so cheerful at the dinner table?

The answer became obvious when Matthew glanced at Margaret and saw her smile. It was a contented smile, a grateful smile, a smile that accompanied a sense of relief. She was buying everything that Paul was selling. Lea was smiling too.

Matthew realized that he was the only one at the table who was worried, and he knew why. Paul had accomplished what he'd set out to do. He was throwing the hounds off the scent. If Margaret and

Lea thought Paul was fine, they'd go home. Paul would be left on his own.

* * *

Eric paced from one end of the living room to the other. Ever since Matthew's call, he'd been thinking about the situation that Matthew was dealing with. At first, he'd told himself that he shouldn't worry. Matthew was a very capable person. He could handle himself when things got stressful. Matthew proved that when it came to managing Eric's flight from reality.

Of course Paul Glass might be another matter. The psychiatrist was a bit of a wild card. He was definitely unpredictable. Plus, Matthew wasn't exactly a Paul Glass fan. So how would he handle someone like that?

Eric checked the time. It was eleven p.m. Chicago time. He'd give Matthew a call, just in case he could help. He only had to wait for a ring and a half for Matthew to answer. "Hello, Matthew, hope I'm not calling too late."

"No, I just got back from dropping off Lea and Margaret at their apartment."

Eric took a seat on the sofa. "Did your evening with Paul go well? Is he as depressed as before."

"Paul Glass is a total pain in the ass. He should get an Oscar for the performance he gave tonight."

"What performance?"

"The women were going to stay at his condo just in case he needed them, but Paul snowed them completely. Now, I have to take their place."

"Why?"

"Because I'm afraid the jerk might try to kill himself."

"You're kidding." Eric sat back, trying to process the information. He hoped he could find that clear space where he sometimes tuned into future events. "Thankfully, I'm not seeing anything like that."

Matthew paused. "It doesn't matter. I'm going back to his condo and spending the night."

"Matthew, like I said before. Be careful."

"I know, dammit, I should have left well enough alone. But no, I had to get involved."

This time, Eric got a very clear picture. Matthew sounded exhausted. "Matthew, you can't fight this thing head on. Back off enough to get your thoughts together."

"Eric, are we like Paul? Will we spend our lives patching up people only to get old and find there's nothing left of us?"

"Is that how Paul feels?"

"Yes, it is."

"Matthew, I'm sure that not everybody feels like that?"

"I bet your dad did."

Before Eric could respond to the statement, Matthew hung up.

* * *

Paul answered the door and hesitated. "I thought it was you. What now?"

Matthew pushed past Paul in silence and walked into the living room. His face was dark and sullen as he slumped down on the sofa.

Paul frowned too. What was he dealing with? He'd never seen Matthew look so upset. He had to be on his game and prepare himself. He had a feeling that the surgeon was ready to hand out another lecture.

Paul took a seat on the couch too. "So spit it out, Matthew. You came here to tell me something."

Matthew's focused gaze was hard and angry. "What do you want from all of us, Paul?"

"I don't understand."

"Neither do I. All I know is that you claim that your life work was about helping people, but I've been thinking about that on the way over. And I figure if your intentions were so noble, you'd be more of a man than the one I see in front of me."

"Did I ask you to come here?"

"What choice did I have? You knew what you were doing when you spewed out that crap about your life. You wanted me to know that you were thinking about checking out."

"Don't I have a right to my feelings?"

"Your feelings? When we were all at the Ferguson mansion you told me that you didn't deal in singular perspectives. You said something about all of us being in the soup together. But now you've switched gears. And it all comes down to some small-minded bull about your life's work being over." Matthew grimaced and looked away. "You and Eric's father have a lot in common. Neither of you could face up to yourselves. You both went through life holding on to your blinders and your pain. In the end, Eric's dad died with a heart attack. I don't know how you want it to end. But I know that you do want it to end."

Paul leaned forward, clasping his hands. "Let's say that you're right. If so, what do you suggest?"

"You're supposed to be the wise, old man. So you tell me. Because I want to know if I'm looking at you and seeing my future."

Paul laughed. "Nothing could be further from the truth, Matthew. You could never end up like me."

"Why is that?"

"You might think that you're a loner, but you're not. You took a chance on life and let yourself love someone. And you held on to that love no matter what. That's the difference between you and me."

"Well, you're not dead yet."

Paul couldn't help but smile. Matthew had a straight-forward way of looking at life. "But it's beautiful on the other side."

"What other side?"

"Matthew, when I choked, I left my body and saw heaven."

Matthew laid his head back and closed his eyes. "Heaven?"

"Yes, you know, the afterlife."

Matthew stretched out his legs and crossed his arms. "I don't want to talk about some airy fairy concept called heaven. It's not relevant."

"Why?"

Matthew let out a weary sigh. "Because even if there is such a place, the point is that we're here now. And I figure we should respect that fact and do our best here."

Paul's brows furrowed as he struggled to fully understand Matthew's statement. As he let his mind mull over the concept, something clicked. "My god, that makes sense." He sat up more attentively and blinked back a couple of times. "I guess what you're saying is that Mother Nature or some Divine force put us here for a reason, a reason I've failed to understand. But that doesn't take away from the importance of embracing my life in the here and now."

When Matthew didn't respond, Paul got up and checked on his guest. Matthew had fallen asleep, but his brows were still narrowed and solemn. Paul chuckled. "Out of the mouth of Matthew Howell. Words of wisdom. The man would be appalled to know he's a philosopher."

Paul grabbed a large cashmere throw from a side chair and carefully draped it over the surgeon. "Thank you, Matthew," he whispered. "Thank goodness you had the strength to call me out on my shortcomings."

Paul had once had the potential for Matthew's kind of strength, but he used his father's death as a reason for holding back. He needed to rethink his decision. But it took courage to truly live up to one's potential. Was he prepared for the road ahead, even the rocky, painful parts?

Paul sighed as he thought about those who looked up to him. Like Matthew said, individuals were also part of a group. As they traveled together, they either inspired each other or helped to bring the others down. Paul had taken a bad turn recently, but he'd seen lots of people pull themselves up after they found themselves in the mire. Maybe he could find a way back too.

Thirty-Seven

LEA RAN A hand over the white, linen table cloth. Its edges were decorated with embroidered birds and flowers. Like the rest of Nicky's apartment, the table cloth was simple, but there was also a warm, cozy factor.

Sitting next to Matthew, Lea felt like she could relax even though she didn't know her hostess, Nicky, or Matthew's partner, Ralph. "It was so thoughtful of you both to have Margaret and me over for dinner."

Ralph returned a warm smile. "It's great to get acquainted. Matthew doesn't say a lot, but he seemed anxious to have us all get together."

Matthew scowled. "What's this 'anxious' business? You invited me to supper, and I suggested that Lea and Margaret come too."

Margaret sat on Matthew's other side and stared up at him. "Matthew, please, I think Ralph is trying to say something nice about your feelings." She smiled at Nicky and Ralph. "It's so lovely to meet the two of you and to know that Matthew's friends are so considerate."

Nicky laughed. "Well, we hope Matthew considers us friends. He's very picky." She glanced across the table at Lea. "But he certainly knows it when he sees a beautiful and talented woman."

Lea laughed. "I only wish I could remember what my talents were."

Margaret immediately leaned forward and pushed Matthew back enough to look at Lea. "Dearest, you are wonderful and talented in every way. Please don't ever doubt that."

Lea looked down and blushed. "I was so fortunate that Margaret and her son, Eric, took me in when I lost my memory."

Margaret's blue eyes filled with regret. "I couldn't believe it when Eric told me that he hit Lea with his car."

It was Lea's turn to push Matthew back and frown at Margaret. "Mom, please, you know very well that witnesses saw me run out in front of his car."

Margaret sucked in a breath. "Still—"

Lea continued. "But I must say that if someone was going to hit me, I was lucky." Her face lit up when she turned to Nicky and Ralph. "I'm convinced that Margaret's son is part angel, right Matthew?"

Matthew snorted out a sigh. "I don't know about an angel, but he's very caring."

"Very caring?" Ralph's eyes widened. "That's high praise coming from you, Matthew."

Nicky reached out to Margaret. "You must have a very special son."

Margaret nodded. "I do, but when my boy was in trouble, no one could be more thoughtful than Matthew." She swiped at her eyes with a tissue. "When Eric fell down some stairs, Matthew was so concerned. He never left my son's bedside until he was positive that Eric was going to be okay."

Ralph sat up straighter, looking confused. "Are you talking about my partner, Matthew Howell?"

Margaret grabbed Matthew's arm and squeezed it. "I think your partner must be part angel too. No matter what, he's the most generous man I've met in a very long time."

Matthew grimaced. "Please, Margaret, you're exaggerating. Ralph knows the real me. I'm terrible when it comes to people and being nice."

Lea quickly grabbed Matthew's other arm and stared intently at Ralph. "You'll have to forgive Matthew, Ralph. I think he's extremely empathic and very sensitive to the pain of others. That's why he avoids certain situations. How else would he be able to do his job as a surgeon except to put up some walls?"

Ralph narrowed his brows thoughtfully. "I guess I can understand that. And it does explain a lot."

Nicky smiled. "Margaret is right. Matthew was certainly there for me when I was ill. I wouldn't be sitting here if it weren't for his caring nature."

Matthew tried unsuccessfully to loosen the tight grip that Margaret and Lea had on his arms. "Please, can we change the subject? Everyone at this table has the wrong idea about me."

Margaret let Matthew's arm go and took a deep breath. "Matthew's right. We need to respect his wishes. He's still having a very hard time accepting praise, the poor dear." She leaned in towards Nicky and Ralph and lowered her voice when she spoke. "Like Lea said, the only way that Matthew knows to protect himself is to put up walls."

After Margaret's statement, Matthew's face turned a bright red, but he seemed incapable of saying anything more.

* * *

While Nicky, Margaret and Lea were talking in the kitchen, Matthew suspected they were still gossiping about him. Their voices were often hushed, and they giggled a lot. "Bringing Lea and Margaret here was a mistake," he sighed. "What an embarrassing evening."

"Why? Any other man would be ecstatic to have those two on their side. And they're right. You're a good man."

"Come on, Ralph. It's just you and me now. Cut the BS."

"I mean it, Matthew. I agree you're a pain in the butt when it comes to patient interaction, but as far as your ability to serve is concerned, you take cases that no one else will touch. And most of the time, you succeed in helping people where others would fail."

"I have a good ego and excellent skills, that's all."

Ralph laughed. "Whatever you say, Matt, but there's a reason why I've put up with your bad temper and fits. I guess I've always known that you have to blow off steam after all the stress you face with your job."

Matthew stood up and headed for the kitchen. "That's it. I'm collecting the women and going home."

"Geez, Margaret is right about you, Matt. You have zip capacity for praise."

Matthew turned and scowled at Ralph. "I can't afford to buy into any of that crap."

"Why is that?"

"I don't want to care about what others think, good or bad. I enjoy being my own person."

Ralph curtailed a smile. "Of course, I get what you're saying. You have a very healthy attitude."

Later, after Matthew dropped Lea and Margaret off at their apartment, he refused their offer to come in and talk. He had no more time for conversation. He had to decide what to do about a very serious situation.

He could be in trouble if Margaret and the rest were right about him being kind and generous. What if he started to care too much about every patient he faced in the OR? What if he cared so much that he couldn't do his job properly? What if a patient died because he couldn't keep his emotions in check and lost his objectivity?

He thought about Eric Lloyd, Doc Angel Eyes. "Oh hell, what if his gift ends up destroying my career?"

Matthew had criticized Paul for being so small minded, but now, facing a similar fate, he didn't feel as sure about his advice. What would he do if his surgical career came to an end? "I'll be working alongside Eric in some damn pet shop. And I don't even like animals."

* * *

Eric was about to get into bed when his phone sounded. It was Matthew's ring tone. He quickly took the call. "Matthew, is there a problem with Paul again?"

"No, I'm calling to say 'thank you.'"

"For what?"

"For redirecting my career and getting me that job in your pet shop."

"Pet shop? Matthew, I don't know what you've been drinking, but—"

"I'm stone-cold sober."

"Well, you don't sound like yourself."

"Exactly, after years of honing a personality that suited my needs, I've lost everything I worked at. And it's because of your precious gift."

"You've lost your personality? I don't think that's possible, is it?"

"Of course, it's possible! Lea is nothing like she was. Once you got hold of her, she became someone who's sweet and agreeable and totally not the Lea I knew!"

Eric sat down heavily on the side of his bed. "Are you saying that you don't love Lea anymore?"

"Of course I love her. But she's too nice. And I'm becoming some sappy, irrational person who's not worth a damn when it comes to my career. After all my years of study and diligence, my future is doomed. I'll be doing all my doctoring at some animal shelter, putting a splint on some damn puppy's broken leg."

Eric started laughing. "That's total nonsense. I can assure you that your precious personality is fully intact."

"How can you know that?" Matthew barked back.

"Because you sound exactly like that jerk who once barged into my house and nearly broke my jaw."

There was a long pause on the other end, followed by a more reasonable tone of voice. "You're not just saying that to make me feel better, are you?"

"Matthew, the bottom line is that you'll never be another Mother Teresa. You've simply had to deal with a lot of interpersonal issues that have you rattled. Once everyone settles down, you'll be back to your comfortable, grumpy self."

"You better be right, Lloyd, or else."

"Is that a threat?"

"Absolutely. If this 'caring' crap doesn't end soon, I'm holding you responsible. So pray that things return to normal, and I don't have to storm your house again."

"I'll be seeing you before that happens. Teresa and I are coming out this weekend to surprise Mom. We'll see you in a few days."

Thirty-Eight

LEA CLOSED HER laptop and walked over to where Margaret was sitting. "Mom, I've been thinking about something."

Margaret looked up from her book. "Thinking about what?"

"I might have a little surprise for you."

Margaret sat back and put her book aside. "What kind of surprise?"

"I've talked to my dad, and he told me that he'd like to fly us to Blacksburg, Virginia. Then we can rent a car, and drive to Elkville."

"Oh, my goodness."

"Yes, I want to visit the place where you lived and raised your family. Do you think you'd like that too?"

Margaret's eyes welled up with sudden tears. "Oh my goodness," she repeated.

Lea stared back anxiously. "Did I upset you? I'm so sorry."

"No, you didn't upset me." Margaret got up and hugged Lea in a firm embrace. "I'm just so happy." After a moment, she stood back. "I forgot how much I missed Elkville until you said I could go back."

"I'm so glad. And it's exciting for me too. I've tried to imagine what Elkville is like."

Margaret frowned. "Please don't get any ideas about it being pretty or very big. It's not."

"I don't care. I just want you to share it with me."

"When can we go?"

"What about this weekend? I cleared it with Dad already if that's not too soon."

Margaret hugged herself nervously. "I just can't believe it. This weekend will be perfect."

* * *

Matthew blinked back at Lea, trying to keep his voice steady. She'd just presented him with an idea that had his heart pounding. "You're going where? Elkville?" They were in one of his favorite diners, meeting for a late lunch. Matthew scowled and shoved his plate aside. "When are you thinking of going?"

Lea smiled. "Can you believe it? Dad is going to fly Mom and me to Blacksburg, Virginia this Saturday. Then we'll rent a car and drive to Elkville from there."

Matthew reached out for her hand. "Lea, please, Eric's told me stories about that place, bad stories—"

"It's fine. Mom lived there for forty years."

Matthew sat back. "I don't care. The place sounds primitive. And the people? Do you know that Eric talked about a person named Wild Nelly? And she was one of the nice ones."

Lea frowned. "I thought you might like to come along with us."

Matthew grabbed for his chest. "Me? Is Elkville even on a map? Do they have city water? Lea, they probably have rural wells, contaminated wells."

"Mom is perfectly healthy."

"Sure she is. She's developed an immunity to god-knows-whatever's in that water, but it's probably stuff that could kill you or me."

"Fine, so we'll load up on bottled water before we leave Blacksburg."

"What if you had an accident on one of those mountain roads? There are no medical facilities. No doctor. No hospital. Nothing!" As he talked about the dangers that were rapidly filling up his mind, Matthew sat back and rubbed his temples. "Oh god, you're right, I better go too. If anything happened, you might not make it back alive."

"So you'll come? That's wonderful!"

"Oh, wait a minute. I just thought of something." Matthew let out a relieved exhale. "Margaret can't go. Eric and Teresa are coming to Chicago on Friday night. They're surprising her."

286

"How perfect! They can come too."

Lea took out her phone. "I'll text Eric right now and ask him to call me. This is going to be so much fun! You and me on another adventure!"

"Maybe this is your idea of fun, but—"

Lea didn't seem to notice his anxious look. After she finished her text, she put her phone back in her purse. "Matthew, I want to clear things up between us."

"What things?"

Lea hesitated and tore at her napkin.

Matthew leaned in anxiously. "What's wrong? Did I upset you with my complaining? I'm sorry, but I don't relish the idea of going to some hamlet that God forgot."

"It's not that." Lea raised her eyes to meet his. "Matthew, I've been wondering. Are we still engaged?"

Matthew's nervous frown deepened. "That depends. Do you still want to be engaged?"

"Every day, I think about you and want us to always be together, but maybe you don't think in those terms."

Matthew's frown slipped away. "So what you're saying is that you want that engagement ring back."

Lea sat up, lifted her chin and crossed her arms. "Yes, I do. If I'm going to spend the night with you—"

"You want to spend the night?"

"Yes, if that's okay."

"I'm surprised." Matthew hesitated and reached into the inside pocket of his jacket. When he looked back at Lea, he was holding a small box. "I know this sounds crazy, but this morning I saw this sitting in my drawer, and—"

"My engagement ring! You have it with you?"

Matthew stood up, grabbed a napkin off the table, and spread it on the floor next to Lea's chair. Swallowing the lump in his throat, he went down on one knee. "Lea, for the second time, and I hope the last time, I'm asking you, will you marry me?"

Lea threw herself at him with such fervor that she nearly sent him falling backwards. "Yes! I will marry you! Yes, yes, yes!"

Lea's announcement was so loud that most of the other patrons in the diner stopped eating. Instead of enjoying their food and conversation, they directed their attention and frowns at Lea and Matthew.

* * *

When Matthew asked her to marry him, Lea couldn't help herself. She let out a shout of joy as she threw herself into his arms. "Yes, yes, yes!" Her enthusiastic response was so spontaneous that she even surprised herself. She hadn't realized how much she'd been holding back her feelings.

Ever since she'd taken an apartment and been living on her own, she'd tried to focus on finding her place in the world. She wanted to be that individual who had self-confidence, a person who others could depend on. That was all well and good, but another part of her also wanted expression. She loved Matthew. He was always in the background, buoying up her thoughts. And her longing for him got stronger with each passing day.

In truth, she didn't want to live on her own. Ever since she woke up in Matthew's arms, she felt like it was where she belonged. She'd tried to ignore that feeling. She did everything she could to be strong and self-reliant on her own. But when Matthew got down on his knee and asked her to be his wife, to be with him forever, she knew it was exactly what she wanted. That's when all of her pent up feelings came to a head. She didn't have to fight her heart's desire anymore. Her ache would finally be satisfied.

Or would it? While she was floating in some wispy cloud of bliss, she realized that Matthew wasn't experiencing anything of the sort. His face was flushed with embarrassment. Instead of looking back at her with adoring eyes, he was glancing around the room. He spoke to her in an irritated tone of voice.

"Lea, please, I'm glad that you're happy, but please, keep your voice down."

It was such a simple, seemingly innocent statement. But Lea knew better than accept it without question. Matthew's condemnation, though minor, went directly to her core. It was a blow that took the air from her lungs. It made her glance around the room in a breathless attempt to understand what had happened.

That's when she noticed that people were frowning back at her. She wouldn't have cared if Matthew's face wasn't frowning too. Like the rest, he was letting her know that she'd acted improperly. Instead of celebrating the moment, Matthew was thinking about the patrons in the diner, making their opinions more important than Lea's.

When Matthew stood up and reached out to her, she immediately backed away. She began to think about all the ways he had tried to explain how different they were in how they thought about everything. That would have been fine if she felt like he loved her in the way that she loved him. She accepted him as he was, and she expected him to except her completely, too.

She stared back at Matthew. His appearance told the story of how he conducted his life. He was always perfectly groomed and impeccably dressed. Pressed suits and jackets. Crisp, spotless shirts. Everything was controlled and exacting.

She was attentive to her appearance and dress, but she wasn't exacting like Matthew. Far from it. Her fears gushed out of her just like her joy had gushed out. "This is all wrong. I've been fooling myself or maybe you think I've been acting like a fool."

Matthew reached out for her hand. "What are you talking about?"

She jerked away before he could touch her. "You're ashamed of me. I see that now."

"Lea, I just suggested that you don't shout in a public place."

"Or maybe you're afraid of who I am. I've been talking to my dad about my early childhood, before the nanny got hold of me. And Dad said that he'd never seen such an impulsive child. He said he didn't know how to calm me down when I laughed too loud or ran around a restaurant because I wanted to fly."

"So you were a boisterous child, so what?"

She put her hand on Matthew's chest. "You're a good person, Matthew. And for a little while, I thought we fit together. But we're too different. You need someone who's meticulous and proper like you. But I'm not like that."

"That's ridiculous. I love who you are."

"Really? When you asked me to marry you, the world disappeared. All that I saw was you. But instead of looking at me the same way, your focus was on what other people were thinking."

"You're reading too much into what I said."

"I wish that was true. But I'm still boisterous, and I embarrass you. That's not going to change. And I want to be happy with who I

289

am even more than I want to be your wife. So I'm sorry. This isn't going to work."

Without waiting for Matthew to reply, she picked up her purse and quickly ran out of the restaurant. By the time she got outdoors, the tears were already streaming down her face. Without a backwards glance, she quickly hailed a cab.

* * *

When Eric got Lea's text, he called her as soon as he had a break in his work day. As he waited for Lea to pick up, he hoped she was okay. She didn't usually call him. When she finally answered, he listened attentively. "Lea? Have you been crying?"

Lea paused and sniffled. "Matthew asked me to marry him, and I said no."

"But why? Don't you love him?"

"Of course I love him."

Eric sat back in his office chair. "Sorry, but I don't think that I'm understanding the problem. If he proposed to you, that means he loves you too."

"Maybe, but he's ashamed of me! And I refuse to be with someone who can't accept me for who I am."

"Whenever Matthew talks about you, he seems smitten."

"Please, Eric, let's drop it. I don't want to talk about Matthew. I want to talk to you about a trip. This weekend, Mom and I are flying out early to Blacksburg, and then we're driving on to Elkville. But Matthew said you were going to surprise Mom by coming here. Maybe you could join us instead."

"Elkville? Why are you going there?"

"Your mom still misses your dad . . . a lot. I think she wants to go back to visit his grave."

Eric closed his eyes, picturing his father's funeral. His mother dressed in black. Her trembling hand holding on to his father's casket. It was a devastating affair for both him and for his mother. "Lea, I wonder if that's a good idea."

"I know it's not healthy, but Mom can't seem to move on. I hoped this might help her to have a little more peace in her life. But now, talking to you, maybe I shouldn't have interfered."

"You have good instincts. Who knows? This might be what Mom needs."

"What about you? Mom doesn't know you were going to surprise her. So if you want to wait, you could put off your trip and forget about Elkville too."

"No, I want to be there for her. So I'll change our tickets and fly directly to Blacksburg. We'll meet you there."

* * *

Paul brought a carafe of coffee over to where Margaret was sitting at the bar in his kitchen. "Margaret, you don't have to keep checking up on me. I'm feeling much better."

Margaret held out her mug. "Actually, I wanted to ask you something."

"Paul filled her mug and went back to the counter and replaced the carafe. "What is it? If you need something, please tell me."

Margaret sipped her coffee and smiled. "I wondered if you'd like to take a little trip back east. Lea and I are going to visit Elkville."

"Isn't that the place where you and your husband—" He stopped himself as soon as he remembered how powerfully Margaret had expressed her feelings about her dead husband.

"Yes, Elkville was our home. Anyway, if you come with us, it would get you out of this place for a weekend."

Paul frowned. He hadn't expected Margaret to extend such a generous invitation. "That's kind of you, but I'm sure this will be a very special time for you and Lea. I don't want to intrude."

"Don't be silly, Paul. I've seen how you stare out the window. You don't like being cooped up for too long."

Paul shrugged. "I do like seeing new places. I think I have a little gypsy in my blood."

"Then it's settled. You're coming with us. The fresh mountain air will be good for you. And you'll love how beautiful everything is at this time of year. Many of the trees will be newly leafed out and gorgeous."

Paul felt a rush of adventure grab hold. He'd never visited the Appalachians, but he'd been curious, especially after listening to Eric's accounts. "Thank you, I'd like that very much."

291

Margaret nodded. "Now for the bad news. Lea and Matthew had a falling out."

"What? I thought they were doing so well."

"I know, but Lea won't talk about it. Every time she tries, she starts crying."

Paul sat down on one of the bar stools. "That is so disheartening."

"Paul, do you think you could talk to Lea?"

"Margaret, you said it yourself. I've already made way too many mistakes."

"Maybe I was too hasty."

Paul rubbed the counter distractedly. "Let's wait and see if Lea and Matthew figure out things for themselves."

Margaret took another sip of coffee and sighed. "I guess you're right. When it comes to love, things can get so complicated. Maybe it's best not to interfere."

Thirty-Nine

MARGARET SAT NEXT to the small, plane window and glanced out. "I never thought I'd be in a private jet. Do you think it's safe, Paul?"

Paul was in the seat next to Margaret's. "I'm sure we're perfectly safe. I've had many clients with their own planes." He glanced around. "But I must say that Raymond's jet is very nice."

"Still, it's much smaller than a regular plane. What if we run into bad weather?"

"Try to enjoy yourself, Margaret. The people who pilot these planes know what they're doing."

"I wish Lea would get back. She said she needed a breath of air before we take off, but she still looks so upset. Poor thing, her heart is broken."

"Did you ever find out what happened?"

Margaret let out a deep sigh. "It's so sad. Matthew proposed, and she refused him. She claims she doesn't think he really loves her."

"I don't get that impression."

"Neither do I. I think Matthew is totally devoted, but Lea has made up her mind." Margaret leaned in closer to her window. "Oh, my goodness."

"What is it?" Paul asked as he leaned in too. "Speak of the devil, is that who I think it is?"

"Yes, but what's Matthew doing here?"

Paul leaned in even more. "He doesn't look too happy, does he?"

"No, but I can't blame him. The poor man doesn't seem to get a break. Still, he does look very handsome today. Look at his fancy sports jacket and those newly pressed slacks. When I lived in Baltimore, I tried to keep Eric looking his best, but he's more relaxed than Matthew." Margaret pulled away from the window. "Paul, sit back, he'll be boarding the plane in a moment, and we don't want him to see us gawking at him, do we?"

Paul settled into his seat with a smile. "No, we don't."

Margaret patted down her hair and leaned in close to Paul. "Should we say anything to him about . . . you know, Lea and the breakup."

"Maybe we should let Matthew do the talking."

Margaret took another peek out the window and quickly pulled away. She nudged Paul. "Shh, he's right outside!" After a short wait, she glanced up and saw Matthew coming up the narrow aisle. She tried to do as Paul advised, but that didn't mean she couldn't be cordial. When Matthew paused next to their seat, she smiled.

Matthew gave her a nod. "Hello, Margaret, Paul."

Paul was very cordial. "Hello, Matthew. Good to see you again."

Margaret's smile slipped away after a moment and was replaced by a look of concern. "Matthew, you don't know how happy I am that you're flying with us."

Matthew frowned. "Why is that?"

Margaret clasped her hands. "It's this little plane. Paul seems to think it's fine, but I keep remembering all those famous people who've died in small planes."

Matthew returned the slightest smile. "Statistically, we're very safe. So try not to worry."

Margaret nudged Paul. "See that, Matthew always has a way of making things better."

"Matthew! What are you doing here?"

Margaret turned around and saw Lea. The young woman had boarded the plane again. Now, she stood a few feet behind Matthew with a scowl on her face.

Matthew looked at Lea too. When he spoke, his tone was measured and low. "Did you forget that you invited me to come, and I agreed?"

Lea stiffened. "Well, I didn't expect you to show up since—"

"Since you decided to walk out on me a second time? Unlike you, I don't abandon the people I care about. If something unfortunate happens in Elkville, I'll be there like I promised."

Margaret clasped her hands again. "Matthew, are you worried about Lea going to Elkville?"

Matthew pushed back his broad shoulders and returned a thoughtful look. "I'm sorry, but from what Eric has told me, it's a very remote area. And no matter what Lea thinks, I care very much about what happens to her."

Lea reacted to Matthew's statement by pushing her way past him. Her voice was strained when she spoke. "Excuse me, but I think we're going to take off shortly. We should take our seats."

* * *

The flight to Blacksburg was uneventful. No one had much to say after takeoff. Margaret read her book, and Paul seemed engrossed in some scientific articles. Lea sat by herself, and Margaret didn't know how she spent her time. Matthew slept away most of the flight. Perhaps, he was trying to catch up.

When they landed in Blacksburg, Margaret got a wonderful surprise. Eric was waiting for her. Margaret knew that she'd missed him, but she hadn't realized how much. He had the most wonderful smile, a smile that melted her heart. As he held her in an embrace, she tried her best to think about the promise she'd made to herself. She had to stop holding on to him. He had a life to live, and she wouldn't impose on his freedom. "Where's Teresa?" she asked as they walked through the airport.

"She was going to come, but you know how it is, an emergency came up. She wanted to take care of her patient personally. But she said to give you her love."

"She's very special, Eric. I'm so happy that you found each other."

Eric had Margaret's arm in his, and he pulled her closer. "Thank you. I'm very fortunate."

Margaret paused and glanced back. "Let's wait for the others."

Eric looked back too. "I didn't think I'd be seeing Matthew. What's he doing here?"

Margaret lowered her voice. "I know. The poor man is determined to take care of Lea even if she's thrown him over."

"But why did Lea turn him down when he proposed?"

"Eric, I don't know what's going on. I've never seen this side of her. She's become very stubborn and unforgiving."

"Did Matthew offend her in some way?"

"If he did, I don't think he meant to. From what I can tell, Matthew is truly concerned about her welfare. He's afraid something could happen to her when we get to Elkville."

"Oh hell, that might be my fault. I told him some stories about what Dad was up against. If I know Matthew, he's probably very spooked by it all."

Margaret found out just how right Eric was about Matthew's state of mind. When they stopped for bottled water and groceries, the surgeon combed the pharmacy section of the store. He loaded up on every kind of first aid item from sterile gauze pads to latex gloves. When Eric commented and tried to put Matthew's mind at ease, Matthew merely gave Eric a dismissive glance and went on to purchase the numerous items in his cart.

* * *

The seven passenger SUV rental that sped towards Elkville was roomy and comfortable. When Lea had asked for a volunteer driver, Eric ended up behind the wheel. He was familiar with the route and seemed at ease as they traveled further and further away from the main highway.

As they neared their destination, Eric became much more attentive, especially when the roadway became narrow and twisted. He skillfully put the SUV through its paces as it navigated the hairpin curves and hump-back terrain. The car climbed one steep grade after another. Once the vehicle crested a hill, Eric was careful to shift into a lower gear. It was a prudent decision, one that prevented the car from attempting a hair-raising, downhill descent.

The scenery was as wild and breathtaking as the roller-coaster ride. The greening mountains were feasts of rugged beauty. As bold examples of the untamed glories of nature, they dominated every point of view. They could frighten a city dweller who usually woke up to buildings of concrete and steel.

TRACES OF HOME

* * *

The trip from Blacksburg to Elkville would always be a memorable one for Matthew. He was in the front passenger seat of the SUV. Its generous windshield gave him a perfect view of every heart-wrenching moment of the journey. He found himself bracing one hand on the dash during most of the trip. It helped a little. He told himself that he could prevent disaster if he held on to it tight enough. Margaret and Paul sat in the seats behind him. Lea had elected to sit by herself in the last row of seats. There was very little conversation between passengers. For whatever reason, everyone seemed caught up with their own thoughts and maintained a code of silence.

When they arrived in Elkville, Matthew felt like he'd gone back in time. Except for the SUV that he was traveling in, there was no sign of the world he was accustomed to. The small, barely accountable village had a half dozen buildings clustered together. Matthew blinked and the main street was already behind him. He was just thinking that he'd been spared looking too closely at the derelict buildings when he was presented with even more frightening instances of human shabbiness.

Elkville's sparse neighborhoods had dirt yards that hosted numerous decaying vehicles and an occasional outdated washing machine. Fences that edged properties were missing slats and any sign of maintenance. The residents Matthew glimpsed hadn't fared any better. They looked faded and dismal too, perfect compliments to the trashy yards and dented trucks with missing tires.

When Eric finally pulled up and parked in front of the Lloyd house, Matthew had to hold back a gasp of panic. Somehow, he'd imagined that the residence would be different than the rest. And, in some ways, it was. There weren't any vehicles in the yard. That was a plus, the only plus.

As he stared at the rundown structure, the novel, "Grapes of Wrath" came to mine. He figured the house was in its prime around the same time that the story was published. As he stared at its peeling paint and sagging porch, he tried his best to rally. But it was an impossible task. He'd entered a foreign, hostile environment that had no mercy on buildings or people.

Matthew noted that he wasn't the only one having a problem. Eric seemed disturbed too. When he got out of the car, he stared at his childhood home with a scowl. He gave his mother a questioning glance. "You should have told me that I wasn't giving you enough to keep up the yard and repair the house. My goodness, the grass must be a foot and a half tall."

Margaret walked over to where Eric stood and sighed. "You gave me plenty, but there was always someone who needed some help. So I told Florence to give the money to those unfortunate souls."

Eric grimaced back. "I'm going to have to do something about the yard."

"Eric, don't worry about it."

"I can't help it. The place never looked this bad. But in the meantime, let's get the car unloaded."

Margaret handed him a key. "Do you want to try your luck with that old lock? You've always been better at getting it open."

Eric nodded, then turned to the people who were still sitting in the car. "Come on, everyone. Let me introduce you to our humble abode."

* * *

The others had already gone inside the Lloyd house, but Lea hung back. The urge to cry had plagued her ever since they left Chicago. The reason was obvious. Instead of being engaged to the man she loved, she was stuck with her judgmental attitude. The situation left her in a state of continual turmoil and weepiness. And she had no one to blame but herself. It was all her fault that she was in the position she was in.

After she had time to think about Matthew's proposal, she realized she was the one being the needy person. She wanted Matthew to love her on her terms instead of realizing that a relationship involved give and take. But once she went down a road of self-righteousness, she didn't know how to extricate herself. Her stubborn, prideful side made itself known. And every time she talked to anyone about her breakup with Matthew, that prideful side took over.

Now, Matthew was being the gallant one in the situation. He'd come to Elkville because he was worried about her. He wasn't letting his pride stand in the way of being the loving person that he was. She wanted to be just as giving and caring, but she didn't know how.

She stood on the street side of the SUV and used it as a shield. If she was going to cry, she didn't want people watching her. But as she gave herself permission to let out her frustration, her tears dried up. All she felt was that she was all alone in a strange place that scared her. After a few minutes, she decided to join the others in the group. She turned and started for the house.

Forty

MATTHEW STOOD AT the living room window of the Lloyd residence. He stared out the dirty panes and watched another accident waiting to happen. When Margaret joined him, he crossed his arms and asked her a question. "What is Eric trying to do out there, Margaret?"

Margaret shook her head. "Maybe he's trying to take his father's place. His dad used to mow the lawn, and Eric would do the trimming and weed the flower beds."

"I assume there was a lawnmower involved, not a sickle."

"The grass never got so out of hand."

"Margaret, may I be frank with you?"

"Yes, Matthew, say what you have to say."

"Eric told me that his 'skills' in some areas are sometimes lacking. And I'm afraid he's proving that now."

"He wasn't always awkward. But I noticed that as he got older, he had a harder time handling certain jobs. At times, I think he has too much on his mind."

"I think this is one of those times."

Margaret stepped closer to the window and peered out. "Oh my, you're right. He looks upset. I don't think he's thinking about what he's doing."

Matthew agreed. Eric's movements had no rhythm. Instead, he whacked away at the overgrown lawn in a way that was uncoordinated, haphazard and dangerous. "He's going at that grass like a soldier in battle, but I don't think that's the way to use a sharp implement like a sickle."

300

Margaret's breath caught. "I better go out there and stop him."

"I don't know if you can. Remember, you've already tried."

"A mother couldn't have a more caring son, but sometimes he gets something in his mind, and he won't listen to me."

Matthew thought about the night at the Ferguson mansion. Eric was determined to leave no matter what. "He does have a tenacious side to his personality."

Margaret turned imploring eyes on Matthew. "Would you speak to him for me, please?"

Matthew thought about his options. He could talk some sense into Eric, or he could wait until an accident happened. Then the rest of his day would be spent trying to patch up Eric's maimed body. "Yes, I'll talk to him."

Margaret smiled. "Like I said before, you're the brother Eric needs in his life."

Matthew nodded, but he didn't want to encourage Margaret's need to make him Eric's sibling. "Where's that lawnmower your husband used?"

"It's in the shed out back, why?"

"I have an idea that might work."

Margaret was clutching at her hands again. "I'm so happy that you came. I don't know why, but somehow you always make me feel like things are going to work out."

"Yes, that's very nice, but I don't think Lea feels that way about me."

"Matthew, don't forget that she was once very frightened, frightened of herself. She shared some of her diary with me, and I got the idea that she's afraid she can't make you happy. So she pushes you away."

Matthew rubbed his temples. "I guess I forgot about all that. She's been so different lately."

"Yes, but that frightened little child is still inside. When Lea doubts herself, I think it takes over. In fact, when she first came to live with Eric and me, she got very upset when she made the slightest mistake with whatever she was doing."

"What did you do?"

"We both kept encouraging her, and little by little, she began to trust herself."

Matthew noted Margaret's face. There was so much kindness in the way she was looking at him. "Thank you, Margaret. That makes sense."

Margaret smiled back. "Lea loves you so much. I've done some crying in my time, but this past week, she could have filled a bathtub with her tears. So please, don't give up on her. She had that with her father when she was growing up. She might not survive if you stop believing in her too."

Matthew took a much needed breath. "Don't worry, I have no intention of giving up on her. But for the time being, I better check on Eric."

* * *

Eric stood in the tall grass, not wanting to, but remembering the last time he'd helped his father with the yard. They'd had an argument. It was rare for him to engage in conflict, but on that occasion, Eric couldn't hold his temper in check. He'd come home for a visit, and he was worried about his father's health. But, as usual, his father wouldn't listen. In fact, his father was openly resentful when Eric had tried to use his expertise as a cardiologist to prove his point.

Eric Richard Lloyd was a proud man. He didn't appreciate a son who questioned his authority. He let Eric know that his opinion wouldn't be tolerated. A short time later, his father had a fatal heart attack.

"Why couldn't he just listen for a change?"

Eric lashed out at the grass, and he wanted to keep lashing out. He hated arrogance and pride, and that's what he'd been dealing with whenever he tried to talk some sense into his father. Now, he was back in Elkville, helping his mother cope with her loss, a loss that could have been prevented.

Eric was also trying to deal with his own loss. In spite of everything, he'd loved his dad, even thought of his father as his hero when he was younger.

"Eric?"

Eric paused and looked over his shoulder. "Yes, what is it, Matthew?"

Matthew held out a bottle of water. "Thought you might need a drink. It's a warm day."

Eric wiped the sweat off his brow. "Thinner atmosphere at this higher elevation. That's why the sun can feel warmer." He reached out for the water. "Thanks."

"I was thinking. After traveling, I could use some exercise. And this job would go faster if we worked together."

Eric laughed. "Are you kidding? Look at yourself, Matthew. Fancy slacks, fancy shirt. You can't work out here in those clothes."

"Is there a store around where—"

"Are you talking about a clothing store? The closest we have here is the general store. It has coveralls, stuff the local folks use."

"Fine, I'll pick some up there."

"You're joking. Matthew Howell dressed up like a farmer? I don't think so."

"What about jeans? Do they have jeans?"

"Maybe, but you don't have to help out. I can take care of this mess."

"Tarnation, Doc Lloyd, dont ya be gettin' stubbrn on me. Lea already fancies that job."

"Yes, I noticed." Eric took a drink of water and replaced the cap. "Seemin that ya be pinin' over that woemern—"

Matthew held up a hand. "Stop, you may have a bit of a southern accent, but your attempt at hillbilly lingo is worthless."

"My father constantly corrected my speech. If he heard any hillbilly lingo, he'd have a fit." Eric took another drink of water and scowled. "Look at this place. After all of my father's hard work and dedication, the only things that he left behind were a house that needs to be torn down and a yard full of weeds and overgrown grass."

"What about you? Didn't he leave a son behind, one who's just as dedicated as he was?"

Eric avoided Matthew's eyes. "My father made it clear that he didn't want what I had to offer."

"Join the crowd. My father won't even speak to me."

"Why?"

"I was supposed to take over the family law firm. Instead, I went to med school."

Eric dug the car keys out of his pocket. "I don't know why our dads bothered to have us."

Matthew laughed. "That's an easy one. They each wanted a mini-me, a son who would grow up and be just like them."

"Well, I may be dedicated, but I'm not like my dad."

"Good, then we have something in common."

When they got to the general store, Eric went directly to the clothing section. He was checking out the inventory when he realized that Matthew had wandered off. The surgeon was checking out the tool section. He had a scythe in his hands. "See something interesting, Matthew?"

Matthew was examining the scythe's two foot blade. "Yes, this would do a better job than the sickle. I could finish clearing the grass, and you could use a lawn mower to even it out."

"You think you could use one of those?"

Matthew let out a huff. "Peasants used them in the middle ages. I think I could manage."

"Okay, it's your call. But I have some bad news about the jeans. All they have is overalls."

Matthew frowned. "Whatever, I'm not going to ruin these new slacks. And I better buy one of those flannel shirts too."

Eric smiled as he picked out the only large size available. Its pattern was a bright red and navy blue plaid print. "You're in luck, Matthew. They're on sale."

* * *

Paul Glass decided to take an afternoon walk. While Margaret and Lea were fixing supper, and Eric and Matthew tackled the yard, he would get a much needed breath of air. For long hours, he'd been sitting on a plane and then riding in a car. He needed to stretch his legs. He also wanted to explore the area, and there was never a better way than on foot.

As he passed by the dozen houses on Margaret's street, he couldn't help but notice their run-down condition. When he thought about Margaret and her husband working in such an impoverished area, he had to admire both of them. For Margaret's husband, the year in and year out grind of being the only medical doctor in the area had to be exhausting. And while her husband was tending to the sick and injured, Margaret had to keep the home fires burning, literally.

Paul shuddered to think about the work involved in staying warm when the town was in the midst of a hard, cold winter. Margaret probably had to continually stoke the ancient stove in the living room. Paul had checked the heating unit out and decided it probably wasn't very efficient.

Thankfully, it was a nice spring day. The weather was mild enough for just a sweater. The sun was warm overhead as Paul continued down a road that led out of town. He was relieved to see the landscape changing. Trash still littered the areas closest to the road, but Paul concentrated on the trees beyond and the scent of the woodsy loam.

The quiet was calming. It was a perfect environment to forget about everything. He'd put off the idea of moving indefinitely. He needed to figure out what to do with the rest of his life before he went anywhere. Eventually, he might think about writing his memoirs, but for the time being he didn't want to think about his past.

He took a deep breath of the mountain air and coughed. His lungs weren't used to air that was so clean and pure. Still, he was sure he could get used to it. He could also appreciate the rich mixture of oak and pine trees that populated the landscape and bordered the winding road. They were beautiful, mature examples of their kind, and they towered over the land like majestic overlords. Birds made the woods less intimidating. Their chirps, tweets and lively song added a light, playful feel to Paul's stroll.

After he'd gone a good mile, he was grateful that his body was quickly recovering. He'd been fortunate. His heart attack had been very mild. Still, he wouldn't press his luck. He'd turn around and go home. Dinner would be ready, and he didn't want anyone waiting for him.

He was about to reverse directions when a movement caught his eye. He paused and stared at the road ahead. "Probably just a rabbit." The explanation didn't feel right, and he decided to take a closer look. As he walked towards a weedy area on the side of the road, an animal raised its head for just a moment and whined. "Oh hell, I bet a dog's been hit by a car."

Paul hadn't had a pet since he was a boy, but he still had a soft spot for animals, especially dogs. The one he'd had as a child had been his best friend. It was during a time when Paul had trouble fitting in with other boys his age. Paul's mother told Paul that he was too serious. When the dog died, Paul had taken it very hard. He'd vowed never to own another one.

As he got close to the animal lying on the side of the road, he wished he'd turned back sooner. He didn't want to see any animal suffer, but the one staring up at him was the most heart-wrenching case of abuse he'd ever come across. It looked like a shepherd mix, but it was so thin that it wasn't much more than bones and fur. The fur around its shoulder was matted with blood.

Paul knew he shouldn't let himself connect to the animal, but he tapped into the animal's energy anyway. Fear and pain filled his mind. "Oh my goodness, someone shot you." The animal panted as it looked back at Paul. Clearly it didn't understand why it was suffering.

It was definitely an older dog. Its muzzle was peppered with gray, and its dirty fur looked rough and dull. Paul slowly reached out a hand to see how it would react. Instead of growling, the dog licked the air and whined again.

Paul shook his head. "In spite of all you've gone through, you're still willing to take a chance on me."

As they stared at each other, Paul knew he had to do whatever he could for the injured creature. He took out his phone to call for help, but he couldn't get a signal. That meant he had a choice. Go back and get the SUV, or he could try to carry the dog to Margaret's house. Watching the animal shake with chills, he chose the latter. He knew in his heart that if he left now, the dog would be dead before he got back.

"You're beyond your prime, but you have a right to life, old boy," he said as he took off his sweater. He decided to wrap the garment around the animal to provide a little warmth. The dog only cried out once when Paul moved it onto the sweater. Afterwards, Paul hoisted the animal up and held it close. It was a chore for his recovering body. Even though the dog was a bag of bones, it was still a large animal.

As Paul started walking, he felt a little better about his life. Maybe his abilities with people were in question, but as he cradled the dog against his body, he knew he had a place in the world of healing again. The dog seemed to second the motion. With great effort, it raised its head just enough to look at him with appreciation.

"I'll do my best to get you home, boy, but I can't promise I'll make it." It was the truth. Paul didn't know if his heart could take the strain.

* * *

Matthew walked into the kitchen and leaned a hand on the chipped counter. He needed a very large drink of water and a long, hot shower. Eric was trailing behind him and looked in need too. The cardiologist's face and neck were covered in a film of dirt.

Margaret stared at both of them with an appraising eye, but when she turned her attention to Matthew, she smiled. "My goodness, Matthew, if you weren't a bit dirty, you could be a model for work clothes in the Sears catalog I used to get."

Matthew wiped his brow with the back of his hand. "A person needs heavy-duty clothing when they're facing a jungle of weeds."

Margaret's tone turned teasing. "It's a good thing one of those women who live in the mountains wasn't around to give you the eye. They might have snatched you up and taken you home."

Matthew returned a slightly terrified look. He'd noted how strong Margaret could be. He couldn't imagine the strength of a true mountain woman in her prime. "No thank you. I'm very happy with Lea." He paused and looked around. "I thought she was helping you in the kitchen. Where is she?"

Margaret glanced upwards. "She wanted to put sheets on the beds while I was finishing dinner." She looked at the clock. "It's Paul that I'm worried about. I checked outside and called for him, but he wasn't to be found anywhere."

Matthew frowned. "I saw him walking up the road earlier in the day."

"Even if he wanted a walk, don't you think he should be back by now? It's getting late," Margaret insisted.

Eric tapped Matthew's arm. "Let's take the car and look for him. He couldn't have gone far."

Matthew returned a disappointed look. After hours of physical labor, he was starving. "I wish he'd been more considerate and not gone off without telling someone."

A shout interrupted Matthew's grumbling. It was followed by the back door being thrown open. When everyone looked to see what was going on, Paul stood in the doorway looking gray and shaky. His hands were covered with blood.

"I need help!" Paul shouted. "He's bleeding again! And I can't stop it!"

Margaret turned, looked at him and instantly panicked. "Paul? Whatever happened?"

Eric rushed to the door, slipped past Paul and quickly went outside. Matthew followed close on his heels.

Paul turned to go after them. "Help him, please."

Matthew pulled back and grimaced when he discovered the "he" that Paul was referring to. "Hell, Paul, I thought you were talking about a person. It's just a dog, and a mangy one at that."

Paul pushed Matthew aside and knelt down by the dog. "I don't give a damn what you think! He has a chance if you'll help him!"

Eric had been bent over the animal, but he stood up slowly and looked at Paul with sympathetic, blue eyes. "I'm sorry, Paul, but I don't think it's got a chance. It's too far gone."

Paul lifted the dog's head and put it on his lap. "Poor old boy, nobody gives a damn about you."

Matthew took Eric's arm and leaned in. "Paul doesn't look too good."

Eric nodded and approached Paul again, but when he tried to encourage Paul to leave his post, Paul threw off his hand. "Leave me alone, both of you! You're both unfeeling reprobates!"

Margaret came over to Matthew and signaled for him to come back into the kitchen. When she spoke to him, her voice was a soft whisper. "I've seen people get like this before. For some reason, Paul has become attached to that animal. You have to try to help. Even if the dog dies, at least he'll feel you tried. Please, Matthew, Paul needs to know people care about what he thinks."

Matthew gestured Eric into the house too. "Do you think the animal has any chance?"

Eric shrugged. "Maybe, a very slim one. And if you want to try to help, we could use my dad's office. It's set up for minor emergencies."

* * *

Matthew couldn't believe it. His nightmare had come true. He'd had terrible visions of how he'd be operating on mangy mutts instead of people. And that's exactly what he was doing. He was working on a dog that looked like it had visited hell before gracing Paul Glass's path.

He looked up at his assistant, Eric. They were gathered round a make-shift operating table. "In spite of this creature's deplorable condition and blood loss, I guess it has a chance," he said as he dropped a bullet into a nearby trash can.

Eric smiled. "Good thing my dad had some surgical supplies on hand."

"Right, at least I'm not using one of Margaret's kitchen knives."

"My dad saved a lot of lives with the little that he had to work with."

"Do you think he might have had your gift?"

Eric shrugged. "I never thought about it, but I think that most doctors have a few angels helping out in the wings."

"If there are any angels in the wings now, this animal is going to need them."

"Matthew, thank you for doing this. Paul looked like he was falling apart earlier."

"Your mother said the same thing."

"My mom has seen so many crazy people living in this place. You wouldn't believe how many times my dad's life was threatened if he didn't save somebody. But in the end, most people knew that he always gave his all."

Matthew was thankful that he worked in a more civilized environment. "Tough job. Anyway, we're about done here, and the dog is still breathing."

"Paul will be happy. He's upstairs lying down. I'll give him the news."

"Let's just hope he doesn't think of us as unfeeling reprobates anymore."

"That statement really bothered you."

"What bothered me is that Paul isn't able to remain rational. That's not good. It seems a waste for a man like him to lose it."

"Matthew, you once inferred that my father gave up. Why did you say that?"

"Not just your father, but a lot of people who put everything into their work. When they get older, they don't know anything else. Look at Raymond Ferguson. The man built an empire, but look how fast he fell apart when it came to handling other parts of his life."

"So will we end up like them?"

"Paul said he didn't think so. Hopefully, he's right."

* * *

When Matthew came out of the little medical addition of the house, he was surprised to see Lea waiting. "In case you're curious, Paul's animal is still breathing."

Lea immediately walked over to him. "That's good, but can I talk to you?"

Matthew was tired, hungry, and in no mood to listen to more reasons why he'd failed Lea, but he kept his mouth shut. He remembered what Margaret had said about Lea being unsure of herself, and he was determined not to reinforce that insecurity. "Yes, let's talk."

Lea gave him a weak smile and took his hand. She led him into the old office that Eric Lloyd, Sr. had used to see patients. But once there, she seemed unable to explain what she wanted. She let go of his hand and stared at her feet.

Matthew sucked in some air and started the conversation. "I'm sorry if you feel that I wasn't there for you in the diner."

Lea shrugged. "I'm sorry, too. I don't know why I got so upset."

Matthew felt his weariness peaking. "I don't want to disappoint you, Lea, but I do. Again, I'm sorry."

"Don't you understand? I disappoint myself."

"What do you mean?"

"In my diary, I wrote about my nanny yelling at me, telling me that I was a horrid child. I don't remember any of that, but sometimes the feelings are there. I try to do what's right, but I always end up doing something I shouldn't."

Matthew took hold of Lea's shoulders. "Look, let's get something straight. You didn't do anything wrong. And if I could change what happened in the diner, I would. My actions hurt you, but there's nothing I can do about it now."

"You didn't do anything wrong either, Matt."

"If that's true, why are we in this situation?"

Lea hugged herself. "I don't want it to be like this."

"Neither do I, but I can't guarantee that I won't upset you in the future either."

Lea blinked up at him. "I think trying to be perfect is what drove me slightly crazy. I don't want you to carry that kind of burden."

Matthew frowned. "What do you want?"

Lea put her hand on his cheek. "I want us to be together no matter what. Like you said, we're both going to make mistakes, but I'd rather live with some mistakes than give up what I feel when I'm with you."

Matthew suddenly felt more energized. "So are you saying that it's nice having me around?"

Lea's eyes lit up. "Of course! When you showed up on the plane, all I wanted was to be in your arms."

"You didn't act like it."

"I didn't know how to let go of my stupid pride."

"And how about now?"

"Matthew, the bottom line is that no matter how I act, I'll always love you."

Matthew started to smile. "That's a thought I can live with."

Lea straightened and stared back. "Matthew Howell, I hope you can be a little more specific about your feelings."

Matthew laughed as he pulled her close. "How's this for specific. I'll always love you, too."

Lea leaned in and snuggled against him. "It's perfect."

With Lea tucked under his chin, Matthew nuzzled her hair. "It's been a hell of a day, but I think things are finally looking up."

Lea hugged him more enthusiastically. "I agree."

A whine from the next room interrupted their embrace.

Matthew groaned. "Oh hell."

Lea pulled away and smiled. "Matthew, that sounds like the puppy."

Matthew winced. "Puppy? Lea, that animal is ready for the doggie retirement home."

Lea grabbed his hand and pulled him towards the adjoining room. "Come on. I want to see him. I didn't get a chance when Paul brought him here. I was upstairs crying."

"I thought you were making the beds."

311

"I started to, and then I thought about sleeping alone. Anyway, that's behind us now. Let's see this dog you saved."

"Do we have to?"

Lea let go of Matthew's hand and hurried over to a corner of the room. The injured animal was lying on a makeshift bed. He was covered up except for his head and his tail. She stared at the dog and let out a cry of distress. "Poor baby."

"Lea!" Matthew warned. "Maybe you shouldn't get too close!"

Lea glanced back and smiled. "Look at his tail. It's wagging. That means he wants us to pet him."

"Please be careful! If he bites you—"

Lea paused and walked back to Matthew. "You're really worried, aren't you?"

"Of course I am. That's why I came. But when I was working on that animal, I kept thinking that I wasn't prepared for a real emergency." Matthew reached out and pulled her close again. "If something happened to you—"

Lea held him too. "Matthew, please don't say anything to Margaret, but this place frightens me. I thought it would be quaint, but I didn't have any idea—"

"That you were entering an untamed wilderness?" Matthew nuzzled her hair again. "Believe me, you're not alone. This place scares me too."

Lea pulled back. "Really? I didn't think many things scared you."

"I'm smart enough to know when I'm up against something bigger than me. These mountains, the people . . . they swallowed up Eric's father, and I suspect they almost did Margaret in. I'm glad she decided to move back to civilization."

Forty-One

THE EARLY MORNING light was streaming through the bedroom window as Margaret stood in front of her old dresser. Looking at herself in the mirror, she realized that her image wasn't crisp like it was in the mirrors in Baltimore and Chicago.

She stepped closer and examined the mirror itself. This one was cloudy and had a number of black spots showing. It was an indication that the silver backing on the mirror had deteriorated. She'd never noticed its flaws when she was living in Elkville. But what could she expect? Unlike the Ferguson antiques, her aging furniture had never had much value to start with. When she and Ricky furnished the house, the furniture was second hand and already old.

Eric tried to renovate the house and its furnishings when he was making more money, but Ricky had taken Eric's suggestion as an insult. As her husband got older, he got more set in his ways. And Margaret hated when he and Eric disagreed.

"And you were the troublemaker, Ricky," Margaret sighed. "You took all his proposals as proof that you were a failure, that you'd failed me."

She bit her lip. She'd seen the way Ricky looked when Eric came home and fussed over her. She could practically read his thoughts. He wanted to be the one who suggested a shopping trip for new clothes. He wanted to be the person who got her other new things, like a washing machine to replace her ancient model.

Ricky had always tried so hard to be a good provider, but he could never succeed in giving his family what he thought they deserved. Luckily, when it came to Eric's education, Eric was exceptionally bright and got a scholarship to college. His uncle, Frank, helped out too. Frank insisted on taking care of Eric's other expenses.

Eric's uncle was a successful business man who never had children of his own. Margaret suspected that Frank sometimes pretended that Eric was his son. He was extremely generous, but Ricky only accepted his generosity because he wanted Eric to be a doctor. Otherwise, he would have shut out Frank like he shut out most people. Ricky could be wonderful with strangers who had a medical need, but he didn't want any personal connections outside of the family.

Margaret stepped back from the mirror, satisfied that she looked presentable. It had been two years since Ricky's passing, and she wanted to honor his memory. Later that morning, she planned on going to the cemetery with Eric. Lea, Matthew and Paul all wanted to pay their respects. Margaret felt fortunate to have their support.

Before going downstairs to make breakfast, she closed her eyes, promising herself that she wouldn't make a scene at Ricky's graveside. She didn't want to cry anymore. She wanted to get on with her life.

But being back in Elkville ignited countless memories. They were like small fires that burned everywhere she looked. There wasn't a square inch in the house that didn't have Ricky's stamp on it. He'd been a passionate man whose energy branded everything he touched. Sometimes, she felt like he'd branded her so deeply and with such adoring obsessiveness that she'd never know herself as anyone but his wife and the mother of his son.

* * *

Eric got up early to visit the cemetery. He wanted to clean up the area around his father's grave before his mother saw it. Like the yard, the space was overgrown with weeds. The air and the ground were still damp from a recent rain. Unfortunately, he'd forgotten to bring along his work gloves. He should have gone back and retrieved them, but he didn't want to take the time. Instead, he pulled the weeds barehanded.

There was no place like a cemetery to resurrect unwelcome images. Beneath the gravestone, his father's lifeless body lay in a casket six feet down. As Eric tugged and yanked at the unsightly weeds, he contemplated the distance between the casket and wherever his father's spirit resided. If his father was enjoying an afterlife, Eric was unaware of it. Their relationship ended the moment his father's heart stopped beating.

That didn't mean he could stop thinking about his father. When a boy grew up in an isolated area with someone like Eric Sr., the experience was always just a breath away. Perhaps for some, fathers were a comfort, a person who made you feel safe. For Eric, he remembered his father with an uneasy breath, an anxious breath.

If only he'd been able to go to school like most kids. But he was schooled at home. He could never leave the classroom. Was he keeping up with his math? What about history and geography? Had he properly memorized all the parts of the human anatomy?

"But Dad, I'm tired!"

Eric should have never made statements like that, even if he was only nine. He knew better, even at that young age that his reward would be a very stern look and possibly a lecture too.

Lloyd men weren't supposed to give in to their bodily discomforts.

"Do you think that being tired is a good excuse for neglecting your studies? What if I let someone bleed to death because I was tired? You have to train yourself, Eric! Train yourself to be stronger than you think you are!"

Eric tried to be strong, but sometimes, he had to get away. When his father was out on a call, he'd sneak out of the house. Tired or not, he'd run as fast as he could to a nearby woods. No one lectured him there. The woods were a quiet place where he had a favorite spot. He liked to sit on a fallen tree log. He'd clasp his hands and wait. If he stared into space long enough, the world would slip away, and his mind would take flight. He didn't know where it went, only that for a few moments, he felt free.

Of course, he always had to come home again. And his mother would be in the kitchen. Her face was often hot and damp when she was tending the oven and something she was baking. She'd give him a brief smile and tell him to wash up for dinner.

As the years of his childhood went by, and he got older, his father would take him along on his calls, always teaching him about "doctoring" and a man's conduct in the face of adversity.

Sometimes, Eric's young mind would wander, wanting the woods and quiet again. But his father's eye was as sharp as a raven's. He was always watchful, always ready to bring Eric back from his attempts to fly into the ethers.

"There's no room for daydreaming, Eric! When are you going to learn that you're on this earth for a purpose, not to be some self-indulgent good-for-nothing?"

As Eric knelt at his father's grave, he realized how long it had been since he'd sat in the woods. There was always too much to do. His patient load often demanded very long hours. By the time he got home, he was tired. And now there was Teresa to think about. He wanted to be there for her.

But the more he dug out the deeply rooted weeds and dandelions, the more he wondered about what he shared with her. As his fingers ferreted out weeds and his mind toiled over the time he spent with the woman he loved, he grimaced with disgust. "I do what my father did with my mother."

Eric told his fiancé about his cases. He described the problems that people had with their hearts. It was very depressing stuff at times, but it was the profession he'd chosen. Or had his father chosen it for him?

He paused and thought about the night he'd fallen down the stairs at the Ferguson house. Before the incident, he'd told his mother he was giving up his career as a doctor. It was like he'd slapped her. Her face was flush and unbelieving.

Eric let out a bitter laugh. "If Dad had heard me, he would have turned over in his grave."

The thought made him go at the weeds with more fervor. Had he ever made an important decision on his own? Or was Matthew right? Was he Eric Sr.'s mini-me? "My father groomed me, day in and day out, until he made me into his image." He snorted out his anger. "I was the grand offering he gave himself."

He paused, gripping the lowest part of a reedy-grass, pulling at it, trying his best to remove it. He was determined to get it out, root and all. But no matter how he tried, he ended up only pulling off the upper part of the plant. The root was still in the ground. Soon it would send up new shoots to replace what he'd pulled away.

He sat back and looked at his hands. The tough grasses had been merciless. As he focused on his task, he'd ignored his body's pain. It's what he knew to do no matter how much something hurt.

"Dad, please, don't! My knees hurt even more when you use that stuff."

"A little pain is good for you, Eric, and wipe away those tears! I didn't raise a cry-baby, did I?"

With his father's voice still echoing in his ears, Eric stood up and stared down at the grave site. It wasn't perfect, but at least he'd made it somewhat presentable. As for his thoughts, he had to push them aside. This was his mother's day. Her needs came first.

He turned and started for home. As he walked, he hardly noticed his old neighborhood. He had to clear his mind of any thoughts that might stir up unwanted feelings. When he arrived at his house, he climbed the stairs to the front porch and found his mother waiting at the door. When she saw him, she immediately stepped outside, looking very upset. "Eric, where have you been? And my lord, look at your hands!"

Eric paused and did as she directed. Some of the cuts were deep and bleeding, but he didn't care about his hands. He couldn't care about anything but keeping an inner storm from reaching ground and hurting his mother. If he could keep it contained for just a little longer, he'd deal with it on his own.

He smiled at her. "Pulled some weeds. It looks worse than it is." How could he tell his mother the truth? He didn't feel any pain in his hands because he'd been taught to ignore it, just like he couldn't shed a tear. What he couldn't ignore any longer was the fact that another person had completely controlled his life. And he'd let it happen. Even as an adult, Eric towed the line of strict obedience.

But the price for such a virtue was dear. Eric bent over and kissed his mother's cheek. "I'll go wash up," he said in a soft, steady voice. He'd get through the funeral gathering, and then he'd deal with the tattered remains of his life.

* * *

After Matthew checked on the mangy creature that Paul had brought home and found it still alive and looking better, he wanted to relax. It was a pleasant morning, and he enjoyed sipping his coffee and catching up on some reading. Lea was sleeping soundly when he left their bed. Luckily, he'd had the foresight to buy two inflatable beds before they left Blacksburg. Paul was using one bed in the old surgery. The second one was set up in Eric's old room. It was a tight squeeze, but the full size mattress fit into the space.

Matthew smiled thinking about how wonderful it was just to hold Lea in his arms again. But that was the extent of their passion. The bedroom's walls were thin, and both Lea and Matthew knew they wanted privacy when they did more than cuddle.

At nine o'clock, Matthew was sitting in the living room, paging through a science article when Margaret came up to him. She was wearing her "frown" face, the one that said he wouldn't be reading for long. It seemed Eric had come home with some problem, and Margaret needed Matthew to check on him . . . again. She said something about Eric having some cuts on his hands.

Matthew did as he was asked, but he did it with a groan. He was still sore from the day before. When he stood up, his entire body protested. Wielding a scythe for hours used different muscles than the ones he used at the gym.

After he climbed the stairs and stood in front of the bathroom, he told himself that Eric probably needed little more than some brotherly advice and some minor first aid. The thought brought a bit of comfort as he rapped on the door. At least he wouldn't be fighting an overgrown yard in coveralls. "Eric, it's Matthew. Can I come in?"

When there was no reply, Matthew opened the door and saw Eric standing at the sink. "Margaret said you hurt your hands. Do you want me to take a look?"

When Eric still didn't answer, Matthew walked over and glanced down at the small lavatory. Eric had his hands submerged in water that was polluted with dirt and blood.

"What are you doing soaking your hands in that filthy water?" Matthew demanded.

Eric looked up and blinked a couple of times. "Matthew, what is it? Do you need something?"

Matthew grabbed Eric's wrists and lifted his hands up for inspection. "What happened to your hands? They're a mess."

Eric shrugged. "I had to pull some weeds. No big deal."

"No big deal? Did you mix it up with the wrong end of a weed wacker?"

Eric pulled away and let the water out of the sink, rinsed the sink and grabbed a small brush off the lavatory. "Really, I'm okay."

Matthew stood back as Eric was about to use the brush on his cuts. "Don't use that! It's missing half its bristles, and I'm sure it's not sanitary."

Eric stared back with distracted eyes. "It's fine."

Matthew grabbed the brush from Eric's hand and tossed it aside. "Eric, I don't know what's going on, but you look like you looked that night at the Ferguson house. Your eyes aren't focused."

"What? Not focused?"

Matthew studied Eric's pale-blue gaze and shook the man's shoulder. He felt like he was dealing with a sleepwalker. Maybe if he could get Eric to come back to the moment, he'd return to his normal self. "Eric, look down at your hands. Tell me what you see."

Eric stared at the wall instead. "No, it's better if I don't."

"Why?"

"I don't want to see or feel any of this. If I can just get through this day—" Eric reached out for the rubbing alcohol.

Matthew grabbed the alcohol bottle from Eric and snapped his fingers. "Eric, you're a doctor. You know this isn't good for your cuts. Besides, I'd think your hands would be hurting enough already."

Eric glared back. "If I let any of this matter, I won't be able to stop what's coming."

Matthew heard the desperation in Eric's voice. "What's coming?"

Eric swayed and had to grab hold of the sink. "I can't hurt my mom again, that's all." He finally let his gaze settle on Matthew. "But if you insist, you can help me clean myself up. But please, don't ask me any questions."

Forty-Two

PAUL SAT ON the floor next to the dog he'd rescued. He'd even spent the night in the same room, sleeping on an air mattress. Since it looked like the dog would survive, he'd named it after the animal he had as a boy. This Duke wasn't much to look at, but Paul liked him anyway. As he ran a hand over Duke's head, he realized that they were both survivors.

Paul hadn't suffered the physical abuse that Duke had suffered, but his childhood had scarred him. He'd never wanted to admit how affected he was by what he'd experienced, but he now knew he couldn't minimize his suffering either. As he had the thought, Margaret knocked and stuck her head in.

"Paul, do you want some breakfast," she asked.

Paul put Duke's head down and stood up. "Yes, that would be very nice. Can I help?"

Margaret smiled. "Yes, if you get cleaned up first."

Paul looked at his hands and nodded. "As soon as Duke is better, he's getting a bath."

"Duke? So you named him? Are you planning on keeping him?"

Paul hesitated. "I guess I am."

Margaret frowned and turned to leave. "Well, hurry up now. You'll have to use the kitchen sink. Eric is in the bathroom upstairs."

Paul followed her to the kitchen and went to the sink. "Where are Lea and Matthew?"

"Lea is still sleeping. Matthew is upstairs helping Eric. I don't know exactly what happened, but Eric came home filthy and his hands were a mess. He said he was pulling weeds, so I suspect he was at the cemetery."

"Yes, the cemetery, when do you want us to be ready for the service."

"It's not a service, just a gathering. And I thought we could go after breakfast. Now, set the table, please."

"Margaret? Are you alright, I mean, I know that going to—"

Margaret took some biscuits out of the oven and set them on a trivet on the counter. She turned to look at Paul. "Are you talking about going to my husband's grave?"

"Yes, I'm sure it can be difficult—"

Margaret put the potholder down. "I keep thinking about being in your kitchen with you just before you almost choked to death. I know I was quite adamant about my feelings for Ricky."

"Yes, you were."

"Being back here, I realize that I sometimes forget all the difficulties I weathered with Eric's dad. But I think it's good that I'm getting more of the whole picture. I can see that I need to make peace with all of it."

* * *

Lea couldn't believe that she'd slept till ten o'clock. It was the best sleep she'd had in weeks. Being in Matthew's arms was so perfect. His strong body, so close to hers, always rekindled that feeling that she was where she belonged. A surge of joy filled her chest as she realized how lucky she was. Matthew was truly there for her.

As she dressed and brushed her hair, she could smell coffee and biscuits. It added to the happy moment. Margaret was in her element, preparing breakfast for the people she cared about.

When Lea went downstairs, she heard people talking and headed to the dining room. Everyone was gathered around the table eating, but they stopped to greet her when she came into the room.

Matthew stood up and came over. "Good morning, sleepyhead," he said as he bent over and kissed her cheek.

Lea took his hand and squeezed it. "I guess I was more tired than I thought, but I feel totally rested now."

"Are you hungry?" Margaret asked as she stood up. "I kept your plate warming in the oven."

Lea glanced at the food on the table and smiled. "Looks like you made one of your omelets, and I'm starving."

"Sit down and I'll get you some juice and that plate," Margaret insisted.

As Lea was about to sit down next to Matthew, Eric stood up and quickly excused himself. Lea noticed that his face was pale and he looked more serious than usual. She turned to Matthew. "Is Eric alright? Why are his hands bandaged?"

Paul spoke up too. "I'm wondering the same thing, Matthew."

Matthew looked towards the kitchen and leaned in. When he spoke, his voice was almost a whisper. "I guess he took care of his father's grave this morning. It was probably overgrown like the yard. Now, I think he's worried about Margaret. But he asked me not to say anything."

Lea sat back, thinking about Eric and Margaret. The two people had encouraged her to believe in herself. When she felt like she'd lost everything, their continued kindness helped her to hold on and not give up. "When are we going to the cemetery?"

Margaret came back into the room carrying Lea's plate and a glass of juice. As she served Lea, she sighed. "I thought we could go after breakfast, if that's alright with everyone."

Lea patted Margaret's arm. "Would you rather that we stay here so that you and Eric can have that time alone?"

Margaret glanced around at the table and its occupants. "No, it'll be nice to have everyone there."

* * *

Lea stood in the cemetery wondering about some of the old graves. A number of them had broken headstones that were losing the battle to weeds and the passage of time. Some grave markers looked more recent, like the one she and the others were gathered around. As Margaret spoke about her beloved husband, Eric Lloyd Sr., their group was there to listen and pay their respects. Eric stood close to Margaret's side. Paul stood across from them. Lea was happy that she was next to Matthew. His presence, so near, was comforting on the solemn occasion.

At first the weather was mild with the sun out, but as Margaret recounted some of her memories of being a doctor's wife, the weather began to change. The tall, still trees that dotted the grounds began to stir. When Lea glanced up, she was amazed at how fast the blue skies and puffy white clouds were yielding to heavier, darker vapors. As the sun was lost to the gray clouds, Lea buttoned up her sweater. Matthew seemed to notice her shivering and quickly put an arm around her shoulders. As he pulled her closer, his warmth helped her to ignore the chilly breeze.

Lea turned her attention to Margaret again. Her dear friend was talking about her husband's dedication and how much he had given to the people in the area. Lea grabbed a tissue and dabbed at her eyes as Margaret's voice broke with emotion. Margaret's unhappiness was accompanied by a sudden gust of wind. A cold front was moving in.

Eric tried to protect his mother from the increasing winds and the pain that was evident in her voice. He quickly removed his suit jacket and put it around her shoulders. As he did, Margaret turned to him and cradled his cheek. She spoke about how proud his father had always been of his son, and how she was sure Eric Sr. was still there with both of them.

Lea noticed that Margaret's statement didn't seem to bring any comfort to Eric. She'd been around him enough to see that he was struggling with emotion too. His chest rose and fell with frequent breaths even though he wasn't exerting himself. His pale face made her think of when he'd come home with a flu bug, and she wondered if he was getting sick. She wished she could reach out to him, but she'd wait until Margaret finished and they went back home.

Thankfully the gathering was a short one. As the group made their way to the car, the weather grew fiercer. The sway of the newly leafed out tree branches shifted dramatically. Within minutes, they whipped the air in a frantic, wind-induced dance. Lea eagerly climbed into the back seat of the SUV as the temperature dropped even more.

In the short time that it took to drive back to the house, a few drops of rain were pelting the car's windshield. Everyone in the SUV quickly exited the vehicle, everyone except for the driver, Eric. He excused himself, saying he'd be back in a little while. As the car pulled away from the curb, the group hurried into the house. Lea stood at the door as the car disappeared down the road. She was even more convinced that Eric was in trouble. But what could she or anyone do? They didn't have a second vehicle. There was no way to go after him.

By midafternoon, everyone was worried about Eric. A heavy rain and winds punished the house and grounds. After hours of the continued downpour, there were puddles in the yard and on the street. Matthew stood at the living room window, peering out silently and fervently wishing that they were all back safe and sound in Chicago. He didn't like Elkville, and with a storm raging and Eric missing, he knew he never wanted to make a return trip.

Finally, Margaret made a statement that expressed what everyone was thinking. "Eric wouldn't stay away this long. He knows how worried I'd be. He must have had an accident."

Matthew heard what Margaret didn't say. She was terrified that her son might have perished in the mountains. The roads were difficult on a sunny day. Matthew couldn't imagine what they'd be like if their ruts and lack of shoulders deteriorated even more. He offered a comment, hoping to ease Margaret's anxiety and his own concern. "Maybe he's just stuck somewhere, but safe."

"I guess that might be true," Margaret said in a breathless voice. She sat in a chair by the wood stove. When the house started to get chilly, she'd made a fire as routinely as someone would turn on a light when the sun went down. But the stove and the heat it was giving off didn't seem to help Margaret's condition. Her face was grim as she wrapped her arms tight around herself.

Paul Glass sat on the sofa. He'd been very quiet, but he spoke up too. "Is there anyone we can call in a situation like this?"

Margaret shook her head. "No, not really."

Lea sat on a dining room chair that she'd put next to Margaret. "Mom, Eric was raised in this area. Surely he's good at navigating the roads, don't you think?"

Margaret shrugged. "I guess. It's just that I hoped I'd never have to feel this way again. It scares me to death to think about how easy something could happen to him."

Matthew glanced back at Margaret. "Margaret, come here. Someone is pulling up in front of the house. Maybe you know them."

Margaret jumped up and hurried to the window. She squinted at the rain and an old vehicle and let out her breath. "I think that's Donnie Campbell's old truck. I recognize the big dent in the rear fender."

"Somebody's getting out and looking this way," Matthew announced. As he spoke, he was already headed for the front door. Without hesitating, he went out on the porch and got a better look at the truck. The driver waved him over. As Matthew left the porch and ran down the sidewalk, the rain was coming down so hard it only took a minute for his shirt to be soaked and for his body to feel the chill.

The truck's driver was hurrying over to the passenger side of the vehicle and yelling out to him. "He'p me git'em into the house!"

By the time Matthew got to the other side of the truck, the older man was struggling to help Eric out of the passenger seat and trying to keep him upright.

Matthew quickly grabbed Eric's other arm. Together, they managed to get Eric into the house.

* * *

Donny Campbell's account didn't include what had happened to Eric's vehicle, only that he found Eric a couple of miles up the mountain, stumbling his way down the road towards town.

Donny stood in front of the wood stove, trying to warm himself. He'd refused a blanket, but he looked at Margaret with appreciative eyes when she handed him a cup of hot coffee.

"Thank you for bringing my boy home, Donny," Margaret said with tearful eyes.

Donny took a long sip of coffee and shook his head. "Didn't recnize em at first til I got alook at his eyes. Then I knew em. I recollect those eyes from when hes jusa boy. They was scared then too. Hard times for yorn child with his pappy always being hateful with em. Yorn doc was a good man, but he weren't one to go easy on his son, Ms. Lloyd."

After that Donny didn't have anything else to say. He downed his coffee and left.

Margaret didn't know what to think after Donny's declaration. She watched from the living room window as the older man ran back to his truck and took off down the road.

Earlier, at the cemetery, she'd meant every word about her husband, how good he was and how proud he was of Eric. She always wanted to think that Ricky had guided Eric with a loving hand. But was it true? So many times, she tried to ignore Ricky's raised voice when he was upstairs going over the homework he gave Eric. Eric never complained about his father, but he didn't smile around him much either.

When Lea walked into the living room, Margaret turned to her with questioning eyes. "How's Eric doing?"

"Matthew and Paul got him out of his wet clothes. He was half-frozen. I guess he must have been out in the elements for quite some time."

Margaret closed her fists and grimaced. "I wish we hadn't come here again. Eric tried to tell me how he felt about this place and his dad when we were at your parent's house, but I wouldn't listen. I don't know if I ever really listened to him. I just had it in my mind that his dad was a dedicated man, the man I loved and left it at that. But goodness knows I can't be certain of anything anymore. Donny just told me that Ricky was a very hard man when it came to Eric."

Lea put her arms around herself. "I'm sorry. This trip was my idea."

Margaret looked up and saw Lea's eyes going dark with remorse. She quickly went over and put her arm around Lea's shoulder. "No, I wanted to come back. I wanted to be close to—" She put a hand to her mouth. "You couldn't have known—"

Lea brightened a little. "Neither of us knew that Eric would be here too."

Margaret tried to smile. "That's right. So don't take any of this on yourself."

Lea sucked in a breath. "Being a parent must be an awful burden. Rita acted so upset when she talked to me. She told me that she didn't want a child, but that my dad forced it on her. But I've been thinking about how young she was. I think my dad met her when she was only seventeen. Rita said she'd been very poor, and my dad gave her a way out. I don't think she knew anything about being a mother."

Margaret made her way back to her chair by the fire. "Eric's childhood slipped by so fast that I don't remember that much. I just remember trying to keep my family fed, washing the clothes, and scrubbing the floors. Always being busy. I know your mother wasn't there for you, but maybe I wasn't there for Eric either."

"Please, you're not like Rita. You love Eric. You always have, and he knows it."

"But does he know that I believe in him and accept him as a person, not just a son? I wonder. I thought he should be like his dad. I was happy when he became a doctor. I think Eric just tried his best to please both of us. But what did he want?"

Forty-Three

MATTHEW SAT IN one bedroom chair and Paul sat in the other. They were in Margaret's room, talking and keeping an eye on Eric. Because of the crowded conditions, Eric had been sleeping on the downstairs couch at night. Now his mother insisted that he recuperate in her bed, and she'd take the couch.

Matthew looked around the bedroom with its faded wallpaper and old furniture and decided he couldn't let himself dwell on how depressing the room could be. He was already depressed enough thinking about his visit to Elkville. People were falling apart again, just like they had at the Ferguson mansion. He glanced at Paul. "Paul, you're the shrink. What the hell is going on with everybody, with all of us?"

Paul returned a contemplative look. "I can only tell you that when one person changes, it can have a domino effect on the others who are involved."

"Yes, well, Eric looks like he was hit with a brick, not a domino. If that Donny fellow hadn't picked him up when he did, Eric might have died of exposure. He didn't even have his jacket to help keep in a little body heat."

"You've had your hands full this trip, haven't you? First with Duke, now Eric." Paul paused. "By the way, Matthew, thank you for all that you did for Duke. And I'm sorry for my outburst. It was uncalled for."

"You did get very upset."

"Yes, and again I'm sorry."

"All that I know is that I wish all the hell that's going on would get some resolution. I'm sure you saw Margaret's face when we

328

brought Eric in. She could be the next one who goes haywire." Matthew's brows narrowed even more. "Got any thoughts about it all?"

"A few. It's an interesting dynamic if we retrace some events. We came together to help Lea. That's when Raymond found out that Rita had handed over their child to a sadistic nanny. Rita fell apart trying to cope with Raymond's reaction and her guilt. Then Margaret found out that her secret was out, and Eric learned about the full extent of his father's background. Then I started making mistakes in how I handled the situation."

Matthew scowled. "You left out the part where I spilled the beans to Lea and then to Margaret about Eric Sr.'s track record."

Paul smiled. "Yes, but something was festering in all their lives. The secrets that came out just opened up old wounds. But you know about such things. Sometimes you have to open a wound and purge whatever is foreign in there. It can pave the way to healing."

"I should have been more attentive to Eric's condition this morning. I knew something was really bothering him, but he didn't want to talk about it."

"Matthew, one of the first things you have to understand is that you can't force people to move faster than they're prepared to move. If Eric refused to open up, it was his choice."

"Yes, but then he took off without a warning."

"Oh, there was a warning. Didn't you notice how he looked at the cemetery? He was very upset, but I could tell he wanted time to think. He's been told what to do his whole life. He didn't want more people adding their opinions."

"Is that what you think? That he never learned to stand up for himself?"

"Consider his background, Matthew. From what little I've gathered, Eric was raised in an almost totally isolated environment. A child that grows up like that doesn't even know to ask questions. It takes something like what he's been going through recently to make him reexamine his life."

"Well, I think he's definitely in that process."

"Yes, and let's hope he finds some answers soon." Paul stood up. "If you need me, let me know. In the meantime, I think I'll go down and check on Duke. He ate a little something earlier. Maybe I can get him to eat some more."

"About this Duke, are you planning on taking him back to Chicago?"

Paul shrugged. "I don't know. I might stay here for a while. I'll have to ask Margaret if it would be okay."

"Stay here? In this primitive outpost? Are you crazy? If you find another suffering animal in your path, I won't be around to patch it up. Or what if your heart—"

Paul smiled. "Stop worrying, Matthew. It's not good for a person like you to start getting so concerned."

"You're right. It's not in my nature to—"

"Get involved? I know. So go back to Chicago and do what you do best, get busy with your work."

Matthew watched Paul leave and stiffened. When he thought about going back to a routine, he wondered why the idea wasn't as appealing as it once was. Maybe it was because he was caught up in the drama that was going on around him.

His musings were interrupted. Eric was stirring in his bed. Matthew got up to check on him. He hoped that the craziness everyone was experiencing was on the wane.

* * *

Eric lay very still as he slowly came back to the world. He didn't dare open his eyes until he went over what had happened on the mountain. As he recalled the experience, it almost felt like a dream.

After he'd taken his mother and friends back to the house, he was relieved to have some time to himself. The weather was turning cold and rainy, but he wanted to drive up the mountain anyway. He needed some quiet contemplation time. At the cemetery, it had been difficult to rein in his feelings. Every time his mother had said something nice or wonderful about his father, Eric had an opposite reaction. He remembered more times when his father had been overly harsh and demanding, not some loving parent.

At the time he'd had the thoughts, they felt blasphemous. On the other hand, he knew he'd never treat a child of his own in the way that Eric Sr. had treated him. And if he took the ideas a little further, he realized that he was still paying the price for his upbringing.

330

On the drive up the mountain, he hardly noticed the weather. The rain had started to pelt his windshield in a heavy downpour. His thoughts were centered around his father and his mother's commentary at Eric Sr.'s grave. According to Margaret Lloyd, her Ricky was akin to a saint. She only saw his dedication and service. She didn't seem to understand the reality of the situation. A lot of what the man had taught Eric was nonsense. A case in point was Eric's recent injuries.

He'd glanced at his bandaged hands and resented the fact that he wasn't supposed to feel his body's pain. As a doctor, he knew it was there for a reason, to tell a person that something was wrong. Dr. Kasner had put it another way. She said that when a person denied their suffering, they also denied life itself.

But Eric's father lived by and enforced a different code of conduct. As Eric reflected on the results of that kind of model, his anger escalated. He wasn't able to stifle the sudden outburst of feeling that shook him bodily.

"Maybe if my dad had listened to me and paid attention to his chest pains, he'd still be alive! Mom and I wouldn't have to be visiting some damnable cemetery!"

A well of emotions started coming up after that. The more Eric had pondered his father's views on personal conduct, the more he clenched the steering wheel. He didn't think about the elevation. It was getting steeper. He didn't notice how the hard, driving rains were affecting the overall condition of the roads.

When his hands had started to hurt, he finally slowed down a little. But he couldn't slow down the purge of feelings that insisted on coming up. He began to have flashes of his trips up the mountain with his father. How he couldn't escape the man's enraged lectures on how Eric wasn't doing enough. How his father insisted that Eric work harder or else. How Eric sat there, trapped in the passenger seat, praying that he could run away to the woods and knowing he'd never be free from his father's dominating ways.

The memories started coming so fast that Eric almost panicked. Was he losing control? Not knowing what else to do, he tried, but he couldn't shut out the pain or the memories.

There was one bright spot in it all. He remembered Matthew's counsel. Earlier, when the surgeon was bandaging Eric's hands, he'd advised Eric to be his own man, to realize that both their fathers were fallible human beings. He told Eric to have faith in himself.

Recalling that advice had helped. With effort, he began to shift to a better mindset. As he did, he pressed a little harder on the accelerator. But he wasn't driving his Porsche. He was piloting a large SUV that wasn't nearly as responsive. When he took a curve a little too fast and tried to correct, he would have made it if it hadn't been for a washout. There was no road where the shoulder should have been. One of the SUV's tires hooked onto the uneven edge.

Eric had known enough not to try to correct too quickly. It would have sent the car out of control. But he was in a no-win situation. The edge dropped off even more as he maneuvered the uneven gullies. By the time he was able to come to a stop, the SUV was angled sharply on a steep decline.

What followed scared the hell out of him. He heard a shout. He heard his father yelling at him. "Get out! Get out now!"

The order was so firm and insistent that Eric didn't question it. He immediately braced himself and undid his seat belt. Getting out of the car wasn't as easy. In fact, it proved to be almost impossible. He used all his strength to try to push open the door, but he was fighting a steep pitch and a howling wind that buffeted the driver's side of the car.

Panic almost set in. Even though he was in good, physical condition, he wasn't strong enough to do what had to be done. It was everything he could do to maintain the right position to push against the door.

There was another shout from his father. "Don't be a quitter, Eric! Push harder!"

Again Eric had obeyed, thinking to wedge his feet against the center console. It helped him to give the door everything he had. When the door yielded a little, he kept pushing until he was able to open it enough to get out.

It was a harrowing event. By the time he managed to get to the safety of the road, he was shaking and already soaked to the bone. It wasn't a moment too soon. More of the road's edge gave way. It was the part that the two left tires were resting on. The SUV began to slide down the muddy slope.

Eric had watched with pounding heart and heaving breath. When his mind cleared a little, he realized his father had been there for him. It was a horribly confusing thought. He'd been cussing his father out one minute and feeling like he needed to be thankful the next.

His muddled thinking didn't last long. The weather and the wind were unrelenting, and he was soon numb with cold. As he started walking down the mountain, he couldn't think anymore. It took everything he had to put one foot in front of the other. Eventually, a truck came along. He vaguely remembered a man's face and getting into the truck. After that, everything was fuzzy.

Now, as Eric came back to reality and opened his eyes, he was grateful to be in a bed. He was grateful not to be freezing with cold. When he looked up, Matthew stood by the side of the bed, looking down with concern. "I guess I made it home," he managed.

Matthew put a hand on Eric's forehead. "Hope you don't have a fever."

Eric pushed Matthew's hand away. He could still hear the tone of his father's voice, yelling at him again. But this time, it saved Eric's life. "I'm a little sore, but otherwise, I feel alright."

"You're lucky to be drawing breath. You nearly froze to death."

Eric pushed himself up and stared at the familiar surroundings. "Am I in my mom's bedroom?"

"Yes, you are."

"I need to talk to her. Where is she?"

"She's downstairs. Do you want me to get her?"

"No, I'll go down." Eric sat up and looked at himself. "I guess I have you to thank for thawing me out."

"Paul helped."

Eric forced himself out of bed, steadied himself and took a deep breath. Physically, he was well enough, but the confusion was back. He didn't know how to integrate the experience he'd had on the mountain. Maybe, he'd been wrong. Maybe it was better not to feel anything. "I need to get dressed, Matthew. Can you get me some clothes?"

* * *

Eric sat next to his mother on the sofa in the living room. Lea, Matthew and Paul were gathered around close to the wood stove. Eric looked at each of them with a feeling of unease. "I wanted to tell everyone about my dad. I didn't say anything at the cemetery this morning, but now, I think it's time."

Margaret put her hand on his arm. "Eric, that's alright. You don't have to say anything. After doing some soul searching, I realize that your dad wasn't always the man I thought he was."

Eric frowned back. "Mom, he was there for me today, when it counted. If it weren't for him, I wouldn't be sitting here."

"What do you mean?"

Eric glanced at the group by the woodstove and back at his mother. "This is going to sound very strange, but I heard him when the SUV was ready to slide down the mountain. I don't know if his voice was in my mind or not. It felt like it came from the back seat. I know he also helped me to get the car door open. There was no way that I could have done it myself."

Margaret smiled and sniffled. "You might not believe me, but he did care about you, and he tried to be a good father in the only way he knew," she said in a sob.

"Please don't cry—"

Margaret swallowed back her tears. "He never told you about this, but he grew up in a very rough part of Baltimore. Things were so different back then. His home life was very difficult with his father drunk and beating him for no good reason. And he had to fight the neighborhood bullies just to survive. They wanted him to join their gang, but he wouldn't. He did everything he could to find a way out of that life. He was smart, like you, Eric. And he thought that being a doctor was something good to aim for."

Eric put his arm around her shoulders. "I wish he would have shared some of his life with me."

"He didn't want you to know about any of it," Margaret said as she pulled away. "And he didn't just run away to some worthless backwoods town. When he lost his license in Maryland, he wanted to find a place away from cities and all the horrible things he'd grown up with. He thought Elkville was the answer. We both had dreams about 'country' life back then. When we moved here, we got more than we bargained for. But your dad stuck it out, especially when the need for a doctor was so desperate. After a couple of years, he couldn't leave the people who depended on him. But it was so hard, and he was always so worn down by it all. He could never get ahead. Still, he tried to give you something, an education and the code he lived by. He wanted a better life for you, the life he couldn't provide for either of us."

Eric felt his face go flush. His mother's feelings were so powerfully expressed that he was completely overwhelmed. If his father was a hero and a saint, where did that leave him?

Suddenly the room was stifling hot, and he couldn't get enough air. He struggled to keep his feelings to himself. He wouldn't confront her, but his mother had shamed him again. Her message was simple. Eric should be grateful for his father's guiding hand, not thinking of him as ignorant. He got up and gave his mother a weak smile. "Sorry, I need some air."

* * *

Lea had been watching Eric again, just like she had at the cemetery. She was still worried. As Margaret started explaining how wonderful Eric's dad was, Eric looked like he was getting ready to pass out.

Lea didn't want to be disrespectful of Margaret, but she had a different take on Eric's father. During the time that she'd lived with Eric and Margaret, Eric had shared a few experiences that he'd had with his father. He didn't make a big deal out of them, but Lea got the picture of how controlling his father had been. His stories were backed up by what Margaret said. Neither wife nor son sounded like they had any say in their lives.

When Eric asked to be excused, Lea stood up and asked to be excused too. She tried to smile at Margaret as she walked out of the room, but it was a forced smile. Once she was in the hall, she saw the front door closing. She quickly opened it and stepped outside. She paused on the porch. The rain was still coming down, and it was cold. But when she saw Eric standing by the side railing, she forgot about the weather. "Eric, what's going on?"

Eric turned around and stared at her, but he didn't answer.

Lea went over to him and put her arms around him. "I'm here for you, just like you were there for me."

Eric didn't seem to hear her. Instead of returning her hug, he remained very still and stiff.

Eric's behavior was telling. He was drifting just as she had drifted. Both of them knew ways to shut out the world. She also knew how hard a person could be on themselves. "You're my angel, Eric, do you know that?"

Eric finally let out a breath. "I'm not an angel, Lea. My father's the one who was a saint. I'm his ungrateful son, a son who goes around thinking his father is a jerk."

Lea tightened her hold on Eric when he tried to push her away. "I never met your father, but I've listened to Margaret and what she had to say about him."

Eric let out a bitter huff of laughter. "I can just imagine."

"Listen to me, please. Did you know that your mom once had lots of dreams? She was an artist, but she didn't hold on to her visions. She married your dad instead. After that, she let him define everything about their life together. And now, she just sits around in our little apartment, looking lost."

Eric stared down. "What are you trying to tell me?"

"No matter what drove your father's actions, he never made room for his wife or his son to express what they wanted. Now you and Margaret both seem oblivious about who you are. From what I can tell, you've both been shut down for so long that neither of you value yourselves."

Eric looked away. "Where'd you learn all that crap?"

Lea smiled. "Some of it came from Doctor Kasner, but most of that crap came from someone who helped me rebuild my life. It came from you, Eric."

Eric sucked in some of the cold air, but he remained quiet. A long moment of silence was interrupted when the door opened and Matthew stepped out on the porch. "What's going on out here?" he asked as he came over to where Lea and Eric were standing.

Lea quickly spoke up. "Our angel's in trouble, Matthew! We have to help him!"

Matthew crossed his arms. "What's this about, Eric?"

Eric's jaw tightened. "I want to make peace with my father, especially after what happened on the mountain, but I'm still angry at a man whom my mother claims was a male version of Mother Teresa."

Matthew's scowl deepened. "Are you talking about the guy who tried to make you deny your feelings when they didn't agree with his?"

Eric shrugged. "I don't know. I'm too confused to think clearly anymore."

Lea still had her head against Eric's chest. His heart was pounding in her ear. She let him go enough to look up and study his face. "Eric, you've been through a lot today."

"Yes, I ran off like a fool, and now we don't even have a car to get out of this place."

Matthew clasped Eric's shoulder. "I guarantee we'll get out. Even if I have to buy one of those beat up pickups, we will not be stuck here."

Eric's eyes brightened a little. "Is it that bad being here?"

"I thought the Ferguson place was hell," Matthew replied, "but Elkville has it beat. And another thing, your father wouldn't have had to save you on that mountain if you weren't upset about him in the first place. I care about your mother. She's a good woman, but she's misguided. All that crap she spouted off at the graveside invalidated your entire painful childhood."

"He's right, Eric," Lea said. "That man, Donny, told your mother the same thing. He said your father was a very hard man, not a saint."

Eric looked down at her, nodded and finally hugged her back. "Thank you. I thought it was just me. It's nice to know that I'm not a totally misguided idiot."

"You're fine," Matthew insisted.

Lea extended an arm in Matthew's direction. "I agree, Matthew, now come over and join in a hug."

Matthew's eyes widened as he stepped back. "Sorry, but I'm not the group hug type."

Lea gave him an imploring pout. "Oh come on, please do it for me."

Matthew came forward with narrowed brows and put his arms around both Lea and Eric. "Fine, for you, Lea."

Lea giggled and shut her eyes as she enjoyed the moment. "Now I have two angels in my life."

"But this angel is in his shirt sleeves and is getting cold," Matthew protested as he escaped Lea's hug. "Let's all go back in the house and figure out an escape plan."

337

Eric laughed. "I just remembered something. I can call Bucky's Garage. It's in a neighboring town. They usually have an extra vehicle sitting around. I'm sure we can work something out."

* * *

After Eric, Lea and Matthew suddenly exited the room, Margaret knew she'd said the wrong thing again. She got up, walked over to the woodstove, and sat down next to Paul. "Can I talk to you?"

Paul looked up and smiled. "Of course."

"What's wrong with me? Eric keeps reaching out, and I keep pushing him away. But it's not what I want to do."

"What do you want?"

"I want Eric to be happy of course."

"And?"

"I guess I want him to be proud of his father. Is that wrong of me?"

Paul didn't answer at first, but finally offered a weak smile. "I'm sure both you and your husband always did your best for Eric."

Margaret clasped her hands and stared down at the floor. "Yes, but why do I feel like I always have to defend Ricky? During our marriage, I thought about the burden he carried. Like I told Eric, he tried so hard, but he was hardest on himself. Or so I thought. I don't think I let myself consider Eric's feelings."

"And now?"

"Sometimes I feel like one of those old mules that farmers used in the fields. They just kept pulling the plow 'til they dropped. They don't know anything else."

"Margaret, you're a bright, beautiful woman, not some animal in the field."

"Am I? When I think back, all I see is living the same way every day, thinking the same thoughts. How do I put all those years behind me?"

"It can take time to establish new patterns, new ways of thinking about yourself."

"Paul, you asked about staying here, and I don't see any reason why you shouldn't except for the lack of adequate medical care. What about your heart?"

338

Paul smiled. "I figure we're on this earth until it's time for us to leave."

"Eric didn't feel that way when his dad died. He said that Ricky should have taken better care of himself."

"I understand that, but my doctor said that I'm doing fine. And there's something about this place that gives me a sense of peace. I like walking out in nature and breathing the clean air."

"How would you feel if I stayed here too?"

"Margaret, please don't stay on my account."

"No, it has nothing to do with you."

"Do you miss Elkville?"

"It's what I know, but maybe it can be more than that. Maybe it can be a place where I come to grips with my life."

Forty-Four

WHEN MATTHEW SHOOK her awake, Lea groaned in protest. She wanted to sleep a little longer, but he reminded her that they needed to get on the road as soon as possible. Hopefully, they could be aboard the Ferguson jet by early afternoon, flying to Chicago.

After packing, it was still early morning when Lea set her suitcase down in Margaret's bedroom. Margaret was sitting on her bed. "I guess we'll be leaving soon. Are you sure you don't want to come back with us?"

"I'm sure," Margaret said.

Lea sat down next to her. "I don't think I understand why you want to remain in Elkville."

"It's a confusing time for all of us, my dear. I only know that if I'm going to pick up the pieces of my life, this is where I need to start."

"Why is that? Why Elkville?"

Margaret smiled. "It must seem strange to think someone would want to live here. When I see how you and Matthew look at this place, I see the panic in your eyes."

"Well, maybe not panic."

Margaret laughed. "Really? Have you seen how Matthew stares at the wood stove or my old kitchen appliances? And when he goes into Ricky's old office, he cringes."

Lea laughed too. "Yes, I suppose you're right. It is different than what either of us are used to."

"In my case, I've lived here for so long that I don't think very much about appearances. I just think about Elkville as my home."

"But it's more than appearances, isn't it? I mean the area and the people are—"

"Are what?"

Lea looked down and scuffed her feet against the threadbare carpet. It had tattered edges, and its once red flowers were faded. The rug's glory days were long gone. "Don't you find it all a little depressing? When you talked about going to Paris and painting, you seemed excited about the beautiful things in the world."

Margaret shrugged. "I know you're right. That's why I need time to reflect. I can do that here. And I won't be alone. Paul will be here too."

"Are you saying that you like him?"

Margaret frowned. "Not in the way you might be thinking. But he is becoming a friend, someone I can talk to."

Lea frowned too. "I'm going to miss you."

"And I'll miss you, but let's both look at the bright side."

"What bright side?"

"Like you told me in Chicago, we're kind of starting over. I don't know what that means exactly, but I'm willing to explore some possibilities."

Lea looked up and studied Margaret's eyes. They had a little more sparkle than earlier in the visit. "Do you really believe that?"

"I didn't before. When I thought about my life, all that I felt was emptiness. But if Eric can start believing in himself, maybe I can believe in who I am."

"Eric would love that."

"Yes, we had a very frank discussion last night. And for the most part, I finally kept my mouth shut. When I listened to Eric, I found out more about who he really is and what he wants. I realize that I want more too. Instead of some definitions about being a wife and mother, I want to know the person that I am. Maybe I'll even start painting again."

Lea smiled. "That's an exciting thought."

Margaret got up and went to the window. The sun was just beginning to brighten the room. "I used to look out at the mountains a lot. I know they can be hard and unforgiving, but they're also so beautiful. Maybe I'll paint them someday."

* * *

The sun streamed through the kitchen window as Matthew carried his mug over to the sink. After the storm, the ground was water-logged, but the skies were clear. Matthew glanced back at Eric. He was still finishing his coffee at the kitchen table. "It looks like we're going to have a good driving day."

Eric nodded. "Are you and Lea packed?"

"Yes, at least I am. Lea is talking to Margaret. She was surprised when she found out that your mother is staying here."

Eric's jaw tightened. "Yes, with Paul Glass. Can you believe it?"

"Is that a problem? They're just friends. Besides Paul is a shrink, maybe he can help Margaret. I think she's still dealing with some guilt about what happened this weekend."

Eric stood up, went to the sink, and stared out the window. "Mom should come back to Baltimore. If she wants to talk to someone, I know some very good people."

"Would these people you know all be women?"

Eric grabbed a dish cloth and began drying the dishes stacked in the dish drainer. As he polished a plate, he glanced at Matthew. "Tell me, how would you like it if your mother were in the same situation?"

"I'd be worried about Paul. My mother has an interesting hobby. She's very good at crushing male egos."

"Thankfully, she didn't succeed with you. You've been very helpful, Matthew. I'm grateful, and I'm sorry for constantly overreacting since we've been here."

"Are you kidding? Talk about being a survivor, I've only been in this place for a couple of days, and I'm about to lose it."

"Paul Glass says he finds it tranquil."

"He's also attached to a hound that looks like it escaped from the bowels of hell. I guess he has a different take on things."

Eric smiled as he put the plate in the cupboard. "It's strange, Lea says you have a reputation for poor people skills, but you've been a good friend since I've known you."

"Yes, but you're the one with the angel eyes."

"Listen, Matthew, if you ever think you'd like to relocate, think about Baltimore."

"Thank you, but I'm staying as far away from Elkville as possible."

"I don't think living in Chicago is much of a deterrent, not with the Ferguson's plane at Lea's beck and call."

Matthew huffed out a breath. "Don't remind me. I think Lea and your mom are talking about another trip in a month or so."

"What are you going to do?"

"Hell, I don't know. With any luck I'll get hit by a bus, and Lea will have to nurse me back to health for a few months."

When Eric laughed and started to grab another plate, Matthew reached out for his arm. "How are your hands?"

Eric held them up for a quick inspection. "They're doing great."

"Yes, they are. It's rare to see someone heal that fast."

"Sometimes the gift works on me. Unfortunately, it didn't help me feel better about my mom staying here. I hope she'll be okay."

Matthew leaned against the counter and crossed his arms. "Don't underestimate your mother. If I were a betting man, and it was a contest between my mom and yours, I'd put my money on Margaret. She's a very strong woman."

"Really?"

"Think about it, Eric. She lived here with practically nothing. Yet she never lost her ability to be kind and generous. And she raised a son who's as dedicated and dependable as they come. What else can I say?"

Forty-Five

CHICAGO'S SUMMER WEATHER was hot and humid. Luckily, the church's air conditioning was doing an adequate job. At least Eric thought the temperature was fine. "Hold still," he ordered as he finished straightening Matthew's white bow tie.

Matthew fidgeted in spite of Eric's caution. "It's too hot in here. I'm going to start sweating."

"The temperature is fine. I think it's your nerves."

"You'd be nervous too if Teresa had a record of running off. What if I get to the altar and find out that Lea's disappeared again."

"That's ridiculous. I saw her earlier. She's practically glowing."

"Are you sure? She didn't have a car waiting in the back? Or a ticket to Alaska in her purse?"

"She was her beautiful self, and she told me that she felt like the luckiest woman in the world." Eric glanced at his watch. "Anyway, it's about that time, Matthew. Are you ready?"

Matthew stepped back. "Eric, can I ask you something? We've both been through some crazy times. Now, I want to believe that the craziness is over."

"You said it yourself. You told me that you and Lea have been doing great these past months." Eric smiled and held up a hand that displayed a wedding band. "And look at me, I have a beautiful bride. By the way, thanks again for being my best man last month."

Matthew's eyes suddenly became introspective and troubled. "But are you happy?"

"What are you getting at?"

"I never worried about my feelings until I lost Lea. Every day, I woke up, did my job and at the end of the day I went to sleep. I never considered whether I was happy or not. Then she ran off, and I went through hell."

"And now?"

"I think about everything a lot more, and I wonder." Matthew turned and began to pace. "When one of my patients is under anesthesia, they don't feel anything. And sometimes, when I think about losing Lea again, I don't want to feel anything either."

"You're asking if the happiness is worth the pain."

"Yes, I guess that's it."

"I only know that people like my father tried to outrun his pain. In the end, his obsession with trying to forget his past left him angry and empty. His emptiness gobbled up both my mom and me."

Matthew paused. "Your gift made me feel like I didn't have a choice. I wanted more out of life. But I kept thinking, even hoping, that the feeling would wear off."

Eric walked over and shook Matthew's shoulder. "Sorry, I don't think either of us can go back now."

Matthew stared back with a critical eye. "So tell me, are you over your personal craziness?"

"Who knows? Taking a chance on myself and going my own way can get overwhelming, but I refuse to live like my dad. I'd rather have the pain than sleepwalk my life away."

Matthew frowned. "I've always taken a chance on myself. It was taking a chance on someone else that almost did me in."

Eric laughed. "Give me a break, Matthew. I've seen how you look when Lea smiles at you. You're doing okay."

Matthew threw back his shoulders, adjusted his tux and glanced over at the small, ornate mirror hanging on the wall. After a long pause, he smiled. "Yes, I suppose I am."

* * *

As Lea slowly walked down the aisle on her father's arm, she could barely contain her happiness. If she gave in to her impulse, she'd rush down the aisle in a fit of excitement. But glancing ahead and seeing Matthew waiting for her with his face all solemn and still, she decided to restrain from any outward display of emotion. After all, she didn't want to embarrass the most wonderful man in the world.

At one time, Eric had held that title, but her viewpoint had changed. After the past months that she'd spent with Matthew, she knew he deserved to move to the top of the list when it came to wonderful men.

Of course, being wonderful didn't mean that Matthew didn't have his faults. He could be impatient, cranky, and overbearing if he felt the people around him weren't performing their duties properly. The caterers that Rita hired almost quit after Matthew dressed them down. They had showed up late for a meeting to discuss the meal selections, and Matthew was not happy. He'd had to wait an extra thirty minutes at the Ferguson mansion. However, Rita seemed pleased to know she had an ally in her quest for punctuality.

On the other hand, Matthew always did his best when he was with Lea. They'd had a few quarrels, but Matthew was very good at holding his tongue and giving her breathing room.

During those times his eyes could become hard beacons of determination and willpower. But that didn't mean that Matthew was unreasonable. His staunch attitude was always tempered with an unyielding strength and commitment to Lea and their relationship.

In turn, Lea was learning how not to take things personally. After their discussion in Elkville about her stubborn, judgmental side, she was careful not to jump to conclusions. It was taking patience on her part, but she didn't allow herself to shut Matthew out. She stayed put until their disagreement was resolved.

Lea loved when they made up after an argument. She sometimes teased Matthew about having a wild side and that's when he'd allow a smile to creep in. She loved that acknowledgment because she had her own wild side. And the more she trusted in who she was, the more she indulged her playfulness. And if she noticed that Matthew could only go so far in dropping his serious approach to life, she was learning that it was okay to be different.

As Lea neared the altar, and her father released her arm, she glanced over and saw Matthew looking back at her. The connection was immediate. Only one thing was important. They belonged with each other. It was a feeling that started in Lea's heart and spread all the way through to her fingers and toes. And from the way Matthew stared back at her, she knew that he felt the same kind of love.

Forty-Six

MARGARET OPENED A lower cabinet in Paul's Chicago kitchen. She was helping Paul to pack the items that he wanted to take back to Elkville. She took out some pans and smiled. "I keep thinking about Lea and Matthew's wedding and how perfect it was. Now, they're off on their honeymoon in Kauai."

Paul continued putting some knives in a special packing container. "They picked a beautiful place. I enjoyed my visits there."

Margaret paused and frowned. "Paul, you've been very quiet today. Is something wrong?"

Paul closed up the box. "I suppose I'm in a rather contemplative mood now that all of our lives are changing so dramatically."

"But Paul, you have a choice about selling this place. Are you sure it's what you want to do. You've told me that you loved living here. And when we were driving back, you had a twinkle in your eye that I rarely see."

Paul stared down at his clasped hands. "I'd be lying if I said I'm absolutely sure about what I'm doing. But I know it's time for something different. And with the money I'll have after selling this condo, I can make a real difference in the Elkville area."

Margaret walked over to where Paul was standing. "Maybe you're moving too fast. First, you bought that little, dilapidated house a couple of doors down from me—"

"Which I'm renovating. It'll be very nice once I put in a new kitchen—"

"And replace the roof, put in new plumbing and central heating, and have the outside completely redone."

"Yes, but I am giving the local folks some much needed work."

"You also sold your beautiful car and bought a truck. Now, granted, it's a very nice vehicle, but it's not sporty like the car you had."

Paul laughed. "My Audi didn't fit my new lifestyle."

"Paul Glass, you're like my Eric. You like something sporty and that new truck is anything but."

Paul went over to the counter and sat down. "I guess after my heart attack, my desires have changed. I realize that I want to contribute more than I have."

Margaret sat down on the stool next to Paul's. "But Paul, think about it. You're not only relocating permanently to Elkville, now you're thinking about building a new medical facility there. That's a huge undertaking."

Paul's anxious face finally softened. "You're right, and I didn't know if I had sufficient funds to do what I wanted. However, when I talked to Raymond Ferguson at the wedding reception, he told me he was interested."

"Why would he be interested in Elkville?"

"I guess Lea's been telling him about the area, and how Matthew almost hyperventilates every time she wants to visit. The subject got him thinking that Matthew is right. There's a real need in the area. Plus, I think Raymond is a little like me. He's getting to that age when he wants to leave behind some kind of legacy."

Margaret frowned. "Why didn't you say something about Raymond's thoughts sooner?"

"Margaret, I know how much you care about Elkville. I didn't want you to get your hopes up. Raymond wasn't ready to commit when we first talked."

"Oh, I see, so Raymond might not be serious."

"Actually he called me a little while ago."

Margaret straightened attentively. "What did he say?"

Paul returned a big smile "He wants in. And he's willing to fund whatever is needed."

Margaret put a shaky hand to her chest. "Oh my, when you first talked about a medical facility, I thought it was just talk. I thought you'd change your mind, or that it would cost too much. Now, to think it might really happen seems like a miracle."

Paul hesitated. "What's wrong? You look like you want to cry."

Margaret quickly got up, retrieved a tissue from her purse and dabbed at her eyes. "I'm sorry, I know this is your dream, Paul, but—"

Paul came over. "Did I do something wrong? I don't understand."

Margaret shook her head. "Bringing proper medical care to Elkville was Ricky's dream too. He never talked about it because he knew it was just a pipe dream. It was all he could do to keep us fed and buy an occasional piece of equipment to update his practice. In the end, I think his dream became something else that he failed to achieve."

"I'm so sorry, Margaret."

Margaret shrugged. "No, don't be. You're such a kind and generous man, Paul. I'm grateful for all that you've done for all of us. Now, to think you're willing—" She paused and looked around at the beautiful kitchen she was standing in. "You're willing to give up everything here and—"

"Margaret, stop it, please. I'm not giving up anything. I'm excited about what I'm doing. If you see any confusion on my part, it's because I don't know if I'm up to the task."

Margaret stiffened and felt her tears go instantly dry. "Paul Glass, are you telling me that you doubt yourself?"

"Perhaps I do, a little—"

"That's ridiculous. I've been watching you these past months, and I think I know quite a bit about the good and capable man that you are."

"Really?"

"And I'm not the only one. My friends have been telling me about the kind deeds you're always doing around Elkville. My goodness, there's that library program you started to help people read—"

Paul sighed. "I've only had one taker so far."

"And then you helped out old Ned at the store. For years he's had problems with keeping his books. But recently, he said you've been teaching him how to use an adding machine, and it's made all the difference. Anyway, the list of your helpful activities is getting pretty long."

"Margaret, those are just simple things."

"But you seem to know how to relate, Paul."

"Thank you. That means so much to me."

"Well then, stop your worrying. I might not know much about building a medical facility, but I'll do what I can to keep your 'confusion' in line."

Paul smiled as he leaned over and kissed her cheek. "I appreciate that."

Margaret returned a little smile and went back to packing a sauce pan. "You know, Paul. After all my years in Elkville, doing the same thing day in and day out, I'm getting excited too. I'm beginning to welcome the idea of a change." She paused and smiled. "I can't believe it, a medical facility in my little town."

"But do you think Matthew Howell will like what I'm doing?"

"Matthew? Why would he object? He should be thrilled that there will be adequate services."

"I think Matthew's dream come true would be to forget that Elkville exists."

Margaret sighed. "Oh, I see where you're going. Do you think Lea will get involved since her father is helping to fund the project?"

"Well, she might take after her father in some respects. I was surprised when she began to take business courses."

"She's been wanting to find a career. But you're right, I never expected her to think about doing something in the business world."

"You mentioned how she and her father have been talking and sharing. Maybe that's where it started."

"Raymond was eager to tell Lea about his company, and I think Lea indulged him at first. Gradually, she took an interest."

Paul nodded. "He told me that Lea seemed proud of him when she found out about his medical and pension plans."

"Yes, that's all well and good, but he ignored what was happening at home. And look at how Lea suffered because of his neglect."

"Raymond is very aware of that. Maybe that's another reason why he wants to build this medical facility. He wants to find a way to ease his guilt."

"Do you think he told Lea about his plans?"

"No, in fact he asked me not to say anything. He wants to surprise her."

Forty-Seven

MATTHEW FELL BACK on the bed, glanced at Lea and heaved out his breath. "Wow!"

Lea returned a sparkly-eyed look and giggled. "I've never heard you say the word, wow, before."

"I've never had an experience like that."

Lea reached over and ran her hand over Matthew's bare chest. "I have a confession."

Matthew gasped in another breath and settled deeper into the plush bed. "Confession?"

"As you know, Rita and I are able to share a little more now. And she seemed like she wanted to help make our honeymoon extra exciting. So she gave me a book with some great tips."

"That was very thoughtful. Thank her for me. And Lea?"

"Yes?"

"Please, keep reading."

Lea sighed dreamily. "This has been the most wonderful getaway ever."

Matthew put his arm around her and pulled her close. "It almost makes up for that year of hell I went through."

Lea snuggled against him. "But I think it all worked out, don't you?"

"If a year of hell is what it took for you to find yourself, it was definitely worth it."

"That is so sweet."

Matthew smiled. "No, not sweet, but I do consider myself quite special."

Lea kissed his cheek and laughed. "And you're modest too."

"It's one of my many gifts, but this modest person better get up and get showered. We have a dinner reservation."

"Thank goodness, I'm starving." Lea started to pull away and hesitated. "Is there room for me in that shower?"

Matthew returned a happy smile. "Of course, there's always room for you."

He wasn't accustomed to such a rush of happiness. It made him aware of how lucky he was. The real Lea, the one who was behind all the anger and attitude when they met, had come back to herself and to him. She was a gorgeous woman who shouted in restaurants and in his bed. She could also be a mysterious temptress who seemed as eager for him as he was for her.

Every day was like that dream he'd had when Lea was missing, only so much better. The word, miracle, came to mind, but he had to remind himself that he didn't believe in such things. Then he thought about his experience with Eric Lloyd. Maybe he'd simply never recovered after old "Angel Eyes" had demonstrated his magic touch. Whatever the case, he wouldn't fight the change in his life, at least not while he was on his honeymoon.

He got out of bed and stretched. It was wonderful to finally feel almost stress-free. However, when he glanced over at Lea, a moment of concern crept in. She was staring at him with a slight frown on her face. "What is it?"

"I'm looking at you and thinking that you're wrong."

"I am?"

"Yes, you deny it and refuse to see it for yourself, but you are sweet. And you're also kind, thoughtful and extremely capable of making a woman feel desirable. In fact, looking at you now, I think you're the most delicious, sexy man on the planet."

Matthew blinked back and smiled. What could he say? He walked over to her and gathered her up in his arms. "If you'd like, we could order room service instead of going out."

Lea giggled again. "Excellent idea, Doctor Howell. I'd like that."

Matthew was about to kiss her when Lea's phone rang. He stepped back. "That's your dad's ring tone. I hope he and Rita are alright."

"They were fine at the wedding. Maybe Dad's just checking in. We've talked a lot these past months." Lea let go of him and picked up her phone off the night stand. "Dad?"

It was Matthew's turn to cross his arms. He had a weird feeling in his gut and suspected that Raymond Ferguson had more on his mind than a casual call. "What now?" he grumbled.

As usual, Raymond's voice was overly loud, but Matthew could only hear bits and pieces of the conversation. One word that he did catch was a word he didn't want to hear. Raymond had mentioned Elkville in a very excited tone.

Matthew waited impatiently. This was their honeymoon. No interruptions were allowed, except in the case of an emergency. However, Lea smiled as she listened to her father. When she finally hung up and turned back to Matthew, her eyes were dancing with excitement.

"Matthew, guess what? I have wonderful news! My dad and Paul are going to build a medical facility in Elkville. And it's going to be called The Lloyd-Howell Medical Building. Isn't that fantastic news?"

Matthew's arms dropped to his sides. "Medical facility?"

Lea rushed over and hugged him again. "Yes, it's your dream come true. After you told my father how scary the situation was in Elkville, how you feared for my life every time we visited, he wanted to help. When Paul mentioned his desire to bring proper medical care to the area, my dad agreed. They've joined forces and are going to build something together."

"Elkville? A medical facility in Elkville? With my name on it?"

Lea hugged him tighter. "Yes, my sweet Matthew. You won't have to worry anymore. We can visit anytime, and you'll know it's okay. In fact, Paul and my dad are depending on you to specify what's needed. You can customize the facility as you see fit. It's my father's gift to us. And do you know what else? My dad wants to build a little house for us there. Whenever we're visiting, we'll be comfortable. It'll be our little, vacation home away from home."

Matthew carefully pulled away from Lea's embrace and stumbled over to the bed. He picked up Lea's phone and handed it to her. "Lea, my darling?"

"Yes?"

"Call Eric and ask him if his gift works when his patient is staying at a distant location."

"What patient?"

Matthew sat down on the bed, laid back and pulled the covers up. "Sweetheart, that patient would be me. Tell Eric that my blinding headache has come back. If there's something he can do, I'd appreciate it."

Lea's eyes filled with concern. "Oh my, I forgot how much you dread the idea of Elkville. I'm sorry." She caressed his cheek lovingly. "But there's no reason for worry. I promise not to be pushy. If you're overwhelmed, that's fine. We'll figure something out that takes the pressure off."

Matthew had been staring blankly at the ceiling, but he gave Lea a fleeting glance. "Really? You're not just saying that?"

"You're wellbeing always comes first. And I promise, if I can possibly prevent it, there'll be no more hellish years in your future."

Matthew found his mind wandering into areas he'd hoped to forget. "Those mountain roads are so treacherous. Eric barely made it home alive. And then there's our last visit in June, remember?"

Lea frowned. "You mean when Donny Campbell's son showed up with his pregnant wife, and you delivered her ten pound baby?"

Matthew began to rub his temples. "I was damn lucky she had the bone structure needed for giving birth to such a big child. If she had been a smaller woman, she might have died."

"I just remember her yelling, 'It's coming,' but you stayed so calm."

"I wasn't calm. I was dumbstruck with terror. I came out of Margaret's house and saw a screaming woman who was squatting in the back of a filthy pick-up. My only thought was that she was bearing down with all her mountain-woman strength, and her baby was going to be jettisoned out and sustain brain damage when its head hit the truck bed."

"I know it was a tough situation, but you caught the baby, Matthew."

Matthew reached out. "Please, Lea, don't make me go back to Elkville. I'm not emotionally equipped for those primitive conditions."

Lea squeezed his hand firmly. "I won't, but you have to admit that little Matthew was an adorable baby."

"I don't understand why the parents insisted on naming their child after me."

354

"Because they appreciate you. Do you know that you shine your brightest in a crisis?"

"But I don't want to shine. I simply want to do my job in a place where I can give people the proper care that they deserve. Is that asking too much?"

"No, it isn't, but things are going to change in Elkville. Dad says that he'll find a young doctor to run the medical facility, and he'll pay him or her a very good salary to stay in the area for a few years. After that, Dad is going to set up a trust fund to keep things going indefinitely."

Matthew felt his muscles ease a little. Maybe he was panicking too soon. If Raymond delivered on what he planned, there would be benefits in store for him. If he had to visit Elkville again, he'd be off the hook when it came to delivering ten pound babies. "How soon can they get started?"

"Soon, very soon. Paul already found a piece of ground that he thinks will be perfect."

Matthew breathed a sigh of relief. "Maybe you're right. Maybe it is good news after all."

"Of course it is. Everything is going to keep getting better and better. I know it."

Matthew pulled her into his arms and kissed her lightly. "I'm glad one of us is so optimistic."

Lea kissed him back, her eyes sparkling playfully. "And no matter what, if you do feel brave someday, you'll have your own vacation home waiting for you."

The End of Book One
Book Two is Now Available:
TRACES OF ANGELS

Note From The Author

Thank you for taking the time to read *Traces of Home*, the first book of my series, OPEN WIDE MY HEART. If you enjoyed my story, please consider telling your friends. Word of mouth is an author's best friend and much appreciated.

Warmest wishes, S. S. Bazinet.

For more information on my books or to find out what's new, please visit my website. Go to SSBazinet.com.

Other Books by S. S. Bazinet

A LIGHT SO BRIGHT SERIES
Book One: A Mother's Love

WHEN THE GODS COME BACK SERIES
Book One: Use Caution It's Earth

HOLIDAY ROMANCES
Holiday Hiccups
A Warlock Under The Mistletoe

IN THE CARE OF WOLVES SERIES
Book One: My Brother's Keeper

THE MADONNA DIARIES
Book One: Dying Takes It Out Of You

SENTENCED TO HEAVEN
An Inmate's Tale from the Other Side
Book Two: A Vampire In Heaven

www.ingramcontent.com/pod-product-compliance
Lightning Source LLC
Chambersburg PA
CBHW031427240626
47154CB00001B/236